Praise for *In the Shape of a Boar:*

"With this novel [Norfolk] has produced a forceful and impressive work."   —*Library Journal* (starred review)

"Telling prose of hypnotic sensory immediacy . . . Fiercely brilliant, sustained displays of virtuoso writing."
—*The Guardian*

"An immensely ambitious novel, one which makes most contemporary English fiction look like a game of Scrabble."   —*The Spectator*

"Enthralling . . . Lawrence Norfolk has constructed a seductive tale out of shadowy uncertainties."
—*The Times Literary Supplement*

"A wonderful achievement, as intellectually provocative as it is gripping to read, and it confirms Norfolk's reputation not only as one of the most exciting novelists around, but also as a writer unafraid to evolve."
—*The Literary Review*

In the Shape of a Boar

In the Shape of a Boar

of a Boar

Lawrence Norfolk

GROVE PRESS
New York

First published in Great Britain in 2000 by
Weidenfeld & Nicolson, London, England

Printed in the United States of America

FIRST GROVE PRESS PAPERBACK EDITION

Library of Congress Cataloging-in-Publication Data

Norfolk, Lawrence, 1963-
    In the shape of a boar / Lawrence Norfolk.
        p. cm.
    ISBN 0-8021-3967-1 (pbk.)
    1. World War, 1939-1945—Underground movements—Fiction. 2. World War, 1939-1945—Greece—Fiction. 3. Meleager (Greek mythology)—Fiction. 4. Poetry—Authorship—Fiction. 5. Refugees, Jewish—Fiction. 6. Greece—Fiction. 7. Poets—Fiction. I. Title.

PR6064.O65 I5 2001
823'.914—dc21   2001040156

Grove Press
841 Broadway
New York, NY 10003

03 04 05 06 07   10 9 8 7 6 5 4 3 2 1

For my parents, and the people they married.

CONTENTS

'I've often asked myself where I might have got my "boar".
Boars, my dear Walter Jens, – such things do exist.'
Letter of Paul Celan, 19 May 1961

PART I

The Hunt for the Boar of Kalydon

They come from the cities of Pherae and Phylace on the plain of Thessaly, from Iolcus on the Magnesian coast, Larissa and Titaeron on the banks of the Peneus. They quit Naryx and Trachis and march inland, westward, by way of the tusked peaks of Mount Oeta and the hot basins of Thermopylae.[1] Rivers lead them out of Argolis, Emathia and Locris – the Asopus, the Axius, the Cephisus – and from Megara and Athens their routes lie across the isthmus of Corinth. They sail east from Ithaca and Dulichion; west from Aegina and Salamis.

The heroes are the outposts of a shrinking country whose centre is the place of their assembly. They march towards its discovery, each step drawing the ring of the tinchel tighter about the ground where their tracks must meet. They are one another's quarry in a bloodless, preparatory hunt.

Those descending the high ridges of Taygetus or Erymanthus join those marching west from Argos and Alea, north from Amyclae, Sparta, Gerenia or Pylos. From Taenarus, on the tip of the Peloponnese, the route must pass by way of Messenia; from Messenia, Arene; from Arene, Elis. Arcadia is a mountain fastness, cool and untouched. One walks out of the thick mists of Cimmeria;[2] another makes the journey from Scythia.[3] One takes a small boat down the Scamander to cross the Hellespont, sails south of the isles of Imbros and Samos, north of Lemnos. Mount Athos is a beacon on the triple isthmus of Paeonia. Soon the coast of Euboea, and a lucky tide or easterly wind to take him down the strait until its brine runs sweet with water from the flood of the mountain-fed Spercheus. Its mouth will be his landfall, the first since Troy.

---

1 Hdt vii.176.2–3; Paus i.4.2, iii.4.8, x.20.1, x.22.1; qua saepto, Paus i.1.3; qua patria advenarum Doriarum, Paus v.1.2; Apollod ii.7.14; qua situ mortis Herculis, Lucian Hermotimus vii; De Morte Peregrini xxi; Soph, Trach 1191ff., Philoc 801–3; Schol ad Hom, Il ii.724; Diod Sic iv.38.3–8; Ov, Met ix.229ff.; Hyg, Fab xxxvi, cii; Sen, Her Oet 1483ff.; Serv ad Virg, Aen viii.300; Anth Gr vi.3; qua situ sepulcri Deianeirae, Paus ii.23.5; re dente, Lyc, Alex 486, cf. Xen, Cyn x.17.

2 François krater (Florence Mus Arch 4209); Hom, Od xi.14ff.; Strab, xi.2.5, xi.8.6; Archil cit. ap. Strab xi.1.40.

3 François krater (Florence Mus Arch 4209), et vid. Paus xiv.10.1.

The landscapes of their childhoods unfold green cloaks and disclose the men they have become: the horsemen[4] and helmsmen[5] and runners[6] and cripples.[7] The new terrain they tread narrows to the routes which will best bring all to the coincidence waiting in their futures. They are smooth-talkers[8] and swindlers;[9] thieves,[10] the sons of thieves[11] and their accomplices too[12]. Their heavy booty drags along the ground behind them. They would abandon it if they could. They steal cattle and tame horses.[13] They ride dolphins.[14] They kill

---

4 Ov, Met viii.306; Apollod i.9.5, iii.10.3-4, iii.11.2; Asclepiades cit. ap. Hes, Cat fr. 63 ap. Schol ad Pind, Pyth iii.14; Hes, Cat fr. 64 ap. Schol ad Hes, Theog 142; Polygnotus cit. ap. Paus i.18.1; Paus iii.12.8, iii.26.4, iv.31.12; Strab vi.1.15.

5 Apollod i.9.23; Paus viii.4.10; Ov, Met viii.391; Ap Rhod i.188; ii.867–900.

6 Ov, Met viii.311; Pind, Pyth iv.179; neque 1, Paus ix.5.3; Pherecydes ap. Schol ad Ap Rhod iii.1179 et Apollod iii.4.1; Eur, Bacch passim; Ov, Met iii.126; neque 2, Apollod, Ep 5.20; neque 3, Apollod, Ep 7.27.

7 Pherecydes cit. ap. Schol (ΣbT) ad Hom, Il ii.212; Euphorion cit. ap. Schol (ΣA) ad Hom, Il ii.212; Schol (Tzetzes) ad Lyc, Alex 1000; Quint Smyrn, Posthom i.66off. et passim; Cypria fr. 1 ap. Proc, Chrest ii; Aeschin iii.231; Apollod i.8.6; Schol ad Aristoph, Ach 418; Ant Lib xxxvii; Hyg, Fab clxxv; Eur(?) Oeneus frs P Hibeh i.1906.iv.21; Apollod, Ep 5.1; Diod Sic ii.46.5, xvi.87.2; Tzetzes, Posthom 100, 136; Dict Cret iv.2; Plat, Gorg 525e, Rep 620c; Soph, Philoc 445–54; Polygnotus cit. ap. Paus x.31.3–4.

8 Hom, Il xi.123, xi.128; François krater (Florence Mus Arch 4209); fort. Apollod, Ep 7.27 et vid. Hom, Od xvi.245–53 et passim.

9 Ov, Met viii.312; Hom, Il xxiii.665; Paus ii.29.4; Sim fr.114 ap. Athen x.456.c.

10 In toto, Apollod i.8.2-3; Ov, Met viii.304; ap. quos 'Iphiclus', Apollod i.7.10, i.8.3, i.9.16; Bacch v.129; 'Aphares', Apollod i.7.10; 'Evippus', Apollod i.7.10; fort. Hom, Il xvi.417; 'Plexippus', Ov, Met viii.441; Antiphon fr. Meleagros ap. Aristot, Rhet 1379b; Apollod i.7.10; 'Eurypylus', Apollod i.7.10; vid. Aristot, Poet 1459b; fort. Apollod ii.7.8 et Ep 7.27; neque Hom, Od xi.516–21; Lesches Il fr. 1 ap. Proc, Chrest ii; Dict Cret iv.17; 'Prothous', Paus viii.45.6; 'Cometes', Paus viii.45.6; 'Prokaon, Klytius', Stes, Suoth fr.222.1.4 ap. P Oxy 2359.

11 Paus vii.45.7; Ov, Met viii.307, vii.439.

12 Amphora (Berlin Antikenmus F1720); hydria (Boston Mus Fine Arts 67.1006); amphora (Harvard 1960.312); amphora (London Brit Mus B193); hydria (Malibu 83.AE.346); amphora (Mississippi 1977.3.63); amphora (Munich Antikensamml 1416); kylix (Munich Antikensamml 2620); hydria (Philadelphia MS2463); hydria (Toledo 1956.70); amphora (Würzburg Martin von Wagner Mus L248); oinochoe (Austin 1980.33); kantharos (Boston Mus Fine Arts 00.334); neck amphora (Boston Mus Fine Arts 76.41); amphora (Chicago 1978.114); dinos (Cleveland Mus Art 71.46); lekythos (Coll. Denman/ Shapiro 26); amphora (Detroit 76.22); hydria (London Brit Mus B329); amphora (London Brit Mus B161); volute krater (London Brit Mus B364); hydria (London Brit Mus E224); dinos (Paris Louvre E874); volute krater (Malibu 77.AE.11); hydria (Malibu 86.AE.114); neck amphora (Malibu 77.AE.75); neck amphora (Mississippi 1977.3.61); neck amphora (Mississippi 1977.3.71); amphora (Munich Antikensamml 1397); neck amphora (Munich Antikensamml 1562); panel amphora (Munich Antikensamml 2302); column krater (Rhode Isl. RISD 29.140); mastoid cup (Tampa 86.54); kylix (Tampa 86.85); Scopas ap. Paus viii.45.6; Apollod ii.5.2, ii.6.1; Hes, Sh 7off, Theog, 317; Paus i.19.3, viii.14.9; Pind, Isth i.17; Plat, Euthyp 297c–d, Phaed 89c; Eur, Ion 198, Herc passim; Ov, Met viii.310; pseudo-Arist, Mirab Auscult 100.

13 Hes, Cat, fr. 68 P Berlin 9739 et vid. Paus iii.24.10; Pind, Pyth i.126; amphora (Madison 68.19.1).

14 Apollod i.8.2; Ov, Met viii.303; Paus viii.45.6; Hom, Od xi.631; Isoc x.20; Panyasis fr.

centaurs.[15] They are murderers[16] and their victims[17] and their victims' avengers.[18] They owe one another the blood in their veins; these convergent journeys represent flights from such debts and their collection. A rare respite lies ahead, in the task awaiting them, such as was found by some on the deck of the Argo, or in the dust of Iolcus, where they contested in honour of Pelias. His son is here.[19] His son's killer is here too.[20]

They have murdered their brothers[21] and been cleansed and betrayed.[22] Their very beginnings have twinned them with the manner of their ends,[23] which will come as thunderbolts out of the bright sky and burn their images into the ground.[24] Their

---

ap. Paus x.29.9; Diod Sic iv.63.2; Apollod i.8.2, iv.70.3; Plut, Thes 30; Ov, Met viii.303; Paus v.10.8; Schol. ad Hom, Od xxi.295; Hyg Fab, xxxiii; Serv ad Virg, Aen vii.304; Ov, Met xii.210–535; Bacch xviii; Hes, Sh 182; Hdt ix.73.2.

15 Paus viii.45.7; Hom, Od xi.631; Isoc x.20; Panyasis ap. Paus x.29.9; Diod Sic iv.63.2; Apollod i.8.2, iv.70.3; Plut, Thes 30; Ov, Met v.10.8; Schol. ad Hom, Od xxi.295; Hyg Fab, xxxiii; Serv ad Virg, Aen vii.304; Ov, Met xii.210–535.

16 Hippocoontidae ap. quos: 'Enaesimus', Ov, Met viii.362; 'Hippothous', Apollod iii.10.5; 'Alcon', Apollod iii.10.5; Paus iii.14.7; 'Scaeus', Apollod iii.10.5; Hdt v.1; 'Dorycleus, Eutiches, Bucolus, Lycaethus, Tebrus, Eurytus, Hippocorystes', Apollod iii.10.5; 'Eumedes', Paus iii.14.6; 'Alcinus' aliq. qua 'Alcimus', Apollod iii.10.5; Paus iii.15.1; 'Dorceus, Sebrus', Paus iii.15.1; 'Enarophorus' aliq. qua 'Enarsphoron' aut 'Enaraephorus', Apollod iii.10.5; Plut, Thes 31.1; Paus iii.15.1.

17 Apollod i.8.2, ii.4.8; Paus viii.14.9; Eur, Herc 967ff.; Diod Sic iv.11.1; Moschus iv.13; Schol. (Tzetzes) ad Lyc, Alex 38; Nicolaus Damascenus fr. 20; Hyg, Fab xxxii; Hes, Sh 50; Plat, Euthyp 297e; Stamnos (Paris Louvre G192).

18 Diod Sic iv.33.5ff.; Paus ii.18.7, iii.10.6, iii.15.3–6, iii.19.7, viii.53.9; Apollod ii.7.3; Schol. ad Eur, Or 457; Schol. ad Hom, Il ii.581, qv. n. 16.

19 Dinos fr. (Athens Agora P334); François krater (Florence Mus Arch 4209); Ov, Met viii.306; Apollod i.9.27, i.121; Paus v.17.10.

20 François krater (Florence Mus Arch 4209); Chalkidian hydria (Munich Antikensamml 596); fort. dinos fr. (Athens Agora P334); neck amphora fr. (Tübingen Arch Inst S/12 2452); Archikles/Glaukytes cup (Munich Antikensamml 2243); Apollod i.8.2; fort. Xen, Cyn i.2; Paus viii.45.6; Ov, Met viii.380; Hyg, Fab cmxxiii; cum Atalanta, bronze mirror (Vatican Mus 12247); clay relief (Berlin Staatl Mus 8308); scaraboid (New York Metr Mus 74.51.4152); hydria (Munich Antikensamml 596); volute krater (Ferrara Mus Naz T404); cup (Bologna Mus Civ 361); neck amphora (Berlin Staatl Mus 1837); lekythos (Syracuse Mus Naz 26822); skyphos (London Brit Mus 1925.12–17.10); neck amphora (Munich Antikensamml 1541); band cup (Oxford Ashmolean Mus 1978.49); band cup (Munich Antikensamml 2241); hydria (Bonn Univ Fontana inv.46); hydria (Adolphseck Philipp von Hessen 6); hydria (Manchester Mus III.H5); dinos frs (Athens Nat Mus 15466, Acr.590).

21 Pind, Nem v.12ff., iv.95; Lyc, Alex 175; Apollod iii.12.6; Paus ii.29.2, x.30.4; Zen, Paroem i.123.

22 Pind, Nem iv.56 et schol, v.25; Apollod iii.13.3; Schol. ad Ap Rhod i.224; Schol. ad Aristoph, Nub 1063; Ant Lib 38; Schol. (Tzetzes) ad Lyc, Alex 175; Zen, Cent v.20.

23 Apollod iii.10.3; Pal, De incred ix; Aristoph, Plut 210; Ap Rhod i.153–5 et vid. iv.1466; Paus iii.14.7, iv.3.1; sed vid. Hom, Hymn xxxiii.3; Pind, Nem x.61–3; Paus iv.2.7; Schol. (Tzetzes) ad Lyc, Alex 553; Hyg, Fab xiv.

24 Archikles/Glaukytes cup (Munich Antikensamml 2243); Cypria fr.1 ap. Proc, Chrest i.; Cypria fr. 7 ap. Clem Alex, Protrept ii.30.5; Schol. (Tzetzes) ad Lyc, Alex 553; Pind, Nem x.60 et schol. ibid.

acts drag them fowards like beasts whose nature is to loathe one another: fierce lions and fiery-eyed boars yoked together in the traces, who tear up the ground and rake their drivers over the sharp stones.[25] The necklaces of gold which they have looped about their wives' necks become nooses about their own, ploughing them face-first into the earth.[26] They watch their images decay. They feel their skins puncture and split. They bristle with their own broken bones. Their memories are the memories of old men who have seen enough of death, those who watch from the walls, who have ransomed their lives and do not care to survive their sons.[27]

But they are sons themselves and they remember fathers other than the ones they are determined to become. Leaping out into free air to land on the far side of the culvert, one looks up to find a sunburnt arm, knuckles bunched about a chipped scythe.[28] Another watches the grizzled paternal head turn from the sacrifice, his fire-reddened face contorted, hand poised and twitching.[29] A third stares into an open mouth spilling a red mash of tendons, gristle and soft bones.[30] A wolf's eyes look back from behind his guiltless gaze.[31] Their fathers are mortals with the appetites of gods,[32] or gods with the appetites of men.[33]

25 Hom, Il ii.715, cf. Phrynicos Alcestis passim, Eur, Alc passim, Zen, Cent i.18; François krater (Florence Mus Arch 4209); Apollod i.9.15; Soph, fr. 851 ap. Plut, Def Or xv.417e; Ov, Met viii.310 et vid. Eur, Ph 409–29, Suppl 132–50, Hyps 87.

26 Apollod i.8.2; Ov, Met viii.316-7; Xen, Cyn 1.2; Pind, Nem ix.16, Pyth viii.38–61; Diod Sic iv.65.5; Paus v.17.7–8, ix.41.2; Asclepiades ap. Schol. ad Hom, Od xi.326; Hyg, Fab lxxiii; vid. Hom, Od xi.326, xv.247; Soph, Elec 836, Eriphyle frs passim; Lucian Deorum Concilium xii; sed vid. Eur, Ph 1104-11; Soph, Oed Col 1320–3.

27 Archikles/Glaukytes cup (Munich Antikensamml 2243); fort. qua 'Podarces' (1), Hom, Il ii.704, xiii.693; Hes, Cat fr. 68 P Berlin 9739 et vid. Paus iii.24.10 et Apollod i.9.12; aut qua 'Podarces' (2), Apollod ii.6.4, iii.12.3, iii.12.5; Schol. (Tztezes) ad Lyc, Alex 34; Hyg, Fab lxxxix et vid. Soph, Aj 1299–303 et Schol. ad Hom, Il viii.284; Hom, Il xx.237–40; neque qua 'Podargos' (1), Hom, Il viii.185; neque qua 'Podargos' (2), hydria (Florence Mus Arch 3830); neque qua 'Podarge', Hom, Il xvi.150.

28 Hes, Cat fr. 98.16 P Berlin 9777; Apollod i.8.1; neque Ov, Met viii.441; aliq. qua 'Toxamis', François krater (Florence Mus Arch 4209).

29 Paus i.42.6.

30 Schol. (Tzetzes) ad Lyc, Alex 481; Apollod iii.8.1.

31 Lyc, Alex 480–1 et schol.; Hyg, Fab clxxvi; Paus viii.1.4–6; Clem Alex, Protrept ii.36; Nonnus, Dionys xviii.20ff.; Nicolaus Damascenus fr. 43; Arnobius Adversus Nationes iv.24; Eratos, Cat 8; Hyg, Ast ii.4; Schol. (passim) ad Iulius Caesar Germanicus, Aratea Phaenomena; Schol. (Lact Plac) ad Statius, Theb xi.128; Paus viii.2.3 et vid. Plat, Rep viii.565d-e; Paus viii.2.6 sed vid. Paus vi.8.2; Pliny, Nat Hist viii.81; Augustine, De Civitate Dei xviii.17; vid. generalius, Paus viii.38.7; Porphyr, De abstinentia ii.27: Eusebius, Praeparatio Evangelii iv.16.6; et vid. Ael, Nat Anim x.26, Artemidorus, Onirocrit ii.12, Schol. (Eustathius) ad Hom, Od xiv.161.

32 Qua Tyndaridis, Hom, Il iii.236, Od xi.298; fort. Hom, Hymn xxxiii.1; Apollod

And yet here, in the gathering coincidence of the heroes' assembly, and now, between their inevitable beginnings and ends, they may step from the tracks holding them to these destined paths. They may struggle out of the deepening furrows marked and dug by their own footprints, which would bury them deep within the earth.[34] They may find the kernel within themselves which cannot be destroyed.[35] Their straggling journeys draw them ever closer, their lines trace a new, earth-bound constellation. A tendrilled creature creates itself over the terrain's rough fibre; its inky body will mark their meeting. They are each other's destinations.

The country which yet divides them is a place of accidental transformations. Its hinterland has been foreshadowed, its instabilities prefigured. Here, brothers turn into uncles,[36] women may become men[37] and men form themselves in the harsh races of rivers, wade out and stand dripping on the banks, a minute old but full-grown.[38] The terrain narrows with every step. Its coordinates are their untrammelled bodies and what they do. Those who die here can do so only by fluke[39] or carelessness.[40]

But the sons of Aeacus must survive to become the fathers of

iii.10.8; Paus iv.31.9, v.8.4; Ov, Met viii.301; Archikles/Glaukytes cup (Munich Antikensamml 2243); Xen, Cyn i.2.

33 Qua Dioscuris, Scopas ap. Paus viii.45.6; Hes, fr. ap. Schol. ad Pind, Nem x.150; Aristarchus ap. Hes, Cat xviiii ap. Porphyrius, Quaest Hom cclxv; Pind, Nem x.80-2, Pyth xi.94; Hom, Hymn xvii.1; Eur, Or 1689; Theocr xxii.1; Apollod i.8.2, ii.23, i.31; Cypria fr. 7 ap. Clem Alex, Protrept ii.30.5; Euphorion Chalkis, Alex Pleuron, Stesich cit. ap. Paus ii.22.6; Archikles/Glaukytes cup (Munich Antikensamml 2243); fort. Hom, Hymn xxxiii.1, Il iii.426.

34 Ov, Met viii.305 et vid. Apollod i.9.16 et Hom, Il i.264; Pal, De Incred x (quondam xi), etsi Heraclitus Paradoxigraphicus iii.

35 Apollod, Ep i.22 et vid. Hdt v.1; Hes, Sh 179; Paus v.10.8; Ov, Met xii.459-532; Schol. ad Hom, Il i.264; Ap Rhod i.57-64 et schol; Acusilaus fr. ap. P Oxy xiii.133ff. (FrGrHist 2F22); Pind fr. cxxviii cit. ap. Plut, Mor 1057D; Plut, Comm Not i.

36 Apollod i.8.2, i.9.16, iii.9.1; Paus viii.4.8, viii. 5.1, viii. 8.4, viii. 23.3; Hyg, Fab ccxliv; Soph, Mys cit. ap. Schol. ad Aristot, Poet 1460a 32; Xen, Cyn i.2.

37 Apollod, Ep i.22; Serv ad Virg, Aen vi.448; Ap Rhod i.57-64 et scholia; Plut, De Prof i; Apostolius Cent iv.19; Pal, De incred x (quondam xi); Ant Lib xvii; Ov, Met xii.459-532; Hyg, Fab xiv.

38 Ov, Met viii.360; Hom, Il xxi.140, xxi.153-61; Strab vii.fr.38/3e, vii.fr.39/Epitome; neque Paus ix.12.1, Apollod iii.4.1, iii.12.6, et vid. Apollod i.9.3, Paus ii.5.1, Callim iv.78, Ap Rhod iv.1765ff. ad dieg. Milan ad Callim, Iamb viii, Schol. ad Ap Rhod i.117, Statius, Theb vii.325, Schol. (Lact Plac) ad Statius, Theb vii.315; neque Hom, Il iv.295, v.695, Aesch, Pers 959, Plut, Them vii.5.1, Hdt viii.5.

39 Apollod i.8.2; Ov, Met viii.308; Schol. ad Aristoph, Nub 1063; Ant Lib 38; Schol. (Tzetzes) ad Lyc, Alex 175; Pherecydes cit. ap. Schol. (Tzetzes) ad Lyc, Alex 444; Eur, Iph Aul 282; Stes, Suoth fr. ap. P Oxy 2359.

40 François krater (Florence Mus Arch 4209); Chalkidian hydria (Munich Antikensamml 596); black figure vase (Berlin Staatlich Mus F1705); Hom, Il ix.534ff.;

Achilles and Teucer,[41] just as the son of Acrisius must once again be the father of sly Odysseus.[42] The ground will close and inseparable allies will find themselves divided between the land of the living and the land of the dead.[43] They have heard their futures in the songs of halcyons and crows; they sounded like commands.[44]

Their country is a spattering of enclaves now: themselves. Their bodies are kingdoms which ally themselves with their neighbours and rivals. Some merged long ago, spooned like twins in the womb,[45] smooth-surfaced and shelled like an egg.[46] The War-god bellows but his son has fled.[47] The Argo sails away from the kingdom and kingship she was built to reclaim.[48] Her captain never returns.[49]

They are the actors of feats they have compelled themselves to perform and others yet awaiting them. Their footfalls shake oak trees to their roots and set off landslides and small thunder-

Bacch v.117; Paus viii.4.10, viii.45.2–7; Ap Rhod i.164; Lyc, Alex 486–90; Ov, Met viii.315, 391–402.

41 Neck amphora. fr. (Tübingen Arch Inst S/12 2452); Apollod i.8.2; Aristot, Rhet 1389a; Paus viii.45.6; Apollod i.8.2; Bacch xiii.97–101; Pind, Isth vi.19, fort. Nem iii.32–7; Isoc ix.16; Xen, Cyn i.2, i.8–9; Plut, Thes x.2–3; sed vid. Pherecydes cit. ap. Apollod iii.12.6; Paus ii.29.9; Schol. ad Eur, Andr 687; Schol. ad Pind, Nem v.7.12; Schol. ad Hom, Il xvi.14; Hyg, Fab xiv; Diod Sic iv.72.7; Eur, Hel 85–6, Iph Aul 193; Hdt viii.64.2.

42 Ov, Met viii.315; Apollod, Ep 3.12; Hom, Od i.430, ii.99, iv.111; Strab x.2.8, x.2.24; Hom, Od i.189 et vid. Hom, Il iii.201 et Aristoph, Plut 311 et Eur, Hec 133 et Plat, Hipp Min 365a, inter alia.

43 Apollod, Ep 1.23ff.; Paus i.18.4; Hom, Od i.631; Eur, Herc 619; Ap Rhod i.101ff. et schol; Diod Sic iv.26.1, iv.63.4ff.; Paus i.17.4, ix.31.5, x.29.9; Apostolius Cent iii.36; Schol. ad Aristoph, Eq 1368; Virg, Aen vi.392ff., vi.617ff.; Hor, Odes iii.4.79ff., iv.7.27ff.; Hyg, Fab lxxix; Aulus Gellius x.16.13; Serv ad Virg, Aen vi.617; sed vid. Hyg, Fab lxxix; Diod Sic iv.63.5 (sed vid. Plut, Thes 31.4–35.1; Ael, Var Hist iv.5; Paus i.17.4, i.18.4, ii.22.6, iii.18.5; Tzetzes Chiliades ii.406ff.); Aristot, Nic Eth 1171a.

44 Pind, Pyth iv.336; Ap Rhod i.65; Paus v.17.4; Hyg, Fab xiv; Ov, Met viii.316, xii.456; Hes, Sh 181; Ap Rhod i.1084ff., iii.930ff., iv.1502–36; Lyc. Alex 881; Stat, Theb iii.521; Archikles/Glaukytes cup (Munich Antikensamml 2243); hydria (Munich Antikensamml 596); Paus v.7.10; Thebais fr. 5 ap. Asclepiades cit. ap. Schol. ad Pind, Ol vi.15–17; neque Schol. (Tzetzes) ad Lyc, Alex 427–30, 980; Hes, Melamp fr. 1 ap. Strab xiv.1.25; Pherecydes cit. ap. Strab xiv.1.27; Hyg, Fab cxxviii, clxxiii; Plut, Def Or 45; Apollod ii.243, 245, 265; Paus vii.3.2.

45 Ov, Met viii.311; Paus ii.15; Apollod i.9.16; volute krater (Ferrara Mus Naz T136).

46 Ov, Met viii.308; Hom, Il ii.621, xi.709, xiii.638; Pind, Ol x.25; Paus v.1.10, v.2.1, v.2.5, vi.20.16; Schol. ad Hom, Il xiii.638–9, xi.709; Eustathius ad Hom, Il xi.749; Ibycus fr. 34 ap. Athen ii.50; Pherecydes ap. Schol. ad Hom, Il xi.709.

47 Hom, Il i.307; Hes, Sh 179; Paus x.29.10; Apollod i.8.2; Ov, Met viii.307.

48 Archikles/Glaukytes cup (Munich Antikensamml 2243); Apollod i.8.2; Ov, Met viii.302; Hes, Cat fr. 13 ap. Schol. ad Hom, Od xii.69; Schol. ad Hom, Il iii.243; Hes, Theog 997–1000; Theocr xxii.137ff.

49 Apollod i.9.17; Lyc, Alex 1310; Pind, Pyth iv.12; Schol. (Lact, Plac) ad Stat, Theb v.402, v.455.

storms. Cattle flee and sheep miscarry. They collapse limestone caverns bunkered deep beneath the earth, or glide over fields of heliotrope without bending a stalk. They wear the armour of their pasts and futures.

Look: the highlands of Taygetus and Erymanthus are deserted, the plains of Elis and Thessaly silent. They have moved on, leaving behind a seismic quiet. The armature of what they mean cases them in its brittle glaze; these are lives which can only be enacted. It will be a weary meeting when they at last look across the gulf and know they may shuck off these encrusted skins.

Almost there.

They are the generation of Heracles: only they would gather in this manner, in the luxury of this long moment. Their sons will destroy one another at Troy. They know this and know that their tale will be twisted there, betrayed by one of their own and recast as policy.[50] The sadness they will forget here is that the armour they shed must encase them again, that their names must swag themselves in epithets, that the sentences they carry will still be here on their return, patient as ferrymen and reproachful as widows. The boats will be waiting and the earth heaped.

The presences of some will leave no deeper imprint than a stylus in wet clay as it lifts and strands them, frozen in strange attitudes in the following silence. For some there will be only that.[51] For others, the scratch of the quill over the papyrus's

---

50 Hom, Il ix.529–99.

51 François krater (Florence Mus Arch 4209); Archikles/Glaukytes cup (Munich Antikensamml 2243); qua 'Pausileon', Ov, Met viii.312; qua 'Pauson', Aristot, Poet 2½2; Aristoph, Ach 854; qua 'Thorax' Larissae, Hdt ix.1, ix.58; qua 'Thoas' (1) Aetolus, Hom, Il ii.638 et passim; Hom, Od xiv.499; Apollod, Ep 4.40, 3.12; qua (2) patre Hypsipylae, Apollod i.9.17, iii.6.4, Ep 1.9, 7.40; Paus v.3.6, x.38.5; Strab vi.1.5; qua (3) rege Tauricae, Ant Lib 27; Eur, Iph in Taur 1–32 et passim; Apollod, Ep 6.27; qua (4) ignoto, Hes, Cat fr. 85 ap. Choeroboscus i.123.22H; Tit Liv xxxv.37–45, xxxviii.38; Pol, Onom xxviii.4; qua (5) gigante, Apollod i.6.2; qua (6) filio Icarii, Apollod iii.10.6; qua (7) proco Penelopae, Apollod, Ep 7.27; qua (8) rege Corinthiae, Paus ii.4.3; qua (9) comite Thesei, Plut, Thes 26.3; qua (10) nomine priore Acheloi, Strab x.2.1; 'Thornax' (1) qua monte Corinthiano, Paus ii.36.1 et vid. Stephanus Byzantinus cit. ap. Strab viii.5 conj. Meineke; qua (2) urbe Laconide, Hdt i.69; Paus iii.10.8, iii.11.1; 'Antandros' (1) qua urbe Cilicia, Alcaeus fr. 65 et vid. Strab xiii.1.51; Thuc viii.108.4, iv.52.3, iv.75.1; Xen, Anab vii.8.7, Hell i.25–6; Hdt v.26, vii.42; Apollod, Ep 3.33; Diod Sic xii.72–3; qua (2) Virg, Aen vii.631; qua (3) ductore Messeniano, Paus iv.7.4, iv.10.5; qua (4) Megalopolitano, Paus iv.10.5; 'Aristandros' qua sculptore (1) Paus viii.30.10, iii.18.8; (2) Arrian iv.4; Pliny, Nat Hist xvii.243; 'Simon' qua (1) sutore, Diog Laert ii.122 et vid. ii.124; qua (2) sculptore Paus v.27.2; qua (3) scelere, Aristoph, Nub 352, 359; qua (4) socio Amadoci, Dem xxiii.10 et passim; 'Kimon' qua (1) patre Militiadidis, Hdt vi.34, vi.39, vi.136; Plut, Cimon passim, Pericles passim; Paus i.28.3–29.8, iii.3.7.

surface decrees contradictory lineages and mad progresses which will send them sailing between Argos and Colchis,[52] drive them from the well polluted by the body of Chrysippus, or tumble them into the labyrinth which will be built by their sons. They glare in the lights from different altars and their shadows battle among themselves. But those dark spartoi are not themselves; they are competing plausibilities.[53]

Such are the futures which tug at them, from whose grasp they have slipped to make this journey and to whose insistence they now deafen themselves with the noise of their own common purpose. As they near the gathering place they shout out their names to those arrived, to be known among them.

... *Euthymachos, Leucippus, Ancaeus, Echion, Thersites, Antimachos, Panopeus, Iphiclus, Aphares, Evippus, Plexippus, Eurypylus, Prothous, Cometes, Prokaon, Klytius, Hippothous, Iolaos, Theseus* ...

They are heard here, this once and never again.[54] Those who survive will remember this clamour as the true beginning of the hunt. Shout follows shout until together their names raise an edifice of air in which all find shelter from the futures racing towards them, be it exile to the islands in plain view before them,[55] or to fall in the hills rising across the water,[56] to flee Trachis and be taken at Oechalia,[57] to know that their prime has passed.[58]

... *Pirithous, Enaesimus, Hippothous, Alcon, Scaeus, Dorycleus, Eutiches, Bucolus, Lycaethus, Tebrus, Eurytus,*

---

52 Ov, Met viii.360 (MS 'U') qua 'Hippalamon', aliq. 'Hippalamus', aliq. 'Hippalcimus'; Hyg, Fab lxxxiv; Schol. ad Eur, Or 5; Apollod iii.11.8; Schol. ad Pind, Ol i.89; Paus vi.20.7; Schol. ad Hom, Il ii.105; qua 'Euphemon', Ov, Met viii.360 (vid. emend. Slater) et vid. Apollod i.9.16, Ap Rhod iv.1754ff., Hyg, Fab clvviii; Ov, Met viii.360 (Codex Planudes, Paris 2848), qua 'Eupalamon', aliq. 'Eupalamus', Apollod iii.15.5, iii.15.7; Tzet, Chil i.490; Schol. ad Plat, Ion 121a; Schol. ad Plat, Rep viii.529d; Hyg, Fab xxxix; Serv ad Virg, Aen vi.14, sed vid. Paus ix.3.2; Diod Sic iv.76.1; Pherecydes cit. ap. Schol. ad Soph, Oed Col 472; Plat, Ion 533a; Clidemus cit. ap. Plut, Thes 19.

53 Ex Locri, Ov, Met viii.312; ex Amyclae, Apollod iii.10.1; Paus i.44.3, iii.1.1, iii.12.5, iv.1.1; ex Megara, Paus i.39.6, i.42.6; ex Caria, Aristot cit. ap. Strab vii.7.2; Hdt i.171; ex 'Asia', Hom Il, x.429, xx.96; ex Troezena, Ov, Met viii.566.

54 Apollod i.8.2; Ov, Met viii.312; neque Xen, Cyn vii.5; neque qua 'Hylaeus', Apollod iii.9.2; Virg, Georg ii.457, Aen viii.294; Prop i.1.13.

55 Strab x.2.20; Apollod ii.5.5, ii.7.2, iii.10.8; Diod Sic iv.13.4, iv.36.1; Paus v.1.10, v.3.1; Schol. ad Hom, Il xi.700; Prisc, Inst vi.92; fort. Hes, Cat fr. 67 cit. ap. schol. ad Eur, Or 249.

56 Hes, Cat fr. 98.16 P Berlin 9777; Bacch v.118.

57 Apollod ii.7.7, i.6.16; Hyg, Fab xiv, clxxiii; Ov, Met viii.313, viii.371; Paus ii.13.2; Iamb, Pyth xviii.23; Diog Laert viii.84.

58 Ov, Met viii.313; Xen, Cyn 2.

*Hippocorystes, Eumedes, Alcinus, Dorceus, Sebrus, Enaro-
phorus, Iphikles, Acastus, Peleus, Lynceus, Idas, Admetos,
Amphiaraus, Podargos, Toxeus, Ischepolis, Harpaleas, Castor,
Pollux . . .*
The discus has been launched, thrown so high it will take
decades to descend. Beautiful Hyacinthos turns to his brother, as
though about to speak.[59] The heroes shout and each shout is
taken up by those gathered here until their names thunder about
them.

*. . . Caeneus, Cepheus, Pelagon, Telamon, Laertes, Mopsos,
Eurytion, Cteatus, Dryas, Jason, Phoenix, Pausileon, Thorax,
Antandros, Aristandros, Simon, Kimon, Eupalamus, Lelex,
Hyleus, Phyleus, Agelaus, Hippasos, Nestor, Kynortes,
Meilanion . . .*
The last of these[60] shouts loud for the last of all, who is his
cousin and the lone huntress admitted among their number.
. . . Atalanta.[61]

---

59 François krater (Florence Mus Arch 4209); Paus iii.13.1; Apollod i.9.5, iii.10.3.
60 Archikles/Glaukytes cup (Munich Antikensamml 2243); fort. dinos fr. (Athens
Agora P334); François krater (Florence Mus Arch 4209); neck amphora fr. (Tübingen Arch
Inst S/12 2452); neck amphora fr. (Tarquinia Mus Naz RC5564); Xen, Cyn 1.2, 1.7; Paus
v.19.2; Apollod iii.6.3, iii.9.2; Callim iii.215; Hellanikos fr. 99; Ov, Ars Amat ii.185–92,
iii.29–30; Prop i.1.9–10; fort. Eur, Mel fr. 537.
61 François krater (Florence Mus Arch 4209); Chalkidian hydria (Munich
Antikensamml 596); dinos fr. (Athens Agora P334); neck amphora fr. (Tübingen Arch Inst
S/12 2452); Archikles/Glaukytes cup (Munich Antikensamml 2243); 'Atalanta' vase
(Athens Nat Mus 432); exaleiptron (Munich Antikensamml 8600); dinos (Vatican Mus
306); hydria (Florence Mus Arch 3830); dinos (Boston Mus Fine Arts 34.212); pelike (St
Petersburg Herm B4528); kantharos (Athens Nat Mus 2855); hydria (Paris Louvre E696);
hydria (Copenhagen Nat Mus 13567); amphora (Trieste Mus Civ S380); volute krater
(Berlin Staatl Mus 3258); clay relief plaque (Amsterdam Allard Pierson Mus 1758); clay
relief plaque (Berlin Staatl Mus 5783); alabaster relief urn (Florence Mus Arch 78484);
sarcophagus (Athens Nat Mus 1186); sarcophagus (Rome Mus Cap 822); cum Meleagro et
apio: amphora (Bari Mus Naz 872); stamnos (Perugia Mus Civ); bronze mirror (Berlin Staatl
Mus fr. 146); bronze mirror (Paris Louvre ED2837 inv.1041); bronze mirror (Indiana Art
Mus 62.251); bronze mirror (ex Munich Antikensamml 3654); wall painting (Naples Mus
Naz 8980); wall painting (Pompeii VI.9.2(1), Casa di Meleagro); mosaic (Cardenagimeno,
Burgos, vid. B.Arraiza: nondum prolatum); wall painting (deletus: ex Pompeii VI.2.22.c,
Casa delle Danzatrici); opus tessellatum (amissus: ex Lugduno); id. (locus ignotus: ex
Domo rubri pavimenti, Antiochus); sic venatrice cum venatoribus, neck amphora
(Toronto Royal Ontario Mus 919.5.35); hydria (Ruvo Mus Jatta J1418); hydria (Vienna
Kunsthist Mus 158); hydria (Athens Nat Mus 15113); hydria (Würzburg Martin von
Wagner Mus 522); wooden relief (Kypselos, vid. Paus v.19.2); wall painting (Pompeii
VI.13.19.(h)); wall painting (Pompeii VI.15.6.(1)); mosaic (Paris Louvre MA3444); cum
Meleagro et Oineo, sarcophagus (Rome Mus Cap 1897); post venationem, sarcophagus
(Istanbul Arch Mus 2100); sarcophagus (Autun MusÂe Rolin 66); sarcophagus (Rome Mus
Cap 623); Parrhasios cit. ap. Suet, Tib xxxxiv.2 ; sic athleta sola, cup (Paris Louvre
CA2259); scarab (Etruscan, amissus); sic luctatorem cum Peleo, dinos frs (Athens Nat
Mus 15466, Acr.590); hydria (Manchester Mus III H5); hydria (Adolphseck Philipp von

11

Their first hunt is for each other and now it is done. They search in one another's faces for the men behind the names. To the south, the claw of the Peloponnese grasps at the sea, its peninsular fingers reaching after the islands escaped from its coast. North is where they are destined. They look across the water.

A narrowing plain runs along the face of the far shoreline. A range of hills rises behind it and far inland lies the great spine of the Pindus. The sea glitters in their faces. On the other side of the gulf, the one who called[62] them here is waiting.

The land drops in terraces to the shoreline; two enormous

Hessen 6); hydria (Bonn Univ Fontana inv 46); band cup (Munich Antikensamml 2241); band cup (Oxford Ashmolean Mus 1978.49); neck amphora (Munich Antikensamml 1541); skyphos (London Brit Mus 1925.12-17.10); lekythos (Syracuse Mus Naz 26822); neck amphora (Berlin Staatl Mus 1837); cup (Bologna Mus Civ 361); volute krater (Ferrara Mus Naz T404); hydria (Munich Antikensamml 596); scaraboid (New York Metr Mus 74.51.4152) clay relief (Berlin Staatl Mus 8308); bronze mirror (Vatican Mus 12247); in cursu, calyx krater (Bologna Mus Civ 300); clay relief roundels (New York Metr Mus 17.194.870); glass bowl (Reims MusÅe 2281); glass beaker (Corning Mus 66.1.238); sic athleta cum cetero, cup (Rome Villa Giulia 48234); cup (Ferrara Mus Naz T991); cup (Paris Cab Méd 818); bell krater (Oxford Ashmolean Mus 1954.270); imagines diversas, lekythos (Cleveland Mus Art 66.114); calyx krater (Milan Mus Civ St.6873); bronze cista (Berlin Staatl Mus 3467); wall painting (vid. Pliny, Nat Hist xxxv.17); wall painting (Naples Mus Naz 8897 ex Pompeii VI.9.2(38), Casa di Meleagro); fort. Atlanta, cup (Paris Louvre E670); clay relief (Athens Nat Mus ex Tegea vid. Jacobstahl MR pl. LXVIII); bronze statuette (Vienna Kunsthist Mus VI2757); alabastron (Ruvo Mus Jatta 1349); Apollod i.8.2, i.8.3, iii.9.2; Paus viii.45.2, viii.45.6; Eur, Mel fr. 530, Ph 1108; Callim iii.215–24; Xen, Cyn xiii.18; et vid. schol. ad Eur, Ph 150; schol. ad Theocr iii.42; schol. ad Ap Rhod i.769; ex Arcadia, cum Meleagro aut Meilanio aut Peleo, Apollod iii.9.2; fort. Plat, Rep 620a; Soph, Oed Col 1322; Aristoph, Lys 785–96; Xen, Cyn i.7; Ael, Var Hist xiii.1; Prop i.1.9–10; Ov, Ars Amat ii.185–92; Mus, Hero 153–56; Theog 1287–94; Diod Sic iv.41.2, iv.48.5; ex Boetia, cum Hippomene, Hes, Cat fr. 14 ap. P Petrie iii.3 et Schol. ad Hom, Il xxiii.683 et P Grec ii.130; Paus iii.24.2, v.19.2, viii.35.10; fort. Plat, Rep 620a; Theocr ii.1.40–2; Hyg, Fab clxxxv; Ov, Met x.560–707; Serv ad Virg, Aen iii.113; perturbationes de leonibus et filiis, Pal, De incred xiii et Heraclitus Paradoxigraphicus xii; Ov, Met x.681–704; Aesch, Sept 532–3, 547; Soph, Oed Col 1320–2; Eur, Ph 150; Thebais fr. 6 ap. Paus ix.18.6; Hecataeus fr. 32; Antimachos fr. 29; Serv ad Virg, Aen iii.113; schol. ad Theocr iii.40; Nonnus, Dionys xii.87–9; Aristarchus ap. schol. ad Soph, Oed Col 1320; Philokles ap. schol. ad Soph, Oed Col 1320; Hellanikos fr. 99; Apollod i.9.13, iii.9.2; Hyg, Fab lxx, lxxxxix, cclxx.

62 According to Apollodorus, they 'assembled' after 'Oeneus called together all the noblest men of Greece' (Apollod i.8.2). The sons of Hippocoon 'were sent' by their father (Ov, Met viii.314), as was Ischepolis by Alcathous (Paus i.42.6). Homer has the heroes 'gathered' (Il ix.544). Holzinger's commentary on Lycophron's Alexandra (ad Lyc, Alex 490) notes, 'Two Ancaei are known to mythology – Ancaeus of Arcadia and Ancaeus of Samos. Of the latter – who is often confused with the other – it is told that when planting a vine it was prophesied that he would never taste its fruit. Just when he was about to drink the wine of its grapes, *there came the news* of the Calydonian Boar . . .' (italics added). Xenophon notes the reaction to a certain Zelarchus, who 'set up a shout; and they rushed upon him as though a wild boar . . . had been sighted.' (Xen, Anab v.7.24).

steps lead down to the water. The heroes fell stands of poplars and alders[63] and build boats,[64] or lash the trunks together to fashion rafts.[65] Or they call up dolphins and ride them,[66] or throw themselves with a shout into the gulf and strike out[67] for the far shore.

63 Hom, Od v.238–42. Fir was used for masts.

64 The first ship was believed to have been built for Jason and called the Argo after its builder, Argos, son of Phrixus (Ap Rhod i.524, iv.560; Apollod i.9.16). Pagasae, where it was built, is perhaps so-called in commemoration of its 'construction', although 'pagae' also 'means "fountains" which are numerous and abundant' there (Strab ix.5.15). Representations on a metope of the Sicyonian Treasury and a red figure volute krater (Ruvo Mus Jatta 1501) are uninformative regarding the Argo's construction: it was presumably sturdy, despite the story that, many years later, its poop fell off and killed Jason, who was asleep beneath it (Staphilus fr. 5 ap. schol. ad Ap Rhod i.4; schol. ad Eur, Med Argumentum). The boat in which Paris abducted Helen was built by Phereclus (Apollod, Ep 3.2), whose father and grandfather, Tecton and Harmon (Hom, Il v.59ff.), are identifiable by their names as shipwrights. Homer equips it with sails, mast, forestays (Il i.432–5), backstays (Od xii.423) and an anchor-stone (Il i.435); two dinoi supply a cathead for raising and lowering the latter (Chicago 1967.115.141; Cleveland Mus Art 71.46). One krater adds landing ladders and steering oars (London Brit Mus 436). Stern cables (Hom, Il i.436) and tackle (Hom, Od ii.423), made of ox-hide (Od ii.428), were liable to stretch (Il ii.135); halyards and brailing ropes likewise (dinos, Cleveland Mus Art 71.46). Prows of warships were carved in the shape of a boar's head (amphora, Boston Mus Fine Arts 01.8100; amphora, London Brit Mus 436; dinos, Cleveland Mus Art 71.46; François krater, Florence Mus Arch 4209). Vid. also a terracotta boat unearthed at Phylokapi (Atkinson et al. *Excavations at Phylakopi in Melos* (1904), p. 206, fig. 180) and Cinyras's deception of Menelaus by fashioning out of clay the boats he had promised for the Trojan expedition (Apollod, Ep 3.9; Eustathius ad Hom, Il xi.20; the 'Odysseus' once ascribed to Alcidamas offers the more conventional ruse of bribery). The most densely figured fragment of a silver rhyton includes men usually interpreted as poling a boat ashore (Evans, *The Palace of Minos*, vol. III, p. 81, figs 50–6, cf. Theochares, *Archaeology*, 15, 1958, Kouroniotes, *Ephemeris*, 108, 1914, Blegen, *Hesperia Supplement*, viii, 1949, pl. VII, Kirk, *Annual of the British School at Athens*, 117, 1914, fig. 5, Schaeffer, *Encomi-Alasia* (1952), pl. X, fig. 38, and earlier, Kunze, *Orchomenos* (1934), vol. III, pl. XXIX and III). The spiral found as a characteristic Cycladic motif (Blegen, *Zygouries* (1928), pl. XX, 9, Tsountas, *Ephemeris* (1899), pl. X, Zervos, *L'Art des Cyclades* (1957), pl. XXIX, inter alia) alludes most plausibly to rope coiled on the deck of a ship.

65 Hom, Od v.238–58; Apollod, Ep 7.24; Brennus's Gauls improvised rafts from their shields to cross the Spercheios at a point seventy miles north-east of here (Paus x.20.8). The raft sailed from Tyre by Heracles was drawn ashore at Cape Mesate by ropes fashioned from the hair of the Thracian women and was preserved in the sanctuary of Heracles at Erythrae (Paus vii.5.6). Thracians, apparently, could not swim (Thuc vii.30.2). Vid.n.67.

66 So Theseus (Bacch xvii, qv.), Melicertes (Paus i.44.8, ii.1.3) and the Spartan Phalanthus (Paus x.13.10). Arion's arrival on dolphin-back at Taenarus was proverbial (Hdt i.23.1; Plat, Rep 453d); the animal is ubiquitous on that city's coinage. A youth astride a dolphin (lekythos, London Brit Mus 60.55.1) may be any of the above. Pausanias reports a tame dolphin at Poroselene which gave rides in gratitude for its rescue by a local fisherman (Paus iii.25.7; Ael, Nat Anim ii.6; Op, Hal v.448–518). Safe passage might be sought within the dolphin's form rather than on its back: so Nemesis's attempted escape from the attentions of Zeus (Cypria fr. vii ap. Athen viii.334b) and, less deserving but more successful, the Tyrrhenian pirates driven overboard by Dionysus's conjured lion and bear (Hom, Hymn vii.47–54; krater, Toledo 1982.134). Elsewhere, the dolphin is a frequent motif in scenes depicting the flight of women from various pursuers (column krater, Oxford Ashmolean Mus 1927.1; Nolan amphora fr. Boston Mus Fine Arts 03.789; hydria,

But they cross the water and its currents wash away their sweat and grime. Nearing land, the brine mixes with freshwater springs which bubble up from the seabed, tasting sweet after weeks of groundwater. The steep limestone peaks of Chalkis[68] and Taphiassus slide by to the east of them; the coast chosen as their landfall is a triangular lagoon fronted by a line of tiny islands.[69] Inland, the looping ridges of Mount Aracynthus rise over them. They wade through reed-beds and abandoned salt pans. As prelude to the hunt they will be feasted tonight in Kalydon.

The ground turns from mud to marsh to baked earth. The sun which steals the damp from their chitons takes with it the last taints and tangs of their journey here, the harsh woodsmoke of their campfires, the burnt fat of the animal slaughtered for good fortune when they left their hearths. That was long ago and the rain's black curtain has fallen behind them like sleep or forgetting. They come ashore in ones and twos and comb the water from their hair with their fingers: a colony of individual silences.

A dog barks. Atalanta looks up. The mud on the greaves tied about her shins is drying. She taps at it with her bowstave. She

Bowdoin 1908.3) or towards the safety of a protector, usually Nereus, the women being his Nereid daughters, whose primary function in Attic art is to run screaming towards him with the news of their sister Thetis's rape.

67 Alexander the Great either could (Diod Sic xiv.17.2) or could not (Plut, Alex 58.4) swim; in this he was typical of the Greeks. Odysseus swam to the land of the Phaeacians after the wreck of his raft by Poseidon (Hom, Od v.375ff.), but later in that poem, 'Few have made the escape from grey sea to shore by swimming' (xxiii.237–9). Two unnamed youths contemplate swimming the River Centrites but find it fordable (Xen, Anab iv.3.12), while brackish Lake Acragas would support even those who could not swim at all (Strab vi.2.9) and bathers in the hot springs at Methana had to be dissuaded from swimming in the sea afterwards (Paus ii.34.1). Of the Persian sailors wrecked with their fleet off Cape Athos, 'those who could not swim were drowned' (Hdt vi.44), implying that some of them could. Barbarians were not swimmers: at the battle of Salamis more died by drowning than by force of arms, while the Greek sailors swam to safety (Hdt viii.89). Swimming was proverbially an accomplishment as basic as spelling, according to Plato (Laws 689d), who alludes obliquely to a form of backstroke (Phaed 264a), but the ability was not universal (Hdt viii.129). Onomarchus's Phocians were proficient enough to attempt escape by that means (Diod Sic xvi.35.4–6), only to be captured by Philip of Macedon's Thessalians and put to death – by drowning. Several writers (Plut, Tim 25.4; Nepos, Tim 2.4; Diod Sic xvi.79.4–8; xiv.114.1–6) warn against the dangers of trying to swim while wearing armour.

68 Thus Homer (Il ii.640) and Artemidorus and Apollodorus as cited by Strabo (x.2.4, x.2.21, cf. Thuc ii.83, Statius, Theb iv.105, Ptol iii.13–14, Schol. ad Nicander Theriaca 215). The eponymous mountain bird (Hom, Il xiv.291) has not been identified (Plat, Crat 392a).

69 The lagoon has been claimed as a harbour (Paus vii.21.1), a port (Thuc ii.83) and a 'great lake full of fish' (Strab x.2.21) among which the 'labrax' was particularly tasty (Archestratus ap. Athen vii.311a).

watches her black-eyed and white-haired animal nose its way out of the reeds: Aura.[70] Next she drops to one knee, gulps air into her stomach and hawks up a thin lozenge of leather. Unrolled, it becomes a tongue of leather cut to the shape of her fingers; within it is the tight coil of her bowstring. Dry.

She unravels the cord and ties it to the bowstave then slips the leather tab over her wrist and fastens its flanges to her fingers. She flexes her knuckles. The twisted rope of cloth is unknotted from her waist and draped over her shoulders. The sun will dry it. Aura barks again. The dog has scented her and approaches now at an easy trot, keeping close to the line of the reeds. Atalanta undoes her pouch and upends it: twelve arrowheads, a bone needle, strips of leather, a pair of bronze ankle guards, a knife. She checks each in turn then repacks them. Around her, the rest of the hunters are absorbed in similar business: unstrapping and cleaning weapons, scraping mud, knotting or unknotting scraps of cloth and leather, fitting blades to shafts. These are well-rehearsed preparations.

A little way down the shore, Ancaeus holds out his double-headed axe[71] between two of the sons of Hippocoon, who sharpen their spearheads[72] against it. The metallic rasp rings out in a complicated rhythm. Her dog has picked up a different scent. The land slopes up from the shoreline in gentle ridges of powdery yellow soil tufted with scrubby grasses.[73] Atalanta

---

70 Aura (Pol, Onom v.45).

71 He is depicted with it on the front gable of the temple of Athena at Tegea (Paus viii.45.6) and in a fragment of Euripides's otherwise lost play *Meleagros* (vid. ap. TGF frs 525–39). This is presumably the same double-headed axe hidden in a granary by Ancaeus's grandfather Aleus in an unsuccessful attempt to prevent Ancaeus joining the Argonauts (Ap Rhod i.163ff.). Hephaistos carries a double-headed tool (calyx krater, Harvard 1960.236) which may be either a hammer or the axe with which he released Athena from the head of Zeus (Apollod i.3.6; Pind, Ol vii.35; Schol. ad Hom, Il i.195; Schol. ad Plat, Tim 23d). Achilles offers ten such instruments to the winner of the archery contest at Troy (Hom, Il xxiii.851). Clytemnestra dispatches Agamemnon with one (Eur, Elec 161–5, Tro 362–5), as does Theseus Procrustes (neck amphora, Munich Antikensamml 2325; skyphos, Toledo 1963.27).

72 Boar-spears 'must have blades fifteen inches long, and stout teeth at the middle of the socket, forged in one piece but standing out; and their shafts must be of cornel wood, as thick as a military spear' (Xen, Cyn x.3). The huntsman must 'grasp it with the left hand in front and the right behind, since the left steadies while the right drives it . . . taking care that the boar doesn't knock it out of his hand with a jerk of his head' (Xen, Cyn x.11–12).

73 Homer supplies Kalydon with the epithets 'rocky' (Il ii.643) and 'steep' (Il xiv.116), probably in allusion to Mount Aracynthus, but softens the description with orchards (Il ix.543), vineland and ploughland (Il ix.581); Bacchylides mentions 'vine-rows' and 'flocks' (v.108–109). Strabo twice describes the coastal plain as 'fertile and level' (x.2.3, x.2.4) – in which he is supported by a fragment of Euripides quoted by Lucian – and the interior as

watches the line of hackles on the animal's back twist as it climbs the incline and disappears from sight. She frowns, puzzled. One of the spear-sharpeners pauses. Further down the beach a head rises from its task. Meilanion? Too distant. The moment stretches and then is snapped by a volley of sharp yelps.

She snatches the knife and is running before she knows it, taking the ground in long strides. She has outrun stags but this is not her terrain. Cold forests and uplands, freezing streams: Arcadia. She reaches the top of the ridge.

Dogs are snarling and scuffling for position. A pack of them surround her animal: Molossians and Castorians,[74] heavy-bodied brown-and-white brutes. She lunges to get an arm around Aura's belly and feels claws scrape down her forearm. She lifts her dog clear. Jaws snap at her forearm and close on air. She knocks the aggressor to the ground. Then, faint yet distinct through the tumult of yelping and barking, she hears the scrape of metal behind her. A sword being unsheathed.

There is no time to think. To hunt is to guess weights, dimensions, angles. The man is behind her and to her left. She must catch him high up, divide him between ducking his head and protecting his face. Cut his throat. Hang his head in a tree. Take his genitals for trophies. She turns on the ball of her heel, planting her other foot forward and raising her arm. She has not touched a man before today, or been touched herself.

But the man stands with the sun behind him, a black shape against the brightness of the sky. His sword is drawn. Atalanta checks her movement. She can smell him. Was this how she smelled to Rhoecus and Hylaeus?[75] A crested helmet covers his face to the chin, leather body armour sheaths his limbs. She

---

'having excellent soil' (x.2.3), although Aetolia as a whole is noted for its 'ruggedness' (Ephorus cit. ap. Strab x.3.2). Agesilaus captured 'herds of cattle and droves of horses' in neighbouring Acarnania (Xen, Hell iv.6.6), but reached the safety of the southern coast 'by such roads as neither many nor few could traverse against the will of the Aetolians; they allowed him, however, to pass through' (Xen, Hell iv.6.14).

74 Molossians were first bred in Epirus (Hdt i.146, inter alia) in the shadow of the Pindus. One such animal was, or will be, indirectly responsible for Heracles killing the sons of Hippocoon, who 'had killed the son of Licymnius. For when he was looking at the palace of Hippocoon, a hound of the Molossian breed ran out and rushed at him, and he threw a stone and hit the dog, whereupon the Hippocoontids darted out and dispatched him with blows of their cudgels. It was to avenge his death that Hercules mustered an army against the Lacedaemonians' (Apollod ii.7.1). Pausanias reports that the animal was a house-dog (iii.15.4). Castorians were named after Castor, who first bred them for hunting (Xen, Cyn 3.1).

75 The two centaurs who attempted to rape Atalanta in the wilderness of Arcadia and

signals her dog to be still. She is unarmed save for her hook-bladed knife, too small to be of use. Her chance has disappeared. She sees the sword stiffen in his grip as though the hand holding it were bronze too, and the arm, the shoulders, a whole body concentrated in the blade. The man stands a full head taller than her, taller than any of the men on the shore, save perhaps the brutish Idas.[76] No part of him moves except his eyes, which move over her. She waits for his advance.

But instead of approaching he calls off the dogs, one by one and by name.[77] The animal she knocked to the ground rises last and slinks back to join the pack. The man's shadow almost covers her. Her thread of life continues in its lee, binding her to a confusing tangle of fates, but none of them this one. He shifts balance in a delicate movement which sends his shadow forward as though it were a liquid dousing her and soaking her body, an obscure incursion, or insult. To step back, she thinks, means retreat. But to remain may mean acceptance. She has known no body but her own. She understands movement – pursuit, the flat arc of an arrow. And stasis – waiting, impact, the weakening judder of the prey and its last twitch into stillness. Which now?

Then a footfall. She hears someone climbing up the slope. Her cousin's head comes into view. Atalanta sees his eyes narrow at the sight of the two of them. Meilanion is carrying a bundle of arrow-shafts, a gift for her.[78] He drops them at her feet and eyes the armoured stranger. She watches both. The man sways back in concession and sheathes his sword. He pulls off his helmet,

---

who were killed by their intended victim (Apollod iii.9.2; Ael, Var Hist xiii.1; Callim, Hymn iii.222–4).

76 Phlegon of Tralles's Perithaumasiai cites 'Apollonius' (Historiai Thaumasiai, MS Palatinus Graecus 398) on the discovery of Idas's grave in Messene. Its exhumation yielded gigantic bones, three skulls, and two sets of teeth. Pausanias reports that the grave was claimed by Sparta (iii.13.1) but thinks Messenia a more likely location.

77 Labros, Methepon, Egertes, Eubolos, Corax, Marpsas, Ormenos (François krater, Florence Mus Arch 4209); Leukios, Charon, Gorgos, Thero (qua 'Theron': dinos, Athens Agora P334), Podes (band cup, Munich Antikensamml 2243); Loraos (neck amphora, Tarquinia Mus Naz RC5564). The inscriptions on two cups (Malibu 86.AE.154, 156) are meaningless. Xenophon recommends short names, 'so as to be able to call them easily', and offers a list of examples (Cyn 7.5).

78 The incident is confusing and perhaps confused. To Aristophanes, Meilanion is a by-word for misogyny (Lys 782ff.), while to Xenophon he is the image of uxoriousness, eventually capturing his beloved through 'love of labour' (Cyn 1.7), which Ovid glosses as carrying her equipment while hunting (Ars Amat ii.185–92). The Meilanions of other writers range accordingly from affectionate to hostile, cf. n. 60.

and then she knows him. His hair is a deep gold in colour, the badge of the one who has gathered them here: Meleager.[79]

*　　*　　*

The men waiting on the foreshore ape craftsmen. They flet and oil arrows. They rub dried salt from their scalps. Soon their weapons will be sharp enough to carve marble, or split stalks of grass. The archers among them gouge deep pocks in the soil as they bend bowstaves to slip the knot between the horns. There is nothing to sustain them on this terrain but what they bring to it. The bowstrings hum as the tensed staves snap them tight.[80] None of their habits are casual.

Heads rise at Atalanta's return. She walks ahead, nervous Aura settling and snuffling about her calves. The two men follow, her heavy-footed attendants. Meleager's dogs mill be-

79 Meleager is 'fair-haired' (or 'yellow-haired') according to Homer, albeit also dead (Il ii.643); his shade tells Heracles the story of how he came to be so (Bacch v.79–170; Apollod ii.5.12). He was the son of Oeneus, King of Kalydon, and Althaia, daughter of Thestius, King of Pleuron (Hom, Il ix.543, xiv.115–18; Apollod i.9.16). According to other authorities (Apollod i.8.2; Zen, Cent v.33; fort. Hes, Cat fr.98.5 ap. P Berlin 9777; Eur, Mel fr. ap. Plut, Mor 312a) the father was Ares or, according to Hyginus (Fab clxi), both Ares and Oeneus. Other references render Meleager as insensitive to others' sensitivities (Antiphon Mel. fr. ap. Aristot, Rhet 1379b), as a suitably patriotic exemplar for Strepsiades of Thebes (Pind, Isth vii.26–33), as susceptible to his wife's properly organised argument (Antiphon Mel. fr. ap. Aristot, Rhet 1365a), as cleverer than his (half-)brother Tydeus (Eur, Suppl 904, although the passage is emended), as the husband of Kleopatra, and thus the nephew of Idas, and the father of the wife of the first man to die in the Trojan War (Paus iv.2.7). He was taught to hunt by the centaur Chiron, as were Atalanta and Meilanion (Xen, Cyn 1.2). His iconography typically consists in a spear, a dog, a dead boar and a head of curly hair (sardonyx, Munich Antikensamml A3174; carnelian, Munich Antikensamml A2084; statue, Vatican Mus 490, attrib. Skopas, and numerous copies of which one found at Kalydon; dinos fr. Athens Agora P334; dinos, Vatican Mus 306; exaleiptron, Munich Antikensamml 8600; neck amphora fr. Tarquinia Mus Naz RC5564; amphora, Bari Mus Naz 872; stamnos, Perugia Mus Civ (uncatalogued); bronze mirror, Berlin-Charlottenburg Staatl Mus fr. 146; bronze mirror, Paris Louvre ED2837 inv. 1041; bronze mirror, Indiana Art Mus 62.251; bronze mirror, Munich Antikensamml 3654; wall painting, Naples Mus Naz 8980; wall painting, Pompeii VI.9.2(1), Casa di Meleagro; opus tessellatum, Cardenagimeno, Burgos vid. B. Arraiza, unpublished; wall painting (lost), ex Pompeii VI.2.22.c Casa delle Danzatrici; Chalcidian amphora, Paris Louvre E802; caeretan hydria, Paris Louvre E696); pelike, St Petersburg Herm B4528, inter alia).

80 Odysseus appears to string the bow used to kill the suitors of Penelope while sitting down (Hom, Od xxi.243–5). The suitors, however, attempt the same feat standing up (Hom, Od xxi.143–51) as does Pandarus (Hom, Il iv.112–14). Herodotus describes bowstringing as a show of strength among both the Ethiopians (iii.21–3) and, more predictably, the Scythians (iv.9–10), albeit at the instigation of Heracles. Plato argues the converse (Nic ix.3). The bow itself is present here, in the possession of Eurytus, who received it from his father Hippocoon. Eurytus will give it to his own son, Iphitus, who will in turn give it to Odysseus. It is, or was, composite (Hom, Od xxi.12); its 'hum' is, or will be, remarked by Odysseus (Hom, Od xxi.410–12), who strings it as though it were a lyre.

hind him. She turns away from them and strides along the
foreshore. Her bowstave lies where she dropped it, but her
pouch has been tossed aside. Its contents are scattered over the
ground.

Her eyes follow the rough arc in which her arrowheads have
fallen, the tracks of a brazen bird, the last glinting print its heave
into the air. She bends to pick them up. The insult is furtive: a
coward's challenge. To whom among the men does it belong?
The men do not want her here. Atalanta spits on the ground and
looks about for the culprit but no one is watching her. They have
turned to Meleager. She moves to join them.

He has mounted the bank to address the men. At first, he
speaks as though their presence here were in question, but the
the note of supplication soon fades. He throws out names and
heads rise. The named men nod and smile. His voice rolls
through the words, the dogs motionless behind him, the men
silent before him while the sun sinks somewhere beyond the
distant terminus of the gulf, turning its waters red. Such
challenges have sought them out so many times. He frames the
expectation forming among them. Their shadows lengthen until
the greater dark of Mount Chalkis overtakes and swallows them.
Then they are black silhouettes waiting for Meleager to issue the
call. He frames the task and shapes their enemy within it.

Whether by accident or design, at the festival of First Fruits,[81]
Meleager's father sacrificed to all the gods but Artemis. In
revenge, the goddess sent a boar to this country to lay it waste.
The boar is her anger, whose shapes are as numerous as the
animals burnt to appease it, for it uproots trees, flattens corn,
rips the vines from the soil and sends the herds and flocks
stumbling down the hillsides with their grey-blue viscera trailing in the grass.

---

81 The Thargelia followed the grain harvest in the latter half of May, the 'Thargelos'
being 'the first loaf made after the carrying home of the harvest', according to Crates (cit.
ap. Athen iii.52), or a yet more primitive 'pot full of seeds', according to Hesychius (s.v.
'Thargelos'). The Thargelia and Thalusia were practically synonymous (Athen iii.52;
Eustathius ad Hom, Il ix.534); both were ancient rites (Aristot, Nic Eth 1160a) whose
typical offerings grew more sophisticated over time and culminated, through ignorance
and fear, in 'the luxury of flesh' (Porphyr, De abstinentia ii.20). By the time Nestor came to
sacrifice to Athena after his return from Troy, the offering of grain was already an
affectation of earlier, simpler habit (Eustathius ad Hom, Od iii.440, et vid. Plut, Quaest
Gr vi). The offering of vegetal and carnal offerings together (Eur, Elec 804–5) signals a later
confusion, or even conflict (Pind, Ol vii.47 et schol.), between the different orders of gods.
Chthonic deities were necessarily vegetarians. Their Olympian successors preferred meat.

The heroes call back to the gold-haired man who stands before them, as they must. Acceptance issues from their lips and gathers in the succeeding silence, becoming their commission. They are here to hunt the boar.

Atalanta is not named. She plucks at the folds of cloth about her waist. Her chiton has dried. She covers her breasts and ties the garment in place. The men pay her no attention, gathered together on the twilit shore and melded by the shadows and Meleager's challenge. The dusk settles on them all like a rain of dust or ash, the rain they have fled. Their pasts are carcasses, toted shoulder-high as trophies,[82] as is her own. Her father left her wailing on a mountainside. She sucked bear's milk in place of her mother's.[83] She was the bear-girl.[84] Now she is the

---

82 'It would seem that in days of old the beasts were much more formidable to men,' notes Pausanias (i.27.9). Atalanta carries the cadavers of her centaurs (q.v. n. 75), Theseus his sow (Apollod, Ep 1.1; Bacch xvii.23ff.; Diod Sic iv.59.4; Plut, Thes 9ff.; Paus ii.1.3; Hyg, Fab xxxviii) and Minotaur (Diod Sic iv.77.1–5; Plut, Thes 15ff. et Eur cit. ap. ibid.; Hyg, Fab xl; Apollod iii.1.4; Schol. (Lact, Plac) ad Statius, Achill 192; Schol. ad Eur, Hipp 887), Jason his bronze-hoofed bulls (Apollod i.9.24) and fertile-toothed dragon (Apollod i.9.16; Ap Rhod ii.1268–70, iv.123ff.). Peleus reduced his trophies to a bag of tongues (Apollod iii.13.3).

83 So Apollodorus (iii.9.2). Theognis has her fleeing when a woman rather than abandoned as an infant (Theog 1287-94). She shares with Paris the fact of her exposure and an infantile taste for bear's milk (Apollod iii.12.5).

84 Callisto, daughter of Lycaon of Arcadia and mother of Arcas, from whom the Arcadians traced their lineage, followed the huntswomen of Artemis until impregnated by Zeus (Apollod iii.8.2; Hes, Ast fr. 3 ap. Eratosthenes Catast fr. 1; Eur, Hel 375–80; Ov, Met ii.401–530, Fas ii.155–92; Serv ad Virg, Georg i.138; Hyg, Fab clxxvii), whereupon she was turned into a bear, either by Zeus, fearful of Hera's anger, or by Artemis, angry at her follower's incontinence – so angry that in some versions she shoots the transformed Callisto dead. The metamorphosis was performed at Nonacris in Northern Arcadia (Araethus cit. ap. Hyg, Ast ii.1). In other versions, Zeus further transforms her into a constellation of stars (Hyg, Fab 155, 176; Schol. ad Lyc, Alex 481; Schol. ad Statius, Theb iii.685). Surviving fragments of Asius (PEG fr. 14), Pherecydes (FrGrHist III fr. 157), 'Epimenides' (FrVk III fr. B16), Amphis (cit. ap. Hyg, Astron ii.1 et vid. Schol ad Arat, Phaen xxxviii aut CAF fr. 47), an allusion to Eumelos (PEG fr. 14) and a scholium to Euripides (ad Or 1646) add nothing but confusion. Callimachus (fr. 632 ap. schol. ad Callim fr. 487 ap. Choerob ad Theod, Can iv.1) has Hera ordering Artemis to shoot Callisto; Pausanias has a similar version (i.25.1, viii.3.6). Palaephatus disbelieves them all (De Incred fr. xiii). Her son Arcas's and father Lycaon's later transformations into wolves are loosely linked to these events. More latterly, the Arcadians' wearing of bearskins is noted (Paus iv.11.3). The cult of Brauronian Artemis reunites the elements of Callisto's story. Young girls would dress in bearskins and dance for the goddess (Aristoph, Lys, 645 et schol.), whose offerings included blood drawn from a man's throat and the robes worn by women who had died in childbirth (Eur, Iph Taur 1458–67). The goddess's image was supposedly brought by Iphigenia in flight from her immolation at Aulis (Paus i.33.1, iii.16.7) and later removed by Xerxes as a trophy (Paus viii.46.3). Zeus's role seems to have been unwittingly played by the Pelasgians of Lemnos, who, 'since they well knew the time of the Athenian festivals, acquired fifty-oared ships and set an ambush for the Athenian women celebrating the festival of Artemis at Brauron. They seized many of the women, then sailed away with them and brought them to Lemnos to be their concubines' (Hdt

huntress, the bitter virgin, the centaur-killer: her own monsters, of which the most insistent and insubstantial is her own circling shadow. A bronze arm points her forward at dawn. Midday, and an arm of iron warns her back. She has looked up through the breaks in the forest canopy expecting vast slow-beating wings but there was nothing and nobody save herself.

She hovers at the rear of the gathering. The outsiders have already found one another here: Pausileon, Thorax, Aristandros, and others[85] whose names she has forgotten or never knew. High above them the west-facing peaks and highest ridges of Aracynthus are still sun-lit, but fading into the dusk. Meleager's voice sounds again. Tonight they will march to Kalydon, where his father Oeneus holds court and awaits the men who will rid his land of Artemis's beast.

The men nod as Meleager falls silent. Their succeeding murmurs echo then amplify his words: they talk of the bowls of cool wine and the women they will enjoy in the palace of Oeneus. Their tones are unsurprised, weary. Drifts of briny air roll off the waters of the gulf. The dark body of men breaks up.

The heroes move off the shore. The ridges bring them on to level ground, a plain bounded by the sea at their backs and by the slopes of Aracynthus. Ahead, beyond the interruptions of Chalkis and Taphiassus, a break in the ground snakes towards them then veers away again. The terrain rolls upward, into the vale of Kalydon and the mountains of the interior. They hear the soft scuffs of their sandals over dusty ground, spears and axes held high. Atalanta ties her arrow-shafts in a bundle and slings them over her shoulder. Her arrowheads chink in their pouch. The heads and weapons of the heroes bob, merge and separate in noiseless intersections of metal and flesh.

To their left, the gentle descents of Aracynthus's foothills descend to the plain, subsiding into humps and long mounds, or shallow buttresses which echo one another and mark the stages of a deceptive progress. Distances stretch forward, or disappear. The river is to their right but they cannot see it yet. The rising of

---

vi.138.1, iv.142.2). The inclusion of Callisto's father among the heroes of the present expedition to Kalydon is troublesome: Callisto was Atalanta's great-great-great-great grandmother.

85 Simon, Antandros, Kimon.

the moon restores their shadows and flattens the bare scene before them. When they round a rise in the ground and reach the first of the orchards it seems to have been dusted with grey powder, or petrified. For a moment they do not recognise the evidence of their eyes.[86]

Broken branches are strewn between the fallen trunks. Those few still standing have been cut and gouged; milky sapwood glistens in the wounds. The ranks of ruined trees stand as an army of wounded and dying men who, unable to muster arms, hold up between them the corpses of the dead. Comprehension arrives here and there among their number. The boar has visited his violence here, according to his compulsion, just as they must visit their own upon him.

They thread paths between the broken trees, their feet sinking in the mess of rotting apples. Atalanta moves to the head of the men about her, five or six, who soon slow their pace. Slipping light-footed around the splintered boughs, Aura keeping close, she hears the squelching progress of the men behind her grow fainter. The fumes thicken in her throat. She stops and thinks. The main body of the men is ahead and to her right. She swings out, away from them. The gold-haired man and her dark-browed cousin will be watching for her. They wanted her. Or have wanted her, or will want her. But they cannot be rivals here. Not yet.[87] Faint laughter sounds somewhere behind her. She finds a rhythm which takes her through the breaks and gaps in the fallen trees. The arrow-shafts bump against her shoulder. She has left her companions behind. Then the trees give out and

---

86 The orchards of antiquity begin with this one (Hom, Il ix.534, xii.312–15). One of those present, Podargos, will return to Troy to plant the next, and be renamed 'Priam' after his ransom. Lycaon will be captured there by Achilles while gathering sticks (Hom, Il xi.34ff., xiii.746ff.; Apollod, Ep iii.32), later sold, ransomed, returned to Troy, and killed by his original captor, who was himself raised 'as a tree in a rich orchard' (Hom, Il xviii.58) by his mother Thetis. The most idyllic orchard was that of Alcinous (Hom, Od vii.112–21), the most tantalising that of Zeus (Hom, Od xi.589). Odysseus's remembrance of the apple trees given him in his youth by his father was one of the signs by which he identified himself to Laertes (Hom, Od xxiv.328–45); the other was the mark of the boar (ibid.).

87 A fair 'Xanthos' and a dark 'Melanthos' contended in single combat, although the dispute was over territory rather than a woman (Ephorus cit. ap. Harpocration s.v. apatouria, FrGHist 70F22; Hellanicus cit. ap. schol. ad Plat, Sym 208d). There, and then, 'Melanthos' won by trickery according to an oracle quoted by Polyaenus and others (cit. ap. Strategemata i.19; Frontinus cit. ap. Strategemata ii.5.41), or through the intervention of Zeus (Lexica Segueriana s.v. apatouria), or Dionysus, who dons a black goatskin to aid his dark champion (Plut, Quaest Conviv vi.7.2.692e; cf. schol. ad Aristoph, Ach 146; schol. ad Aelius Aristides Oratio Panathenaia 118.20. Nonnus, Dionys xxvii.301–7).

the ground rises. She is clear. Turning back, she overlooks the ruinous scene through which she has passed, ash-grey in the moonlight.

She is standing on a ridge of land, a rib which curves up behind her to join the slope of Aracynthus. A ribbon of darkness marks the treeline. Her head begins to clear. The dizzying fumes masked some more virulent poison: the boar's musk? But the smell is no longer in her nostrils and slips from memory as she reaches for it. The boar obliterates, she thinks.

Tiny movements in the orchard signal the progress of the men within it. Some have regrouped on the far side. She sees that they might have skirted this obstacle, had they wished. Meleager chose to lead them through it. There he is, pacing the far perimeter, gathering those who have chosen to follow him. An obedient tail of dogs sweeps back and forth at his heels. Her gaze ranges again over the orchard. The men who accompanied her into the trees, and whom she outpaced, have not emerged. She can hear but not see them. She picks out Meilanion's slight figure. Aura waits beside her. Her late companions crash about, stumbling and falling, rising again. But each time they resume the interval of silence is longer and the last reaches after a moment in a future too remote to be conceived. There is no more sound. They fell behind, she thinks. All gathered here have thrown themselves among their possible futures, which may end with the boar, or in the city they march on, or here.

Leave them.

Let them rot with the apples, thinks Meleager. The early drop[88] is the earth's due.[89] He sees Meilanion walk clear of the trees to

---

88 Summer, even late summer, is not autumn. An apple is not a quince. The Greek term encompasses both 'apple' and 'quince' (and 'sheep', 'goats' and 'small cattle' in Homer, and 'a girl's breasts' in Theocritus), the former tree blossoming later than the latter, hence the synonyms for and confusion between 'spring apples' (Androtion cit. ap. Athen 82c, distinguished there from 'apricots') and 'winter apples' (Phylotimus cit. ap. Athen 81c). The 'pomegranate' (Euphorion fr. 11 ap. Athen 82a; Nicander fr. 50 ibid.) adds a needless complication. It is plain that the orchard is mixed, the fallen fruit are quinces, and the trees still in blossom (Hom, Il ix.542–4) bear apples, or would do had they not been destroyed.

89 The precedents for gifts of apples were unfortunate. According to Pherecydes, the golden apples given by Ge to Hera on her wedding day so delighted the wife of Zeus that she planted them in the garden of the Hesperides beside Mount Atlas, whose daughters promptly began to steal them (frs ap. Eratos, Cat iii; ap. Hyg, Fab xxx; ap. schol. ad Ap Rhod iv.1369ff. et vid. Hes, Theog 215ff.; Eur, Herc 394ff.; Diod Sic iv.26; Paus v.11.6, v.18.4,

be greeted by Ancaeus. What had the younger man decided, watching his, Meleager's, shadow creeping up Atalanta's body? Meilanion had avoided his eye and the two men had exchanged no word as they followed her back to the others. Might the youth have understood his intention so soon? Where is he?

Atalanta rounds the last rank of trees and sees Meleager ahead, unmoving, his dogs scuffling behind him. The leather soles of her sandals unpeel themselves from her feet and readhere with every step. The sugary juices of the fruit dry on her calves. The men stand in groups, as they had on the foreshore. Before she reaches them the nearest begin to move off.

The slope of the land becomes shallower. Grasses rustle and crunch beneath their feet. Atalanta keeps to the higher ground on the right, a coincident satellite to the rough mass of the men. The sound of gurgling water reaches their ears, growing louder as they near the lightless break in the ground glimpsed earlier. At the bank, they look down into the river.[90] Heads turn upstream and downstream. She watches from a distance, sees Meilanion striding along the water's edge and thinks of the cool water washing over her skin. The men resume their march. Meleager she cannot see.

She and Aura loop behind them all to reach the river's edge.

vi.19.8; Ov, Met iv.637ff., ix.190; Hyg, Ast ii.3). Thus angered, Hera set a serpent to guard them. Heracles killed the former and stole the latter, or tricked Atlas into doing so in his stead (Ap Rhod iv.1396ff. et schol.; Apollod ii.5.11). A golden apple, inscribed 'To the fairest' (Schol. ad Lyc, Alex 93) and thrown among the guests at the marriage of Peleus and Thetis was to lead, eventually, to the Trojan war (Hom, Il xxiv.25ff.; Cypria fr. 1 ap. Proc, Chrest i; Eur, Tro 924ff., Iph Aul 1290ff., Hel 23ff., Andr 274ff., Apollod, Ep iii.2; Isoc x.41; Lucian, Dial Deorum xx; Hyg, Fab lxxxxiii). Further golden apples, supplied by Aphrodite from either Cyprus (Ov, Met x.644ff.) or the garden of the Hesperides (Serv ad Virg, Aen iii.113), were to trick the Boeotian Atalanta into marriage with Hippomenes (Hes, Cat fr. 14 ap. P Petrie pl.III.3; Apollod iii.9.2), which union ends with both condemned to pull the chariot of Cybele, having been transformed into lions (Pal, De Incred fr. xiii; Ov, Met x.681–704).

90 Formerly the Lykormas (Strab vii.7.8, x.2.5; Bacch xi.34), renamed the Evenus after the son of Porthaon and father of Marpessa. Evanus challenged each of his daughter's suitors to a chariot race and, when they lost, cut off their heads and nailed them to the wall of his house (Bacch xv.1–12; Simonides fr. 213 ap. Schol. ad Hom, Il ix.557; Eustathius cit. ap. ibid.). Idas, furnished with a winged chariot by Poseidon, carried off Marpessa. Outraged at his daughter's abduction, Evenus pursued the lovers as far as this river, where, despairing of catching them, he slaughtered his horses and threw himself into the waters (Hyg, Fab ccxlii; Schol. ad Lyc, Alex 561–3; Paus v.18.2, quoting an inscription on the chest of Kypselos). Strabo offers an unverifiable account of the course of the Evenus (x.2.5) and Hesiod appears to assert that it received its name from Tethys (Theog 345).

She looks down on a shelf of crumbling earth. Beyond it, a sheet of fast-flowing water is broken here and there by the smooth rocks of the river-bed. This would be a torrent in spring. Now, late summer, the descent is an easy jump. She splashes water against her calves and works her fingers between her toes. Aura dabs her paws one after the other in the flow. The streams familiar to Atalanta do not flow like this. They tumble, or skid, or foam. Whorls and jets of their icy waters strike rocks then leap up and break against one another, or stand in perpetual fountains. These streams are nameless, each one sounding its single liquid syllable until the confluence of their croaks and gurgles melds in the great valley rivers and their names: Alpheus,[91] Ladon,[92] Erymanthus,[93] Eurotas.[94] Such rivers and

91 The Alpheus rose at Phylace in Arcadia (Paus viii.54.1–2), where stone lions marked its source (Paus viii.44.3), then sank underground for ten stadia (Polybius xvi.17) to rise again near Asea (Strab viii.3.12), after which it shared the course of the Eurotas for twenty stadia. Both rivers disappeared underground and separated there, Alpheus reappearing at Pegae and continuing north-west through Arcadia, Elis and past Olympia for eighty stadia (Strab viii.3.12) until falling into the Ionian Sea. The waters of its 'untiring' (Bacch v.180) and 'beautiful stream' (Bacch xi.26) were 'wide-whirling' (Bacch iii.7; v.37) or 'silver-whirling' (Bacch viii.27, xii.42, although the latter text is mutilated) or 'wide-flowing' (Pind, Ol v.18), particularly in the river's lower course (Hom, Il v.545). Its eddies were deep (Hom, Hymn i.3), but it was fordable at Thryon, near its mouth (Hom, Il ii.592–4; Hymn iii.423), which was choked with rushes (Strab viii.3.24), and also upstream by the shrines of Pelops (Pind, Ol i.90–4) and Zeus (Eur, Elec 782, Hipp 535–9) and again at Olympia (Pind, Ol ii.13; Paus v.13.2), eddies notwithstanding (Ephorus cit. ap. Strab x.3.2). On its banks Hermes discovered the art of fire (Hom, Hymn 105–9), Apollo made love to both Evadne (Pind, Ol vi.31–5) and Melampus (Apollod i.9.11), the Olympic Games were held (Bacch xii.191; Eur, Elec 863; Pind, Isth i.67, Ol i.21; Anon. ap. Cy, Epig i.28, inter alia) and the first wild olive trees grew (Paus v.14.3), from which were fashioned the wreaths crowning the victors (Paus v.15.3). Heracles's diversion of the Alpheus to clean Augeus's stables is little-attested (Diod Sic iv.13.3) and the addition of the Peneus (Apollod ii.5.5) geographically implausible. Among its tributaries may be noticed the Cladaus (Xen, Hell vii.4.29; Paus v.7.1, vi.20.6, vi.21.3), the Brentheates (Paus v.7.1, viii.28.7), the Naliphus and an Acheloos (Paus viii.38.9–10), the Helisson (Paus v.7.1, viii.3.3, viii.29.5, viii.30.1–2), the Buphagus (Paus v.7.1, viii.26.8, viii.27.17), the Aminius (Paus, viii.29.5), the Celadus (Paus viii.38.9), the Gatheatus (Paus viii.34.5), the Malus (Paus viii.35.1), the Mylaon and Nus (Paus viii.36.1–2, viii.38.9), the Gortynius (Paus v.7.1, also called 'Lusius'), which joined the Alpheus at Rhaeteae (Paus viii.28.4), the Scyrus (Paus viii.35.1), the Thius (Paus viii.35.3), and most notably the Erymanthus (Strab viii.3.12; Paus viii.24.4 et vid. n. 93) and the Ladon (Paus viii.25.12 et vid. n. 92). As a river-god, Alpheus was the would-be seducer of Artemis (Telesilla fr. 1 ap. Hephaestion lxvii), who disguised herself by smearing her face with mud, and of the nymph Arethusa, who was pursued by Alpheus under the ocean as far as Ortygia (Pind, Nem i.1; Paus v.7.2–3, viii.54.3; Ibycus fr. 24 ap. schol. ad Theocr i.117). Nestor's ships carried ensigns showing Alpheus, conventionally enough, as a bull (Eur, Iph Aul 273–6) and a bull was a sacrifice appropriate to the river-god (Hom, Il xi.726–7).

92 The Ladon rose midway between Lycuria and Kleitor (Paus vii.20.1–21.1), disappeared underground at Pheneus (Diod Sic xv.49.5), then reappeared at Leucasium, flowed past Mesoboa, Nasi, Oryx, Thaliades, Thelpusa (Paus viii.25.2) and Onceium, where Demeter bathed after the rape by Poseidon (Paus viii 25.4). The Tuthoa joined it at

their valleys have never been her place. Soon they will run as black by day as the Evenus does here and now by night. They may be dark now.

Across the water from her, thorn bushes[95] choke the opposite bank. Atalanta looks downstream to where the river narrows and the ground is bare. A cairn stands – to mark a crossing, she thinks. But then she sees that the cairn is built from bones: rib-cages, knouted femurs and segmented spines are piled up to form a platform. Four horse skulls rest on top. To mark a death, she decides, and wonders whether it lies in the past or is yet to come.[96] Here a once-living being found the hadal current which

Heraea, and the Ladon itself fell into the Alpheus at the Island of Crows (Paus viii.25.12). There was no better river (Paus viii.25.13) nor more beautiful waters (Paus viii.20.1). Heracles shot the Cerynitian hind as it crossed the Ladon (Apollod ii.5.3; sed vid. Pind, Ol iii.53ff. et schol; Eur, Herc 375ff.; Diod Sic iv.13.1; Hyg, Fab xxx), slowed perhaps by reeds (Corinna fr. 34 ap. Theod, Can s.v. 'Declension of Barytones in -on'). Act and locale were to inspire at least one imitator (Antipater Anth Gr vi.111): Leucippus, the would-be lover of Daphne, was killed by her and her companions when discovered as a man while bathing there (Paus viii.20.2–4; Parth, Er Path xv.4; pseudo-Pal, De Incred fr. xxxxix). Like all river-gods, Ladon was the son of Tethys and Oceanus (Hes, Theog 344).

93 In the texts, as in the topography: Mount Erymanthus overshadowed its eponymous river and also formed its source (Paus v.7.1), the particular peak being Mount Lampeia (Paus viii.24.4). Thereafter, the Erymanthus 'passing through Arcadia, with Mount Pholoe on the right and the district of Thelpusa on the left, flows into the Alpheus' (Paus ibid.; Strab viii.3.12). There was a crossing-point at Saurus, just upstream of the confluence (Paus vi.21.3–4). In Pausanias's account, Heracles's capture of the Erymanthian boar took place at this river (v.26.7). Apollodorus seems to agree (ii.5.4).

94 The bankside flora of the Eurotas included reeds (Theognis 783–8), rushes (Callim, Aet lxxv.23), flowers (loutrophorus, Malibu 86.AE.680) and mint (Callim, Hec fr. 284a.16). The latter attracted horses (ibid.) and the horses attracted Castor and Pollux (Callim, Hymn v.24; Aristoph, Lys 1300; Eur, Hel 205–11). It was hard to cross in winter (Diod Sic xv.65.2), but there were fords between Amyclae and Therapne (Paus iii.19.4–7; Xen, Hell vi.5.30), at Pitana (Pind, Ol vi.28), and later, when the latter settlement was incorporated into Sparta, a bridge there (Xen, Hell vi.5.27). Rising at a spring next to the source of the Alpheus, then sinking with the latter at Asea (q.v. n. 91) 'the Eurotas reappears where the district called Bleminatis begins, and then flows past Sparta itself, traverses a long glen near Helus and empties between Gythium, the naval station of Sparta, and Acraea' (Strab viii.3.12). Its name derived from the creator of its lower course (Paus iii.1.1), which was first conceived as a drainage project, although 'Eurotas' can be translated as 'the fair-flowing' and the drainage was ineffective (Paus iii.13.8). It was synonymous with Laconia, whence Helen was abducted by Paris (Eur, Hel passim, Tro.133–5). The 'youthful labours' (Eur, Hel 210–11) supposed to take place on its (inevitably) 'reed-fringed' banks (ibid., 349, 493, Iph Aul 181–2) remain obscure.

95 Bacchylides claims these were as roses (xvi.34).

96 Nessus was among the centaurs driven by Heracles from Pholus's cave, whence he fled to the river Evenus (Apollod ii.5.4). Here he served as ferryman, carrying travellers across the water on his back. In their second confrontation, Heracles shot him with an arrow dipped in the blood of the Lernaean Hydra for attempting to violate Meleager's sister Deianira during the crossing. In revenge, the dying Nessus described to Deianira the deadly mixture of his semen and poisoned blood as a 'love potion' to be used if Heracles were tempted to betray her (Apollod ii.7.6; Soph, Trach 555ff.; Diod Sic iv.36.3ff.; Strab x.2.5; Dio Chrys,Or lx; Eusebius Praeparatio Evangelii ii.2.15ff.; Schol. ad Lyc, Alex 50–1;

twists in the waters of all rivers. Or a still-living being was moving towards it now, unknowing as the men who entered the orchard behind her, never thinking that its broken trees would mark their graves. The cairn might even be her own. The ordination of the hunt will loosen and the boar's marks grow contradictory. One of them may deal the death-blow: hurl the fatal spear, swing the double-bladed axe, thrust the sword, or loose the single arrow that may find the animal's red eye. Their roles wait to claim them, hovering in the instants outside their beleaguered present.

Atalanta looks up from the surface of the river in search of the peaks seen earlier from the shoreline. The stars overhead mark out the lesser of the Bears;[97] the moon is sinking. She looks over her shoulder to find the Virgin,[98] glimpses bright Arcturus[99] off to the west. Then she springs to her feet.

Meleager stands on the bank above her. He wears his helmet as before. His body appears to lean out over the water, as though his feet were rooted in the ground above her. The current tugs at her and her toes curl about pebbles concealed by the water. She holds herself still, waiting for him to speak,

---

Tzet, Chil ii.457ff.; Ov, Met ix.101ff.; Hyg, Fab xxxiv; Zen, Cent i.33; Serv ad Virg, Aen viii.300; Schol. ad Statius, Theb xi.235). The stench of the centaur's rotting body was one of several hypotheses offered for the malodorous air of neighboring Ozolian Locris (Paus x.38.2–3). Another was 'the exhalations from a certain river' whose 'very waters have a peculiar smell', which accords with Strabo's belief that Nessus was buried on Mount Taphiassus and that his corpse polluted its springwaters (ix.4.8). At the time of the present expedition, Nessus lived, Locris smelled sweet and Heracles was enslaved to Queen Omphale of Lydia (Apollod ii.6.3, i.9.19; Soph, Trach 248–53; Diod Sic iv.31.4–8; Lucian, Dial Deorum xiii.2; Paus i.35.8; Plut, Quaest Gr xlv, Thes vi.5; Tzet, Chil ii.425ff.; Schol. ad Hom, Od xxi.22; Hyg, Fab xxxii; pseudo-Seneca Herakles Oetaeus 371ff.; Statius, Theb x.646–9; Pherecydes cit. ap. schol. ad Hom, Od xxi.22), who dressed him in women's clothes and, according to some traditions, spanked him with her sandal (Ov, Her ix.55ff., Ars Amat ii.216–22).

97 The Lesser Bear, or the Lesser Wain (Hom, Od v.272), or Cynosura, the 'Dog's Tail' (Arat, Phaen 52), was traditionally associated with Callisto (Apollod iii.8.2; Eratos, Cat i; Schol. ad Lyc, Alex 481; Hyg, Fab clv, clxxvi, clxxvii; Ov, Met ii.409–507; Serv ad Virg, Georg i.138; Lactantius Placidus ad Statius, Theb iii.685).

98 Hyginus alone asserts that 'Parthenon' (the Virgin) was the daughter of Apollo and Chrysothemis (Ast ii.25.2). Whether any identification with the mother of Parthenopaeus may be allowed is doubtful. A rival Attic account claimed the virgin was Erigone, who hanged herself at the murder of her father, Icarius, who was similarly catasterised as Boïtes, or Arcturus (Callim, Aet 178).

99 'Arcturus' (the Guardian of the Bear) was traditionally Arcas, whence 'Arcadians' in general and, five generations later, Atalanta in particular (Ov, Met ii.409–530, Fas ii.183; Hyg, Fab clxxvii; Apollod iii.8.2). The morning rising of Arcturus marked the beginning of autumn (Hes, WD 610; Plat, Laws 844e; Soph, Oed Tyr 1137; Hippoc, Epid i.2.4; Thuc ii.78), the evening rising the beginning of spring (Hes, WD 567).

or act, to disclose his purpose. But he does none of these. She turns her head to spit in the river. When she turns back he has gone.

*   *   *

The moon disappears. The landscape loosens. The heroes march up the valley to Kalydon.

Darkness raises low humps and ridges from the terrain, spectral exaggerations which nudge them hither and thither across the valley-floor. Gradients curve into cliffs which dissolve on approach, becoming terraced slopes which slant down to the river whose dull gurgling is an unreliable guide, batted back and forth between invisible walls of stone. Sometimes the river seems to sink into the earth on one side and re-emerge on the other, and then a moment later the reverse. At times its faint splashings come from both sides at once and their land-borne Argo sails down a canal of terrafirma, which closes behind them, becoming an isthmus, then before, an island: they are marooned, or adrift, or landlocked in the valley's beaconless night. Coarse grasses and asphodel crunch underfoot. The stars are white-hot splinters marking any number of shapes in the darkness of the sky.

The Athenians move to the fore, the Arcadians to the rear. Meilanion lingers, allowing himself to fall back through the men. Atalanta was towards the rear when last he saw her. He cannot see her now. Ancaeus draws level with him and grips him by the arm. They will be eating their fill in Oeneus's halls soon enough. The bowls of cool wine, roasted fat and meat, the women who will serve them . . . Meilanion nods. The older man will not let him go.

The column stretches. Behind and to his left, he hears someone send a cascade of pebbles skittering. Someone else coughs, further back again. Male footsteps, by the rhythm. He calculates such matters without thinking. He was named for darkness[100] by his father Amphidamas of Tegea,[101] brother of Iasus, who was the father of Atalanta, who carries the arrow-shafts she accepted

---

100 Aristoph, Lys 785–96.
101 Apollod iii.9.2.

28

from him, slung over her shoulder, somewhere in the surrounding lightlessness. Tegea too has its dark places,[102] its trails set with snares and bristling with lime-twigs, its night-hunted woods.[103]

He glances about. Atalanta is not in view. He tracked her into the orchard and found the men who had followed her, slumped against the fallen trunks or face-down in the rotting fruit. She was gone.

The men pass through bushes whose stems scrape at their greaves and tangle about their ankles: vines, but all broken or uprooted. They cross the dry bed of a gully. Ancaeus nudges him. The Athenians have stopped.

---

102 Its 'melanai' according to an oracle quoted by Polyaenus (Strategemata i.19). To the Lacedaemonians who inquired after the grave of Orestes the Pythoness of Delphi sang: 'A certain Tegea there is of Arcadia/ In a smooth and level plain, where two winds breathe/ and blow falls upon blow.' Her description was interpreted as a smithy (Hdt i.67.4–68.3; Diod Sic ix.36.3; Paus iii.11.10, iii.3.6). A further prophecy from Delphi sent the Lacedaemonians marching on Tegea carrying chains to enslave the population there. The attackers ended by wearing the manacles themselves while working the fields of the Tegean plain (Hdt i.66.1–4), presumably the 'Manthuric' Plain, extending fifty stades from the city (Paus viii.44.7, viii.54.7). Oak forests lined the roads to Mantinea (Paus viii.11.1), Thyrea and Argos (Paus viii.54.4–5), thus surrounding the plain, but were penetrable even with half a foot missing if the escape of Hegesistratus of Elis is credible (Hdt ix.37.1–3 et vid. n. 103). The road to Argos passed between Creopolus (Strab viii.6.17, but otherwise unknown) and Mount Parthenia (Hdt vi.105.1), which was where Auge, being marched to execution, gave birth to Telephus (Alcidamas, Od 14-16), and which was infested with tortoises: local farmers protected them in superstitious deference to Pan (Paus viii.54.7). The mountains to the south fell within the district of Sciritis and formed a natural barrier against Spartan incursions (Diod Sic xv.64.3). Agesilaus was forced into complicated manoeuvres to avoid ambush in the narrow valley leading to the Tegean plain (Xen, Hell vi.5.16–18), which offered an exposed, yet advantageous position (Xen, Hell vii.5.7–9). In contrast, Arcadian forces opposing Agesilaus were able to travel from Alea to Tegea even by night (Xen, Hell vi.5.15).

103 Xenophon's 'hunters by night'were professionals (Xen, Mem iv.7.4). The invention and use of nets (Op, Cyn ii.25) were censured by both sportsmen (Ar, Cyn xxiv.4–5) and moralists (Plat, Laws vii.822d–24a), but snares were set the night before even the most sporting hunts (Xen, Cyn ix.11–16) and deer, attested on Mount Parthenia (Apollod ii.7.4, iii.9.1), were notoriously difficult to catch by day (Xen, Cyn ix.17) unless one were Achilles, who simply outran them (Pind, Nem iii.51–2). Among the equipment dedicated to the gods on a huntsman's retirement are found hunting nets, nooses, foot-traps (Anth Gr vi.107), spring-traps, cages, bird-lime (Anth Gr vi.109), hare-staves, fowling-canes (Anth Gr vi.152), fowling-nets (Anth Gr vi.181), and quail-whistles (Anth Gr vi.296). All are proper to the night-hunt. Hegesistratus's escape from Sparta to Tegea prompted the region's most notorious night-hunt: 'made fast in iron-bound stocks, he got an iron weapon which was brought by some means into his prison, and straightway conceived a plan of such courage as we have never known; reckoning how best the rest of it might get free, he cut off his own foot at the instep. This done, he tunnelled through the wall out of the way of the guards who kept watch over him, and so escaped to Tegea. All night he journeyed, and all day he hid and lay concealed in the woods, till on the third night he came to Tegea, while all the people of Lacedaemon sought him.' (Hdt ix.37.2–3). Tegean night fishermen seem to have met with a lack of success comparable to that of Hegesistratus's pursuers (Simonides fr. 163 ap. Aristot, Poet i.1365a).

Ahead, a corona of red light glows above a rise in the ground. The men advance, then veer around to the left. Again the Athenians at the head signal a halt.

The heroes are still and their sudden silence lifts a thin sound high into the night air. Animals. Meilanion distinguishes the lowing of cattle and the bleating of sheep. The men around him ready their weapons. The gully narrows and deepens as it continues. There is a smell of burning in the air. The bank to their right has become a wall, a foundation for a great stone terrace which looms over them as they pass along the length of its base. The light is coming from above. They hear the dull roar of a fire and voices shouting. The smell is recognisable now. The wall shields them in shadow from the firelight which pours its red glare over the edge, still high above their heads. But the ground is rising and brings them up at last at the far corner of the terrace: heads, shoulders, then bodies emerge as though struggling out of the soil.[104] The first men to clamber onto the stone apron of the terrace walk forward and come to a halt at the sight which meets them. Those at the back shoulder their way through and stop too.

A furnace of heat and light roars across the distance of the terrace. The roof and walls of the temple on the far side struggle to hold the blaze. At a hundred paces the men shield their eyes from the red flames which lash the interior walls and sheet the roof in fire. The columns of the temple shimmer, melting and re-forming. The men who toil to feed the conflagration are charcoal-black – stick-like figures scratched in a wash of blazing

---

104 Deucalion and Pyrrha repopulated the earth after the flood by throwing stones over their heads on Mount Parnassus at the bidding of either Zeus (Apollod i.7.1, iii.14.5, Pind, Ol ix.41–5) or Themis (Ov, Met i.367ff.). Deucalion's stones grew into men, Pyrrha's into women. Cadmus peopled Thebes by slaying a dragon and sowing half its teeth (Eur, Ph 656; Pind, Pyth iii.167, Isth vi.13; Ov, Met iii.32). Jason repeated the act, sowing the remaining teeth in Colchis (Ap Rhod iii.1178ff.). The descendants of these 'aboriginal sons of the dragon's teeth' (Plat, Soph 247c) could be recognised by a birthmark in the shape of a spearhead (Aristot, 1454b; Dio Chrys iv.23). Athens traced the lineage of its kings back to three 'Sons of the Soil': Cecrops (Apollod iii.14.1), Cranaus (Apollod iii.14.5) and his usurper Amphictyon (Apollod iii.14.6, sed vid. Mar Par 8–10; Paus.i.2.6). The Athenians claimed to have been 'planted' there by Hephaestus and Athena (Plat, Crit 109d). Their autochthony was a source of some pride (Eur, Ion 29, 589; Aristot, Rhet 1360b; Plat, Menex 237b) and the pride an occasion for ridicule (Aristoph, Lys 1082, Vesp 1076). Other centres claimed other 'Earth-born' founding fathers: Pelasgus (Hes, Cat fr. 30 ap. Apollod ii.1.5; Apollod iii.8.1), Lelex, son of Cleocharia (Apollod iii.10.3), Aetolus (Strab x.3.2, although the inscription quoted is ambiguous) and Locrus (Hes, Cat fr 82 ap. Strab vii.7.2).

orange. One or two glance across at the gathering heroes but most do not look up from their labours.

The men and women carry animals. Four men are wrestling a goat towards the fire. They look up as the heroes fan out across the platform, but then bend themselves again to their task. Braces of chickens beat their wings against the hands which grasp them by the feet and a bullock being manhandled onto the terrace tries to kick against its puny guards.

But such rebellions are rare. Cattle, sheep, goats and pigs appear to quiet themselves as the temple is approached and its deep roar begins to shudder through their skulls. Their resistance ends, or their rage and panic is borne by their sacrificers, who bellow to one another as they take hold of a leg or clutch a fleece to raise the animal high. Then the fire appears to suck each body through the air, breathing its own fierce life into placid flesh and bone. The animals seem to dance.

Meilanion watches with the others, a deep unease seizing him as his gaze is led further up the slope by the long chains of men and women who move up and down it. Pens cover the hillside. Those nearest are empty, but the remainder are crammed with livestock. Drenched in the red of the fire, the crude enclosures crawl with movement as the animals within them shift about. It was their noise that the heroes heard from the slope below.

The goat, like the others, gives up its struggles as it is lifted shoulder-high. The men throw it forward and turn away before it lands. The bullock follows it with as little ceremony. The gangs pass back and forth with their cargoes: the same spectacle is repeated over and over until the moment when the furnace wraps each beast in its burning cloak, hiding their bodies from prying eyes until they are consumed.[105]

---

105 The sacrifice to Artemis Laphria was witnessed by Pausanias at Patrae, where it was performed by Kalydonians displaced there in 14BC on the orders of Augustus: 'Round the altar in a circle they set up logs of green wood, each sixteen cubits long. On the altar within the circle is placed the driest wood. Just before the time of the festival they smooth the ascent to the altar, piling earth upon the steps . . . For the people throw alive upon the altar edible birds and every other kind of victim. There are wild boars, deer and gazelles. Some bring wolf-cubs or bear-cubs, others the full-grown beasts. They also place upon the altar fruit of cultivated trees. Next they set fire to the wood. At this point I have seen some of the beasts, including a bear, forcing their way outside at the first rush of the flames, some of them actually escaping by their strength. But those who threw them in drag them back again to the pyre. It is not remembered that anybody has ever been wounded by the beasts' (Paus vii.18.11–13, et vid. Paus iv.31.7). Lucian Samosatae reports a yet more

Meilanion feels his own disturbance ripple among the heroes. Those hauling their livestock to this exorbitant slaughter pay them little attention. And no wonder, thinks Meilanion. This is one of their futures: the future in which the boar is the victor, in which a divine anger rages and will not be appeased, but must be propitiated for ever, through a sacrifice without end. In this here and now, the heroes are no more than memories of the victims they were destined to be, empty-handed ghosts whose corpses lie rotting and unlamented in Kalydon's trackless interior, where they joined with the boar in battle and were overcome. There is no role for them here.

And there will be no 'cool wine' in Kalydon, he knows then. No women to serve them roasted fat and meat, no Oeneus to welcome them to his halls. Perhaps no Oeneus at all. He looks about him at the different comprehensions surfacing on the faces of his companions. Meleager is pushing his way through the men. There is no sign of Atalanta. A gust of wind scoops a cloud of oily smoke and sends it rolling across the terrace towards them. It smells of their defeat.

Meilanion turns and looks back. The heroes' giant shadows stretch over the stone terrace until the edge, which cuts them in two. Beyond is darkness. Meleager's dogs burrow through the heroes and cluster about their master, who takes his stand before the mouth of the temple. It is hard to look at him. The fire behind him is too fierce.

Atalanta and Aura emerge from the dark and pad towards the back of the body of men. Her gaze skates over Meilanion and comes to rest on Meleager, who is addressing them. Meilanion turns from her as she approaches. Meleager's arm sweeps out as

---

horrible rite (De Syria Dea xlviiii). The animals' pacifism was a condition of the sacrifice (Aesch, Ag 1297; Plut, Pel xxii; Porphyr, De abstinentia i.25; Inscr Kos xxxvii; Dio Chrys, Or xxii.51; Apollonius Paradoxographus, Mirabilia xiii). The goddess was surnamed Laphria 'after a man of Phocis, because the ancient image of Artemis was set up at Kalydon by Laphrius, the son of Castalius, the son of Delphus' (Paus vii.18.9), or possibly in derivation from 'Laophorus' ('Protectress of the Way' or 'Carrier of People') or 'Elaphos' (the Deer-Goddess). Horns of cows and calves have been found at the site, along with boar-tusks, tortoise shells, locust remains, horse bones and horse teeth but no antlers. Related festivals were the Elaphebolia at Hyampolis and that of the Kouretes at Messene (Paus x.1.6; Plut, Mul Virt 244). Heracles's self-instigated immolation on Mount Oeta must post-date the festival of Laphria (Pind, Isth iv.67–74; Schol. ad Hom, Il xxii.159). As late as Xenophon, pigs were burnt alive as offerings to Zeus Meilichios (Xen, Anab vii.8.4 et vid. Schol. ad Thuc i.126), but these were a relatively cheap sacrifice.

though to include the pens which cover the hillside, or higher up perhaps.

Beyond the first slope is a shallow saddle of land, its spine marked by a road paved with white stones. Its course scores the darkness of the valley beyond as if a fiery arrow has been loosed, its after-image fading and disappearing with distance, but then exploding into tiny pinpricks of distant light. Meleager is pointing there. He shouts louder, but the fire roars, the animals bellow or bleat, those hauling them towards it likewise. The heroes cannot hear him, nor do they need to. They have always known that they would gather here.

The men around Meilanion are restless. He is jostled by someone behind him but he does not turn. A hand grips him by the shoulder and pulls him about. Atalanta stands before him. He feels the imprint of her fingers, the fire's heat behind him, the slow disturbance of the men surrounding them both. They gather themselves for the last leg of the march. The lights in the darkness are Kalydon.[106]

---

106 Rather, they are congruent with Kalydon. The lights which punctuate the darkness of Ancient Greece send indirect or ambiguous signals. A great relay of beacons and torches built of pinewood, dried heather, kindling and mountain-wood (Aesch, Ag 288, 295, 305, 497-8) stretched from Mount Ida to Lemnos, from the summit of Mount Athos to the watch-towers of Makistos and Messapion, from there to Cithaeron overlooking the plain of Asopus and Mount Aegiplanctus, across the waters of Gorgopos, then past the headlands of the Saronic Gulf to the watch-tower by Mount Arachnaeus, and so to the palace of Atreus in Argos (Aesch, Ag 281-317). The fires told Clytaemnestra of Agamemnon's return from Troy. Beacons from Sciathus carried news of a lost naval battle to the Athenians' allies at Artemisium (Hdt vii.183.1), where, much earlier, Lynceus had learned of Hypermnestra's flight from Larissa by the same method, and she of his (Paus ii.25.4). A blaze of nocturnal light bright enough to 'cast shadows on the earth' presaged disaster for the Lacedaemonians (Diod Sic xv.50.2-3) and another – possibly a comet (Aristot, Meteor 343b.23) – preceded the sea's engulfing the cities of Buris and Helice (Callisthenes ap. Sen, Quaest Nat vii.5). Yet the same phenomenon augured well for Timoleon's expedition to Sicily (Diod Sic xvi.66.3). Athena led the Furies from the palace of Atreus to the Underworld by torchlight (Aesch, Eum 1022-4) and Artemis transfixed her prey in the same glare (Paus viii.37.4). Trepidant maidens followed processions of flaring twigs (pyxis, London Brit Mus 1920.12-21.1; stamnos, Mississippi 1977.3.96) to the marriage-altar (Eur, Med 1027, Ion 1474, Hel 723), but their sacrifices were made in darkness: only mad Cassandra lit the tapers in celebration of her own 'marriage' after the fall of Troy (Eur, Tro 308-52). Torches raised by Orestes and Capaneus signalled the murder of Hermione (Eur, Or 1573) and the fall of Thebes (Aesch, Sept 433); that held by the laughing Thais provoked the answering laughter of Alexander as he watched Persepolis burn (Diod Sic xvii.72.5). Compare the 'flash of torches' by which Iphigenia hoped to cleanse her brother's pollution of the sanctuary at Taurica (Eur, Iph Taur 1224) with those tossed into the pit in honour of Demeter at Argos (Paus ii.22.3); or the light by which Cimon's troops were rallied (Diod Sic xi.61.6-7) with the light shining off the bald head of Odysseus (Hom, Od xviii.354), who was old by then and mocked by the men he would shortly kill. All these lights have yet to shine and the light by which Meleager sees Atalanta turn to the man at her side and speak to him must be a more teasing illumination, such as came from the torches which

*　　*　　*

They had entered the city by the southern gate, found deserted streets, silence, a lightless riddle. The city promised to them hid within a city taken and plundered. They moved through Kalydon's streets, listening and watching, being listened to and

---

illuminated the secret rites of a 'Great Goddess', but never to the extent of naming her (Soph, Oed Col 1049). He cannot hear, and the lights of Kalydon flicker like the stubs of lamp-wicks (Aristoph, Nub 56–9) floating in salt and oil (Hdt ii.62.1–2), badly trimmed (Aristoph, Vesp 249–54), purple-flamed (cup, Paris Louvre G135) and purple-smoked (skyphos, Paris Louvre G156), choked with the ashes that foretell rain (Aristoph, Vesp 262). Castorberry oil (Hdt ii.94.1–2) would give a better light and olive oil better again (Xen, Sym vii.4).

The heroes move forward. The city is a silent torch race run amok (Paus i.30.2; bell krater, Harvard 1960.344) or a loose glitter in which every glint is a lamp and what it might reveal: a man poring over his ledgers (Aristoph, Nub 18), a woman intent on her toilette (Aristoph, Lys 825–8; bell krater, Harvard 9.1988; kylix, Mississippi.1977.3.112) or working a hand between her thighs (Aristoph, Eccl 1–18). They shift, reform and echo one another: the tents burning on the beach at Troy (Eur, Rh 43) will be mirrored in the light streaming from Helen's chamber (Tryphiodorus, Excidium Il ii 487–521) and replaced by Sinon's treacherous beacon (Apollod, Ep 5.15). The Greeks will deceive, their ships sail; across the sea, Nauplius's answering beacon will draw them onto the rocks of Capheria (Apollod, Ep 6.7, ii.1.5; Eur, Hel 1126–31; Schol. ad Eur, Or 432; Quint Smyrn, Post xiv.611ff.; Schol. ad Lyc, Alex 384; Hyg, Fab cxvi; Sen, Ag 557–75; Dict Cret vi.1; Virg, Aen xi.260 et Serv ad ibid.; Lact, Plac ad Statius, Achill i.93; Ov, Met xiv.472). For each Mycerinus lighting lamps to turn night into day (Hdt ii.133.4–5) there is an Antigone sweating beneath a sun she cannot bring herself to look upon (Soph, Antig 879); and for every pair of buffoons burning off one another's body-hair (Aristoph, Thes 237) there are the dozen flames of the jury come to indict them (Aristoph, Vesp 219). In the darkness to the east, oaks and olives cover the foothills of Mount Oeta; the upper slopes are pines. Heracles's pyre is still virgin forest (Soph, Trach 1193–1205). The heroes file up the paved way to the city and the lights multiply and spread to either side (Hom, Il viii.555–66). They tow cargos of consequence – Hera's burning temple (Paus ii.17.7), Athena's blazing face (Hom, Od xix.33–4) – which grow larger in the eye until they blot out everything around them (Eur, Cyc 663). As the heroes approach the gate, Kalydon's lights scatter. Meleager has lost sight of Atalanta. His dogs bark to the dogs within and are not answered. Where is the real signal?

'Athena's lamp' was redesigned by Callisthenes and furnished with a wick of fireproof 'Carpasian flax' (Paus i.26.6–7). The fire stolen by Prometheus hides among its countless progeny (Aesch, Prom 1–11). Kalydon exchanges the lines of its streets for a geography of pinpricks. They are akin to the false fires sometimes glimpsed by sailors (Hom, Il xix.375–6), or the nonsense signals sent from Plataea to Thebes, among which the true signal was jumbled (Thuc iii.22.7-8), or 'the tapering flame which gives decisions on two points, being a sign of both victory and defeat' (Eur, Ph 1255–9). The gates open for the heroes. Kalydon is host to a thousand lidless glows; they muster at the far ends of the streets then scatter like embers raked from a fire. The heroes raise their heads and rub their eyes; they do not recognise these new constellations whose red stars light nothing but themselves. The dogs draw together. But the lights surrounding them are not so distant as stars. They are the red of falling coals, or drifting sparks, or tiny after-images of the pyre in the temple, each pair set in a solidifying darkness. The heroes trace the forming shapes as the lights of Kalydon encircle them. Such lights are unrecorded in the sources, yet they exist. Beyond the limit of the record lies the terrain where their acts will leave no mark or trace: where the boar may be hunted. They watch the glowing eyes which watch themselves. Then the first animal leaps.

34

watched themselves by shapes that formed beyond their sight. Their fears were the fears of hunters who track in silence or wait concealed, their weapons raised and poised; in the moment before the fatal strike, they see themselves reflected in the black of the quarry's eye and, in the moment following, they feel its terror shuddering through the shaft. The heroes were noiseless, each one listening while the animals gathered around them. They recognised another of their futures. To be the hunted is the hunter's fear.

*   *   *

Glowing points of red drifted in the darkness above them, winking in and out of view, tracking the heroes' progress towards the high ground of the sanctuary at the city's northern limit. Passing through a narrow and high-walled passage, Meleager's dogs began to bark. The heroes quickened their steps. Herded together too close to use their weapons, the knowledge of what was about to take place took hold of them, stranding them between advance and retreat. To where? Atalanta looked up. Bodies swelled behind red eyes, lining the roofs to either side. The men at the head of the column turned and tried to make their way through those behind. Those trying to advance jostled them. Someone shouted for order and a moment later their assailants leapt down from left and right.

There was clumsy chaos, a confused grappling. The first victim cried out, and then there was panic. The hunters could not win there and weakened by that first assault they had split, had tried to reunite, had failed. One group had continued to the precinct of the sanctuary. The other had scattered.

Atalanta, Meilanion, Ancaeus and the Cimmerian found themselves running together. Something had scraped against her face. She batted it away. Then something caught her ankle. She had lost her footing and would have fallen, would have been left there. A hand had hooked itself under her arm and scooped her up. They were running again.

The city raised walls of darkness around them and the heavy bodies of the men thudded against one another until their flight slowed, their pulses pounding. The street widened and ended in a courtyard with a cairn of stones at its centre.

Ancaeus muttered then that they were Arcadians, ignoring the Cimmerian, and had cursed Meleager, the captain who had led his men into ambush.

They took their stand about the shrine, each facing out to quarter the open ground but seeing nothing. She did not know how long they waited before they heard a scrabbling, moving towards them over the roof tiles. She watched the hot points of their eyes blink into being all around them. Six, eight, ten, twenty. She slipped on her finger-guard and reached for the first of her arrows.

The Cimmerian had loosed his own shafts until no more remained, then had unstrung his bow and used the cord as a garrot. They had massed upon him. Meilanion had moved to help him and she had heard her own voice blended with that of Ancaeus, both barking at the youth to hold still. There were two sharp cries of pain from the lost man and then a brief respite for the three survivors as the smell of his blood drew the pack. She fought with her knife between her teeth, Aura at her feet darting out to dispatch those she could not finish. Ancaeus swung his axe in a never-ending roll, left and right and left again, swapping it between his hands, his legs rooted and immobile as oaks. She felt the blood from his kills splash her back and shoulders. Meilanion jabbed with his spear, grunting with the effort, but it was she and Ancaeus who bore the brunt of the assault. For the animals attacked in waves – she lost count how many times – and a strange weariness draped itself about her neck, a monotony that hummed and murmured to her in a voice she remembered but could not place. She waited until the last moment before loosing each of her arrows, eyes finding the target, arm reaching back, fingers notching the shaft, bending the bow, her heart slowing and steadying. Then the wait, a yawning interval in which she heard the thin cries of men in distant parts of the city, the grunts of the men guarding her back just as she guarded theirs, the skittering of claws more suited to earth and grass than to Kalydon's smooth stones. These intervals seemed to stretch moments into seasons; there was so much time in which to let the arrow fly. The bodies fell at her feet and when the kill was clean she gripped the shaft below the head to pull it through the corpse and fire again.

When dawn had come they had faced each other filthy from

the slaughter, as though they, not their weapons, had pierced the slick flesh of their victims, had cut their sinews and felt the suck of their fat as they were drawn out again. But no trophies would be taken from their victory. The battle had left no trace. The cadavers of their victims had disappeared and of the Cimmerian there was no sign.

The three survivors skimmed the scum off a water trough set against the far wall and cleaned themselves. Atalanta watched the two men watching as her skin shed its crust of drying blood, then she gave herself up to the sensation of the cold water washing over her body. A burst of laughter from Ancaeus brought her head up in time to witness Meilanion, and his excitement at the sight of her. She felt blood race to her cheeks. The younger man turned away and she plunged her head back into the water until it throbbed from the cold.

Those who had survived the night gathered beyond the west wall of the city, their faces grey from fatigue. Meleager strode about the walls, calling to the missing. But by midday, when the sun drove them to slake their thirst from a stream running off a spur of Aracynthus, the names called were met by silence. Atalanta recalled the thud of the Cimmerian's body when their dark assailants had pulled him down: a soft sound. Meilanion's grunts of effort had been higher-pitched than those of Ancaeus, almost gasps. His manhood was new to him and untried. The hand which had pulled her up off the street had felt smooth, even as its fingers dug into the hollow of her armpit and twined themselves in the tangled nest of her hair: a man's touch. The nightmare-monotony of the attacks was rolling back and away, a dying thunderclap.

Or the fading crash of the pillars wrenched last night from the airy palace they had raised on the far shore of the gulf, composed of their shouted names, she thought, as Meleager echoed their calls, shouting out to the missing for the last time, expecting no answer now and the catalogue serving as obsequy for the lost: *Agelaus, Dryas, Panopeus, Eurytus and Cteatus, Amphiaraus, Panopeus . . .*

And all the sons of Hippocoon, and a dozen besides, as she counted them. She looked up at Aracynthus, which rose over the remaining hunters, its blunt peak filling the sky. Their proper rites could not be observed here.

The survivors prepared for the march ahead. Down the valley, the animal pens were empty and there was now no sign of Kalydon's dispossessed citizens. The temple stood deserted. In daylight it appeared diminished, no more than a lodge marking the entrance to some far grander construction, obliterated long ago. The fire had scorched a black tongue of soot into the stones of the terrace. Meleager walked between the seated huntsmen. Their glory would be all the greater, the fewer of them survived to share it. It would burn brighter, prove more durable. He pointed to the route, which led back down the valley, towards the sea and along the shore between the water's edge and the foot of Aracynthus. His dogs rose to their feet.

Thersites' foot had been cleft in two, as though a claw had hooked it and his panicked motion had drawn the talon through the flesh, tearing it along its length. Acastus and Peleus supported him between them. The sons of Thestius closed about their injured brother Cometes as though to guard him from the curiosity of the others and bore him along on a crude palanquin improvised from their spear-shafts. Podargos limped. Lynceus carried one arm in a sling. The others bore the cost of their survival in gashes and cuts which stung and throbbed as the sun dried them. Their feet dragged in the dust, which soon enough rose to coat them and parch their throats. Atalanta and Aura took their own path off to the left.

At the foot of the valley their route swung west. Below them, to their left, the salt marshes through which they had waded on the previous day shimmered as the sunlight glinted off the brackish waters and the gulf breezes set the reeds and rushes quivering. Above them, the heights of Aracynthus were a jumble of vast boulders tumbled off the mountain long ago and embedded in the earth wherever chance had brought them to rest. They rose in perspectiveless tiers which turned the dense maquis into a seeming forest, gullies into valleys, sand into scree. Giants had played here once and later conjured themselves into the battered mortals who stumbled in broken line beneath the ruins of their pleasure-ground. Meleager led. Atalanta felt her presence in his thoughts, something flickering at the edge of his vision. He had not spoken to her or approached her since appearing above her on the river-bank.

The wound in her hand was oozing a clear fluid which would

scab by sundown. She had not felt the barbs puncture her skin as she pulled her shafts from the bodies of her victims, nor the deepening of the cut with every repetition. The fingers were stiffening. She flexed them and looked up as Thersites yelped. He was being transferred to the supporting arms of Nestor and Meilanion, who avoided her eye. What kept the younger man distant now? Meleager? The presence of the others?

It took them the best part of the day to reach the last spur of Aracynthus. Beyond, the upper part of the lagoon came into view. Yesterday's landfall was now far behind them. The sun turned the water red, as it had the previous night. Dusk tried the air and was accepted. The line of little shoals standing sentinel between the lower lagoon and the gulf which sought to include it studded the water and cast lengthening shadows, little wakes of lightlessness towed by smooth-backed sea-creatures swimming after the fireball now sinking into the western sea. More of them clustered further down the coast, more than she remembered, although who among them had troubled to count when they had looked across the water on the previous day, when their shouts had built the palace of sound in which they had set their names one by one, as refuge from the sentences suspended over them, in which their tales were foretold?

None.

But there were more of them – she saw it now – and the little islands moved. They were closer and smaller than she had first thought. They emerged from the mouth of the Lycormas, twenty or thirty of them. A flotilla of tiny craft was crossing the gulf, inching behind the sandbanks which they aped and whose own stasis betrayed them, in which creatures who must be men were carried, one to each, and which were bestirred by their motions. She thought first of the townspeople, disappeared that morning, who had abandoned their mad sacrifice. But there had been hundreds of them, perhaps thousands. She shook her head and turned to shout her discovery.

Meleager stood before her, a man-shaped absence against the red glare of the sun. He too had seen the flecks of darkness moving over the water, or had known that they were there and had held his tongue just as he held her in his gaze now. The grey shadow of dusk sped into the gulf to blend together its waters and whatever moved upon them. She held him too: by an acquiescence which was part-submission to the man who had stood above her on the bank of the river but had not dared to approach and part-bestowal of the gift he sought from her now, beneath the shadow of Aracynthus, and here, surrounded by men he had led into disaster, and which took the form of her silence.

Meilanion might track the beast they sought; Meleager might kill it. But neither both. Her choosing between them must weaken her, she reflected, when time should come to choose.

*   *   *

The hunters' dream that night was of the boar. To the north and west a storm flashed and fizzed over the low peaks of the Acarnarnian range, lighting their slumped bodies in its flashes. Rolling over the lake of Trichonis it broke against the northern mountains, sending down rain in silent sheets which pooled on the unaccepting ground. Thunderclaps rumbled south, stretching, fading, redoubling so that their din reached the sleeping men and entered their dreams. They lay where they had sunk and the distant storm echoed in their heavy heads, becoming the drumming of hooves. For when the beast rouses himself from his marshy hide and leaps onto hard ground the earth seems to rumble.

The hunters had been listening for his signal and listened for it now. It was the last sound that Idmon heard, gored in the groin and buried in the lee of Cape Acheron by the Argonauts. There, Peleus and Idas dispatched the beast and left the hide and head to spoil. The thunder rolled on, echoing between the stilled Symplegades and speeding back over the sea to the country about Phthia, where a brother once listened for the same sound and another two dissimulated. This hunt is a pretext. The hapless Phocus will be bundled down a well. Peleus and Telamon will be guilty, and then banished, and then find themselves here, in the dream. Laertes sees two men, one young, one old, picking their way through a forest of myrtles and laurels. They carry spears of cornel wood. The younger looks up: a faint rumble has hovered at the threshold of their hearing and now leaps to a new, urgent level. The older fixes his eyes on the underbrush. The two men resemble himself: as he was and

40

as he will be. Their heads come about with such agonising slowness. Some other force operates this dream, a pervasive languor which turns their limbs to lead and the dreamer's teeming brain to wind-smoothed and sun-warmed stone, whence the dream shimmers in radiated heat. Admetus strains against the chain leashes which gyre and tug as lion and boar resist the traces that will give him the daughter of Pelias. Their roars and snorts grate on his ears. His back is flecked with their foam.

The boar leaps and capers about the red circuit of their campfire. Their heads twitch from the impact as the animal lands with a grunt among them and piles up small earthworks. They are breathing citadels under siege. Their futures are undefined, compounded of their pasts, which are tangles of obligation and challenge. The ground bristles and ripples, then settles. The fire's red eye dulls with the passing of the hours. Morning comes. The surviving sons of Thestius – Iphiclus, Aphares, Evippus, Plexippus, Eurypylus, Prothous, Prokaon, Klytius and Hippothous – are gone. The hunters raise their heads from slumber and find the deserters' token, which may signify good or ill and prove either a gruesome totem or melancholy relic: Cometes' abandoned cadaver sits propped against the broad trunk of an alder at the edge of the grove, his spear tied to his hand.

*   *   *

The dogs fanned out and scampered forward, heads dipped and noses sweeping, sniffing after scent. Aura barked at them, wanting to follow. Soon the animals were white or tawny dots of movement, indistinct against the bare earth and rain-starved grass. They had rounded the southernmost spur of Aracynthus. It was early morning and the western slopes were in shadow.

Meleager had loosed his dogs and set them on the trail of the sons of Thestius. The hunters followed the animals and their quarry into night-cooled air which rolled down from the upper slopes leaving drifts of thin mist in its wake. A heavy dew soaked their feet and all except Lynceus blinked as they turned their backs on the glare coming off the surface of the gulf and advanced into the shade. Then, as though the mountain sensed

41

their invasion of its purview, a strange cry drifted out from its slopes, thinned by distance to a single falling note which carried in the still air and reached them as a drawn-out shout. A human cry.

They looked up, counting one, two, three heartbeats before the sound was cut off. Nothing moved on the mountain. They looked down again, all except Lynceus who listened after the fugitive sound. His gaze carried through the mountain's coarse surface to the successive overlapping washes of alluvial soil which draped the hard limestone in soft armour. The inner mountain churned. Countless tiny shelled creatures swirled in a congealing sea of rock and darkness. Idas tugged at his arm. Lynceus seemed to stare at nothing and yet could not turn away.

Atalanta watched without curiosity: Lynceus was the far-sighted one, just as Theseus and Pirithous were inseparable, as Peleus and Telamon were the killers of their brother Phocus, and Jason the singular captain of the singular ship. Just as she was the bear-girl or the virgin. Or the victor over the boar. Idas dragged his brother forward by the arm. The hunters continued along the invisible trail of the men who had fled in the night.

The column stretched and the two brothers soon fell far to the rear, joining Nestor and Phoenix, who carried Thersites.

The flight of the sons of Thestius was a kind of lure or bait, or intended as such, thought Meilanion, who walked at the rear of the column. The cries of a tethered fawn will draw its mother; carrion will breed both crows and maggots. Through the dogs to the fleeing men, through the men to the boar. For the beast would take the smaller group first. And through the boar to Atalanta. Through Meleager too. The one who would lead them into disaster, as he must, just as his dogs were leading them astray now. All but himself. He searched the terrain for confirmation of his suspicion, his eyes sweeping up the mountain, then down to the water, back and forth. There was something in his memory, or something yet to be encountered.

They inched around the base of Aracynthus and the gentle incline they traversed began to steepen. A ribbon of spiny oak scrub which had paralleled their path for most of the morning thickened now, descended the slope and forced them nearer to the water. The sun cleared the peak of the massif and fell full upon their heads. The lagoon below and to their left narrowed to a waist some way ahead, then broadened into the still lake which was its terminus. The distant dogs had stopped at a fast-running race of water which had cut a channel down the slope on its way to the lagoon below. They sniffed up and down the banks of the streamlet in an attempt to pick up the trail. Up the slope, the gully disappeared beneath impenetrable oak scrub. The dogs moved down towards the water, baffled.

Little sandbanks broke the lagoon's surface just before its narrowest point. The heroes came off the mountain's lower slope and gathered at the edge, where tall rushes fenced the water. Idas and Lynceus stumbled down, the former guiding the latter, who now moved like a blind man and waved his un-injured arm in a strange motion, as though against malevolent insects. Thersites and his bearers were further back. The waiting hunters looked back for the stragglers, who reached the gully then descended its course until it met the flat ground of the foreshore and split into innumerable rivulets. The dogs now ran among these in frustrated confusion. It was as if the sons of Thestius had ascended into the sky. The trail was dead.

Meleager tamped the ground with the butt of his spear. Atalanta saw Ancaeus rise, his brow furrowed by a thought she could not read. The Arcadian swung his axe onto his shoulder and looked about him, then frowned again. She tried to catch his eye, but his gaze roved instead over the main body of the men, themselves now rising. The dogs yapped in desultory fashion. Aura snarled in response. The path now was through the reed-beds.

Spurge: its downy stems rose up among the reeds. The heedless tramping of those at the head broke its stalks and those following felt its milky sap coat their legs and thighs. Soon enough their skins began to itch and burn. Swathes of it lined the lagoon, concealed amid the rushes and alternating with mallow and flax, whose pink and blue flowers guided them through short-lived respites from the stinging sap. They heard Thersites shouting with pain until he fell far behind, his bearers tiring. Further out the reeds grew to head height and the damp ground turned to true marsh. They lost sight of each other and drifted out one by one, splashing through brackish water and pushing aside the the fibrous stems which rose all around them. The sun hung overhead and they wandered shadowless through the tall stems, guided by the depth of the water, which increased as they drifted further from the invisible shore.

The reeds swayed around Atalanta, their topmost shoots brushed by light gusts which the convecting air sent scudding across the lagoon. There were no winds worthy of the name on this side of Aracynthus. The rustlings and soft commotions swept up the cruder crashings of the men. They moved about her in diffuse formation; the plashing of their feet betrayed them. A soundless shadow swept over, sunlight flaring about a dark span, neck gathered under a heron's yellow-beaked head, gliding. Gone. The boar was known to favour bogs, whose cloudy waters cooled his belly. The after-image of the passing bird hung in the reeds and twitched with the movements of her eyes. Aura panted. The sounds of the men grew fainter. She felt their presence peel away from her and her own luxurious solitude take its place. The idea of the two men retreated. But they would come at her, necks locked like contesting bullocks. She was the arrow to pierce and pin them both. These were vague thoughts, drifting from her as she reached for them.

The lagoon petered out in shallows. Heads, shoulders, then torsos broke the surface of the bristling reeds: the heroes waded out onto a foreshore in front of a low cliff. Water-starved trees clung to the rising rock-face, their roots bridging the dark splits of the fissures. The widest of these breaks cut the cliff from top to bottom, forming the entrance to a narrow pass. Stands of stunted oleanders and terebinths choked its mouth, suggesting that the level of the lagoon had once risen and lapped at their roots, then receded, leaving them stranded on the hard white limestone. From time to time, the winds probing the far side of the mountain would find this passage and drive a cloud of yellow dust out of the mouth of the cleft. Little stones fell from the heights and landed with loud cracks on the echoing floor.

The sun emptied its afternoon heat into the sky. Idas and Lynceus, then Thersites' bearers, pushed aside the last curtain of reeds and stamped their feet on solid ground. There being no shade, the heroes turned their backs to the sun and stared into the white mouth of the cleft. The dogs' tongues hung in the heat. Sweat ran over Ancaeus's furrowed brow and his eyes moved from head to head. He was counting, Atalanta realised. Meleager moved among the prostrate men, whose limbs were

44

blotched with rashes. When he came to the broad-shouldered Arcadian some words passed between them and then Meleager too scanned the area in which they were gathered. Both turned and looked down the lagoon's long shore. The green of the reed-beds darkened and lightened as the stems swayed in the breezes. Otherwise nothing stirred. She examined her injured hand; the wound had not reopened. Ancaeus was pointing back beyond the reeds. Whatever troubled him now had troubled him first there. It did not concern her. She wondered if the water here at the top of the lagoon was as foul as that below. Aura would not drink it. She thought that their fates would be settled in the mountains of the interior where streams boiled and foamed as they hurtled over pebbled beds. She wanted freezing water, familiar terrain. Ancaeus and Meleager had stepped back from one another. Those nearest were watching this unexpected alliance: Theseus and Pirithous, Jason a little apart from them, four or five others gathered about Peleus and Telamon. Thersites and Lynceus muttered to themselves in their private worlds of pain. Nestor seemed to be asleep. Who else? Castor and Pollux had walked to the mouth of the narrow canyon and were staring up at its walls. Acastus was sharpening the blade of his spear, using a smooth shard of stone which rasped against the iron. The others were idle. They would move off again soon, she thought, then thought again. They would all move off, except one. She looked about to confirm her suspicion, then turned back to Ancaeus and Meleager, who were still staring down the shore-line: reeds, water, the slope of Aracynthus. But no movement there. No sign. Meleager faced her then and she felt herself back on the little ridge above their landfall, his body moving to cover her own and his eyes on her before the younger man had appeared to interrupt the wordless transaction. But there would be no interruption here – the fact was written in his face – and Ancaeus had known before any of them. Very well, she thought to herself. Meilanion had disappeared.

*   *   *

A shape gathers at the back of his mind. But reach and it recedes. The night-hunter understands these things: that a dog thinks with its nose, that the prey will reek when chased, that water

45

carries no scent but its own. The dogs' confuson at the gully running down the slope of Aracynthus had given him another point of the forming shape. The channel ran up as well as down, ascending and disappearing beneath the impenetrable thicket which covered Aracynthus's lower slopes. The flight of the sons of Thestius had taken them into the stream which cut its way to an invisible destination high above. And then?

Meilanion glanced about at the other hunters, a casual turn of the head. The gully was a steep-sided trench half the height of a man cut by an agitated flow of water which flexed and quivered as it raced down the slope. A single moment and its single movement would take him out of view. The others had turned to the lagoon below; the hunt recorded in their footprints would give out at the water's edge and be resumed wherever they regained land. His own would leave no trace at all, but his would be the one to succeed. The losses in the abandoned city, Oeneus's absence, the inordinate sacrifice in which their pre-figured failure resounded in the cries of the animals as they burned. They were all beyond the hunt's posterity now. And this trackless territory was his, proper to the night-hunter: himself.

He jumped down into the channel, crouched and waited, counting seconds. No shout pursued him. He crawled forward.

The day-hunter is solar. The night-hunter's double lives in the fall of sunlight. He glows with heat. The day-hunter becomes one with his prey, bound to it by the mutual pounding of their feet along the trail or of the blood within their veins. They are close, at the finish. But the night-hunter drapes himself in nets and bristles with lime-twigs and little cages. He knows the moon's face better than his mother's and the forest paths are more familiar to him than the lines in the palm of his hand. The light by which he hunts is cold.

The spiny branches of the dense oak scrub closed over Meilanion's head. A little further up and he would be indis-tinguishable from the shadows. He paused and listened again for the sound of pursuit. He heard the yapping of the dogs far away down the hillside. Water surged against his wrists and knees. The sides of the gully were formed from slick yellow-brown clay into which his hands sank as he advanced. His knees bruised themselves on the stones collected in its bed. The oak scrub thickened above him and prickled with glints of sunlight. It was a half-lit world. He braced his feet against the sides of the channel and forced himself on, marvelling that the sons of Thestius had left so scant a record of their passage, for the clay recorded his own scrabblings and scrapings in the form of gouged handholds and footprints.

The shaft of his spear tangled in the dense branchwork above. He pulled it free. His knees were raw; he felt the sting of the water in the cuts. The gully was too narrow to turn about and inspect them. Clay smeared him from head to toe, dried on his skin, flaked, and was replaced by a fresh coating whenever he missed a foothold, for he was forced to flatten himself in the bed to prevent his sliding down the incline. The thorny canopy above reached down and scraped at his back. From time to time the stream received trickling tributaries. Above each of these his narrowing channel would shrink and press him harder. The incline seemed to extend to the height of the sky. He measured his progress in the jerks and lunges by which he pulled himself forward and which grew clumsy as his limbs tired. He stopped to rest but it cost as great an effort to brace himself as to continue. Sunlight broke through the screen of branches, the hot shafts falling on his back. His mind drifted about the clay-coated body which housed him and which the sun's kiln baked to a brittle skin. He was outside the man climbing the slope of Aracynthus, in a future where he rattled in a tomb of sun-baked clay which aped the form of his flesh. His memorial would be shards of empty armour. The spiny branches would wreathe his shell and wind themselves about its limbs until they too dried in the hot wind, burned, and left his soot-blackened carapace exposed to curious eyes and inquisitive fingers. Whose? And whose lips would then form the name inscribed upon his parchment skin, the record of the creature he had been: Meilanion?

He had halted. He drew breath and pushed forward again. Ahead, the course of the channel bent to the left where an outcrop of limestone broke through the soil. He pulled himself around the obstacle. Was the thorn-scrub less dense than before? The sunlight seemed stronger.

The roof of his world broke open. One moment there was nothing but the sides of the gully, whose lines converged until they merged in the thickening shade, the next he was pushing aside a swathe of thick grasses, rising and standing upright in full sunlight.

He had reached a truncated ridge which jutted from the cliff. The face continued above him, riven with cracks from which water seeped, running down and pooling between the tussocks of lush grass. To either side, the ground fell away into deep ravines. The air was thinner and colder. He looked down at the lagoon far below. Nothing moved there except a single bird making a wide circuit of the shoreline. He turned and gazed up at the cliff, shielding his eyes from the glare of the sunlight reflected by the white stone. Its base offered handholds and little ledges, but thereafter its slope appeared sheer and smooth. He thought of the clay which lined the gully, in which nothing and no one had left its mark. Except himself.

He scooped water from the shallow pools and began to wash the clay from his body. Could Meleager, following his dogs, have been right and himself wrong? Might the sons of Thestius have descended to the lagoon and waded out far enough to lose the pursuing pack in its waters? For all its heat and light, this was a night-hunt, a pursuit through country where paths would double back on themselves or lead into traps. The real trail would always be the least likely. And the quarry he pursued, that too was a lie: a shape-shifter. The sons of Thestius huntsmen who had become the hunted, bait for the boar, who would replace them. They led to the beast, and the beast led further, being the token for the final prize.

The cool water was red with clay rinsed from his skin, red as the water in the trough that morning, after the slaughter. He frowned then, recalling Ancaeus's laughter and the sight of Atalanta, unperturbed, plunging her head into the tainted liquid. Straightening, her face had seemed to run with the blood of those they had killed. She had said nothing, her thoughts turning to his sun-blessed double. He did not know. She had turned away in search of other survivors and Ancaeus had drawn him aside to tell him that the tales told of her were partial. Rhoecus and Hylaeus had tried her in the forests of Arcadia, it was true, but she had not shot them. The huntress had cast away her bow; the virgin had feigned willingness. And then, Ancaeus had continued, in the midst of their pleasures, she had torn off their genitals. The centaurs' howls had echoed down the valleys as she harried and tormented them, allowing them no respite while they bled to death. She was untouched because untouchable. Ancaeus had laughed again at the expression on his face. The boar alone would give her to him.

He looked down from the cliff, into the ravines to either side, two steep chutes gouged from the stone as though by gigantic heels scraping down Aracynthus's sides. A furring of brushwood concealed the final footprint. He picked out heaps of stones which the winter frosts had prised from the face and sent tumbling down. He felt a heaviness in his limbs; his knees and ankles were stiffening. He would have to move soon. Patterns of handholds led right and left, then disappeared. Which to take? He thought forward to the ebb of his energy as he clung to the rock-face, unsure whether to press on or turn back, the stumps of his fingers being peeled from their handhold and the final lean back into airy space.

He remembered the drawn-out cry which had raised their heads to the cliffs that morning. He had tried to remember something then, but it had lain in his future not his past: here. That morning it had been a man. He screwed up his eyes against the glare and stared down. One of the sons of Thestius had walked with his brothers that morning, had scrambled with them up a clay-lined channel, had rested here, and then had begun to climb. But he had tired, or slipped, or lost his head. He had fallen, and now he was no more than a blood-stain baking on a limestone boulder far below.

Meilanion turned from the distant dead man to the rockface. The sons of Thestius had climbed from this ridge. One had fallen. But eight had survived. He slung his spear over his shoulder and began to climb after them.

*　　*　　*

Behind them were the lake and the reed-beds. Before them lay the break in the cliff, the entrance to a canyon. The hunters pushed through the trees choking the mouth. Beyond was a channel cut from white stone and the sunlight beating into it. The camber of its floor pushed tamarisk scrub and tufts of grass to its sides, where their roots scrabbled in drifts of gravel and pebbles or sought out cracks in the stone.

The walls were worn smooth to the height of a man but thereafter cracks began to appear in their sides. Jagged overhangs jutted out higher yet as if a thick cord of sinew had been pulled from the body of the mountain leaving an open wound which the sun had baked to stone. Some way ahead the course of the canyon bent towards the north and the shadow cast by the west wall cloaked the stone in a darkness that their sun-blinded eyes could not penetrate.

And so the first trickle of water, advancing and filtering through the till and low mounds of pebbles in the lee of the shadowing wall, sucked at by water-starved roots, spilling in and out of cracks, went unremarked until it began to splash about the larger rocks and its noise called them to kneel and slake their thirst.

Aura lapped at an arm of water which curled about a smooth-sided boulder, her yellow teeth and quick pink tongue visible as she twisted her head. The shade was a cool balm. Atalanta cupped her hands and scooped water which ran down her arms and dripped off her elbows. Her skin remembered faster streams, foaming and colder. She looked up. The nearest of the men was Ancaeus, who crouched some way downstream of her and bent to immerse his face. The other men kept their distance from her. They cast down their weapons and cupped their hands, all save Thersites, who lay flat on his belly, and Lynceus, who approached the trickling stream then retreated from it, back and forth until his brother pulled him down and dashed the water into his open mouth. Meleager's dogs waited for their master's command, given when the last of the men had had their fill, and then they too leaped forward to drink.

Atalanta rose. Nestor and Phoenix supported Thersites but in the heat haze the three men appeared to her as a single figure staggering under the weight of his frame. The others were thin as twigs, merging and dissolving. The heat of the canyon blended and collapsed them into one another, all save herself.

A prohibition fenced her and held the men away. Her continuing presence and Meilanion's disappearance were alike inexplicable to the huntsmen, part of the same mystery in which the two of them were bound together. She thought of the frame of bones that an animal carries in the case of its flesh, its articulations and flexings and possible shapes. The youth was a space in their ranks and whatever deeds were marked out for him were now among their omissions. But she was their excess. A hunter might dispatch the quarry with a single cut of the knife and then find himself in the grip of its death, stabbing at the carcass over and over. An avenger might take the life beyond the one owed him and turn restitution into a blood-feud, a blood-feud into a war. They feared what she might mean.

Atalanta, in her turn, thought on what their fear might mean to her. Meleager strode ahead with his mane of yellow hair heavy in the heat and his dogs advancing in line with him, heads held high, for the sun had scoured any scent which might have been laid here. Rhoecus and Hylaeus had reared up expecting her to turn and run so that their hooves might knock her down, crack her bones and pin her motionless, face-down on the forest floor. But she had not turned and in their confusion they had made easy prey. She did not know if she might resist Meleager, if he should come for her. And she did not know whether Meleager might break the prohibition in which the others had immured her or whether, being hers and she his, he would find himself bound within it.

The canyon's sides rose higher. Aracynthus's flattened peak would be far above them, to the left. It was invisible from the canyon floor. The stream – it had broadened to merit the name – gurgled in its channel and its noise echoed off the walls. The bottom of the canyon began to narrow. The sinking sun sent a black shadow creeping across the floor and up the eastern face. They walked in the bed of the stream, which now reached as high as their calves. The dogs jumped from rock to rock, panting to keep up. The air cooled.

They halted where the canyon bent off at a different angle. From a distance it had appeared that their passage might have come to an abrupt halt. Peleus and Acastus marched forward to investigate. The rest sat down to await the stragglers. Phoenix and Nestor were struggling to carry Thersites over this more difficult terrain and Theseus and Pirithous had dropped back to add their efforts. Idas and Lynceus had yet to come into view.

The stream rose again.

But among those waiting on the near side of the bend – Eurytion sharpening a short-bladed knife, Telamon standing guard over the spear of Peleus, Ancaeus sitting beside him,

Caeneus lying propped on his elbows, Laertes squatting, Eurytion slumped, Castor and Pollux drawing lines in a pan of dry gravel, Jason speaking to a nodding Podargos, and Admetos spreadeagled on a sun-warmed rock, arms outstretched along an axis linking nothing to nothing unless it be Meleager and Atalanta, both alone – and among those to the van and rear, none noticed.

For water is devious by nature. It infiltrates and forms its shapes between rocks and roots, in their concavities and sharp angles. It penetrates, waits out the winter in the form of ice and peels shelves of stone which crash down the high sides of mountain in thunderous tumbles of loose rocks and lethal rains of stones. And in summer the same mountains trigger catastrophic downpours which the baked earth will neither channel nor accept and which gather in fragile sumps, deceptive lakes with brittle boundaries. Noiseless, distant, unsignalled and without warning, seepage becomes a drip, then a trickle, a steady and fattening flow which batters down its dykes and hurls their fragments forward. Rock will float, in a flood.

Atalanta watched motes of gravel no bigger than olive pits form curling ridges and grooves in the clear water. The streambed wavered and drifted. Thersites and his bearers had stopped to rest some way short of the main body of men; Theseus and Pirithous were not to be seen. She recalled the sharp peaks she had seen from the far coast of the gulf and wondered at the decision which would have to be made when they were reached. For their route must be taking them towards the mountains where the maimed man and Idas's raving brother would hinder their progress, if not bring them to a standstill. She looked up at the unscalable walls and wished herself clear of them.

The men lazed and yawned. The canyon now was an airy channel through which shade flowed. Meleager's dogs nosed at his feet. She watched him out of the corner of her eye as he reached to retie the thongs of his sandals, intertwining them in a lattice. The sinews rose in his arms. The others would play the parts of his functionaries, for now. But not herself. And not Meilanion. She dipped the tip of her toe into the water. The cold pricked her flesh. Thersites' grunted curses reached her ears across the intervening distance – Nestor and Phoenix were preparing to lift him again – and then, far behind these three, Lynceus at last came into view.

Theseus, Pirithous and Idas were clustered about him so that at first she could not make sense of their movements. They proceeded in a chaotic zig-zag, all four of them lurching over the broken ground. Then she saw that the men were bound together. They had tied two cords about Lynceus's wrists and a third about his neck. His mouth hung open but no sound issued from it, or none that she could hear. His head tossed up and down and he strained his arms against their restraints, but these motions were undirected and random, compelled by some interior torment rather than directed against his keepers. So they led him forward like an animal. When he stumbled they lifted him to his feet and continued.

As she watched their advance, the water touched her again. She looked down. The stream, which had been crystal clear, was now clouded with mud. When had that happened? There were sub-streams within it, strata of sorts, composed of oxides and mudstone which deepened as she watched their idle collisions, growing richer and redder so that her thoughts turned to the glow of the sun's dying torch as it fell through the line of bristling firs forming hackles atop the ridged back of Erymanthus, or its pinkened morning echo sounding over Mount Cyllene, bright poisonous berries and rusty lichens, the autumn leaves of the middle slopes and the hides of wily stags clip-clopping through them, almost invisible in their own autumn colours. Arcadian scarlets, russets and reds.

But this was the red which waited in the moment at the end of the chase, when her arm would rise and fall in an arc whose terminus was her victim's twitching neck. Then the blood would come. The streams of Arcadia, too, had run red when Rhoecus and Hylaeus became hers, so that someone standing far downstream might have watched a tongue of scarlet stain the water and lap about his legs, and wondered whose death it tokened, as she did now. Except there was no mystery here, for the lives dissolving before her eyes belonged to the pair sent forward: Peleus and Acastus. The boar must be close, she realised. She jumped to her feet and would have shouted out, but the cry died in her throat.

A dull rumble was rolling down the canyon. It echoed off the canyon walls and for a few moments it seemed to be dying away. But then it deepened and grew louder again, moving towards them, and in her bafflement Atalanta understood nothing save that this was not the beast they hunted. This was a sound she had never heard before.

A ridge of water rounded the bend ahead, scended against the wall, broke and fell. For a moment it appeared motionless, then it gathered itself and rolled towards them. She saw Meleager rise, disbelieving, locked in confusion until her high shout broke his trance. Her voice sounded alien to her. The others were rising, grasping their weapons, some fleeing down the canyon, others jumping for the walls. Aura was up. Atalanta snatched her bowstave and sprang from the channel, searching for handholds as the muddy wave swept down the channel. She gulped air and pulled herself tight to the rock, tensed herself against the impact.

But it did not come. She felt the very top of the wave wash over her ankles, then sink away. The stream fell. Down the canyon she saw Nestor, Phoenix and Thersites coughing and spluttering. Lynceus and his guardians were rising to their feet, drenched but unharmed. She turned. Ancaeus was wiping down his axe and Telamon his brother's spear. Or his dead brother's spear. The others were wringing water from their chitons, puzzlement and relief showing in their faces, all except one. Meleager's gaze was directed at herself, but his face was blank. He seemed not to see her or anyone else. He was listening.

Then she heard it too, the same sound as before. This time it was deeper and its noise issued from a mouth whose teeth ground stones and whose swollen tongue thrashed down and drove before it a rolling head of air. Atalanta smelt river-weed, soil and clay. She looked up, wondering how high she must climb to clear the surface of the flood. Aura snarled at her feet. The noise of the flood rumbled louder and deeper, then jumped to a new pitch.

Further down the canyon, Phoenix had abandoned Thersites and was running for the side. Nestor remained, struggling to lift his burden. Or was the injured man refusing to release him? They wrestled, fumbling at each other. Theseus and Pirithous had stayed with the two brothers but Idas was pushing them away with furious gestures. The sound shuddered in her bones, an assault. She jumped and felt her arm lodge against something. There was nothing in her head except the noise of the flood, which would come as a rampart of liquid mud, bristling with tree trunks and hurling boulders before it, scouring everything in its path. She turned away, pressing her cheek to the rock. She heard the impact of the water as it hit the bend in the canyon. She saw Theseus and Pirithous break away from their hopeless task and sprint for the walls, their weapons scattering about them. She sucked air. Then she saw Idas plant his feet, take hold of Lynceus and lift him, raising him above his head as though he might carry him thus to safety. He stood rooted beneath the weight of his brother, a single pillar supporting the pediment of an impossible temple, refusing flight, but whether in defiance or acceptance of his fate she could not guess and would never know, for at that moment the wave fell upon her and she saw no more.

*   *   *

Blood dries to black and fades to brown. His guide was the dying fall of a dead man's cry, a stain on a rock. A man had failed on this climb, where he, Meilanion, had so far succeeded. The same man had died far below, on the rocks. He might have failed at a point below, or one higher up, a point Meilanion had yet to reach but which awaited him as a covered pit awaits its unsuspecting victim. A smooth overhang would bring him to a halt somewhere beyond the point where descent was possible and he would cling there, trapped in his inability and his failing strength; to fall *here* was no less certain than falling *there*. The pads of his fingertips felt the mountain's coarse skin. He must use his hands as tools. There was a narrow place where he could be, a tight crevass whose sides were made of rock and air. Before him rose the face. Behind him lay the drop.

Climbing thoughts.

And below him were the huntsmen whom he had abandoned, whilst above him were the sons of Thestius. A light wind blew, which cooled the surface of his skin even as the sun burned it. His hands and feet were blunt pegs fixing him to the stone. His body hung from them, then pulled them loose, then drove them in again. He continued in a broken rhythm. Behind the sons of

Thestius was a being who tracked them and could think of only that: the night-hunter, who exists between his appetite and its satisfaction.

But the night-hunter's appetites were various and the hunt complex, pulling his limbs into strange attitudes and alliances so that the knuckles of his left hand were braced against the instep of his right foot, his intervening body threaded by the shallow bow of muscle which tensed and connected them, and then – some moments later – his cheek was pressed against the rock and supporting there a tiny portion of the weight which hung below it: the weight which pulled him out into space and the jointed pieces of him which clung and gripped, released and moved in slow passes over the mountain's coarse surface. The rock's stasis was a deception; it was a river whose spate had swept away its bridges. Now it would sweep him off the broken stumps of their piers and hurl him down, were he to miss his footing. And how little of him was accepted – fingers, toes – in the cracks and narrow ledges which punctuated the face, precious enclaves of security from which he hung suspended, midstream in the current that would carry him to his extinction far below.

He had been climbing since midday and he was tiring.

A crack to his left had opened. It ran toward a wider fault which seemed to follow a steep diagonal. He edged towards it twice and each time the featureless stone surrounding the fault forced him back. Its slant was away from him and when he made height to try again, it had receded further. His weight was on one foot. He raised an arm, feeling for a handhold above him. There was nothing. He made the next foothold and repeated the motion.

A tiny ledge. And he could see the end of a horizontal crack, which he now knew he must reach. The ledge must lead to the crack, he told himself. His fingers must search along the ledge and then they must bear his weight. And then he must reach the fault and the fault must carry him to the top. Because he was tiring.

He flexed his knuckles and brought one hand up to join the other. The arch of his right foot tautened and the slack weight of his body hung between these extremities, slung like a carcass from a pole. He could not hold himself here for long. A vague outswelling created an overhang whose brow rolled back out of sight. He thought of the arc his arm must follow and the splayed fingers of his hand, imagining their impact and how his palm would slap the rock and hold. He could not see, or wait any longer. The air burned his throat and smelt of nothing. When his lungs were filled he would push off from his foothold, swing his arm and the ledge would hold him. His chest swelled and tightened, his ribs pressing against the tight membrane of flesh and skin. He launched himself out, swung around and grasped, his fingers searching for the handhold.

Nothing.

An instant later he felt his palm sliding off the smooth lip, his own unbearable mass pressing down on his last handhold, which could not support him. Two wild heartbeats and he was dangling, but how? And from what? He jammed a foot hard into rock, felt pain as it stripped a nail from his toe, reached out again, his fingers clawing for purchase. He could not understand how he was still here instead of tumbling through the air. It seemed easy to relinquish his foothold and, at the same time, slide his hand further along the top of the overhang – a hand's-breadth, a finger's-breadth. If there was nothing, he would fall. If something, he would cling to it. He felt grit between his fingers and an instant later a spray of it dashed against his face, blinding him. It made no difference. Another hair's-breadth would topple him and this too made no difference. When he tumbled into space he would take the mountain with him, bring it crashing down. The tendons in his arm were tight as bowstrings. They would snap before he fell. His hands would detach themselves from his wrists and be left here to scrabble like crabs over smooth rock. He understood then that he had lost.

But his hand closed on stone. The ledge led to the crack. His fingers searched along it and they bore his weight. He hung like a dead man, awakening and disbelieving his reprieve. His body's motions were impossible and he disbelieved these too. He reached the fault.

When his watering eyes had washed out the grit, he looked up and saw a disc of piercing blue sky far above, as though the crevass were a well and he was lodged at the bottom. He could wedge himself between the sides, but the incline was kinder even than he had hoped and irregular enough for him to walk up as though it were a shallow-raked ladder. He pulled the remnant of his toenail from its bed of flesh, spat on his hands and began, once again, to climb. The blue pool of light grew. He clambered over the lip of the rock and stood before a different vista. He had reached the flat summit of Aracynthus.

Tall, purple-feathered grasses covered an undulating meadow whose gentle troughs deepened until, to his left, they sloped down to a thickly-wooded terrace. The tops of the highest trees showed above the drop of the ridge. Ahead, the distance of an arrow shot, the ground fell away into a narrow ravine, its exact contours smoothed by dark green pines. The breeze gusting from the north buffetted the tall grass, flattening and releasing it. Its scent billowed and sank in the cold air.

But around his feet the grass had been trampled flat and a trail of broken stems marked a broad furrow. The sons of Thestius had rested here and then moved on, making no effort to conceal their passing. He felt his muscles begin to ache and shifted from foot to foot, rubbing his arms. In the west the sun hung above the horizon. How long had he been climbing? The mouth of the gulf was a sheet of blue. The lagoon below was in shadow now, while to the north the distant mountains glowed pink where the sun caught their western slopes. His damaged toe began to throb. He tore a strip from his chiton and knelt to bind it. When he walked, he would leave the mark of his injury in every footprint. He pressed his hand to the crushed grass, gauging its resilience. The sons of Thestius had not lain here long.

The men's trail led across the meadow, the fading signal of their passage. He thought back to the hard-packed paths of the Arcadian forests, their reluctance to tell of the quarry's passing. He had read signals in terrain more resistant than this. Denuded trees spoke of hunger, muddied pools of thirst. Dens, nests and lairs were the indices of safety and sleep. He had seen a great flock of starlings arouse itself from late-summer torpor and erupt from the canopy of a dense-leaved lime tree. Trouble below. He had stood far downstream of a place of slaughter, had waited for the neighings and bellowings resounding from the upper slopes to fall back into the forest's chatter, to be transmuted there and emerge in the clear run of water as an encroaching bloodstain in which the hot stenches of horse and man were intermingled. He had seen her red signal then: the killer of centaurs. Even Atalanta left her mark.

But the night-hunter moved in the footprints of others. His places were the forest's spaces. He faded into thickets and rematerialised in the foliar calm of clearings. He moved through undisturbed air and left it still. No trace marked his passing, nor monument the being who had passed. He touched nothing and no one. And she was untouched – terrain on which the lightest step would leave its print, where the soundless brush of a finger would bloom red. Her blood would rise at his touch and flush the surface of her skin: his sign.

The air rumbled.

Thunder? He looked up in puzzlement at the unbroken blue of the sky. The noise came again, but fainter perhaps, and then in waves which broke and died in their intervals, softening and merging with the intervening silences until the last was no more than the rustling of the grass and the brush of the air in his ears. Then silence again: a mystery.

He believed the boar would come in such a manner, leaping out of a deep quiet, hooves thudding and thundering, growing louder and louder again until the noise drove out all thought.

The sons of Thestius would have heard it, and known what it meant in the last instants of their existence. His eye wandered again over the meadow with its luxuriant cover, its constant movement, and he wondered how far the men he had followed here had progressed before that noise had broken over their heads. And then, rising from the ground all bloody and tattered, what would they have made of the silence which succeeded it? The hush on the far side of that noise was now their language, proper to lost men, their memories and their ghosts. The trail of the sons of Thestius ended here.

*　　*　　*

A hammer formed from water and soil had knocked the air from her lungs and pressed her flat against the smooth rock. The flood had driven itself against the wall of the canyon and risen there, its energies gathering. The first shock of cold had been succeeded by a terrible weight as the water buried her. She felt herself driven beneath its mass, deeper and deeper as though she might never fight her way back to the surface. Then the surface itself disappeared and darkness took its place, a liquid dark that wrapped river-weed fingers about her face. The current driving the head of the flood caught her then, shook her like prey in the jaws of a greater and more powerful animal. It pulled one arm from its anchorage and her lungs screamed for her to let the other go, to strike out for the surface, for air and light. She had clenched her hand and hung on.

The flood had strung a bow with water and loosed its arrows. Rocks whirled in the slings of its eddies and clattered in the flow. Something tumbled towards her. But the impact was soft. Let go now. She was dwindling, being sucked down into her own darkness. She was drowning and could hold on no longer. She had closed her eyes and let go.

When she opened them again, the flood had receded. Everything glistened: the humped boulders, the broken-backed crags, the detritus carried down by the flood, the sheer sides of the canyon itself. A slick skin of mud rendered all alike. For an instant.

The mud began to steam. Soft wisps of mist rose in swaying columns which intertwined among each other, collapsed and rose again, peeled themselves from the canyon's sides and drifted in the humid air until they tumbled down as tiny clouds. A smooth pool of vapour settled on the canyon floor and rolled under the soft blows of a near-imperceptible breeze. The boulders which cleared its surface appeared as islands in a steaming sea.

One of the boulders stirred. It unfolded, or opened. It sat up and began to cough. A splintered tree trunk sprouted branches in the form of arms and propped itself upon them. Another halved itself midway along its length and stood upon the ends. An archipelago of hump-backed islands extended peninsulas, spits and spurs whose flexings transformed them into mud-coated bodies: chthonic beings disinterring themselves from their formative clay, bones heavy with damp, eyes crusted and hair matted. One by one the heroes rose and blinked in the unfamiliar twilight of the flood's aftermath, stiff-jointed and raw with the ache of resurrection. How did they come to be alive?

Some looked about for their weapons. Others, yet unable to

stand, rested their heads in their hands or scraped at the mud which covered them from head to toe. Caeneus held up the remains of his hunting spear, its shaft as thick as his wrist and snapped in two.

The boulder nearest Atalanta extended a pink tongue, licked her face, then barked, being Aura. Further up the canyon she saw Laertes and Podargos kneeling over a prostrate figure. Laertes pressed the man's chest until a half-choked cry erupted and both ministrants sprang back. The figure jumped to his feet and stood before them, swaying. He scraped the mud from his eyes and looked about as though he did not recognise these strange, mist-draped surroundings. It was Meleager.

Down the canyon, Jason, Castor and Pollux had drawn together. Ancaeus stood beside them. She recognised them by their silhouettes for the canyon's twilight gloom and the men's encrusted dirt rendered their faces uniform and indistinguishable. The trio were looking back the way they had come and when she stared she too was able to make out a figure which may have been a man. Of Nestor, Phoenix and Thersites there was no trace. Nor of Idas and Lynceus. She thought of the force of the flood as it had struck her, clinging to the side of the canyon. Idas had stood in mid-channel.

She rose to her feet and followed three men who were walking back to the distant figure. Behind her she heard Meleager calling his dogs: Labros, Methepon, Egertes, Eubolos, Corax, Marpsas, Ormenos, Leukios, Charon, Gorgos, Thero, Podes, Loraos.

The single sound to come in reply was Aura's growl, prompted by the sound of their names. Meleager called again but she did not turn back.

Theseus was pressed against the side of the canyon, one arm reaching deep into a narrow crack. He drew back as the three men approached. Sounds of movement came from within the fissure, then a low groan. Atalanta reached the men and peered into the darkness. Two eyes stared back at her. Moments later she made out a mouth. It opened and the groan came again. It was Pirithous.

Theseus shouldered her aside and reached in once again. But try as he might he could not reach the man. His hand closed on nothing but mud which the flood had driven in after his companion as though to seal him in his tomb. She looked at the crack and remembered Pirithous's broad frame, and wondered at the force which had driven him into such confines. For he was held fast there and it was impossible that he should be freed.

Castor, Pollux, Jason and herself stood back. Theseus lunged again at the crack and again his fingers closed on nothing. They waited for him to give up the hopeless task, but he would not, or could not, and showed no sign of tiring, jamming his arm into the crack up to the shoulder as though he might split Aracynthus's bedrock with his bare hands. When Jason placed a hand on the man's back, he shook it off angrily. Atalanta shrugged. Even if he should reach his companion, what then?

The others waited where the canyon angled. Beyond them, Atalanta saw a solitary figure come around the bend. For a moment she thought it was Meilanion, but as the figure drew nearer she noted the heavy-set chest and shoulders. She saw Telamon raise his spear in greeting and she remembered the scouting party that had been sent ahead. It was Peleus, who returned his brother's salute. She made her way back, expecting Acastus to come into view at any moment. Meleager and Telamon went forward to receive Peleus's news. But the man was alone.

She joined the hunters who had gathered about him to hear how the first weak flood had knocked the two of them off their feet, how they had sheltered from the second in a side-canyon and how Acastus had been swept out in the flood's recession. But he did not say how he came now to hold the dead man's spear. The canyon would bring them out by nightfall, he reported. They would have to move now, if Meleager saw fit to do so, he concluded.

At that, they looked back to the group gathered about Theseus, who belaboured the rock with undiminished energy. Jason, Castor and Pollux were gone. Meleager took three quick steps forward, fist clenched about his spear as though he had thought to pursue them. But he stopped and pointed at Atalanta, his mouth opening to frame a curse on her presence, or an accusation.

The others watched him let fall his arm and choke back his words. Then, a gesture of dismissal, he reached for his equipment and motioned for them all to do the same. The survivors walked forward again.

At the bend, the canyon began to widen. She saw Ancaeus step aside and wait for her, nodding as she drew near. Together they turned and looked back at Theseus. Ancaeus filled his lungs and his voice boomed and echoed off the stones. But Theseus remained where they had left him, inseparable from his doomed companion and in the grip of the same strange dance as before, only now it appeared that he was manacled to a twitching sinew anchored deep within the mountain whose random spasms pulled him hard against the rock then released him, over and over again.

Ancaeus turned away. The men walked on and Atalanta fell to the rear again. But the hunters' shunning of her was perfunctory. A dwindling deference to Meleager compelled it, the leader who had led them into this place, who had pointed to herself. She counted the survivors, those the flood had brushed aside. Then she counted the vacant spaces between them, left by those the flood had chosen to take: Eurytus, Harpaleas, Idas and Lynceus, Thersites, Nestor, Cepheus, Echion, Phoenix, Acastus perhaps, and Theseus bound to doomed Pirithous. The palace of their names was crumbling, insubstantial as smoke. All of them except one. Between her own name and Meleager's was the outline of the youth who had seemed to disappear into thin air, or who marched now along his own shadow-trail. Was he lost too?

*   *   *

There were animals whose toes and claws were reversed. Their tracks would lead the credulous hunter backwards to musty dens and middens of bones and dry droppings: the places they had quit. The ripples in the pools from which they drank radiated over the water's stillness and sank in its inertia. They slithered from the womb into shallow bowls hollowed from dry soil and green havens of flattened bracken. He wondered, did such lairs mark beginnings or ends? Beyond birth or death were the unknowable places, where trails became the presumed heavy-bellied stagger of the animals which bore their young and then sank into the haunts of their non-existence. Crows left ragged arcs of clawprints, scatterings of arrowheads or dragon's teeth sown in soil where signs alone would grow. Flightless birds foraged grubs along the forest paths by scraping ovals in the soft soil, whose series the careless tracker took for hoofprints of unknown ruminants. Impossible beasts ambled in cloudy dapplings of broken light, spectres of an eye which scanned for patterns and their disturbance. Meilanion's eye. Meadow-mites crawled down the stems of tall grasses to reach the corms where they laid eggs whose larvae would hatch and feed on the sweet-juiced subterranean stems and thereby reveal the course of the original colony through the meadow, its random drives and turns charted by the destructive hunger of its offspring which toppled the high stems in a single morning, great swathes of them falling as though some vast and low-slung beast had dragged itself through the field, flattening everything in its path and cutting the mark of that progress in the lush shoots, so it seemed.

But that, the night-hunter understood, was not what had happened here.

He found the sons of Thestius in the trees beyond the meadow. The grass gave out at the sun-starved ground beneath the trees whose tops he had glimpsed earlier, and which must have drawn the men here in the first place. Through the sparse branches of the firs he scanned the slope below, which dropped, levelled, then dropped again. The brighter green of chestnut trees ousted the silvery needles of the firs as the second of these giant steps descended, and the same needles, dropped and browned, lay thick on the ground beneath his feet, accumulating in spongy, prickly drifts where the tree roots formed accidental corrals. To his right he saw the gash of the ravine cut its way down the mountainside. The slopes below might have been parched grass or stone for all he could tell. A deep fault broke the bare terrain down there. A bend midway along its course sent it towards the north-west. Meleager's hunters must be within it, there being no other route save his own. He looked down on the landscape, where twilight had fallen. His muscles ached. Each soundless thud of his heart announced a throb of pain in his foot.

Then, a single viscous pearl of liquid eased itself out of the branchwork and fell into the fir needles about his feet.

Meilanion looked down at where the liquid had landed, a bright red bead, and then up at whence it fell.

So it had been here, he saw then, among the clustered firs standing sentinel about a field of wild grass, through which the passage of five men might ape the heavy tread of the boar which had tracked them, or the myriad destructions of a feeding colony of meadow-mite larvae. Here was where the prey's trail had ended and the predator's trail would begin. Their encounter was marked – his eyes roved about the ground – by gouges in the boles of the firs and by great plates of uprooted and overturned turf which lay scattered like the abandoned shields of a routed army.

He listened to the wash of air in the trees. The boar's fury was wanton and would be expended on anything which stood in its path. So the trees were slashed and the earth broken up. He walked to the edge of the terrace and peered down into the undergrowth, then made a slow circuit of the battleground, but if there were hoofprints to be found he failed to spy them. He turned back to the damaged trees. The cuts were cleaner than he had first imagined, as though some tool had been used. And the rounds of turf were too perfect, as though cut by a blade. He squatted to examine one. Teeth, tusks, snout and hooves: but which of those might have produced this?

It was almost dusk and the morning would reveal the boar's tracks, he thought, which would lead down the mountain to the ravine, where Meleager and the others moved. The boar would stalk them from above. Sunlight pinked the tops of the mountains to the north. There, he thought, among the untrodden peaks. The heroes' dowsing in the waters of the gulf, the bloody flurries in the city of Oeneus, his own route up the mountainside, every footprint and snapped twig, ripple and rustle would come to silence and stillness in the mountains. And the sons of Thestius would be wound in the trail that had brought them here and led him after, bound tight in the record of their ended lives.

They were dangling from the branches. They had been spitted on their spears and their cadavers hung as trophies in the trees above his head. Pierced through the neck, or the shoulder. One through the mouth. The protruding shafts were lodged among the forks of the trees and it seemed that the beast had sported with them for their bellies were slashed and their viscera dangled. The lolling heads of the eight sons of Thestius bent to show him their waxen faces.

The boar could not be satisfied: appetite was its nature. He looked at the distant break in the mountain's lower slopes, a black crack of shadow in which the hunters moved, invisible to him: Meleager and those he commanded, his quarry among them, black-haired, long-limbed Atalanta. He could come at her only through the boar himself, through a spray of his splintered bone and blood, his squeals and grunts cutting the thin air, hooves clacking on ground which yielded the animal and the night-hunter nothing and recorded no mark, being stone. The boar's course led into the mountains.

*　　*　　*

Now: Ancaeus, Caeneus, Telamon and Peleus, Eurytion, Podargos, Laertes, Admetus and Meleager. Her companions numbered nine.

The canyon walls fell to low ramparts and the canyon itself widened, becoming a shallow channel whose mouth flared and spat them out on the far side of Aracynthus. The sun had fallen below the mountain's dark bulk long before. In so complete a darkness they could go no further and, muddied and bruised, they lay down on the stony ground to rest. The night settled itself upon them.

Stones dug into Atalanta's back. Her world was a rough oval of sun-warmed stone defined by the span of her arms and the sweep of her hands. In the moonless darkness, she could know nothing beyond its boundaries. From time to time came the scrabble of Aura's claws on the rock as she roused herself from sleep, then the rustle of mud-caked hair as she settled herself once again. Atalanta heard the men's breathing, which rose around her in little towers of sound whose collapses were soundless dispersals, the plumes of dying fires whose smoke rises and disassembles in still air. The night damped their names to near-inaudible whispers which sighed and wheezed, invisible and interchangable. The broken-backed rhythm of the nearest sleeper might have been Telamon or Peleus, both breathing out the death of their half-brother as a column of stagnant damp air lifted whole from the well in which he rotted. Or did its stertorous stops and starts mimic the last thrashings of poor Acastus, throat slashed and head pushed under the rising flood until his limp body's final breath bubbled through the bloody water and burst between the hands of his killer? For Peleus had murdered him near the head of the canyon, she believed, and yet the murderer breathed himself. The softer double-susurration rising under it would be the exhalations of Caeneus and the inhalations of Caenis – breathing out as a man, breathing in as a woman – or Eurytion, whose lungs' inflations and deflations counted the great chain of moments leading to the final rattle. How many now before the succeeding silence? A million? A thousand? A faint bass-rumble pricked her ears and seemed to sink away as she sought its origin: Ancaeus. Podargos and Laertes rasped back and forth between one and another and sent two rough-skinned serpents skywards, their intertwinings rising to the point where they would part and seek out their futures by chasing and fleeing the sun. Admetus panted like a drunkard.

And there was one whose breathings-in and breathings-out could not be distinguished, whose breath seemed to roll in his throat and escaped from his lips in a single continuous sigh. A lament, perhaps, for the city of his father, or for the loss of his men or the drowning of his dogs, or even, she wondered, for herself.

She could not know. Darkness was the place of their ignorance; the night returned them all to infants whose cries had been damped to the suck and blow of air. She had clamped her day-old mouth to the teats of a she-bear and pulled the milk from her, knowing nothing else. As a child her wanderings pushed back the frontiers of a world of mountain peaks and crags, later the tops of tall firs, pines, oaks and broad-leafed chestnuts, then the forests which marshalled them. But the plains to the north and west of her childhood's demesne remained distant blurs of dust, habitats of all she might suspect and not know. Even the later huntress could gaze into the far distance where the horizon met the sky and not know whether the grey train of low-backed creatures marching out of sight was a range of clouded mountains or a vaporous shimmering sea or a mote of dust floating across the surface of her eye. The shrieks and bleats of her prey unravelled in the air until their threads were finer than spider's gossamer; she could not conceive the chamber in which their racket found its refuge. She dug her toes into the forest's rain-soaked soil which oozed up between them and waited motion-less behind tree trunks until she could feel no boundary between her skin and the smooth bark. The shiver of a single leaf, high up, out of sight, struck by a single gust of air and humming down the massive bole would send its faint shudder down her spine. But her world was riddled with cavities and vesicles, places denied her. And when she thought upon them, urged by the rising and falling breasts of her companions, she heard them named in the two words of the sleeping language whose chatter surrounded her, one rising and one falling.

They were 'Meilanion' and 'Meleager'. She was called 'Atalanta'. And Oeneus was the king of Kalydon who neglected the sacrifice to Artemis at the festival of First Fruits, for which omission she sent a boar of surpassing ferocity and size to ruin the land. And so the heroes gathered to hunt and destroy the beast.

Her breath sent its own muted night-cry to join the others. What names did they hear in the filling and emptying of her lungs? The huntress? The bloody-handed virgin? She was all that they did not see in Oeneus' city and everything drowned out in the thunder of the flood. She was of a piece with the spaces in their ranks. Rising. Falling. The stone's hard fingers kneaded her back. They had not dared to venture further to-night, just as none had dared approach her, or try her. They saw in her their own surrounding darkness.

Night.

A tickling of the eyelids and the mind's being goaded back within the body's cage. Aching limbs and grunts and groans and the clang and scrape of metal on stone. When sunrise came she rose with the rest of them, every joint in her body stiff. The tongue of rock on which they had camped extended from the canyon mouth and gave out in still-sodden turf. The flood had battered a stand of wild almond trees and festooned their branches with weeds. The dawn light revealed the 'stones' which studded their sleeping place as unripened nuts. The ground before them sloped down into a rough bowl in which the canopies of broad-leafed trees appeared as monstrous fruits. The flood would have paused here, she thought, gathering force before finding its outlet through the canyon. She sniffed the damp air. The woodland continued into the middle distance before breaking at the shore of a great crescent-shaped lake whose surface, still untouched by the sun's rays, appeared dull and grey. Beyond it, to the north and east, rose the mountains.

The hunters sat to massage life into numb limbs or bent and stretched to ease sleep-stiffened sinews. They gathered and ordered their equipment. The worst of the mud had dried on their skins and flaked off but an ingrained residue resisted their attempts to remove it. They were red-eyed with fatigue. A sour reek rose from them. She pulled at the scabs of mud which clotted her hair and remembered the lice she would pick out of Aura's coat. Ancaeus and Eurytion raised their heads and stared as she rose and walked down the slope towards the wood in search of water.

She found leaf-mould, nettles, a shallow stagnant puddle and then Meleager, sitting on a toppled tree-trunk, his back to her, with a stick in his hand. If he heard her approach he gave no sign. The stick moved this way and that over a patch of earth in front of him; he might have been directing a war between rival colonies of ants or prescribing some complicated dance. She watched in silence. From time to time he would pause and the stick would rise and fall in a measured fashion, then he would continue his scratching. Taking no interest in this, Aura sank onto her belly and fell asleep.

When he reached down to smooth the earth with the flat of his hand, she saw him wince, as though injured. He was filthy, as they all were. His hair – the colour of gold, she had thought, when he first pulled the helmet from his head and stood before her in full sunlight – was lank and matted. She waited. Meleager's arm moved along a concluding arc and then he looked up from his task. She followed his gaze into the recesses of the wood. A thicket of hawthorn scrub grew in a break between the trees. Beyond it, canopies of leaves furred everything in grey shadow. He dropped the stick and rose to his feet. She listened until the sound of his footsteps dragging through the damp leaves and undergrowth was replaced by the faint rustle of the trees. Then she roused Aura and advanced on the image he had left.

Her first thought was the boar. Meleager had scored the damp

69

soil with shallow furrows whose curves and straight lines intersected and cut across one another. Rough crosses decorated the areas thus defined, together with little pits whose excavation she had taken for idle flicks of his drawing tool. Her eye ran over the curve of the boar's belly, found its tusks, its back and then an eye. But where were its legs? And its hackles? She pursed her lips. Aura dabbed an inquisitive paw. She shooed the animal clear. Perhaps its secret was that there was no image to be discovered, that it meant nothing. Yet he had been intent upon it, thinking himself unobserved. There was no animal to be found in these scratchings, nor the means to track one. Perhaps Meleager had groped for a future here and been thwarted. The terrain before them would offer signs but the course that led to the boar's death ran far beyond this country. This Kalydon was no longer the Kalydon of Oeneus, nor even of his son. She swept her sandalled foot back and forth, obliterating the image, then turned on her heel and walked back.

The surviving hunters were readying themselves. She brushed past the man she had espied and bent to gather her equipment.

The country through which they were to pass was broken woodland stretching to the north and east, where it was curtailed by the lake. She wound her bowstring around its staff, then joined the men, who leaned on their spears and attended to their leader in sceptical silence, looking beyond him to the country ahead. Morning sunlight touched the crowns of the trees. Atalanta traced the line of the distant shore and her eyes narrowed.

Meleager spoke now as one whose course was inevitable, its stages marked by the irrevocable acts of the hunt: their gathering by the shore, the march on the city, their journey to this place. The men shifted from foot to foot. They would dig a pit and drive the beast before them. It would run at them and they must drive it back or kill it. It would be forced from its cover and spitted on their spears.

But she saw that they no longer believed this. They nodded, but would not meet Meleager's eye. Peleus alone grunted his assent and grinned at the prospect of the animal's death. The others looked at the ground, then up again as though willing the boar to show itself in the landscape's stillness, to stamp hoofprints in its soil or rip a furrow through its green calm.

For the woodland to the north of Aracynthus tented the plain in a protective canopy of leaves, which softened its ruptures and irregularities so that it appeared to the hunters as a vast empty meadow. When they descended within it and began the trek towards the lake, it seemed impossible that anything might break in upon them save the sunlight which fell in slanting shafts through the branches. The ground rose and their feet crunched in a mulch of leaves bedded on dry soil. They filtered through the woods, dividing about the trunks of the trees and reuniting in the groves. Their loosened assembly loosened further.

Atalanta tasted dust thrown up by the footfalls of the men ahead. She smelt their sweat. Their wake was an airborne river of sour musk. Its vague rampart would confound baffled deer or bears, then, toppling and dispersing in the still air, it would breathe itself into the dry ground, rolling down rabbit holes and filtering through the dens of their enemies, panicking both. Pigeons clattered out of the trees and whirred through the woodland's half-light. The rising hum of wasp's nests signalled rainwater which collected in pools; creeping vegetation hung from the trees which ringed their margins. The merest disturbance of their surfaces sent slow clouds of black mud exploding in silence through the water.

The boar was not possible here, she thought, tramping her own winding path among the winding paths of the men. Aura darted out to left and right and looped her in distracting detours. She felt the tight circle of her awareness break and reform about the dog's peculiar route. When the trees broke, juniper scrub and small-leaved limes sprang up, which they would skirt to re-enter the woods. The scuffing feet of the men preceding her exposed the black soil beneath the dropped leaves. The network of branches above their heads, the pendant leaves, catkins and emerging yellow blossom conspired together to bleach the sunlight pure white even while shielding them from its harshness.

Theirs was a zone of abeyance, an anomalous interruption between the earth's slow churn and the air's unbodied exposure, an eventless enclave. The men were loose in it. Their rambling paths criss-crossed, coincided and parted; they met and would mutter together then drift apart amid nods of agreement, mutual shrugs of absolution. She saw them but was not included. Meleager was apart from this. Meleager and herself.

They walked through the day, slept and walked again. The canopy of leaves which had shaded them began to break up as the gaps between the trees grew wider. They crossed little clearings choked with tall grasses and brambles. These breaks grew larger and more frequent, the ground shelving gently downward, until they passed through a final stand of oaks and hornbeams and, emerging on the far side, they found themselves at the edge of a sea.

No boats floated upon it, nor ever would. Its surface bristled beneath the gusts of a westerly breeze which plucked feathery crests from the green depths, raising them high in its sway, to drop them again in its sag, over and over. Sunlight skimmed the rolling surface, bounced and broke in a tumble of light and shade. The hunters stood and watched the play of wind and light and saw in it a deceiving camouflage. They thought of their quarry, shaping him in their minds' eyes. Then they raised their weapons and walked forward together until the gentle heave of sprays and shoots closed over their heads and they disappeared into the depths.

*   *   *

He had found them sleeping at the mouth of the canyon. He was to lose them in a sea of reeds.

Or they were to lose themselves. For how else could Peleus's javelin reach Eurytion, the brother of his wife, the man who cleansed his hands of his own brother's blood, save through blindness and accident? How else might their failure prove so abject and how else could the hunt reach a conclusion so remote from the palace raised on the shore of the gulf, with Kalydon before them and their names shouted high in the air?

Meilanion watched for dawn from the brink of the canyon, where the hollow of a limestone tusk curled up in defence of Aracynthus's flanks. A scrambling descent through firs and chestnuts had brought him to slopes of grass rooted in thin topsoil and then to the bare white stone beneath. He crouched on his haunches, motionless. Below, the bodies of his former companions sprawled in fitful sleep, arrayed as the scattered spokes of a broken wheel.

He waited for their reveille. He counted their losses and stared in puzzlement at the bare stone passage of the canyon through which they must have passed. Whatever depredation had reduced their numbers remained mysterious to him. Meleager stirred first, reached for his helmet and pulled out the pieces of his leather armour. At first it seemed as though he would put them on, but after examining them one by one he stowed them again in the helmet, rose to his feet and walked down into the woods. Then Meilanion saw Atalanta's head rise and the slow movements by which she stretched her limbs. He sensed his own thought pass between the other huntsmen, themselves awakening now, heads turning to watch her. Her dog stretched and sniffed at the ground. Meilanion glanced up to see if he might work his way about them. A short slope marked the boundary of the limestone and beyond it was the safety of the trees, but the ground between here and there was bare. He could not cross unseen. Atalanta looked about, then climbed down the incline and disappeared into the woods.

Where Meleager was: the night-hunter's red thought. He saw Ancaeus's bulky figure heave itself upright. Another huntsman joined him and some comment passed between them. The others gathered about Peleus. Meilanion watched for what he could not see, in the woods, whose rough verdure extended the false solidity of its surface forward almost to the shore of the distant lake. The light began to prickle there. The mountains sank as they approached its gleam, or rose as they fled it, half-formed animals petrified in the moment of flight. He waited.

The huntsmen waited too. One or two peered out from the huddle formed about Peleus, drawing back for the time it took to glance down into the black of the woods, then leaning in again to catch the man's words. Peleus gestured, his bearded chin jutting forward, stabbing a finger at each of them in turn and then at the ground. They nodded, or remained impassive. Meilanion did not need to hear the words. When Meleager reappeared and gathered them about him, they shifted and fingered their weapons. He saw Atalanta emerge from the undergrowth, her dog in tow. They were preparing to move off. Meleager pointed north, towards the distant lake, or perhaps

73

the mountains beyond. If he fostered any awareness of the men's new disposition he gave no sign of it. When the last of the hunters had disappeared within the greenery and the crash of their footsteps through the undergrowth was little more than a whisper in his ears, Meilanion climbed down and started after them. Meleager's time must be near, he thought, as he passed the mouth of the canyon. Meleager had failed them. He had bound his men to each other and to him. Now he clung to Atalanta.

And here, Meilanion told himself, was where they had lain together. He looked down at the patch of ground where their feet had scuffed the soil, at its scrapes and shallow gouges, noting too an attempt to erase these marks. He dug his hand into the loose soil and rolled the friable grains between his fingertips, imagining her splayed legs and the drumming of her heels, feeling for their fading heat in the bed of dry earth.

The sun dragged its leaking sack of moments across the sky. The night was its exhaustion, emptied of all but a rasping heat. The huntsmen colluded about a drifting fulcrum, a transitory patch of forest which they tugged from side to side, whose centre was the sum of their divergent paths: the *here*, where Eurytion shaded his eyes against an improbable sheaf of sunlight which slotted itself between decked canopies of foliage and Peleus inclined his head to speak in his ear; or *here*, where Ancaeus brought down his axe with a powdery thud on a tree trunk dry with rot and urinated into a clump of ferns; or *here*, where nothing happened save the patient dismemberment of a beetle's carcass by a horde of forest ants; or *here*, where the faint rustle of leaves overhead signalled a breeze too weak to penetrate the forest canopy and stir the still air trapped beneath, where Atalanta paused to glance up and did not see Aura turn and point her snout at something on the far side of a tangle of elder-scrub, something moving among the tree trunks. The dog turned back as her mistress looked down and the night-hunter faded into the undergrowth.

He walked the rolling line of the hunters' periphery, circling, nearing, retreating. The open ground of clearings drove him from his quarry in search of cover. When the trees again closed over his head and the broken sunlight dappled everything in its camouflage, then he could approach. His zone was the margin of their awareness, where a disturbance in the woodland's chiaroscuro might be a wind-bent branch or a thrush flicking itself into the air, where the dry crunch of a careless footfall in a drift of leaves filters through the trees and bushes, disperses its signature in echoes and dull impacts, becomes ambiguous, innocuous, a meaningless anomaly: the ribbon of doubt-riddled terrain in which their eyes and ears could be relied upon to deceive them. Her dog had caught his scent. That he could not disguise. The night-hunter hoards his signals, watches unseen and listens unheard. The quarry feels nothing of the hand which tightens about its neck.

He was imperfect, the zone where he was possible being so narrow and its line so fine. The hunters' wandering paths cut swathes through the concealing woods, sometimes isolating him in the necks of narrowing peninsulas; he could not resist the temptation to move among them. Once he found himself marooned in a leaf-filled hollow ringed by wild pear trees and waited, listening as two sets of careless footsteps moved in from right and left. They passed to either side and he breathed again. Another time he blundered across a long natural avenue of sumacs and oaks and found himself in plain view of a huntsman traversing the same vista, each one too distant to make out the face of the other. The man raised an arm in hesitant acknow-ledgement. He returned the salute and moved on, smiling.

The breaks in the wood began to widen. Clearings intersper-sing the densely-packed trees had appeared to him at first as deep shafts dug out of the wood's substance. Now sunlight washed over the canopy of trees and poured down to fill them. He would avert his eyes, tuned as they were to the wood's interior gloom. These slabs of light sank and spread, becoming expansive sanctuaries whose boundaries were raised against him. He halted at the edge of rank meadows until the last of the hunters had disappeared into the darkness of the trees on the far side and then crept across the exposed ground, arrived within the protective twilight and hastened forward to find them again. There was no pattern to their movements. They scattered and regathered, their pace slowing or accelerating, until he won-dered if this inconsistency might be their signature and if their path was governed by his own movements about them rather than any impetus of their own. For they were no longer the pursuers, whether they understood this or not. Their quarry was no longer before them and their ceaseless interminglings and jostlings for position put him in mind of panicked deer when the first hind has felt the scrape of claws in her flank and her terror leaps faster than she herself, bounding through the rest of the herd and scattering them. The hunters moved not as predators, but as those for whom knowing, believing, suspecting and fearing were not choices but successive resolutions. They moved as prey. And his own trepidation, he realised as he waited, crouching behind brushwood until the last of them disappeared into the far thicket, was baseless. The only monster in their minds was the boar.

The sun was sinking when the trees gave out. Tussocks of sedge rose from waterlogged soil. The ten hunters were walking abreast of one another, towards a palisade of tall green reeds. Beyond the reeds, he knew, was the lake. The mountains rose to the north and east. He picked out Atalanta, then Meleager and Ancaeus. The others he could not distinguish. Their figures dwindled and merged until his eye could no more separate them than it could the swaying stems into which they walked and which closed behind them, engulfing them as though they had marched into the waters of the sea.

They left him then, or he lost them there. He would never learn the precise events of the night that followed. Those who escaped must have passed by him in the darkness. Those who died would have lain undiscovered in the reeds. Of those who survived, Ancaeus alone would push aside the tall green stems, walk back across the marshy ground, his unbloodied axe slung over his shoulder. Grey-faced in the following dawn's grey light, he averted his eyes from the place of his defeat. He would show no surprise at the youth's presence but instead point back to the place he could not look upon and walk on, betraying nothing of what had taken place. Meilanion would know that on the evening of the hunters' disappearance, the sunset was swift and brilliant, that the succeeding darkness was complete, that the rustling of the reeds reached his ears across the intervening distance, although he felt not a breath of wind, that when the earth on which he lay began to shudder he had believed it was the twitching of his own sleep-lulled limbs, that when the trees behind him crashed to the ground it must signal some subterranean collapse, that when that din was replaced by the pounding of the marshland then the mud thrown up seemed to fill the air like mist, choking him, and that when the reeds too began to crash and he first heard the heroes' call to one another, it was not to deafen himself against these sounds that he groped in the darkness for the handfuls of mud which he drove into his ears, but against those he knew must follow them, which were the sounds made by aweless men reciting the lesson of terror.

He would learn none of that, blinded and deafened, stretched out face down in the marsh. She was in there, ahead of him, but she was a question, his single question. There would be nothing else to remember.

So the reed-spears rose again in the grey light preceding dawn and Ancaeus emerged and told him nothing. A broad swathe of flattened or broken stems formed an avenue leading to a wider area of destruction. He remembered the sons of Thestius and the mutilation of their corpses. But, walking forward into the green channel, he saw no sign of the hunters or their specific fates. The reeds rose around him until the peaks of the mountains disappeared behind them. His feet plunged and splashed in the brackish water, raising cloudy explosions of mud. He moved deeper into the reed-bed, the tall stems waving as he pushed them aside, signalling high above his head. He knelt to wash the mud out of his ears. His hearing restored, he listened to the near-inaudible plashing of the lake and the soft scrape of the reed stems. He was a clumsy intruder.

The sounds of the reed-bed were his protection against discovery, if there were any left to find him out. He thought back to their gathering on the far shore of the gulf. They had thought their names would prove a sanctuary, as though they might step off the paths marked out as theirs and stop within its refuge. His name had been the last but one and Atalanta's had been the last. Now, standing alone in the press of reeds, he understood that one could not leave the path. Outside the limits of the trail and its signs was a wilderness or desert and he was a limping creature, one sandalled foot slapping on packed earth, one naked in the raw weather beyond – a straddler of edges. His *eschatia* was the green littoral between a forest and a lake and the mountains. The heroes had fallen here. This place might mark his own limit.

He lifted his feet clear of the water, a fastidious crane. His green kingdom swayed in mockery about him. He stumbled and the tall stems sprang back in alarm. Righting himself, they snapped to attention. A narrow ravine formed from their bent stems marked his passage to this point. His evidence. He could not stir here without leaving it. The sun had risen now and the shadows thrown by the reeds skewed his perpendicular world. Within it, his movements grew careless. Sunlight dashed against the lake's surface and broke against the palisade. He followed little slivers of light through the close-packed stems until they grew to become shafts, then luminous avenues. He found himself at the boundary of the reed-bed. He was standing before the great crescent of the lake, whose surface was a single sheet of light, dazzling him. He blinked and squinted as he searched for the far shore, found it, then followed it as it curved back towards him. A smudge of haze blended the shoreline with a range of hills which rose higher as they approached, becoming mountains which loomed over the wind-stirred waters. A strip of shelving ground ran between the lower slopes and the water's edge, narrowing, then curving in behind a final curtain of reeds. He waded forward and pushed aside the stems.

He saw their weapons and clothes heaped by the shore. Beside the pile lay its complacent guard, stretched out in the sunshine asleep: Aura. Atalanta and Meleager were bathing in the lake.

*   *   *

She held his head in the crook of her arm. Meleager lay back, giving her his weight. His legs floated free in the supporting water. She watched his arms drift out from his sides and the backs of his hands break the surface. The water lapped around his neck. His chest twisted and rippled in the water's refraction and his sex was a blur of white in the dark hair of his groin. She splayed her fingers, ran them into his hair and pulled them free, combing out the knots and burrs.

She stepped back and his trunk and legs lurched upwards then sank again. The water made small cupped sounds as it closed over his limbs. She dipped his head and he spluttered, but when he had blinked his eyes clear and she looked down into his face she saw no change there. She could have drowned him if she had wished.

She had loosed one arrow. She might as well have thrown straw.

There was a disturbance in the reeds: three birds with powder-blue plumage beat their way into the air. She looked over her shoulder.

Her last memory of Ancaeus was of his clutching his knees to his chest and rolling onto his side, his eyes as dead as Meleager's. He had stood with the man she held now when Peleus and his followers had turned on them. He had faced the boar. But the boar had broken him, and Meleager too. The others had been slaughtered or put to flight, she did not care which. They were nothing.

She looked down again at Meleager's face, framed by her hands. A sound reached her ears. Someone, or something, was in the reeds. The twitching tops of the stems flagged its movements. The blue birds were chasing each other in a wide circle over the lake, dipping and rising. Meleager turned his head as though to watch them. Ashore, Aura dozed. A broad black track of ripped turf and soil scored the ground behind the sleeping dog.

When the boar at last had turned from its victims and quit the reeds, the excess of its fury had been expended there. It had torn and trampled, throwing clods the size of a man's head high into the air. They had rained down around her as she cowered in the water.

Now she wondered for whom that fury had been destined, and why they had been spared it. The boar had never come at her, or closed on her. She had heard Ancaeus crying out, like a child, and seen him clutch his spear to his chest to quell his noise as he lay half-submerged in the water. She had seen the worse humiliation yet, which was Meleager's. But if she was intended for the beast's witness, she had failed. She had let fly her single arrow into shadow. She had not set eyes on the boar.

The movements in the reeds drew nearer. She raised the man she held to his feet and scrubbed at the dirt ingrained in her skin. Meleager stood apart from her, waded a few paces further out, then stopped. Her eyes scanned a line of reeds set a little way out from the rest and she wondered at her own lack of concern. If she ran now she might yet reach the shore with time enough to string her bow. From there she would not miss. She would never miss again. But she stood still, realising first that there was no danger, and only then why this was so. Meilanion would again have the pleasure of seeing her bathe. She scooped a handful of water and let it run down the back of her neck, waiting for the intruder to show himself.

*   *   *

Box, lentisc, myrtle and broom brushed their legs and coated them with resins and gums. Aura alternated between slinking along with her belly to the ground and proceeding by a succession of leaps. Sprays of rock roses pinked the grey-green brushwood of the hillside; the animal sniffed at unfamiliar scents and barked.

The vegetation thinned as the slope rose – gnarled wild olives, sun-blasted gorse – but the trail was too obvious to lose. A line of trampled bushes and broken branches marked the boar's path up the hillside, punctuated by areas of more thorough destruction. The soil was redder here and stonier. The boar had scraped, gouged, scattered and climbed on up the hillside.

Above them to left and right, two crags extended ridges which met to form a saddle. The slope steepened as it rose towards the crest. Their pace slowed. Atalanta paused and looked back down the hill. Meilanion was halfway up, near enough for her to see his head come up but too distant to make out his features. He halted, as she had known he would.

It had been the same at the lake. He had watched, but he would not approach. She had strode ashore and covered herself. Meleager had wrapped himself in his chiton, dressing in silence beside her. Both had gazed at the youth as he emerged from the reeds, took a few steps forward through the water, then stopped. Aura barked just once, as puzzled as her mistress. She glanced at Meleager, who regarded the younger man without expression. Meilanion stood there with the water lapping about his waist, making neither sign nor sound. It was then that she had wondered how he came to be here after the mystery of his disappearance. He must have tracked them to this place, she realised, but his sudden halt upon finding them had baffled her. Meleager and herself had set off. When they looked back from the foot of the hill, they saw him wade ashore. He had been waiting for them to leave.

Now she turned away from the distant figure and began to climb again. Meleager moved with a new ease a few steps ahead of her, his helmet swinging from one arm and his armour within it. His battles were over, she thought. If the youth imagined he would find an opponent in the older man now, then he understood nothing. She redoubled her efforts and pulled abreast of Meleager. His eyes ranged over the ground ahead, then herself, mild interest showing on his face, or surprise, but that was all.

The late afternoon sun began its slow fall behind a saw-toothed ridge far off to the west. Soon the ground would begin to return its heat to the cooling air. The final stage of the ascent was steeper yet: a bank of dry earth and loose stones Atalanta scrabbled up on all fours and which Meleager scaled by driving in the butt of his spear and pulling himself up by brute strength. Out of breath, their limbs aching, they gained the ridge, felt the cool dry breeze gusting down from the north and turned their faces into it to gaze upon the vista before them.

Mountains aimed their peaks at the sky for as far as the eye could see. Rank after rank succeeded one another, marching down from the north and in from the east. Where they met, a harsh chaos reigned, as though two rivers of molten rock had collided and dashed each other so high into the cold air that they had solidified there, forming pinnacles, cliffs and overhanging crags. The mountains seemed to ripple in the red light of the sunset. Rivers and streams sliced their way between them, their fiery wires cutting deep ravines in the stone. Rock-faces swept up to blade-like ridges and fell sheer into shadowed canyons. Scars of white unweathered stone showed where overhangs had pried themselves free and crashed down onto the lower slopes, ringing them with walls of broken rocks.

This was the boar's world. Atalanta looked upon it and breathed its thin cold air. She thought of the soft slopes of Aracynthus and the woods which fringed its northern slopes. The boar had led them from that world to this one, culling the heroes until Meleager and herself remained. And Meilanion. Where was his place in the wilderness before her?

She looked back down the hillside. The youth was traversing the slope, taking a rising diagonal to a higher point on the ridge.

She knew his thought. The stags she spied from the ridges of Cyllene and Sciathus would bolt at the sight of her and she would pursue, running after them with a loping stride, losing sight of them as often as not, until they stopped and waited, then bolted again as her form flashed between the trees in pursuit. She drove them up and down the wooded slopes until they would halt and look about, awaiting her inevitable reappearance, a terrible weariness in their eyes. Then she would do as Meilanion did now: move out wide to outflank the prey, which, worn down and habituated to the hunter's presence, would watch as the trap was sprung, even in plain view.

So Meilanion circled her – patient, attentive – just as he had at the lake. But an animal hunted thus and *not* taken could never be taken again and to hunt it then was to begin an endless pursuit. The quarry's path became the hunter's path, its bed the hunter's bed. Chained together in the chase, the prey would drag its predator forward like a bullock to the altar. But there could be no outcome, for where was the altar here? Where was the priest with his bright knife?

She watched the youth's slow movement up the hillside until he disappeared behind the curve of the slope.

Then Meleager, Aura and herself began the descent into the first of the ravines. Looking up from the bottom, she saw their pursuer clambering down after them. Huddled together to shiver their way through that first night, she knew that he too shivered from the same cold, heard the same torrent foaming below him as they heard and awoke to the same cold light. Wherever they passed, Meilanion was the creature who came after them.

She thought of lying in wait for him, knowing he would prove no match for her, suspecting that he would offer no resistance at all. But she marvelled at him too, for the days that followed were harder than she could have imagined when she first looked down upon this wilderness of stone.

They moved along the bottoms of gorges so steep that the sun seemed never to reach their depths and whose torrents soaked them in icy spray. Aura leaped from rock to rock, searching for the boar's scent. From time to time she saw Meleager look up at the strip of bright blue sky framed by the sides of the chasm and fancied she saw in his expression a placid regret for the unreachable sun-warmed world that they had forfeited. It would not have mattered if the boar had left no scent or trail to follow. All their paths had shrunk to one. They shivered in a world of shadow, rock and chill. They slept, and woke and continued.

Meilanion was always there. The track gave out where the stream had cut into the base of the ravine leaving a buttress suspended over the water. They clung to the overhanging rock, feeling for finger- and toe-holds, Aura content to be slung from Meleager's back. Atalanta pressed her cheek to the cold stone and a tiny vein of mica gleamed in her eye. They were making for a low spur further on and when she looked back from that vantage point she saw the youth clinging there just as she had, feeling the same cold stone against his cheek, the same glittering thread stitching his eye to the bare rock as had her own. The chain that bound them was the trail. When she climbed and looked down he was there below her, hauling himself onto the same ledge, scraping his stomach over the same sharp lip. She examined the grazes and bruises which marked her body and wondered if they might not be matched by his, the record of their progress and its damage inscribed twice: in his flesh and her own.

The cold sank into her bones. More than once she thought to take the leather armour which Meleager still carried, without purpose it seemed, in his helmet. He would have yielded it if she had wished. They slept when they could no longer see to walk or climb and woke to resume the march which took them ever deeper into the mountains. Sunlight glittered high above them where mountain springs broke out of the ravine walls and tumbled down in silver cords of water, glancing off ledges and overhangs to thunder into the fast-flowing stream. The cliffs glistened with meltwaters which froze by night and frosted the rocks in the stream's rare meanders. The three of them skated and slithered over thin black ice. Then, after the interval which corresponded to the separating distance between her self and her shadow, her every act and its repetition, Meilanion too picked an unsteady path across the treacherous surface and came after them again.

He was of a piece with the substance of this place, obdurate and cold, she thought. A pebble skittered out from underfoot and the cold air stung her nostrils, as it would his. She was footsore, as was he. All she felt, saw, touched would be felt, seen and touched by him. The ravine was narrowing.

Meleager no longer looked up at the sky. Aura no longer growled when she found the scent of their quarry. Her mistress thought the thoughts of the youth behind her before he had thought them himself. Their futures were indivisible. The boar now. She had not imagined she could still be surprised.

And yet, when the span of the ravine measured no more than that of her outstretched arms, so straitened had its confines become, and the foaming water which before had drenched them from head to toe had shrunk to a tame rivulet contained in a channel no wider than the splay of her fingers, when its course had grown so irregular – twisting, turning, redoubling – that the vista down its length extended no further than the next ten strides, and those at a pace slowed by the expectation of the ravine's final closure and their own eventless defeat, then they rounded a final spur and a single step took them from the confines of the ravine into the place they knew must be their destination.

They stood at the bottom of a vast crater of stone.

The floor of the basin stretched before them, enclosed all around by high cliffs, which rose as though a ring of mountains had advanced on this place, collided and merged. The sides curved up from the floor and then climbed sheer into the sky.

Aura snarled once, a deep gurgle which broke the silence. But the warning was unnecessary. Nothing could exist beyond this place. The boar could be nowhere but here.

Atalanta and Meleager advanced into the crater, their footsteps over the loose rocks and smooth grey pebbles sounding at once too loud and too puny. They might have been giants or insects. There was no scale. The air was cold and very dry. Atalanta narrowed her eyes against the light. There was nothing in their heads but the thought of the animal they had trailed here.

Then Meleager halted. He took the leather armour from his helmet. Atalanta watched as he strapped on ankle guards and greaves, wrapped the girdle about his waist, reached for the thongs of his leather cuirass and tied them. Last of all, he gathered his hair and pulled on the crested helmet. His eyes regarded her from behind the slits in the bronze, moving over her as they had at their first encounter. Now she met his gaze.

84

He toted his spear, feeling its weight, turning its shaft in his hands. He was unknown to her again. He turned from her to a point on the far side of the crater's floor and then she understood his purpose.

The fault in the rock which long ago had allowed a trickle of water to cut the ravine did not stop where they stood. The facing mountain must once have been joined to the massif through which they had passed, for the same fault was visible there too. A shallow incline rose to an opening in the base of the cliff opposite. She might have mistaken it for a shadow. It seemed too narrow, no thicker than the blade of a knife.

The sounds of their footsteps pursued them as they echoed off the cliff at their backs, then, once they had passed the midpoint, ran to meet them from the one facing it. The crater was vaster even than she had thought, or perhaps their pace had slowed. Her sense of time seemed adrift: the constant glare of the sky, the silence, the bareness of their surroundings and the stillness within them. She thought of those moments of excitement, the brief rushes of exhilaration or terror in which time slowed and its moments stretched, when she would spring and seem to hover in mid-air, unable to descend upon the flash of movement that was her escaping quarry. Nothing happened here except themselves.

The entrance to the cave rose before them. Meleager's fingers tightened about his spear. She wondered if the boar might break from his lair and charge them out here in the open, half-hoping that he would. The cave's darkness was part of his armature, familiar to him and as potent a weapon as his tusks and hooves. He would come at them low and crush them against the walls he knew so well, grind them to a pulp. Her arrows would find the yellow-haired man and the white-haired dog instead of their target. He would do to her what he had done to Meleager. The slope leading to the mouth of the cave was littered with stones. They climbed.

She glanced back once before entering. The ravine from which they had emerged was no more than a hairline crack in the rock. Meilanion was standing at its base, a tiny figure whom she understood now. The beardless youth. How still and bare he must find this place where he had hoped to find so much, and how harsh the light of the sky upon it. They were her own

85

thoughts but he could be thinking no others. Her choice was to continue. What was his? He had seen them now. Was he running?

Her questions would not be answered. It was too late and apparent that he, the night-hunter, was the one to be spared.

Consider our ends, she thought, and the ends of our trails, the moment when the prey stumbles and the hunter does not, how the cries of an animal *in extremis* may sound like human cries and how human cries can be taken for those of an animal. The boar too has his song. His guises change but he does not. He has waited a long time and longer. He waits now in the darkness of the cave.

*   *   *

The mouth of the cave tapered to a point, framing a blade of light. Outside, there were pebbles and stones. Here, the floor was smooth sloping rock. The boar took his stand below the lip of the entrance and waited for his assailants.

Here, the outer cold mingled with warmer air which rolled up from the depths of the cave. It settled in the nap of his bristles and he smelled his own compound scent: dried scours, a midden of bones, urine, the lingering whiff of a must which had driven him to grunt through a mouth of streaming saliva and grate the tender tip of his sex in frustration against the unyielding floor. Now these scents were the beacons – his own beacons – which guided him through the twists and turns of the passageways and chambers, warning him of jutting obstructions and sudden drops. His hooves made a clacking sound when he trotted over the bare stone, skipping over treacherous ridges and wheeling himself around the sharp bends.

But the first time the boar had awoken here the darkness had seemed to press upon him and smother him. He did not know how long he had blundered within the bowels of the mountain, nor how he had come to be there in the first place. There were dim memories of panicked charging, collisions and screams – perhaps his own. Exhaustion had felled him. When he awoke, his grazes and cuts had scabbed and begun to throb. He had whined to himself in the darkness.

The old enemy had driven him forth: hunger. Hunger and

stone. He had offered his lament to the surrounding cliffs and they had returned it to him. He had recognised nothing in his new surroundings and remembered nothing of his old surroundings. He had awaited signals. None came.

His belly was a cauldron of acids; it had growled at him, urging him away. The terrain grew easier the further south he moved. After the mountains, a final ridge had given him a vantage point over a different landscape, gentler and greener. A lake had tempted him down. He had cooled his underbelly in its waters and wallowed in the reeds which sprang up in its shallows. In the woods beyond he had rooted in the friable soil and rubbed his mud-encrusted sides against rough-barked trees. A massif of hills merged and rose on the far side, cut by a crooked pass of bare white stone. He preferred to climb and so reached the plateau at the summit. Tall grasses grew and he sported among them for days on end. It might have been longer. The air was cooler there, he recalled.

Now he stood and waited for his pursuers. They would be here soon enough with their weapons and irrevocable intentions. This place was the socket into which they fitted. He had pared them to its dimensions. He scraped his hooves on the cave floor and gauged for the thousandth time the weight of his bones and the dense flesh massed about them. A boar's power resides in his hindquarters, whose haunches are wound tight with wiry muscle. Confronted by hills, his most natural mode of movement is the gallop. But descents are difficult, a boar's forelegs being thick but brittle staves and unused to an animal's full weight pressing down upon them. Overtoppling is a danger. It could not have been any natural urge which had impelled him to descend from his grassy plateau to the lower slopes of Aracynthus. Nevertheless the boar found himself shouldering aside fallen tree trunks, enduring the more or less pleasant scratching from the thorny thickets through which he forced a path, leaping over spring-fed rills and dry meltwater courses. Descending and circling, then descending again, but in a thickening fog of puzzlement. His was not to question and yet, like the reawakened ache of an old wound, or the sudden unclouding of the sun's rays, or the escape of some slippery prey (as slippery, almost, as memory), and so circling and descending.

Why was he here?

Pleasant basks in the afternoon sunlight which washed the middle slopes of Aracynthus were good occasions for considering matters such as these. He found a hollow there, a gentle-sided and grass-lined bowl which was congruent with the spread of a boar's belly, well-suited too to the slack bathing of the striped skeletal muscles in their sheaths of oozy sarcoplasm and the regular contractions of the smooth visceral muscles within, meaning digestion. Anything from the excrement of rodents to the hooves of a bull would pass through a boar. The latter produced pleasant acidic tingles in their through-passage to the sphincter. He observed the city in the valley below and the actions of its inhabitants. They seemed designed to unsettle him. True, his own acts grew more random. Uncontrolled. There were periods of time for which he could not account.

If he could divine the yellow-haired man, the boar had believed, then his own purpose would be clear. Or perhaps that thought had struck him later. The city dwellers had expelled one of their own. They had tossed him out with his hands bound and a sack tied over his head, then beaten him to make him run. He had stumbled down the valley surrounded by his dogs, who were torn between following their master and launching themselves at his tormentors. The animals had tumbled and scrambled about him, carrying him off on a raft of noise. Their barks and yelps had reached his twitching ears as the squeaking of mice. The man had worked his hands free and pulled off the hood. Watching from the cover of the undergrowth on the overlooking hillside, the boar had seen him shake free his hair and known that there was another as singular as himself.

But he had not descended further then, nor even when the city dwellers themselves had fled their city, streaming out by the gates and spreading over the valley with axes, sickles and scythes in their hands. He had welcomed the sight of their glittering blades, their glinting signals meaning – he was sure of it – the resolution he awaited: they were coming for *himself*.

No.

They had carried their tools to the orchards and begun cutting down the trees, then hacking and slicing their roots. The largest trees had been rigged with ropes to the trunks of their neighbours and the ropes tightened until the wood split. The vineyards had followed. Then they had gathered and penned their livestock and lit the pyre in the temple, which had glowed yellow, then orange and red. And then they had begun the burning.

There had been three nights of that, each one seeming longer than the last. The stench of roasted flesh drove him ever higher up the side of Aracynthus and the firelight which illuminated those labouring in front of the temple cast its red glow over all. He recognised one, rose at the sight of him and would have careered down the slope had he not been surrounded by men the like of which he had not seen before. Different from the inhabitants of the city, and a woman among them. The yellow-haired man had gathered them and returned as their leader.

The boar watched as they tramped towards the city, tracking them, his agitation growing. The moon sank from sight and the darkness which followed was blacker than any he had known, save that of the cave. A distant storm flashed and rumbled in the distance to the north but illuminated nothing save itself. He was locked in his blindness as though still pent within the mountain.

The same darkness must have blinded the men, immured that night within the walls of Kalydon. It was a darkness he knew too well, which stretched and flattened, settled itself in the angles of the city. The boar thought of the men crawling through streets and courtyards, stumbling over toppled stones and broken walls while their predators padded across the roofs, mapping their routes. The boar watched for first light to scratch its claws against the underside of the eastern sky, waiting for the weals of pink and yellow-tinged whites when the light reached west and sought purchase in the dark folds of the night's fat, probing for its bones.

But the boneless body of the sky came apart, disintegrating and dissolving, its flow pulling streams of light through the craggy valleys of the east where frost-fractured rock felt the same claws searching for cracks and flaws, prising at its legacy of secret scars as though both light and dark were sleep-blinded animals who had dreamed themselves fighting and then awoke to find it true. The sun vaulted the horizon. A lake of shade drained from the vale of Kalydon. Morning, noted the boar.

The boar took shelter among the trees. Gorse and scrubby grasses tufted the descending slopes. The city lay like a piece of battered armour cast away in the panic of battle, dull-grey in the pre-dawn light, now yellowing to bronze as the sunlight fell full on its stones. Those who had found safe haven were scattered through its length and breadth. From the tree-shaded heights of the valley's head, the survivors appeared no larger than ants and their weapons as tiny fragments of twig or stalk carried by blind instinct. The dawn which had come too late for so many was signal to the living that they must rise and count the dead.

But the depredations which reduced their numbers had taken place in darkness, their exact character unknowable, even to the boar. Curtailed shrieks and screams had disturbed the night-air. The citizens labouring in the pens further down the hillside had raised their heads, some of them slipping away now their work was done. The cries spoke of brief flurries of pain preceding the crunching of windpipes, or the gurgle of blood-clogged throats, fatal slashings and maulings. Matters the boar understood. Acts, he knew, which had been marked out for him.

Now, in the morning light, the survivors ran clear of the silent walls. Kalydon's shadow began to slide down the hill-side, stretching towards the outermost pens, deserted now. The temple stood empty, a shimmer of heat rising off its roof.

The hunters gathered. Arms were raised and waved. The vale of Kalydon became a sheet of baked earth indistinguishable from the plain below. The tiny figures who moved upon it blurred and then fused in its heat; their column was a segmented insect that dragged itself down to the stream to drink and on its return broke apart. It was midday before they moved off the hillside, turning their backs on the mountains, retreating down the valley. Breezes coming off the gulf far below swept their scent up the hillside as far as the concealing tree line, mingling it with wild thyme and the stale charnel-reek of the temple: their fresh sweat, the dogs and their hot nerves. One turned and barked, head angled beyond the ruined olives, eyes probing beneath the dark canopy of the trees. But the boar did not stir. The hunters continued, past the abandoned pens, past the temple, and then, rounding one of the low foothills by which Mount Aracynthus anchored itself to the coastal plain, they disappeared from view.

The boar rose then. He stretched and felt his hackles prickle upright along the ridge of his back. He arched, to prolong the sensation. When the upright bristles extended to his tail, he knew, the red mist would begin to descend. His mouth would fill with saliva and the saliva would begin to foam. Beneath the saddle of compacted fat armouring his shoulders, back and sides, his temperature would rise. His forelegs would itch and he would rub them together – slowly at first – hooves kneading the ground, then faster and faster until his heart would pump his eyes so full of blood that they stained his vision with swirling red. But the twitching muscles of his hindquarters would not be denied, nor his splayed toes and pricked ears. His tusks. He *must* charge.

And then he would be hurt, for the aftermath meant pain. There were acts which took place – always the same acts – but they were unclear to him, lost somewhere in a glorious and greater loss, which was of himself. He was ecstatic there, dissolved in his own fullness. To gallop as fast as one might gallop, to leap and feel the heart's pounding almost to bursting point, to cut and to feel nothing. The boar's pleasures. All too brief.

They had disappeared one by one, he thought now, counting to himself in the cave: one by one by one by one. He waited for the yellow-haired man, and the woman too. Her dog had been the one to bark at him. They had a secret together, an accord which both bound them and held them apart. He should have stayed close. He should have shadowed them. Instead, that day, he had climbed.

Swathes of yellow stonecrop and silverweed had rustled and crunched beneath his hooves, then mulleins and knapweeds when the slope became rocky. Higher yet were deadnettles and broad-leafed borage. The mimosa-smothered walnuts and wild olive trees gave way to chestnuts and oaks, then pines and struggling sun-blasted beeches. Last of all came the endless perpendiculars of the firs which surrounded and sheltered the plateau of Aracynthus. The tall grasses waved their greetings. He stamped his own. The sharp tangs of starch and sap filled his snout and he thought of roots.

Above ground: hunger. Below: sustenance. The surface of the earth was a mirror in which each tree, bush, creeper or flower – even the poisonous walnut and shy crocus – was reflected and distorted. Fibrous mats and thrusting tap roots oozed through the soil in imitation of the colourful sprays and great green canopies above. But these subterranean branches were bare and blanched, all colour washed away by the flow of air-sucked water to the bright greenery of the sunlit world above. A boar's snout could cut a furrow into ground so hard with frost that an iron plough would bounce upon its surface. His own snout twitched and tingled, sensing the soil-cased meadow below the one so abundant and verdant above. Rooting, and then more rooting. He stood in the grasses' soft palisade. The sunlight which pushed through the tall-standing firs fell about him in ragged bars.

Matters might have stood otherwise. The dew condensing in the soft hair of his underpelt and the cool gusts of the Etesian wind pushing down from the north cased him in their different contexts. The continued swayings, abrupt flattenings and rebounds of the resilient grasses leached the original welcome from its gesture and replaced it with mere repetition. Paths ran through the meadow, but not his. He walked along them, hooves sinking a little in the springy turf. And then?

Or perhaps 'Otherwise . . .'? There were gaps in the account, between 'And' and 'Then' or 'Otherwise'. There were gaps which might better have been termed mutilations, for their edges were jagged as the shadows cast by fir trees on wind-waved grass, hard as hooves and sharp as tusks. A boar is built to destroy creatures greater than himself: low-slung with massive armoured shoulders for the upward blow, tusks for the toppled enemy's fall and then the slash. Groin to throat is effective.

Standing amid the grasses of Aracynthus, he had pricked his ears at the sound of muffled grunts and curses. His snout had twitched at the smell of sweat. Men were advancing upon him. His eyes narrowed at the sight of their spears and the sky against which their figures were etched seemed to clog with haze then glow as though the breeze were fanning a dormant ember into life, growing redder and redder. How many? He walked forward, searching for Yellowhair, but he was not among their number. Eight of them. A few more steps. How could these striding men not have seen him? How, when their lifeless bodies were to hang from the branches of the trees could they have advanced on him with their spears and knives? How could that have happened?

The boar stamped his hooves on the stone floor of the cave. They would hear him, the ones who had tracked him here and were advancing upon him now. He heard their footsteps scattering stones outside. They would be able to smell him. They would fear him and their fear would nourish him like milk from the teat. He was a patient feeder, nuzzling under the slack soft warmth of a sow's belly for the ragged lozenge of flesh that was his. He could wait for them a little longer.

He had thought that these 'men', who hunted him and perished, or continued and survived, were brittle and liable to snap. So thin and tall. They scattered, or grew entangled in one another, then split apart again. There were densities of them, places where they were thick and impenetrable so that his more brutish advances crushed them and they crackled underfoot. As twigs did. A flood had carried many of them to oblivion. The survivors had walked through a forest to the lake. Eight cadavers hung in the trees behind him. But forget them now, for here was Yellowhair, his woman and her animal. Of the other dogs, there was no sign. They must have been lost in the flood. The hunters had growled and scraped at the ground in their unhappiness, recalled the boar. They had lurched upright and staggered into the woods. So few of them were left. Might there be wounds which they concealed from him, or a sickness which they were carrying in their bodies? He had followed them into the woods. He drank the water which pooled among the exposed roots of the chestnut trees, then ate the roots and watched the escaping water sink into the soil, darkening it. He ate a worm. His weight sufficed to snap oak branches the thickness of his neck. He had tossed a goat upwards into the air and watched it rise three times its height. The landscape was the collection of things which resisted him. He stood on it.

But the hunters were not landscape and they too resisted him. In the woods they resisted him, for otherwise he could not understand how they remained alive as they split and filtered through the maze of trees. There were times when he was close enough to hear them breathe. A prohibition hung about them which had to do with the woods themselves, with the thickness of the dark trunks and the twitchings of the canopies which they upheld against the rich warmth of the sun. This was not the place where they were to die, just as the reedbed beyond was where Yellowhair and his woman must survive. Light glittered through the leaves and fell in shafts finer and swifter than the path of an arrow. It broke them into creatures of darkness and light. Mixed animals.

They were circling Yellowhair. They were going to snuff out his flame.

No. That came later.

They carried spears, arrows and sharp-pointed knives. They walked through the sun-dappled spaces of the woods. In the reeds of the lakeshore he saw the grasses of his waving meadow grown stiff and monstrous. He felt his bristles rise to horrid spikes at the sight of the tall blades and when his hunters disappeared within the mass of greenery he thought of the fragments of sharp metal they carried with them to pierce him and slice him. They floated in the sea of reeds, borne by currents he could not trace. Their desires, he presumed. He could not wallow there. Their spears would surround him and their arrows fall from the sky in a mockery of his own spiked armour: an inside-out boar with daggers for bristles and spears for tusks. He did not hate them. But the sun fell and left him in darkness, alone with his foaming appetite. The earth began to quiver beneath his hooves and shake the bones in their fleshy sheaths. He heard the furtive scratching at his back which signalled the coming into being of the one he might not, might never . . . The beardless 'him' whom he could not flee, whose tracks were to circumscribe and frame the shape he must assume. He could not *be* when that other's being neared his own.

And so he ran at his hunters, as he was bound to do. He must have run at them and found them cowering in the false sanctuary of the reeds. He must have ripped and trampled, gored and butted and broken them. Eaten them? He did not know. There were gaps. He should have stayed closer, kept their scent strong in his nostrils and his ears pricked for their footfalls, as earlier. He had allowed himself an intervening distance. He would have to gallop, for the ground yawned beneath him and seemed to stretch when all four hooves left the rough turf which separated the trees from the edge of the lake and its lapping waters. There were brief, airborne moments when he knew nothing of the terrain beneath him. He ran towards the acts which were to be performed in the reeds fringing the lake of Trichonis, which were to be recorded in the bodies of the hunters, and then, once done, he ran from those acts. He fled his damage.

He ran here to the cave and waited and now the waiting was all but over.

He heard the scrape of their feet up the incline and the rattling of the pebbles. He saw their outlines rise in the mouth of the cave. First the helmetted and armoured man, spear twisting in his hands, then the woman, her bow strung, and last of all her dog, head low and belly flattened to the ground. They halted at the entrance. The man turned to the woman and spoke to her. She nodded her acquiescence, reached for her quiver and notched an arrow to her bowstring. The boar saw her strain to bend the stave until it seemed it must snap, the bronze-tipped arrow trembling, its point searching for the line that would speed it through air and bury it in his flesh. The boar listened for the note of her single-string lyre, waiting for the hard pads of her fingers to loose the cord and send the signal for his own rough music to begin. Soon, he thought.

His lungs filled and emptied, swelled and collapsed. One more breath, he thought. In and then out.

Now.

*   *   *

The stones cut his feet and cracked against his shins. Meilanion ran, and knew as he ran that he would not catch them. He saw Atalanta turn away from him, reaching for an arrow as she did so. The mouth of the cave breathed a darkness that rolled over them like thick smoke, engulfing Meleager first, then the woman too. She walked into the cave with her dog at her heel and disappeared. Then the crater was bare of everything save himself, silent except for the dying echoes of his footsteps.

And no trail. No hoofmark or footprint or mark of any kind to tell the tale of what had passed. The night-hunter reads signs where others see nothing, but when the signs give out . . . He looked up from the ground to the dark blade of the cave-mouth but nothing moved and no one emerged. Atalanta, Meleager, the boar; they had moved past the point where he could follow. What was he without them?

The cold dry air stung his throat as he heaved it into his lungs. He knew this place, though he had never seen or heard of it. Its sunlit double had been raised on the shores of the gulf, where they had first met and joined, shouting their names as they came together to build a sanctuary of sound whence they would march against the boar. Here was that place's counterpart and cancellation: a silent crater scraped out of stone.

Tied between them was the twisted braid of all the paths which the hunters had followed, which had thinned as each thread had frayed then snapped. And here, here beneath his feet, and now, there was no trace of them at all.

They were in the cave, the survivors, in a place whose darkness resisted him and whose silence thwarted him. He waited in the failing light.

Then, issuing from its mouth, came a sound. It began as a whisper, then gathered as if a voice were urging itself into intelligible speech, or vast lungs were drawing breaths, each one a little deeper than the last. The sound swelled until it filled the air and echoed between the cliffs. He crouched on the ground in the encroaching darkness while the roll-call raised a pillar of noise whose base was the whole volume of this empty place and whose column threw itself into the sky.

He heard first the cries of those who had died among the reeds and the roar of the fire in Kalydon's temple. Then the song regathered itself and he heard the first of the names – the names of the heroes – and he recognised in this the wreck of their palace, raised across the water from Kalydon. Only the names of the two he had tracked here were not heard: Meleager and Atalanta. They were with the beast whose shape was their fate and whose own fate was shaped as they were.

But their shapes were so various and the boar too seemed to frame himself from moment to moment. His epithets glinted, his attributes jangled in Meilanion's ears. In this song he was the pieces of a beast: all the jumbled hoofprints of his trail, the fragments scattered and buried in the soil of Kalydon, on the slopes of Aracynthus and here.

Here was where Atalanta must become 'Atalanta' and Meleager clothe himself in the garb of 'Meleager'. Here was where the boar must be divided as though to make a sacrifice: meat to the men, offal to the gods.[107]

107 Hom, Il xix.249–69, Od xi.131, xxiii.277–84; Soph, Trach 1095ff.; Diod Sic iv.12; Apollod ii.5.4; Paus v.10.9, iv.15.8.

The boar's music broke over the night-hunter's head and the names of the hunters whose company he had quit tumbled in slow confusion. He heard the record of the hunt unbind itself from the shaft yet to be staked in its victim's flesh and come apart: its noises, fleeting odours and flashes of colour, the changing tints of the sky, the corrugations and textures of oak-bark, dry earth, pine needles, the coarse wire of her hair slipping between his fingers. All this must be lost and the gaps left by those losses, the shapes of the absences, these too disappear. Hindsight's tales will fill the truthful silence and flood its darkness with lies.

The true fates of the heroes are to become their own apocrypha. Some of those who escaped the hunt must return to die there; some who perished there must rise again, being destined for graves elsewhere than Kalydon. Agelaus[108] and Ancaeus[109] die in the reeds, gored and trampled by the boar, as does Eurytion, whom Peleus's blind spear finds among the tall stems.[110] But Jason's course veers from the hunt and leads him through the years to the beach at Iolcis, where he is crushed beneath the poop of the long-careened and worm-eaten Argo when it collapses upon him as he sleeps.[111] The twelve sons of Hippocoon are scattered and regathered, then slaughtered by Heracles beneath the walls of Lacedaemon, perhaps for the murder of the son of Licymnius, whom they cudgelled to death,[112] perhaps for the ousting of Tyndareus, whose kingdom they usurped:[113] whichever, they are buried in Sparta.[114] Castor's nemesis is sharp-eyed Lynceus, who falls in turn under Pollux's spear and whose brother Idas is burnt to a cinder by a thunderbolt hurled by Zeus.[115] Toxeus bleeds to death in a ditch.[116] Theseus is driven out of an Athens which has no use

---

108 Bacch v.118–19.

109 Apollod i.8.2; Bacch v.118–19; Paus viii.4.10, viii.45.2.

110 Apollod i.8.2; Schol. ad Aristoph, Nub 1063; Ant Lib xxxviii; Schol. ad Lyc, Alex 175; Pherecydes cit. ap. Schol. ad Lyc, Alex 444.

111 Staphylus fr. 5 ap. schol. ad Argumentum Eur, Med, cf. Diod Sic iv.55; Xen, Hell vi.5.1.

112 Apollod ii.7.3.

113 Apollod iii.10.4; Paus iii.15.1–2; Diod Sic iv.33.5ff.

114 Paus iii.15.1–2.

115 Theocr xxii.137ff.; Schol. ad Hom, Il iii.243; Schol. ad Pind, Nem x.112–20; Schol. ad Lyc, Alex 546; Apollod iii.11.2; Hyg, Fab lxxx; Ov, Fas. v.699ff.; Paus iii.15.4–5.

116 Apollod i.8.1; Hes, Cat fr. 98 ap. P Berlin 9777; and not the eponymous son of Eurytus (Hes, Cat fr. 79 ap. schol. ad Soph, Trach 266; Diod Sic iv.37.5).

for him and is murdered by treacherous Lycomedes on the distant isle of Scyros.[117] Thersites is cut down at Troy by Peleus's son Achilles for defiling the body of his beloved enemy, the Amazon queen Penthesilea.[118] Achilles' son buries Phoenix, his father's aged tutor, somewhere on the road between Tenedos and the country of the Molossians on the march home from Troy, the cause of his death unknown.[119] Peleus himself survives his son to expire of old age in exile on Cos,[120] or Icos,[121] or perhaps in the depths of the sea.[122] His brother Telamon dies in a raid on Elis undertaken with Heracles, who buries him there, perhaps,[123] while Amphiaraus digs his own grave, dragged into the earth by his maddened horses in the ill-fated campaign against Thebes.[124] Caeneus is bludgeoned into his tomb by the centaurs at Pirithous's wedding,[125] or changed into a woman,[126] or a yellow-winged bird according to Mopsos.[127] Mopsos himself meets his end in the deserts of Libya: snakebite.[128]

The boar's music is unmelodious: these are roguish trails. They fork and split and fork again, dragged this way and that by incompatible destinations. Anomalous tracks suggest feints and detours, retreadings and rejoinings among the heroes impelled along them. The last imprint is always a grave.

The other huntsmen fade away. Their strides lengthen. Their footprints thin until the trail becomes a scattered archipelago, their acts marooned on islands separated by eventless oceans. So

---

117 Plut, Thes xxxv; Paus i.17.6; Diod Sic iv.62.4; Apollod, Ep 1.24; Aristot, Ath Con fr. 6 ap. schol. ad Eur, Hipp 11.

118 Schol. ad Lyc, Alex 999; Arctinus Miletus cit. ap. Proc, Chrest ii, cf. Soph, Philoc 441–6 and Plat, Rep 620c, where, in Hades, the soul of Thersites clothes itself in the body of an ape, and Plat, Gorg 525e, where he is partially exonerated.

119 Apollod, Ep 6.12; Euripides's Phoenix is almost wholly lost, cf. Aeschin, i.152; Dem, xix.246.

120 Schol. ad Eur, Tro 1128.

121 Dict Cret vi.7–9; Antipater of Sidon, Anth Pal vii.2.9.

122 Eur, Andr 1253–69.

123 Paus viii.15.5–7.

124 Eur, Ph 172–9, Suppl 925ff.; Apollod iii.6.2–8; Paus i.34.2, v.17.7, ix.41.2; Soph, Elec 836–9; Diod Sic iv.65.5ff.; Asclepiades cit. ap. Schol. ad Hom, Od xi.326; Hyg, Fab lxxiii; Stat, Theb viii.1, cf. Pind, Ol vi.12–15, Nem ix.16–27 et schol., Nem x.9; Hdt viii.134.

125 Apollod, Ep 1.22; Lact Plac ad Statius, Achill 264; Ap Rhod i.57–64; Schol. ad Ap Rhod v.57; Schol. ad Hom, Il i.264; Acusilaus cit. ap. P Oxy xiii.133ff.

126 Serv ad Virg, Aen vi.448.

127 Ov, Met xi.524ff.

128 Ap Rhod iv.1502–33.

Nestor loads the bones of Machaon into his hold and sets sail after the victory at Troy,[129] finds landfall at Poeëessa,[130] then Gerenia[131] and the palace at Pylos. And then he disappears. Laertes is waiting when his son Odysseus returns from the same war; when Odysseus dies,[132] he vanishes. Phyleus takes Heracles's part against his father Augeas, is banished to Dulichium and the Echinades, hunts the boar. But a generation later it is his son, Meges, who leads the islandmen to Troy. Of the father, there is no trace. The heroes' footprints grow ever lighter and their traces appear ever more faint. They reach their own truthful silence, find it useless, and their final steps take them clear of the tell-tale surface altogether. *They were nothing . . .*

Meilanion heard in the fading sounds of the battle within the cave the trail rebounding, as water will when it dashes against a cliff, scends into unresisting air, and its backwash retreats in search of more impressionable terrain in which to stamp its signs: stiff clays and marls, freshly-fallen snow, the damp soil of the forest floor. He listened for the prints of the beast within the cave and read their succession as characters unspooling in a high wind, as ribbons revolve and whip about the thin staves to which they are fixed.

Cleaves and dew claws identify the tracks of a boar, their depth his weight, their grouping his gait.[133] In melting snow such imprints swell, the hooves which made them seem to grow and the boar perched upon them grows monstrous. The tracks multiply and become jumbled: the boar is confused or furious. Broken ground signals his hunger[134] and muddied

---

129 Apollod, Ep 3.12, 6.1; amphora (London Brit Mus 1897.7-27.2); Callim, Aet iii. fr. 80–2; Hom, Il 620ff. et passim, Od iii.102–200; Paus iii.26.10, iv.3.1–2, iv.31.11, v.25.8; Pind, Nem iii.112, Pyth vi.33; Plat, Hipp Maj 286a–b, Hipp Min 364c–d, Laws 711E, Phaed 261b–c; Strab vi.1.15.

130 Strab viii.4.4, x.5.6.

131 Paus iii.26.8–10.

132 Whether as per Tiresias's prophecy (Hom, Od xi.135) or at the hands of his son Telegonus (Eugammon Cyrenicus cit. ap. Proc, Chrest s.v. Telegonia; Dict Cret vi.15; Hyg, Fab cxxvii; Hor, Ode iii.29.8) is unknown.

133 Although, 'Swine are either cloven- or solid-footed; for there are in Illyria and Paeonia and elsewhere solid-hoofed swine. The cloven-footed animals have two clefts behind.' (Aristot, Hist An 499b.12–14, cf. Aristot, Gen An 774b.21, pseudo-Aristot, Mirab Auscult 68.835a.35, Antig Car 66(72); Pliny, Nat Hist. ii.106, xi.44, Ael, Nat Anim v.27, xi.37).

134 Aristot, Hist An 595a.26–8, cf. Hom, Od x.242, Aristot, Hist An 603b.27, Varro, Re Rust iv.2.

pools his thirst.[135] He rubs himself against trees, in either martial[136] or sexual[137] frustration. The boar is the sum of his inscriptions.

Meilanion watched the mouth of the cave, waiting for whoever or whatever might emerge. But nothing now disturbed the air save his own breathing. Where nothing happens, time stands still. He was suspended between the two openings: where the boar had been run to ground and the gorge which had led them to his lair; between preservation and extinction.

And both must happen. The running daughter of Schoineus and the hunting daughter of Iasius describe two different Atalantas. The Meleager who slaughters the sons of Thestius cannot at once be the Meleager who walks into the cave. They grow out of different trails. So too the boar is two-fold: at once flesh and bone, and a spectral beast who emerges out of the prints and traces which will become the tale of the Boar of Kalydon. The beast in the cave will not suffice to consternate and terrorise, as the 'Boar of Kalydon' must. A shadow-boar accumulates in the story's negative space.

But whether he is conceived in the vengeful brain of Artemis or in the womb of the sow Phaea,[138] whom Theseus will later kill, he must swell to fill his allotted shape. Thus he fattens himself on roots, barley, millet, figs, acorns, wild pears, cucumbers, mice and snails.[139] His favoured haunts have been assigned: the quarries of Pentelicus in the Attic mountains, Mount Taygetus in Sparta and the border disputed with Elis, the oak-groves of Phelloe and Soron by the banks of the Ladon, the slopes of Mount Pholoe.[140] Most of all the heights of Mount

---

135 Hom, Od xiii.409, xiv.533; Ael, Nat Anim v.45.

136 'Wild boars, though usually enfeebled at this time as the result of copulation, are now unusually fierce and fight with one another in an extraordinary way, clothing themselves with defensive armour, or in other words deliberately thickening their hide by rubbing against trees or by coating themselves repeatedly all over with mud and then drying themselves in the sun. They drive one another away from the swine pastures and fight with such fury that very often both combatants succumb' (Aristot, Hist An 571b.13–21).

137 'Castrated wild boars grow to the largest size and become fiercest. . . . Wild boars become castrated owing to an itch befalling them in early life in the region of the testicles, and the castration is super-induced by their rubbing themselves against the trunks of trees' (Aristot, Hist An 578a.25–578b.6).

138 Bacch xviii.23–5; Diod Sic iv.59.4; Plut, Thes ix; Paus ii.1.3; Strab viii.6.22.

139 Aristot, Hist An 595a.26–8, 580b.24, Hist An 621a.36–9, cf. Hom, Od x.242; Aristot, Hist An 603b.27; Varro, Re Rust iv.2.

140 Paus i.32.1, iii.20.4, v.6.6, vii.26.10, viii.23.9; Xen, Anab v.3.10.

Cyllene in Arcadia, for the boars who forage there are white.[141] Like himself.[142]

So he grows, and roots, and grubs, and roams, and grows again. He builds his lair from stock materials: in 'a thicket',[143] therefore, 'through which the strength of the wet winds could never blow nor the rays of the bright sun beat',[144] and the thicket itself in some inaccessible location[145] where he can revel in the quiet and darkness.[146] Safe within the lore of his den he feels the ground shudder with impending catastrophe: earthquakes, pestilence, famine.[147] He relishes the cellular swell of enzymes granting immunity from salamanders and hemlock.[148] Outside, his enemies are gathering.

Sheep butt him to the ground and the wild oryx impales him on its horn.[149] He competes with the weasel alone in his hatred of snakes.[150] A boar who ventures into water after suffering a bite from the scorpion of Caria will die; but is his enemy then the scorpion or the water?[151] Henbane causes paralysis. It can be cured by eating crabs.[152] He chases wolves.[153] His hackles rise at the sight of a lion.[154]

The boar girds himself with epithets and fights. He grows intimate with his sources and more complex under their injunctions, which render him at once quick-tempered, ferocious, unteachable, gluttonous, implacable, devoid of justice, a cannibal, and the progeny of a coward.[155] On his wary return to the watering-hole from which he has been chased, whose mud-

---

141 Paus viii.17.3.

142 Cleomenes Rheginus cit. ap. Athen ix.402a.

143 Hom, Il xi.415–16; Apollod ii.5.4.

144 'Nor could the rain pierce through it so thick it was; and fallen leaves were there in plenty' (Hom, Od xix.439–44).

145 'Hemmed in with sheer cliffs and chasms and overshadowed by trees' (Aristot, Hist An 578a.25–578b.6).

146 Hom, Od xiii.409.

147 Ael, Nat Anim vi.15.

148 Ael, Nat Anim ix.28, iv.23.

149 Op, Cyn ii.332, ii.457.

150 Aristot, Hist An 609b.28.

151 Aristot, Hist An 607a.17–20.

152 Ael, Var. Hist. i.7.

153 Aristot, Hist An 595b.1, although the passage is emended.

154 Aristot, Hist An 630a.1–3, but cf. Paus iii.14.7-10, where trained boars are said to have been set upon each other by Spartan youths at the Phobaeum. Vid. Eur, Ph 408ff., Suppl 132ff.; Zen, Cent i.30; Hyg, Fab lxviiii; Stat, Theb i.370ff.; Apollod iii.6.1; Hes, Sh 168–77.

155 Aristot, Hist An 488b.15; 'μολοβριτεσ': according to Hipponax cit. ap. Ael, Nat Anim vii.47, cf. Nat Anim vii.19, x.16; Plat, Lach 196e.

clouded waters have cleared in his absence, he bends his neck to the mirror-like surface and sees in his own wavering image the faces of the men who will one day be compared to him: Hector, Ajax, Heracles.[156]

They were always there, disguised behind his tusks and foaming mouth, peering out through his own fiery eyes. Little by little, in his first awakening moments and days in the cave, he feels a plausible boar's body tighten about his frame. Next, the victims appropriate to such a creature draw nearer.[157] His own particular victims will follow.[158] He is all but perfect for the role which awaits him in Kalydon. Anger rises in his throat until it can no longer be contained; the inevitable acidic foam, his unstoppable hooves, the descending red mist. Almost ready.

There are initial propositions: that the father of Meleager omit sacrifice to Artemis; that the heroes gather for the hunt; that the flocks and herds of Kalydon be numerous and its soil rich; that the trees in the orchards groan under the weight of their fruit and grapes swell on the vines, promising wine.

And there are final propositions: that the vines be torn up by the roots, the wine never made; that the orchards be cut down and the fruit rot where it falls; that the bellies of the sheep and

---

156 Hom, Il xvi.823-7, xii.42-50, xvii.282-5; Hes, Sh 387-93.

157 Atys, Adonis and Idmon, presumably: Hdt i.36.1-43.3; Paus vii.17.9-10; Diod Sic ix.29.1; Apollod iii.14.4 (cf. *Bion I, Bionis Smyrnaei Adonidos Epitaphium*, ed. Fantuzzi; Plut, Quaest Conviv iv.5.3-8; Athen ii.80b; Schol. ad Lyc, Alex 831; Prop iii.v.37-8; Ov, Met x.710ff.; Hyg, Fab ccxlviii; Anon (Anacreon?) ap. Heph, Ench xxxiii s.v. 'Antispasticon'; Apollod i.9.23; Ap Rhod ii. 815ff.; Hyg, Fab xiv, xviii; Valerius Flaccus, Argonautica v.1ff.). Odysseus, although wounded while hunting boar on Mount Parnassus with the sons of Autolycus (Hom, Od xix.429-67), subsequently, and typically, turned the injury to his advantage (Hom, Od xix.385ff.; Anon Odyssey fr. 1 3-4 ap. P Ryl iii.487).

158 Ancaeus is first wounded (Paus viii.45.2, viii.45.7) in the groin (Lyc, Alex 479-93; Ov, Met viii.391-402) then 'killed by the brute', his fellow victim being Hyleus (Apollod i.8.2), or Meleager's brother Agelaus (Bacch v.117), or no one (Paus viii.4.10). It is moot whether Eurytion is the victim of Peleus or the boar (Apollod iii.13.2; schol. ad Aristoph, Nub 1063, who calls the victim 'Eurytus'; compare Ant Lib xxxviii et Schol. ad Lyc, Alex 175, who specify a boar-hunt in general rather than the Kalydonian one in particular). Meleager's death is harder to assign. The death of the boar entails the division of the spoils, which, favouring Atalanta, entails the battle with the covetous sons of Thestius, thence their deaths, and Meleager's, too, either in the fighting (Hom, Il ix.529-99, cf. Paus x.31.3-4 and Apollod i.8.3; Hes, Cat fr. 98.4-13 ap. P Berlin 9777) or by the intervention of his mother, Thestius's daughter, Althaea (Bacch v.93-154; Aesch, Cho 602-11, cf. Diod Sic iv.34.6ff.; Ant Lib 2; Schol. ad Hom, Il ix.534; Ov, Met viii.445-525; Ibycus fr. 15 ap. Diomedes, Ars Grammatica i.323, the last of whom chances on 'Meleager' and 'Althaea' to comment that the formation of a patronymic from the name of the mother is improper; Hyg, Fab clxxi, clxxiv). Surviving fragments of an 'Oeneus' (?Eur, P Hibeh i.4.21) and a 'Meleager' (?Eur, vid. D. L. Page CQ, xxxi, 178) are inconclusive on this point, although the latter mentions

102

cattle be slashed so that they stumble over their viscera as they run in panic down the hillsides; that some of the hunters live while others die, gored or trampled; that Artemis be satisfied in the end.

Their middle term is the boar.

The hunters pursue him and surround him, as they must. There was never a chance of victory or escape. Atalanta's first arrow was loosed even before his conception. The dense fat armouring of his back puckers and sucks the shaft into its rightful sheath. Must he first open his eye to admit the spear of Amphiaraus? The flesh of his flank prickles and itches, waiting for the weapon that will finish him. He senses his purpose as something alien and inevitable inside him: a waiting wound. The events which must now take place have no use for his life. His purpose is to be killed.

He stands his ground to that end. The two hunters advance with slow steps, weapons twitching. He may not move. He thinks of his high meadow, its breezes and softness. They have seen him now. They will suspect his stillness. He counts seconds. He breathes in and then out. His events are done, all but one.

Meleager's spear-thrust comes at him, its force snapping off the crosspiece and spitting him along the length of the shaft. Gut, lungs, heart, throat. Cold bronze inside him. His eyes roll up into his skull like her hands disappearing into Meleager's hair. They will skin him now.[159] They will hack off his head[160] and snap off his tusks.[161] Alive, his fate is to be their justification for killing him. Dead, he becomes their trophies.[162] They

---

159 the hide which the sons of Thestius claimed on the grounds that Iphiclus had been the first to wound the boar (Apollod i.8.3) but which Meleager presented to Atalanta, along with

160 the head (Hom, Il ix.548), according to the Homeric account. The diegesis to Callimachus' 94th Aetion remarks: 'A huntsman . . . upon killing a boar said that it was not fitting for those who surpass Artemis to dedicate [their trophies] to her; so he dedicated the boar's head to himself, hanging it on a black poplar. He lay down to sleep under the tree, and the head fell and killed him.' A boar's head was not to be trifled with, even after the kill. The same may be remarked of

161 the tusks, which 'become intensely hot whenever the boar is provoked' and retain sufficient heat to singe hair even when the animal is dead (Xen, Cyn x.17, cf. Paus v.12.2). Tusks were highly prized as trophies (Hom, Il x.264) and yet the first recipient of this particular pair is unrecorded and unidentified. They

162 were later dedicated to Athena in her temple at Tegea, Callimachus (Hymn iii.215–22) states that 'the tokens of victory came into Arcadia which still holds the tusks of the beast'. They were removed, many years later by the Emperor Augustus. One – broken –

will divide him among them and carry him off. His tracks[163] henceforth will be the footprints of men and their scrawled handiwork will be his markings.[164] The boar's bestial mutations – his rages, his appetites, his strangest shapes and outgrowths – must all accord with familiar needs, for we are the authors of our monsters.[165]

*   *   *

First, the sounds of strife had dulled, as though the combatants were battling their way deeper into the mountain. Then they had grown intermittent, with longer and longer intervals between the outbreaks of noise. Meilanion's straining ears had supplied the faint sounds which he sought, hearing his blood's popping and pulsing in his veins as the boar's dark and fatal flood, the hissing fall of his lungs as the gasps and grunts of his assailants.

. . . with naked feet should they travel who study the dim tracks of wild beasts, lest the noise of their sandals grating

___

was displayed in the Forum at Rome; the other – whole – in the sanctuary of Dionysus in Augustus's private garden. It was the size of a man's leg (Paus viii.46.1–5) and the boar proportionate to such a tusk would have stood taller than a giraffe at the shoulder. 'It would seem that in the days of old the beasts were much more formidable to men,' comments Pausanias (Paus i.27.9), citing the boar of Kalydon, among other monstrous beasts. The hide, 'rotted by age and by now without bristles', remained in the temple at Tegea (Paus viii.47.2).

163 But the scattering of the boar leaves no mark on the landscape: no 'tracks in soft ground' or 'broken branches where the bushes are thick' or 'marks from his tusks wherever there are trees' (Xen, Cyn x.5).

164 Hence the images commemorating him carved in the throne of Apollo at Amyclae (Paus iii.18.15), surrounded by his tormentors on the gable of the temple of Athena Alea at Tegea (Paus viii.45.6), pierced by Atalanta's arrow on the shield of her son Parthenopaeus (Eur, Ph 1108–11), warning of the war that will follow his death on another shield (Callim fr. 621 ap. schol. ad Eur, Ph 134) whose ownership is unrecorded, which is itself lost, and perhaps never existed. Even the boar's 'representations' dissolve into a generalised iconography of enmity and rage (Eur, Ph 408ff., Suppl 132ff.; Hyg, Fab lxviiii; Stat, Theb i.370ff.; Apollod iii.6.1; Eur, Suppl 139–48), and thence the constituent stock epithets which compel his 'foaming mouth' (Hes, Sh 389; Eur, Ph 1381–2, cf. Eur, Bacch 1122–4) and the 'gleaming points of his tusks' (Hom, Il x.262–4, xi.416, Hymn iv.569; Ael, Nat Anim v.45; Eur, Ph 1380; Hes, Sh 388) as instances. They are the elements into which he disintegrates and

165 which thus dictate his later shapes: as winged (Artemon of Pergamon cit. ap. Ael, Nat Anim xii.38), or horned (Agatharcides cit. ap. Ael, Nat Anim v.27), or thundering down the slopes of Olympus in the form of a river (Paus ix.30.9–11), or stunted (Aristot, Hist An 573b.2–5; 577b.27, cf. Aristot, Gen An 749a.1, 770b.7) so that Achilles might prove his manhood at the tender age of six (Pind, Nem iii.44–50, cf. Aeschin, III Contra Ctesiphon 255ff.).

*under their sleek feet drive sleep from the eyes of the wild
beasts . . .*[166]

Then the cave was silent. He thought of waterfowl scrambling
into the sky with their wings grasping for air and their feet
dashing up water until the last beat and kick took them clear of
the lake's surface and they rose into the sky. The birds shrank to
specks and then they were gone with no trace to mark the fact
that they had been there. Water was a surface which offered no
more record than stone of what took place upon it. The night-
hunter must fumble his way over both as a blind man might.

*Even in the dark they slay wild beasts by the rays of the
moon . . .*[167]

Whatever figure might yet be fashioned from his own flesh
and blood, and whatever shape that figure's quarry might take,
they would be 'Meilanion' and the object of 'Meilanion's pursuit'. The youth who stood alone in the void formed by the
surrounding mountains listened to the dull clap of his heart.
Sinews stitched his flesh to its scaffold of bones. His weight
pressed on the balls of his feet. His throat burned. His skin
puckered from the cold.

But 'Meilanion' felt none of this, being insubstantive, con-
venient, accomodating even of his quarry: a swift-footed woman
fleeing him, or the huntress whose arrows sought out the Boar of
Kalydon, or even the beast himself. His role was to pursue, to
approach, to yearn. But never grasp, for then all three would
glove his hands like the silvery-grey gossamer of spider's webs
which tent the dew-soaked grass and are lit by the rising sun of
the poets.

He was at the fork in his trail. Behind him lay the possibility
of his maintenance among the cloudy ghosts of the hunters
whose path he had quit on the slope of Aracynthus. To rejoin
them now would be to preserve himself as they were preserved
and be strung between them as the figure necessary to their
stories. His acts would subsist in the traces of those acts, which

---

166 Op, Cyn i.309.
167 Ibid.

were the swerves and inflections of the hunt for the Boar of Kalydon. To quit their number meant the cave. He looked to the dark mouth which had swallowed the huntress and her consort.

It is the night-hunter who takes the boar . . .[168]

There was no 'soft ground' to record his passage, but stone and the darkness of the cave. The rays of the moon would not penetrate there; he would be blind and helpless with the boar, whose tracks went unrecorded, as his own would, and the two who had preceded him. How many before them, he wondered. How many after?

Did he stand then, his knees cracking, his muscles stiff from inaction? Did he turn away from the narrow opening of the gorge and advance instead towards the cave? There was no means to mark his choice, nor any witness to recall it. And so no one to see him climb the rock-strewn slope, and no record of his pausing at its entrance, to look back for a moment or two, no more. And, once he had taken his first hesitant steps forward into the darkness, no sign betrayed his existence or its passing. A dwindling disturbance stirred the darkness of the opening, then sank within it. He was beyond record, if these events were indeed those that would later prove to have been his fate: to walk into lightlessness and silence, leaving nothing. To be among the lost.

*　　*　　*

A fragment of Palaephatus's *De Incredibile* surviving in a later epitome of that work first records the fates of Meilanion and Atalanta,[169] which are summarised by Apollodorus in his *Bibliotheca*: 'So Meilanion married her. And once upon a time it is said that out hunting they entered into the precinct of Zeus, and there taking their fill of love were changed into lions.' Hyginus reproduces and augments this tale, as do Nonnus and Servius in his commentary on Virgil's *Aeneid*.[170] Later mythographers, following Hyginus, explained the metamorphosis as

---

168 Op, Cyn i.76.
169 Pal, De Incred fr. xiii.
170 Apollod iii.9.2; Hyg, Fab clxxxv; Nonnus, Dionys xii.87-9; Serv ad Virg, Aen iii.113.

punishment for the lovers' incontinence and cited Pliny for the fact that lions mate not with their own kind but with leopards. The transformation prevented them from repeating their sacrilegious act.

But Pliny nowhere states this fact and the other authorities for their fates are contradictory or incomplete. Theognis claims that Atalanta flees her father's house and marriage, takes to the mountains and eventually 'comes to know the end'.[171] The end of love, one presumes. But with whom? Sons – all called Parthenopaeus – are fathered on her by Meilanion,[172] or by Meilanion but not on Atalanta,[173] or on Atalanta but by Meleager,[174] or by Talaos of Argos,[175] or Hippomenes,[176] or by persons unknown.[177]

There the record halts. The trails of 'Atalanta', 'Meilanion' and 'Meleager' run out. Their footprints churn the ground to an illegible palimpsest where all three are reduced to the evidence for their existences, collections of plausibilities, fleeting intersections between the different versions of their history, which meet as collusive armies to battle among themselves.[178] Their bloodless warriors wield soundless weapons as they round the grass-flooded slopes, axes high, cased in black inhuman armour. There . . .

. . . in the cave: Meilanion's sandal scraping over stone . . .

And yet for every history limping along the trail of its confused posterity there is another which consumes itself. Here they leave no mark at all. The prows of their ships cut the surfaces of seas whose waters close behind them and wash up the beach to sweep away the footprints of their crews. They

---

171 Theog 1287–94.
172 Hellanicus 4F99; Apollod iii.9.2, cf. Xen, Cyn i.7; Prop, i.1.9–10; Ov, Ars Amat ii.185–92.
173 Paus iii.12.9.
174 Hyg, Fab lxx, clxxxxi, cclxx, cf. fr. 537N among the surviving fragments of Euripides's Meleager.
175 Hecataeus (FrGrHist I fr. 32); Antimachus (fr. 29 Wyss); Aristarchus and Philocles cit. ap. schol. ad Soph, Oed Col 1320; Paus ix.18.6 et vid. Theb, fr. 6 ibid.
176 Schol. ad Theocr iii.40.
177 Aesch, Sept 532–3, 547; Soph, Oed Col 1320–2; Eur, Ph 150.
178 'The footprints are reversed! Just look at them! They face backwards! What's this? What sort of order is it? The front marks have shifted to the rear; some again are entangled in two opposite directions! What a strange confusion!' Soph, Ich 80–9 ap. P Oxy ix.1174.

march inland and the terrain preserves the trace of their passing only as the country which overlies an underground river maintains the deep secret of the subterranean course beneath it. The shrouds of their lives are draped over them and their features raise short-lived terrains of ridges and gorges. But the mountains dwindle. The basins fill. The countries of their lives settle over their bodies and smooth the heroes away.

. . . heard the sound of breathing. Not his . . .
. . . guarded by the boar. The Anaurus-crossing spear of Me[leager[179]
Lay] broken at his feet as sign that they had passed [this way.
And the] rough stone rasped his skin and [cut him
He left his own] dark mark [on the walls of the cave
With those of] yellow-haired [Meleager and
Atalant]a . . .[180]

179 Meleager's spear was said to have been preserved in the Sanctuary of Persuasion at Sicyon until destroyed by fire, along with the flutes of Marsyas, when the temple burned down (Paus ii.7.9). It was presumably the same spear which he threw across the River Anaurus to win the javelin contest at the Games for Pelias (Simonides fr. 61 ap. Athen iv.172e; Stesichorus fr. 3 ap. Athen iv.172d).

180 The fragment's provenance is uncertain. A 'Meleager' and an 'Oeneus' by Euripides are attested (among 62 others of his plays), as is an 'Atalanta' of Aeschylus (among another 80), and a 'Meleager' of Sophocles (among a further 113). Mention might be made of Charemon's 'Oeneus' and the 26 books of Stesichorus's works, which included the epic poem 'Suotherai' or 'The Boar-hunters'. Nicander may have addressed the broader contexts in his 'Aetolica' and 'Cynegetica', and Phrynichus the conventional aftermath in his 'Pleuroniai', or 'Women of Pleuron'. Anyte of Tegea is most likely to have written the epitaph for the boar and Astydamas to have clarified the parentage of Parthenopaeus.

But these 'titles' stand as headstones over empty graves in the great cemeteries of antiquity: the 'Etymologicum Magnum', the 'Onomasticon' of Pollux, the 'Bibliotheca' of Photius, or the 'Suda'. The bodies of their texts survive nowhere now but in works such as the 'Agrapha' of Phylarchus of Naucratis. The title means 'The Unwritten Things' and announces a compendium of stories never recorded elsewhere. Their existence now subsists in the title alone. Agrapha is lost.

PART II

Paris

'Close your eyes.'

The girl dabbed cold cream on his cheeks and forehead, wiped it down the bridge of his nose, then smoothed it over his face. Quick strokes of her fingers worked around his jaw and down as far as his collar. The paper ruff she had tucked there rustled. He heard the rattle of little pots and compacts, the soft rasp of tissues being pulled from their box. She blotted the top of his head, then paused. Bristles brushed his expectant skin, coating it in powder. Cheekbones, nostrils, the tops of his ears. She raised his chin to tilt back his head. He felt a tissue settle and cling. Her fingers pressed it to the skin of his neck then peeled it away.

'There.'

His head sat on a sagging plate. Its bloodless face regarded him from the mirror. He recognised the widow's peak, a drooping around the eyes. An unexceptional mouth set above an unremarkable chin. His face had lengthened in his late teens, when his appearance had been described as poetic by some. Equine, he recalled, by another. *You sad horse.*

His thirties had rounded him out again and since then this face had been his. Tonight, painted, it would appear on television screens all over the country. Its encrusted forehead would crease with thought. Its grey lips would answer questions. He would wear a clown's face, drained of colour.

'I appear to have died,' he said.

'The studio lights change the shape of your face. It's how the shadows fall.' The girl tried to show him with her hands. 'It's normal to wear make-up. Everybody does.'

Her brush darted at a smudge above his eye. Sol blinked and nodded. This was the most she had said to him since his arrival. He had been escorted in by the producer, who had paid him elaborate courtesies before leaving him in the hands of the make-up girl. She had indicated silently the chair in which he should sit. Then she had set to work. He had assumed that she was nervous. She was young enough to know his work from school. It was part of the syllabus in France.

The door behind them opened and a woman looked in. He watched in the mirror as her head turned left and right, then withdrew. She was the third person to have done this. Sol had looked up expectantly each time, but none of them had been Ruth. She would be somewhere in the building now, submitting to this same process in a room identical to this one. The heads popping around her door would be equally indistinguishable. But she would ask them in a Californian twang who they were, or who the hell did they *think* they were?

The paper ruff was pulled away. The girl crumpled it noisily into a ball and tossed it into a corner of the room. How odd her days down here must be, he thought, painting the priests of the over-lit temple upstairs. She would tell her friends of moles and warts, of pustules and acne-pitted skin. Even one's skin had secrets. He had never appeared on television. He had not given an interview in almost twenty years.

'The Americans have a phrase,' said a voice behind him, which then adopted a mock-American accent. ' "You look a real *picture*." '

This time he had not noticed the door opening. A buzz of noise billowed in from the corridor. Slava's face poked its way into the room, grinning nervously.

'Faucher's asking if you'll join him in the Green Room,' he continued. 'Shall we?'

He directed the question as much to the girl as to the man sitting before her. She nodded: all done. Sol straightened his tie.

'No,' he said.

Slava pursed his lips. He had conducted most of the negotiations with Faucher's people, arguing over details in endless telephone calls. Moderssohn had involved himself too. Ruth, on the other side of the Atlantic, had deputed equivalent figures, Sol assumed. But Slava's interest was obscure. Securing Solomon Memel for Faucher's show was a coup of sorts. Slava's stock would rise, as a man who could secure things. As a fixer. That would be Slava's recompense perhaps. People do things for you, thought Sol. But why?

'Everything's settled already,' Sol said. Let's have a cigarette in the corridor. Then we'll go up.' He took a last look in the mirror. His old grey suit. White shirt. Tie. He pushed himself out of the chair.

The girl extended her hand. 'Goodbye Monsieur Memel. Good luck tonight. I read all your work. I wanted to say earlier.'

Smiling, he gave silent thanks that she had not. He took her hand in both of his. Slava hovered, then reached for his cigarettes and offered one to Sol.

'There's a problem,' he told Sol outside. 'Ruth's been delayed.'

Clusters of people passed the two men, each group composed of a single figure cased in a subordinate shell of assistants. The attendants were thin young men and slightly older women, all smartly dressed. Their conversations spilled times and places to which the central figures either nodded or shook their heads, their faces hidden behind pale bronze masks of powder. Identical, Sol saw, to his own. He pulled on his cigarette and raised his eyebrows.

'Her flight got in only forty minutes ago. Faucher thinks it best to start without her. They'll bring her in when they can.'

'She's not in the building? When are we on air?'

But beneath his irritation he felt a strange relief. There were answers he could give more freely with Ruth snug and distant in the plush capsule of her limousine. He thought of her falling in and out of sleep in its velvety calm while it nosed its way through the backstreets. There was something unstoppable about limousines.

'Twenty minutes,' said Slava.

Beams of light descended in columns from the darkness of the studio's roof. A technician bent back his head and shielded his eyes, pointing to the top of a luminous pillar. It wavered obediently then disappeared. Sol followed the man's gaze up.

Black metal lamps hung like bats from gantries high in the cavernous roof. They spread or folded their wings as directed, producing changes in the fall of electric light. Squinting through the glare, Sol made out human shapes clambering in the darkness above. The lights intensified then began to throb.

'There's Max,' said Slava, standing beside him. The man raised his arm in greeting to someone on the far side of the studio.

Hot after-images glowed and floated in Sol's vision. Across the floor he saw the presenter moving in a barrage of drifting flares.

White, yellow, ember-red. They faded and the familiar figure emerged.

He had first known Maximilian Faucher as a little-regarded writer for the cultural pages of *Paris-Soir*. The presenter had been one of the many whose requests for interviews Sol had turned down during the controversy over his first book. Faucher had written his piece on the 'Memel Affair' regardless. Favourable, Sol recalled. That seemed long ago. Now, Max Faucher was better-known than most of his guests. Every Thursday night at eight o'clock, his face stared out from television screens across the country. He wore his hair swept back and would comb it with his fingers while he listened to those who appeared on his show. He bore a great resemblance to an Italian pianist Sol had once seen perform in Vienna and whose name he had never afterwards been able to recall.

Sol had encountered the critic from time to time. Faucher would nod to him at gallery openings or wave across restaurants and stride up to his table. Prompted by Faucher's attention, other diners would glance across, or stare at him, and a gradual recognition would relay itself among the tables: 'It's the poet, the one who . . .' or, if they were younger, 'Don't you remember reading his poem at school?' Someone might quote a line, dredged from a half-forgotten lesson. It was of a piece with the shy students who sometimes approached him in cafés, or the mad ones who turned up on his doorstep, or the mail he received in languages he could not read, page after page, each incomprehensible except for the laboriously transcribed quotations. Who did they think they were writing to, or talking to? He was forty-nine. The lines they quoted had been written half a lifetime ago. The youth who had crawled into the darkness of the cave had emerged a different creature. His life was no longer the life recorded in those lines and he was no longer the man who had written them: the lines which made him the different being he had become. A long time ago, he had killed a man. The man had been dying. But he had killed him.

That would not be mentioned. The 'Memel Affair' would not be mentioned. If asked he would stand up and walk out, Ruth or no Ruth. She was here to make a film of his poem. He was here for her. Not himself.

Sol watched from the far side of the studio as Faucher made

his final preparations. A little world of attendants and assistants revolved about him, dabbing at him, touching his elbow and murmuring in his ear. Clipboards were carried and boxes ticked. One held up a small mirror and Faucher angled his head to left and right. The presenter nodded, satisfied.

A young woman walked over to Slava and himself, introducing herself as the production assistant. She talked over her shoulder to Sol as she led him back across the studio. Cameras were manoeuvred forward on soundless rubber wheels. Thick black cables snaked about the concrete floor, fixed at intervals by crosses of tape. They converged on a pool of light where two chairs confronted each other across a low table. Faucher was already seated. A microphone was being pinned to his lapel. Its wire was threaded carefully through his jacket to emerge behind and be plugged into a squat box bristling with other such plugs and wires. The presenter rose to shake their hands, Slava first, a perfunctory tug, then himself.

'This is a great honour, Monsieur Memel,' said Faucher while technicians busied themselves about Sol. 'Slava here told you that Madame Lackner has been delayed? Entirely our fault. We should have allowed more time. But you are here and, speaking personally, that is the most important thing. For you to break your silence here,' he gestured about the hangar-like studio. 'It is important for us.'

Faucher talked on, easily and fluently. Sol realised that he was being set at his ease. He pushed away the unbidden thought that this was all wrong, that Ruth was not here, that he had no clear idea of anything he wished to say because he had already said too much to another flatterer of his vanity long ago, that he should walk out of this pool of light, this studio. The agreements worked out with Slava would be worth nothing as soon as his face appeared on all those millions of screens. For what was to stop Faucher asking anything he wished?

Then he saw that the technician threading the microphone leads had a battered volume of his work stuffed into the pocket of his jacket and then that, instead of staring at the real god of this controlled world of artificial light and dark, Faucher's acolytes now were discreetly watching himself.

He was described as 'reclusive' in articles about him and

his work. It was untrue. A burst of sound from an invisible monitor broke his chain of thought. Somebody called for the lights to be dimmed. The familiar music started up. Little red lights winked on and off in the darkness surrounding the circle of yellowish light which held them both in place, he and Maximilian Faucher. Someone said, 'Five seconds'. It was too late.

'Eberhardt'. 'Professor Jakob Feuerstein'. One mention of either, walk out. Damn you, Ruth.

The dim light brightened in an accelerated electric dawn. Faucher turned to a point somewhere to Sol's left and began to speak.

'The worst wounds are self-inflicted. What did humanity become between the years 1939 and 1945? I have spoken with many of the greatest artists of our age, here, on this programme, and whether mentioned or unmentioned that has been the question lying behind many of those encounters. What did we do? How could it happen? Tonight I have as my guest the man many believe to be the true custodian of our uncertainty. And of an answer too, buried – perhaps – in the dense imagery and complex argument of his most famous, or most notorious work. In 1951 a poem entitled *Die Keilerjagd*, or *La Chasse au Sanglier*, appeared from an obscure publishing house in Vienna. It had been written in extraordinary circumstances by an unknown poet named Solomon Memel. Based partly on the myth of the hunt for the boar of Kalydon, partly on events which befell him during the war. . . .'

Parsing Faucher was a simple business, Sol thought to himself as the interview unfolded between them. Faucher used 'perhaps' to test the ground upon which he was about to venture. Meeting resistance, he would retreat to 'Can we agree . . . ?' Outright contradiction elicited 'these are difficult matters', and a change of subject. They danced together, more or less in step.

'For many people, *Die Keilerjagd* expresses the tension between what must be done, what should be done and what can be done in face of the fact of evil,' said Faucher to Sol. 'Ordinary people quote snatches of your poem, perhaps without even knowing where they come from. French schoolchildren study it, learn from it. Children in many other countries too.' Faucher let the train of thought peter out. 'Evil inhabits the boar. He is the principal of violence, of licence. Those who hunt him also hunt that. They *want* it, would you say?'

Faucher shaped his questions with his hands before releasing them. He nodded during Sol's responses; the cloth of his suit rucked about his wrists as he brought his fingers together in unconscious mock-prayer. The lights shone down on the two men, who cast no shadows as they mimed and talked. Words fluttered and fell around them.

'The themes of your poetry are universal because they draw on the events of a representative life, which is to say your own life. Representative, I mean, for the mid-twentieth century: loss, then flight, then resistance, then revenge. Your work has been applauded, discredited and restored in a strangely parallel career . . .'

Outside the circle defined by the harsh lights there was only darkness. Sol heard a scuffle of movement and glanced about vainly for the cause. Faucher's next question concerned the final section of the poem. Reichmann's old criticism would be trotted out and he would reply that poetry did not flow transparently through a life. Sometimes the work replaced it.

But what took place in the cave? And what does it mean? They all wanted to know that.

'A distinguished German critic diagnosed a "fatal ambiguity" in the poem's concluding verses, which led to some heated discussion as I recall.'

Sol knew where Faucher was trying to lead him. The 'distinguished German critic' had retracted the charge but Sol did not mention that. He talked about the core of irreducible doubt which resided within even the most careful recollection. Memories were violent from the inside out. People made them up because they had to. He tried to say this simply.

'These are difficult matters,' said Faucher for the second time. 'You have consented to the making of a film. But a film cannot be ambiguous in the ways available to a poem. One must decide to show or not. Many commentators here in Paris were surprised that you agreed to such an adaptation and by a director known for her, shall we say, uncompromising working methods? Your poem ends in darkness – a Stygian darkness, if I may – where the explanatory gestures of the poem's beginning are absent or indecipherable. But how can one film such a darkness?'

These were the questions intended for Ruth, Sol realised. Her film would be a kind of sequel or postscript to the poem, so far as he understood it. It would be set in an unemphasised present day and would continue the emotional narrative of the hunters and their quarry as if they had survived. The mysteries of his poem would be over long before the film's opening frame. Kept safe. He had known Ruth since childhood, he told Faucher, who pretended surprise then talked about hindsight, the ironies of history. The presenter asked a long and intricately qualified question which Sol answered to half-intended comic effect with a simple 'yes'. There was some gossip about the young actress who was to play the Atalanta-Thyella figure. Their time was almost up.

'I would like to end by invoking the moment of this work's conception, the moment when a young man crawled forward into the darkness to meet his adversary. At the same time, a young poet brought to mind the first line of what would later prove his greatest work. And, in the distant past, an uninitiated hunter waited outside the cave in which his quarry waited for him. And yet these were, in a sense, all the same person, in the same moment, and all facing the same enemy.'

All different, Sol thought. I am not the man I was. How could he be the shivering youth of then? Let it go . . . He spoke of how the body registered events in different ways from the mind, and the memory in other ways again. Faucher nodded wisely, thanked him for his thoughts, and it was over.

Thank you thank you thank you thank you.

'. . . when I will be looking at the work of Great Britain's foremost painter in advance of his first complete retrospective, opening next week at the Grand Palais here in Paris. Once again, Solomon Memel, thank you. And goodnight.'

The lights came up and the little theatre dissolved. The cameras were being pulled back, the assistants moving in. Sol leaned back and closed his eyes. The click-clack of a woman's heels brought his head up. The technician was standing over him, holding out his book. His second collection. Autograph. Over the young man's shoulder he saw a tall woman with long copper-red hair emerge from among the studio's shifting bodies. She walked forward, smiling at him through her fatigue.

'Solomon,' she said.

'Ruth,' he replied, rising to embrace her. 'You're here.'

⋆   ⋆   ⋆

On a hot afternoon in the summer of 1938, a young woman waded in a broad and shallow river. She had knotted the thin cloth of her dress above her knees and picked her way forward, peering down into the clear water ahead of her, leaving a trail of wakes which curled in the current then disappeared within its motions before each step. The river flowed over a sandy bed studded with smooth pebbles. Mid-stream, long tongues of bright red river-weed wavered beneath the surface. The young woman was making for these. She was watched by two young men.

Lying on the bank, Sol saw the young woman stoop to pull up a thick cable of the weed, whose colour darkened and seemed to concentrate when she raised her trophy into the sunlight. She disentangled the strands, shaking the water from them. Droplets fell back into the river and disappeared. She draped the fronds about her neck and turned to him, twenty or thirty metres away. He waved as she ran her fingers through her hair, which was long and red, drawing it out between her fingers. Then she turned downstream and shouted to Jakob, who was paddling in the shallows by the far bank.

Sol lay back and closed his eyes. The river flowed beside him, almost silent. The air was still and he might have slept. But three distant shrieks launched themselves into the air and struggled down the valley, thinning in the late afternoon heat. An image of the young woman swathed in red with her dress bunched about her thighs was banished by an ungainly bird which lurched up before his mind's eye, stubby winged and bristling with organ pipes from which spouted shrill columns of steam, *toot, t-t-toot, to-oot.* He raised his head, eyes blinking against the sunlight which glared off the river.

The afternoon train from Lemberg had sounded its whistle, as it did when it neared the village of Sadagora further up the valley. From there it would set off along tracks which curved in grudging imitation of the river's meanders, nearing the water and veering away, before finally crossing the bridge just outside

119

the town's main station. The station lay at the foot of the hill and from there the trolley-car which met the Lemberg train departed promptly to climb the steep incline to the town's centre. The train whistle was the signal for their departure. Sol propped himself on his elbows and shouted across the water.

'Jakob! Ruth! Come on!'

The whistle sounded again, as though emphasising his words. Jakob waded slowly across from the far bank, a pensive crane. Ruth unwound her ragged scarf and threw it into the water, which carried it away.

The town's main station was a twenty minute walk away, along a dusty road which followed the river on the opposite side to the railway. They walked in silence. The route was over-familiar and there was nothing which had not been remarked a hundred times: stands of beech trees, farm outbuildings, the river, the railway track beyond it, the flat fields which stretched away far into the distance to the east.

They heard the slowing chug of the Lemberg train. The station's glass-domed roof came into view. The locomotive billowed smoke and sounded its whistle again, its brakes squealing just before the bridge. They hurried forward and saw the trolley-car's familiar red and white livery beside the goods shed. The driver was walking down the side of the vehicle, fanning himself with his cap. He climbed into the cab and, a few moments later, they heard the gears clank and saw the trolley-car jolt forward. The motion galvanised them into action.

'Come on!'

Ruth threw her arms apart, Sol and Jakob caught her by the hands and they broke into a run. The trolley-car's tracks joined the road a few metres ahead. The young men pulled her between them, dividing to either side of the tracks as the car trundled up the incline then turned into the road. They held Ruth in the vehicle's path as they all sped forward. The trolley-car rumbled behind them, gathering speed.

'No-oo!' Ruth shrieked, mock-exhaustion sending her into a stumbling run. The car sounded its bell. She tried to pull away: from Sol, then from Jakob, but neither would yield. The trolley-car clanked and squealed, drawing nearer. Ruth's face creased in lavish terror, or pleasure. She felt the weight of the car thundering and shuddering. Her heels pounded the stones. How could they let her go? She briefly drew ahead of them, her hands still gripped tight and her skirts flying up above her knees. The conductor shouted from the trolley-car's platform and the bell sounded again, louder now. This time the clangour went on and on.

Jakob released her. Ruth sprang out of the tracks, spinning about and winding her arms around Sol. The tram rumbled past at a disappointing rate, its brakes squealing as it came to a halt in front of the railway station. Jakob rolled his eyes at the other two and trotted after it. Ruth panted and laughed, still held in Sol's arms. She disentangled herself and followed.

The Lemberg train had deposited a small crowd of passengers, who awaited the trolley-car's arrival. They rose from the benches outside the station and shuffled forward, manoeuvring their boxes, parcels and cases inside. Sol, Ruth and Jakob dawdled until the last of these were aboard, then swung themselves up onto the rear platform, where the conductor shook his head at them in disapproval, red-faced under his cap. He was the father of their classmate Gustl Ritter. Jakob spread his hands in apology and all three squeezed into the rearmost seat. Gustl's father rang the bell and they set off.

Their legs stuck to the slats of the bench through their clothes. Ruth clasped her hands and flexed her arms, then yawned and leaned back her head. Her eyes closed. The summer had deepened the red of her hair and raised a crop of freckles around her eyes. Sol and Jakob exchanged glances across her.

The trolley-car's route wound its way gradually up the hill from the station towards the centre of the town. The three of them jostled against each other as the vehicle took the bends. Houses grew up around them, gaining second and third storeys, and the narrowing streets became steeper and steeper until between Uhrmacherstrasse and the Polish church, a stretch known locally as the 'Hump', the car slowed almost to a halt, its motor whining, its wheels grinding in their tracks. They passed a horse and cart whose driver had dismounted to lead them up and now waited to recover his breath, one careful hand resting on the brake. Ruth's hair smelt faintly of the river. It seemed impossible that the trolley-car should pull its own weight up such an incline, let alone its passengers too.

But once past the church the vehicle picked up speed. It stopped outside the local government office, where a group of men dressed in suits and stiffly starched collars got on, then at the corner of Laurinerstrasse. Gustl's father moved back to stand guard on the platform as the seats filled. Sol asked after the man's son and the conductor shook his head in resignation. Gustl had not gained his certificate. They had all taken their final exams six weeks before, in the Gymnasium, whose airless lecture halls now held only chalk dust and heat, a few streets to the east. Ruth smiled and opened her eyes on the pale cream roof of the trolley-car. Butter, she thought, in the cool of a dairy. The car was stifling.

Suddenly the street widened. The town seemed to fill its lungs and blow the heat out of its body as the tram pulled into Ringplatz, where the sudden recession of the buildings sucked passengers from the car, sending them to mingle and join with those already gathered in the square: men in shirtsleeves, men in dark blue aprons, men in brown or black suits, women carrying baskets or infants. Handcarts loaded with boxes or bottles packed in straw emerged from one or other of the streets, trundled across the sunlit space then disappeared into the shade again. Housewives carried meat parcels tied with fine white string and bulging bags of vegetables. The Rathaus cast a slanted block of shadow over the warm cobbles. The square clock tower extended a further jut. It was seven minutes past four. The town's single traffic light went through its colourful cycle, ignored.

'Coffee,' said Jakob.

'Cakes,' said Ruth.

' "Drinking were too much for me!" ' recited Sol ' "This . . ." something "fills me with sparkling water." ' He paused. 'I thought we were going to the park?'

'Afterwards,' said Jakob, unpeeling himself from the seat. He jumped down from the platform and walked towards the café. Sol and Ruth followed.

The Schwarze Adler stood directly opposite the Rathaus. Its ornate façade extended across the north side of the square almost to the corner, where a narrow street continued the line of shopfronts around a corner towards the old grain market. Each summer the tables of the coffee-house spread as the weather grew warmer until they blocked the entrance to this street almost entirely. Each year, the Prefect would write a letter concerning this problem to Auguste Weisz, the café's proprietor, usually in September. The tables would recede obediently, then disappear altogether; by October it was either too cold or too wet to sit outside in any case. Newspapers from Berlin, Munich, Frankfurt, Graz, Budapest, Bucharest and Vienna, together with the town's own *Morgenblatt*, hung from the racks by the entrance, while the café's interior rang with the accents of Romanian, German, Yiddish, Russian and the patois of the villagers who would venture into town once or twice a month and take a drink here as reward for their courage before trudging down through the Hapsburghöhe to rejoin the horses and carts they had left in the charge of their unruly children at the foot of the hill.

Sol scanned the faces at the tables inside. On some mornings his father did business here but in the afternoon it was rare to find him anywhere other than the timber market. Ruth inspected the cakes and pointed first to an éclair, then changed her mind and chose a pastry smothered in bright yellow cream, topped with a single cherry. Jakob asked for a *mélange* and was directed by the waiter's succinct nod to take a seat. They trooped outside and found a table at the edge of the Adler's ill-defined enclave, where they sat in a row, legs stretched out in the sunlight. Cake and coffee arrived for Ruth and Jakob. The waiter glanced at Sol, who shook his head.

'Rilke says nothing about eating,' he said suddenly. 'Not a single line.'

Ruth and Jakob looked up, creamily moustached.

'Why?' he demanded, provoking stares from two well-dressed women at the table next to theirs.

Jakob swallowed and shrugged.

Ruth licked her fingers. 'What?'

At that moment a fragment of cream toppled from the peak of her half-eaten cake, collided with the cherry which she had moved to its lower slopes, and sent both in a tumble to disappear down the front of her dress. She plucked at the neckline and peered down. Sol and Jakob stared.

'Perhaps one of you might ask Herr Weisz for cake-tongs,' she suggested to her attentive companions. 'Why are you talking about Rilke?'

'I'm talking about eating,' said Sol.

Ringplatz grew busier. A swirl of bodies got up momentum around the three of them as men and women strode into the square. A bell sounded in the distance, signalling the trolley-car's return up Siebenbürgerstrasse. Presently it reappeared, spilled its passengers into the crowd, picked up others, and continued on its route back down the hill. The three seated at the Adler's outermost table watched these comings and goings in silence while the shadows of the surrounding buildings inched forward across the square towards them.

'Come on,' said Sol, stretching. 'The park. Let's go and pay our respects.'

Jakob groaned, but rose nonetheless. Ruth hesitated, holding the cherry between thumb and forefinger, as though inspecting it. She had retrieved it by a discreet contortion involving a feigned sneeze. A small boy being led by the hand stared with unabashed fascination at the red fruit, his head swivelling at an angle which grew increasingly impossible with every step. When it seemed the boy's head must come free of his shoulders if it were to twist about any further, Ruth popped the cherry into her mouth. The boy's face registered such outrage that both Sol and Jakob laughed out loud. An instant later both mother and son disappeared into the crowd.

How many are lost? Sol wondered idly, as they edged their way towards the sidestreet. So many faces are seen only once. Where do they all go? The little boy would cross Ringplatz every day for the rest of his life, until the woman grasping his hand turned into his grand-daughter or the world went up in smoke. He turned to Jakob as though to share this thought. 'They disappear!' Jakob would say. 'They leave and never come back. So what?' Or something like that.

Sol said nothing, falling into step with the other two as they rounded the corner into Theaterplatz, part-shadowed and almost deserted except for the tables of the Kaisercafé. Some decades ago, the town's masters had been distant and Austrian. Now they were Romanian and nearer. In keeping with the change of patriotic spirit, the statue of Schiller, which had stood in front of the theatre, had been replaced by one of Mihai Eminescu. The patrons of the Kaisercafé sat quietly at their tables as if waiting for the adjacent building to disgorge an entertainment.

'The indignity,' muttered Sol to the stone figure who was no longer Schiller.

'And the injustice,' added Jakob.

'Who cares?' Ruth complained. 'It's not as if he's been banned.' A year ago, she had sat through the three parts of *Wallenstein* on consecutive evenings in this very theatre. 'Look, there's Lotte and Erich. And Rachel.'

Three waving arms had been raised from amid the tables of the Kaisercafé. Ruth waved back and walked across, turning on her heel after a few paces to make a face at the two of them, who had not moved.

When she was safely distant, Jakob turned to Sol.

'She's in love with you,' he said.

'Or with you,' said Sol.

Jakob shook his head. Both looked up at Eminescu but there was nothing more to remark in the dark bronze features which looked out over the slow comings and goings in Theaterplatz. Ruth was squatting between the chairs of her friends, who leaned forward to catch her words, their tousled heads framing her face. She stood up suddenly, miming bafflement. The two girls laughed.

'They're talking about you,' said Jakob.

'About us,' Sol replied. 'Or you. Or anything.'

He watched the girls huddle together, telling their secrets or guessing those of others. His fellow students were drawn to what he might represent for them. At the same time they held back from him through fear of discovering that he was no different from themselves. Were he to reach out, to Lotte or Liesl or Edith, they would shrink back in puzzlement at his ordinary need for contact, touch, whatever it was that he craved and did not find. He had known Jakob since he was six years old, Ruth since nine. To the others he was untouchable. He had been their champion at the Gymnasium. When, once, he had stood up to ask Herr Zoller how, if it was so crude a language as he maintained, Shakespeare himself had been translated into Yiddish, then he had felt himself propelled forward by all of them: Lotte, Rachel, Erich, Jakob, even Gustl Ritter who was amiable and simple. Even by Ruth. Zoller had made no answer. But there was no mystery. He spent his time in the libraries of the Toynbeehalle and the University. He spoke French, some

English, his mother's German. He puzzled over Latin and Greek, and the Hebrew his father had insisted on from the age of six to fourteen, after which he had rebelled and given it up. He was apart: an unpoetical *poète maudit*. Ruth was threading her way back through the tables.

He wrote late at night or early in the morning, when he could believe that the only waking consciousness in the house was his own, piling up the stubborn lines until the heap would accept no more or collapse. It was some weeks after his last lesson at the Safah-Ivriah Hebrew School when his father had walked into his room and found him staring blankly out at the bare branches of the chestnut which grew behind their apartment. He had glanced at his son's distracted face, then to the page before him and its mass of crossings-out. 'So that's it,' he had said, prying Sol's protective arm from the manuscript. 'That's how you prefer to waste your time.' The remark had not been clarified at the time. But Sol had recalled it a few days later, and understood it then, when it had been purged of all possible ambiguity. After that Sol had told no one what he did, not even Jakob. He watched his friend watching Ruth walk across the square. Everyone had secrets.

'"Here we are, telling the time at home. Speak! Proclaim!"' Ruth called out as she approached. Three quick steps brought her to them. Then, pushing between them, she reached for their hands and pulled them about to follow her.

'"We are here just in time to tell whatever is speakable and proclaim . . . the It!"' Jakob responded from her right.

Sol sighed. The previous winter he had pressed the ungarbled original of this line upon them, repeating it until even these, his most indulgent friends, had rebelled and taken to spouting it back to him in the form of gibberish. He had stormed off in a temper, stamping through this very square, where the words of his uncle David had come back to him, words to the effect that no one else was ever likely to take him as seriously as he took himself and to persist in this was a near-guarantee of unhappiness. He had forgiven Ruth and Jakob, or they had forgiven him, and the game continued intermittently, gradually becoming a private joke between the three of them. He smiled thinly and thought that his nineteenth year had gone on long enough.

Behind Theaterplatz, the town staged one of its unexpected

disappearances. The houses and public buildings gave out and in their place was Schillerpark. A 'Schillerallee' led to parkland which rose gently before them to a ridge marked by a line of chestnuts, still in full leaf. The roots of one, curving up like hawsers to anchor the trunk in its sea of soil, marked out their three places. A crowd of boys was playing football over towards their right, but they seemed too young to cause trouble. Ruth, Sol and Jakob eased themselves into their accustomed seats and leaned back against the trunk. The slope of the hill fell away in front of them and they looked out over the plain to the distant Cecina mountains, whose slopes were a ripple of grey-blue shadow. The sun bore down on the day's remaining light. Sol felt its ebbing warmth on his face. Ruth had closed her eyes but Jakob watched the boys, whose chaotic game pulled them further and further down the slope of the hill. The three of them had been together all summer, as they had the summer before and the one before that. Their days together ended here more often than not.

'You'll spend the rest of your life missing us,' said Jakob. 'When you leave.'

Ruth opened her eyes.

'If I leave,' Sol replied, masking his surprise. They had had this conversation before. Vienna or Paris, Florence or Berlin; distant cities moved among his thoughts, whirling them through orbits which took him far away from here. An imagined future awaited him, somewhere. The three of them would think about their pasts here, but he would be gone, leading the fabulous existence of those who depart never to return.

'I'll be lucky to get as far as Klokucza,' he said.

He met Jakob's eye but his friend turned away in quest of the football players. They had drifted out of sight yet the still air carried their shrill voices and even the thudding of their boots against the ball so perfectly that they seemed closer even than before, a team of noisy ghosts.

'Perhaps it's us who will go and Sol who will be left behind,' ventured Ruth. 'I have a pretend aunt in Venice. We could live on a canal, just you and I, Jakob. And if he does abandon us, we will buy a cottage right here and recite Schiller to each other.' She was in rehearsal with a number of their schoolfriends for a performance of *Die Jungfrau von Orleans*.

'Our neighbours will evict us,' said Jakob.

'Rilke then.'

'They'll throw stones.'

Jakob smiled quickly as he said this. Ruth was leading Jakob out of the gloomy thicket of his thoughts, of some eventual leave-taking, Sol thought.

Here is the time for the Tellable. Here is its home. Speak and proclaim.

There was nothing to tell. There were no secrets behind them then. He did not understand what Ruth was prompting Jakob towards. Perhaps it was a joke against himself. Where was the time for the Tellable? When was that?

'Or worse than stones,' Jakob continued after a pause. He rose to his feet and glanced down at Sol. 'But you'll be long gone by then,' he said in a hard voice. Then he turned without another word and strode back up the slope.

'Jakob!' Ruth called after him. 'Wait Jakob, what are you doing?'

The two of them got to their feet and Sol made as if to go after their friend. Ruth's hand touched his foream.

'There's no point. Not when he's like this.'

'What do you mean "Like this" '? Sol watched Jakob's retreating back as it climbed towards the ridge. Ruth's fingers closed about his wrist. 'Like what?'

'Stay,' she said.

Only the tops of the town's tallest structures showed above the ridge. Sol and Ruth saw Jakob pause before he dropped down the far slope. For a moment his tight jacket and untidy hair were etched among the towers and spires: a giant sinking into a drowned town. The weather vanes of the churches of Saint Maria and Heilige Kreuz swung in slow synchronicity as an easterly breeze blew in. Next to them in the depthless panorama, the clock tower of the Rathaus was a little temple topped by a double-headed eagle. The two of them walked slowly up the slope and the cupolas of the Orthodox Cathedral rose before them, then the spires and buttresses of the Armenian Cathedral. The last step gave them the strange spirals of Saint Nicholas's stubby towers and the very top of the old wooden church it had replaced. The synagogue was behind it, further down the hill, and invisible. The breeze reached them. Far off to their right, the single pennant of the casino in the Volksgarten fluttered into life, then the tricolour flown by the commissioners of the Toynbeehalle, and last of all the swastika which flew above the Deutschehaus. The town glowed in the sunset's powdery light.

'You look like the saddest horse in the world,' said Ruth. He smiled as she nudged him. 'Don't worry about Jakob. Everything will be fine.'

The walk home took him through the southern end of Schillerpark. The rough meadow narrowed between an avenue of poplars and a row of cottages fronted by vegetable plots, until it was no wider than a path. The path became a street and from here Sol had only to turn left, right, then left again to find himself in Masarykgasse and home. But instead of continuing into the street, Sol made for the first line of trees. He could see the old prison ahead, whose dark barred windows had frightened him as a child. Now it appeared no more threatening than the warehouse it had become. Beyond it was the timber market, surrounded by a high brick wall.

Before they had parted, he had asked Ruth if she were coming back to take tea. A casual shake of her head had reminded him that Thursday was a rehearsal day. He should have thought of it earlier. If they had gone directly from Theaterplatz then Jakob would not have stamped off in a sulk. They might have brought Erich along, and Lotte and Rachel. He should have mentioned it as they walked back from the river. Regret must have shown on his face for Ruth had asked him what was wrong. She did not understand; none of them had guessed. His mother's demeanour was quite normal in the company of his friends. At that point he had contemplated asking her outright to miss her rehearsal and come back with him; even if there were just the two of them. He had choked back the impulse. She had run down the slope and he had begun the walk home.

The rear gate to the timber market was left unlocked until sundown, when the clerks who lived in the town's south-west quarter used it as a short-cut home. He might have passed through unchallenged and emerged on Siebenbürgerstrasse. He thought of his mother waiting for him now, sitting by the window overlooking the street. Were her hopes rising or falling while the minutes ticked away?

Go home, he thought. The streets beyond the southern boundary of the park drew him in. Men in threadbare suits or overalls carrying lunch-pails or briefcases walked with him. Their numbers thinned as they were claimed by their homes until he walked alone down the gentle slope of Masarykgasse. A little more than halfway down the street, a light showed from a window on the first floor of an apartment building. He drew a breath and pursed his lips.

His mother opened the door.

'Your father's out. He'll be out till late.'

She had chosen a cotton summer dress printed with tiny blue flowers. Her make-up was light and her hair casually pinned. He glanced into the front parlour. Biscuits and cakes were laid out on the table.

'Out where?' he asked, although he knew the answer. His father was drinking with Petre Walter, who worked as a finisher in the Lupu furniture factory and lived in Flurgasse. They had a plan to emigrate with their families to South America which both knew would never be put into effect but which nevertheless required lengthy discussions two or three times a week. Before that it had been a venture to build a number of workshops with apartments above them on a small plot of land inherited by two brothers who worked in the timber yard. Before that a haulage-brokering scheme, or had the ill-fated partnership with his brother-in-law, Uncle David, intervened?

'Where are they?' asked his mother. 'Where is Ruth?'

'A rehearsal,' he said neutrally. 'She told you.'

'Mondays and Thursdays,' repeated his mother absently. 'Well,' she said, 'we shall have to make do with Jakob, Lotte and who else? Erich? We had a wonderful talk about . . . What was it last time? There was so much more to say.'

She was peering over his shoulder, searching the stairwell for the guests she knew were not there. There would be no continuation of the discussion of 'last time', which was now more than two months in the past.

'You promised me, Sol,' she reproached him. She gestured vaguely towards the kitchen. 'Why do you make me take up my day with preparations and then not bother to bring your friends here for a simple tea? Why?'

He listened to the rising edge in her voice, swallowing the

impulse to deny that he had said any such thing. The saddest horse. What had Ruth meant? His mother's tone grew bitter.

She shook her head and said, 'You make me so tired, Sol. I feel so tired nowadays.'

It was true, as Sol knew. He often returned and found that she had not stirred from her bed but had spent the day staring up, her eyes fixed on the ceiling. There was something wrong with her and it could not be mentioned. Once he had heard her weeping in the front parlour, had gone to her and told her that life could not continue like this. She had smiled sadly at his concern and told him that he must not worry himself. He had taken her hand in his and spoken plainly. They would have to change, all three of them. She nodded, then freed her hand from his and walked across the room to the sideboard where a vase of cut crystal held an arrangement of dried flowers. Then she had carried the vase out into the tiled hallway and dropped it on the floor.

Now she turned her back on him and walked quickly into the kitchen, closing the door behind her. The clank of crockery and the sound of tea being swilled from the pot. It would have been standing, cold, for hours. The stacking of the plates and saucers and the rehanging of the cups. There was silence for a few seconds. Then he heard his mother begin to cry.

He listened, unable to move nearer or further away. He wished neither to stay nor leave.

Vienna. Paris. Berlin.

'So what have you done to her this time?'

He started at the sound of his father's voice. The older man was panting slightly from his climb up the stairs.

'What have you done?' he repeated.

Sol shook his head and turned away.

'Nothing.'

'That's right,' retorted his father. 'Exactly what you've always done.'

*   *   *

Sol passed through the ritual of his expulsion in a lucid daze: handshakes, make-up removal, corridors, lift. Its doors trundled open on distant glass walls in which images men and women slumped on low couches and armchairs watched screens suspended from the ceiling.

'Madame Lackner has had to go on ahead,' Slava said beside him. 'Her people are already at the restaurant. She left her apologies.'

Sol nodded, thinking it unlikely that such a thought would have crossed her mind. But that was the Ruth of thirty years ago, he reminded himself. He looked about the airy spaces of the foyer. People who knew the value of appearing busy were made to do nothing here, their discomfort policed by uniformed security guards and receptionists. As reward they were permitted to swim briefly in the watery globe of the Cyclops' eye. As he had done.

'There is a car waiting,' said Slava. 'The driver has the address.'

The route began and ended in familiar thoroughfares. The riddle of Paris's backstreets connected them. After a grunted greeting, the driver made no attempt at conversation and Sol was left alone with his thoughts. Ruth's absence sharpened the realisation that he had wanted this short car-ride with her. He leaned back and watched the streetlights strobe over the rear window. One of her hands had clutched at him when they embraced; he had felt her nails through the cloth of his jacket and shirt. But then, when she stood back to look into his face, she had appeared perfectly composed. Over the years he had received news of her triumphs and occasional setbacks at irregular intervals: nominations for awards, a contractual quarrel with a studio, a divorce, acrimonious even by Californian norms, a period of silence, re-emergence as a director. Her first three films had not been released in France, but then she had made *Nothing for Nothing* with Paul Sandor and that had been shown everywhere. Sol had thought the star's performance self-obsessed, and the film had troubled him because he had found in it nothing of the Ruth he remembered. *The Blue Dawn* had followed, loathed by the critics and even more successful. Now *Die Keilerjagd*, or whatever she intended to call it.

They were uncoordinated facts. He did not know the life that connected them – Ruth's life in America – any more than she could know of his. They had spoken twice in twenty-five years, both times by telephone. The latest of these conversations had taken place three weeks ago when the negotiations between Moderssohn and the film's producer had reached a deadlock which, it seemed, only a film director and a poet could resolve. They had talked inconsequentially. He had made a weak joke about her accent and Ruth had asked him what he meant. She had inquired about the weather 'in Europe' at that time of year.

Of the earlier conversation, he remembered almost nothing. Even fifteen years later the few lost minutes in which his drunken self had babbled to a woman thousands of miles distant marked a fissure dividing the man who had waited in his apartment for a distant operator to place his call from the different man who had been woken hours later on the floor of the same apartment by the dropped receiver's angry buzz. The fissure recurred in his dreams. Sometimes he leaped over it, but more often he stumbled as he approached and a terrible clumsiness afflicted him. He seemed unable to save himself, or do anything but postpone his eventual tumble over the edge. He fell, but he never reached the bottom. He would wake in the instant before impact, sweating and shaking. He did not know what he had said to her.

The car's suspension sagged and lurched, softly rocking him as the driver swung the heavy machine smoothly around the corners. Soon the name of the restaurant came into view in blue neon letters mounted high on the white façade of a hotel.

Sol recalled Sandor's face from its appearance every six months or so on hoardings all over Paris. The star's exaggerated features rose out of costumes which came to seem increasingly absurd as his fame grew: cowboys, a boxer, soldiers. He remained Paul Sandor and his movies flowed about him, leaving him untouched. In return, he rendered them ridiculous in some way and as his stardom grew the films themselves began to accommodate Sandor's overbearing vitality at the expense of all else. The better his performance, the more shrunken the film. Then, within a single year, his public had deserted him.

The anecdote from the shooting of *Nothing for Nothing* was that Ruth had taken Paul and a small crew to the Arizona desert to film the final scene. Paul's character has lost home, job, wife, children, friends. He runs into the desert, where the script, as Ruth related in syndicated interviews carried in the French press, had called only for his 'final dissolution'.

She had begun with a series of very long shots which shrank Paul to a speck of black in the vastness of the landscape. A second series, taken with a longer lens, had focussed on his face. Paul walks and walks but seems to get no closer. He does not sweat. He seems not to tire. 'He is expressionless because he does not know who he is or what he should do,' Ruth commented later, which her interviewer had understood as a reference to Paul's character rather than to Sandor himself. 'He is undirected at this point, following an unwritten script.'

There had been mechanical problems with the camera, because of the heat. Paul's face was dry because his sweat evaporated. Each time he neared the camera, Ruth had made them load the equipment into the truck and set up another half-mile away. They did this six times. On the seventh, Paul had broken into a run. They had filmed him running from the back of the truck. Then they continued as before.

The critics had spoken of a new urgency in Paul's performance in *Nothing for Nothing*. With the distance between the camera and his character collapsed, a note of appeal had broken through the star's façade of flawless technique. It had always been there, some argued, but implicit and paralysing. It had taken a bolder director to find it and make it explicit: Paul Sandor's simultaneous need and distaste for what he did.

So Ruth had made him run under a burning sun. The concluding images of *Nothing for Nothing* comprised a montage taken from the hours of footage shot that day: Paul's character trying to stand up; stumbling, then rolling down a shallow slope; raising an arm as if warding off a blow; crawling on hands and knees; attempting to haul himself to his feet. The crew had mutinied when Sandor collapsed, loading the semi-conscious actor into the back of the truck and driving him to a hospital in Flagstaff. This was later denied by Ruth and by Sandor himself.

The car stopped.

The brasserie standing opposite the dark edifice of Gare du Nord was well-known to Sol. It had never replaced its white linen tablecloths with paper ones, nor its green leather banquettes with more easily manoeuvrable chairs. Its L-shaped interior hooked an arm back into the depths of the building. Lamps copied from those mounted on the parapets of pont Alexandre III glowed yellow, their light thrown from wall to wall by bevelled mirrors. Similar mirrors cased the square pillars which punctuated the clangorous space. Sol watched himself approach as he entered the brasserie. Suddenly Ruth's face flashed in the periphery of his vision. A freak of the brasserie's decor had projected her forward in a flicker so fleeting that at first Sol could not decide whether he had merely thought of her or seen her. Sol stopped and turned, looking around the mirrored columns and walls for the chance configuration responsible. But the image had gone and he could not recapture it. Ruth, Sandor and whomever else might be dining with them were nowhere in sight.

A bar ran down the side of the first dining-room. Diners waiting for tables and a large group of youngsters in the mufti of American teenagers coexisted there by ignoring each other and talking as loudly as possible. Sol edged his way through, murmuring apologies.

'Monsieur Memel, this is an honour.' The *maître d'hôtel* materialised before him. 'Madame Lackner's party is already here.' The man glided sideways to usher Sol through, casting a glance over the bar area and adjacent tables as he did so, frowning at the youngsters.

The rearmost corner of the brasserie was raised on a low platform and partly screened from the eyes of the other diners by panels of frosted coloured glass. In this gaudy sanctum the party sat about a large round table, already crowded with half-empty bottles of wine. Ruth rose at his approach, edged around the backs of her neighbours' chairs and kissed him briskly on the cheek. Two of the dozen or so men looked up at him incuriously then resumed their conversations. A third regarded him evenly across the table. That was Sandor.

'Rolf, Vittorio, Julian, Peter, François, Erno, Ethan . . .' They looked up and offered quick salutes as Ruth reeled off their names. 'Basically, the crew. And this,' she raised her voice to call them to attention, 'is Solomon Memel, as you all know.'

Sol stood awkwardly in their collective regard. Those nearest him offered greetings which he strained to catch. The noise from the bar behind reached a new pitch. Suddenly a protesting voice rose out of the din at the front of the restaurant.

'Shit,' muttered Ruth. She squeezed past Sol and strode away through the dining-room towards the source of the commotion.

Sol watched her go and when he turned back Sandor had risen from his seat and leaned across the table to offer his hand.

'I'm Paul,' he said. 'I saw you come in. Look.' He pointed to one of the mirrored columns in the dining-room, where the scene at the bar was just visible in miniature: the *maître d'hôtel* gesticulating, a girl pointing her finger at his chest. Ruth appeared beside her and rested a hand on her shoulder.

'Come and sit down. Drink some of this wine.'

One of the crew, Rolf perhaps, was to Sandor's left, waiting impatiently to resume his conversation. Sandor ignored him smoothly.

'Quite a woman, Ruth. You knew each other before the war.'

Sol nodded, reaching for a cigarette. Sandor lit it and declined one for himself. Huge hands, thought Sol. But delicate movements, how they handled the lighter. 'We grew up together,' he said. 'Then we grew apart.'

The two men began to talk while the table bunched and knotted and unravelled itself into different configurations. People came and went. When their numbers were swelled by the late arrival of four Americans (whose connection to the film Sol was unable to fathom) a second table was pressed into service just outside their glass-walled enclave. Men hopped between the two, leaning forward to rest their palms on the white linen, or crouching down between two chairs, heads turning back and forth like spectators at a tennis match. Apparently whatever had drawn Ruth away was continuing. She had yet to return.

Sandor brushed away some breadcrumbs and settled his forearms on the table, addressing himself to the patch of tablecloth between them. He would speak, then glance sideways to Sol, who made a comment or gave a slow nod of agreement. The cocoon of intimacy between them was Sandor's creation, part of his act. Nevertheless Sol's attention wavered and veered from the actor, who perhaps sensed his distraction for it was he who broke off their carefully-shaped exchange.

'Where's Ruth got to anyway?' he asked abruptly, and at that both men stood up to peer over the glass screen.

Ruth was still talking to the *maître d'hôtel*. She rested a hand on his forearm. The man smiled unhappily. The girl from the bar stood behind them, arms folded, a sulky expression on her face.

'What do you think?' Sandor asked Sol.

Heads had turned to look at the actor from all over the dining-room, a fact which he seemed not to notice. His directness caught Sol by surprise.

'I don't follow you,' he said.

'The girl. You know who she is don't you?'

'No, I . . .'

'She's your Atalanta, or Thyella. Lisa Angludet.'

The girl was dressed in faded blue jeans, suede boots and a loose white blouse. She swung a heavy leather coat from one hand as she waited gracelessly for Ruth to take her leave of the mollified *maître d'hôtel*.

'Not mine,' said Sol. The girl looked over at him for a moment, her thick black hair falling to her collar and framing a full mouth and large dark eyes. No bra, he thought. And too young. What did Ruth think she was doing? The real face flashed unbidden before his mind's eye: stronger, less obviously beautiful. The mask of the woman he had known as Thyella, and Atalanta. In twenty-seven languages. Something sank in his memory, too quick to be caught. He knew her from somewhere, had seen her somewhere. Lisa Angludet was all wrong.

'Monsieur?'

She was standing in front of him, one limp hand outstretched. From a magazine article, he thought without conviction. Her lower lip stuck out a little; perhaps the sulky expression was natural.

Ruth said, 'Lisa, this is Monsieur Memel.'

'I know.' She smiled at him, then turned to Ruth and said, 'I have to go. My friends are waiting.' Ruth nodded and kissed the girl on the cheek. The three of them watched her twirl about and weave a path between the tables, dragging the leather coat along the floor behind her.

'She's a real piece of work,' said Sandor, watching her departure.

'She's perfect,' retorted Ruth. 'Sit down. We should talk.'

The film would be shot over seven weeks in an apartment in the Chaillot district overlooking the Seine. Ruth laid out photographs on the tablecloth. From the windows one could see the Eiffel Tower across the river to the left, then directly below and to the right the long artificial island of allée des Cygnes. A barge was moored there. The bridge would be pont de Bir-Hakeim. The apartment was only a few hundred metres upstream from his own, which overlooked the river from the other side. The scenes would be set up to suggest that the apartment was endless, its rooms always leading to other rooms. One of the men who had been introduced earlier now drifted over and explained to Sol how the lighting would lower the ceilings and stretch the apartment horizontally; Paul and Lisa would appear taller and more distant from one another. 'It is a cave of a kind. Like the one in your poem,' he said. 'But it's not possible to film real darkness.' He shrugged apologetically.

The crew began to gather about Ruth, drifting up to the table in ones and twos. Sol felt the conversation slide away from him. And what is 'real darkness', he wondered.

'Lisa will be nervous to begin with. After that, I don't know. I want you to catch that, Vito. I want her at a loss, uncertain.'

'Her face is hard to light,' said the man who had been speaking to Sol. 'Her eyes don't do anything. Paul's face looks best when the light is coming in low and from the side, but then her cheekbones disappear.'

'Most of the early scenes we're sitting or lying down,' said Sandor. He looked at the photos of the apartment. 'Looks like we'll be lit from above, pretty much.'

'I can balance it out, but I can't turn up into down,' said the lighting director. 'I still think we should use lamps.'

'No,' said Ruth. 'It's not possible. When it's overcast, or there's a thick haze, the light here in Paris is close to the mountain light in Greece. There's a lot of very high thin cloud so the light is chalky, very flat. It's a good light for what we want.'

'Greece?' Sol had spoken before he realised. 'When were you . . . I mean, you never told me.' He did not know how to continue.

'Told you?' Ruth turned and regarded him evenly. There was a new note in her voice and, in that moment, Sol felt that she was distant from him, peering down while he fell away. He did not know her at all. Then her expression changed again and she spoke warmly. 'But there's nothing to tell, Sol. The production office sent a couple of cameramen down there to get footage of the locations. What's the matter?'

He shrugged. Their exchange had drawn the attention of everyone at the table.

'The landscape there is incredible,' said Vittorio. 'Especially in the mountains. How the hell did you survive out there?'

'Luck,' said Sol. 'Boots.'

Vittorio smiled.

'We're going to use it as punctuation,' Ruth continued. 'It'll represent their memories, their previous lives. So there'll be sudden openings in the darkness, an expanse of sky or a lake, the mountains. As if the closed world of the cave, the apartment, is broken open and there's the world they've escaped, where they've lived the lives they can't live anymore.'

'It is a most *expressive* landscape,' added Vittorio.

Ruth laughed, 'OK, OK. There's about two hours of footage. You should watch it, Sol.' She looked up. 'Do we have a screening room yet?'

They began discussing the relative merits of different screening rooms and why none of them were suitable, or had not been secured, but Sol could think only about the flatness of Greek light. There was something wrong in what Ruth had said. He tried to think back the twenty-five years to the last time that light had fallen upon him. Something in what she had said troubled him. Something had slipped by him. He looked up quickly and caught Sandor watching him with undisguised curiosity. A smile spread slowly across the actor's face.

'Boots,' he said. 'Luck. There's no such thing as good light. How in hell *did* you survive?'

'You're drunk, Paul,' said Ruth sharply before Sol could think to reply.

Sol held the actor's gaze for a second or two, then looked away.

'I have to go,' he said.

Ruth caught up with him outside.

'Pay no attention to him,' she said.

'He wasn't drunk. He hardly drank all night.'

'I know. Just forget it. It's meaningless. I'm sorry about tonight. We should have met somewhere away from the others. There's too much to say.'

The light from the restaurant silhouetted her and reflected off the wet pavement on which she stood. It must have rained. He could not make out her expression.

'Now is the time for the Tellable,' Sol intoned.

'Then tell me.'

Her face was unreadable. He hesitated before her.

'There's so much . . . Almost thirty years, Ruth.'

'I wrote to you. Different addresses.'

'I never received anything.'

Ruth shrugged. 'Tell me what you think of Lisa.'

'Young,' he said quickly. 'Too pretty.'

'You should see her naked,' replied Ruth. 'It's worse than you can imagine. But she's good with Paul. They'll work well together, when we put them in their cave.'

Sol nodded. She was soothing him. The two of them stood there, thinking of the third who did not. Ruth was right. Tonight was the time to say nothing.

He had thought that she would walk with him and found himself surprised at their parting, although it was he who raised her fingers to his lips and turned away. Why had he thought their meeting again would settle him when their pasts lay parcelled up between them, taped, stamped, containing bulky unwanted gifts. Ruth had never called back after his drunken telephone call. It had not been mentioned when they had next spoken, fifteen years later. Three weeks ago. How did that seem so distant?

He turned left into boulevard de Denain, which led to place de Valencien, a grandly-named crossroad. Traffic penned and released by the lights further up roared past him and continued down rue La Fayette.

The pitch of the traffic noise changed. A convoy of identical trucks was approaching, the old-fashioned kind with high cabs and oversized wheel-arches. Sol watched them draw near. Their headlights smeared the wet asphalt with yellow. He might have been twenty again, standing by the side of the road while his future rolled past him. But he had not recognised it. None of them had, even when the events of the following days had prefigured what was to come with such exemplary candour. Even then they had not understood. They should have taken to their heels, every man, woman and child, all the thousands and tens of thousands and hundreds and millions, all of them scattering over the fields.

The trucks of the convoy passed him and continued on their way, the wet road reflecting and multiplying their tail-lights. The red glows drifted in the darkness as the vehicles retreated. Sol watched until the last had disappeared.

*   *   *

Seven dull thuds shuddered through the town. A thick column of mud-coloured dust rose slowly from behind the railway station, leaned as the breeze caught it, then toppled into the river. The retreating Russians had blown the bridge.

War had been declared the previous autumn but nothing had happened until the following spring, when the Russians had demanded the return of Bessarabia and northern Bukovina. The retreat of the Romanian units from their forward positions to the north and east of the town had prompted the abrupt departure of the town's police force, most of the university faculty and a significant proportion of the civilian population. Within a single week, the early-morning roar of the markets at the far ends of Herrenstrasse and Siebenbürgerstrasse fell to a polite hum, the crush in Ringplatz to an orderly toing and froing, and Gustl Ritter's father found himself presiding over a near-empty trolley-car. A meagre human traffic interrupted the heat-haze of the streets, squares and parks, a subdued remainder who recast themselves as survivors of some enigmatic catastrophe, moving slowly, jostled only by their memories of those who had left.

This strange calm had been broken by the appearance, on the plain of the Prut, of a Soviet armoured battalion. A tank had been deployed in Ringplatz for the first week of the occupation. The armoured unit had been succeeded by a garrison of red-cheeked Ukrainian peasants costumed in brown uniforms and commanded by thin-faced commissars.

Now, more than a year after the arrival of the Russians, Sol, Ruth and Jakob sat outside the Schwarze Adler, neither eating cakes, for there were none, nor drinking coffee, although the liquid in the cups before them still went under that name. Sol watched the surface of the steaming concoction Auguste Weisz served from the elaborate chrome contraption behind his counter. The liquid shivered as the seven explosions went off, the first triggering an answering volley of pigeons from the building opposite, which had been the Rathaus, then the garrison commander's headquarters, and now appeared deserted.

'The railway station?' he wondered aloud.

'The synagogue,' said Ruth.

'The bridge,' said Jakob. 'Retreating armies destroy bridges. Force of habit.' He tilted his cup to confirm that it was empty.

In the third week of the occupation, the university's fleeing professors had been replaced by a mixture of Ukrainians and schoolteachers from the surrounding villagers, whose ignorance Sol had taken pleasure in exposing with abstruse questions. Three times a week, he and his remaining fellow students were herded into the university's largest lecture hall to listen to a catalogue of Tsarist injustices and the reforms achieved under Soviet communism. The course was called 'History' and was compulsory.

Openings and closures had been haphazardly decreed. Thus the medical department, whose faculty had not been replaced, had closed, while the Yiddish Theatre, closed seventeen years before, had reopened. As direct consequences, Jakob had spent the previous year studying Ancient Greek and Botany and Ruth had taken small parts in the dramatised folk tales and Soviet playlets which the Yiddish Theatre's director, Pessach Ehrlich, had been encouraged to stage. Most of her fellow-actors were cutters and seamstresses from the leather-goods factory at Weinberg, which had closed for want of leather. Ehrlich himself had been a dentist's assistant, until the dentist had fled. A Ukrainian company from Lemberg, or Lvov as its citizens insisted, had been installed at the grander establishment in Theaterplatz, where they put on productions of Shakespeare, Racine and Kulish. Ruth and Sol had spent an amusing evening at the Kaisercafé miming to a performance of *Bérénice*, clearly audible from the adjacent theatre. The troupe from Lvov tended to bellow. The town's new overlords had dispatched four thousand of the town's inhabitants to a new life in Siberia and forbidden the remainder to venture outside the town's boundaries. The timber market had closed and Sol's father had found employment in the office of the Municipal Engineer, where his final task before the Russian withdrawal had been to survey the town's bridges.

But the glove-stitchers and saddle-makers of the Weinberg works could not believe in themselves as actors any more than a dentist's assistant could credibly direct them, or an acolyte of Rilke eulogise tractors, thought Sol. Doctors treated people, not plants, and timber-brokers had no business with drafting tables unless it were in supplying the wood to manufacture them. For the past year, those who had remained in the town had worn the vestments of those who had departed. They did not fit and now the seven explosions, one for each of the seven piers of the bridge painstakingly drawn by Sol's father, announced that these awkward garments were to be discarded. What form would their replacements take? An army of empty clothes was marching towards them, wanting only bodies. Six days earlier, Germany had turned on her ally and declared war on the Soviet Union.

'Shall we investigate?' asked Sol. The trolley-car's bell sounded as it proceeded up Siebenbürgerstrasse.

'Tomorrow,' said Jakob, glancing at the clock tower, which held his attention for longer than seemed necessary. The other two looked up. A bare spike protruded from the top of the tower where the two-headed eagle had been mounted.

'Lotte told me that Erich left,' said Ruth. 'Have you seen him?'

'Erich? Impossible!' Sol scoffed.

'The last time I saw him was two weeks ago. He was terrified,' offered Jakob.

It had been obvious for a month that the Russians were preparing to leave. The train had shuttled between the station at the foot of the hill and its invisible counterpart at Lemberg, taking first the possessions of the Soviet officials, then their families and eventually themselves. When the last train had left, the original inhabitants were told by the commander of the remaining garrison that they should prepare for evacuation to safety and a new life in the Ukraine. Then he and his men had left too.

'Well?' demanded Ruth.

Sol shook his head. A community of artisans whose grand-parents had emigrated from Ukraine and who worshipped at the cathedral on Herrenstrasse had supplied a few hundred refugees, the town's known communists rather fewer, but Erich was neither a Ukrainian nor a communist. They had known him since the first day of term at the Meisler Institute, when they were six years old. It was inconceivable that he should have fled with the Russians. Sol said as much.

'Inconceivable, but true,' retorted Jakob. 'Like so many things.'

Sol frowned. The thought that Erich might have taken flight unsettled him in a way that the more obvious signs of the town's abandonment had not. Erich had been quiet, prone to embarassment, a passable violinist.

'How could he leave without a word to anyone?' Ruth appealed to Jakob.

'If he really has gone,' added Sol. 'Remember when he ran away and hid in the lifeguard's hut? He stayed away three nights.'

'Erich isn't twelve anymore,' Jakob said flatly, 'and he's not hiding in a hut by the swimming pool. He's gone and we don't know why, and that's that.'

Ruth looked down at her lap. Sol felt his temper rise. He and Jakob had argued more frequently over the past year. Now there were grudges between them, trivial disagreements which had been left too long and were beyond resolution. Through his irritation, Sol wondered if this spat were destined to become another. There was no middle ground between what was known and what was not, according to the Book of Jakob. There was no room for doubt. Erich was simply 'gone'. *And that's that.*

And Jakob was wrong, he thought. Erich existed. He was out there, somewhere. Erich's life continued, whether known to them or not, a flickering in the periphery of their vision, a reference to a lost source.

But Jakob would have no truck with any of that. The three friends had collided that summer, rebounded, then collided again. And there was a new element in their relations, a gritty particle which had worked its way between them leaving tell-tale scratches. Jakob had not deciphered those marks.

'How would you know?' Sol burst out in response. He would have said more but Ruth had risen, the legs of her chair scraping over the stones and the sound echoing off the wall of the Rathaus, breaking the near-silence in Ringplatz. Startled, Sol and Jakob looked up but she was already striding away, almost running with her skirt swishing angrily from side to side. She rounded the corner and was gone before either of them could summon the presence of mind to call out.

'Damn,' said Jakob softly to himself. Then, with obscure authority as Sol half-rose to go after her, 'No, leave her be.'

Sol relapsed into his chair, pondering whether he did so in deference to Jakob, or to Ruth's mood, or to the strange lassitude which the hot afternoons brought to the town, when humid air collected in the streets and pressed against the walls of the buildings. Later he would remember Jakob's furious departure from Schillerpark. That was now almost two years in the past: the year of Soviet occupation and the year of waiting which had preceded it. Then, Ruth had stayed his pursuit with the same phrase. Now he stared at his feet and wished he had not spoken. It would have been simple to hold his tongue. He had no doubt that Ruth's anger was directed at himself. An uncomfortable silence descended on the two of them.

'What are we going to do, Sol?' Jakob asked after a minute or more. His voice was level and his eyes unblinking as they sought Sol's own. 'What are we all going to do?'

He was jealous, thought Sol. The suspicion scuttled into his head and clung there. Jakob held his gaze for a second longer than seemed natural. Jakob was jealous because he *knew*.

'I . . .' Sol began to say, then thought better of it.

'What?' Jakob prompted, more quietly than before. 'What do you want to tell me?'

It had happened three months earlier. Ruth had been appearing in her third production at the Yiddish theatre. Ehrlich had adapted a number of folk-tales and linked them to suggest a progress from rural poverty to collectivised and mechanised emancipation. The production grew implausible as dibbuks and trolls strove to recast themselves as landowners and other counter-revolutionary elements. Ruth played an array of erring daughters, and two ill-defined 'hags' for Ehrlich's adaptation necessitated a certain amount of doubling-up among the members of his inexpert troupe. The costume changes had produced chaos backstage, where the hissing of the audience had almost been drowned out by the dresser's cursing of the actors, who would mislay hats, lose boots, or tear buttons off their costumes in an attempt to solve the arithmetical conundrum of seven actors divided between eighteen parts.

Ruth had banned both Sol and Jakob from attending, offering in recompense detailed accounts of the production's nightly disasters. More often than not, one or the other or both of them would meet her afterwards at the stage door from where they would walk with her the short distance to her home while she related that night's catalogue of disasters, extending the route as necessary to accommodate explanation of their absurdity in full. But it had been Sol alone who had been waiting for her three months ago. The two of them had found themselves in the alley running behind Flurgasse, both of them laughing so hard that they had had to stop walking and prop their hands on their knees to recover their breath. They had risen slowly and fallen silent, their faces flushed.

'I. . . .'

But he thought afterward that he had not even managed that single syllable. He had wanted to speak. Everything was clear for an instant as their months of cautious circling spiralled in to the inevitability of what followed. Ruth's urgency had startled and silenced him. She had pushed him up against the fence, parted his lips with her fingers and kissed him without inhibition.

'What is it?' Jakob asked again. He appeared puzzled.

'Nothing,' said Sol. 'Ruth's nervous. We shouldn't forget that.' The sentence sounded ridiculous in his ears.

'And you, Sol?' Jakob asked without a hint of challenge, the solicitude on his face catching Sol by surprise and disarming him so that all he could muster in reply was a forced smile as he said, 'Now is *not* the time.'

He pushed his chair back and stretched. He was rising to his feet when Jakob spoke again.

'Forgive me.'

Sol thought that he must have misheard. He stood there, at a loss how to respond. At that moment Auguste Weisz emerged from the café but, perhaps sensing the oddity of the exchange, paused in the doorway and did not approach. Jakob seemed wholly absorbed in the stained rim of his coffee cup.

'There's nothing to forgive,' blurted Sol.

Jakob nodded without looking up.

Quickly, he had thought in the alley. Ruth had pressed her body against him. He had nuzzled her neck, one of his hands reaching for her under her skirt. She had pushed harder, at once denying him and clamping him in place. Everything was suddenly a flurry of hot breath, the awkwardness of their clothes and the scent of one another mixed together. He had felt her shudder. Then she had softened in his arms and hung there for a second or two, one hand hooked over his shoulder, the other clutching him below his ribs. He would find the marks of her nails there later when he undressed. Then she had exhaled, or sighed, and her own breath had seemed to blow her away from him.

'Never tell him.'

Those had been her first words. She had meant Jakob, of course. He had nodded stupidly, wanting her and thinking that perhaps his agreement would be the price of her continuing.

'Promise me,' she said. 'It would kill him if he knew.'

He had reached for her, grinning at her melodrama. But she had jumped back.

'Promise!'

'I promise.' He smiled more broadly. 'But we make such a good pair of rivals. Especially over you.'

He had thought she would smile, or at least acknowledge the compliment. Instead she had stared at him in amazement.

'Is *that* what you think?'

Her hand flew to her mouth. She had turned on her heel and fled. Her reaction baffled him so completely that he stood rooted to the spot for some seconds before shouting after her, 'Wait! Ruth! Of course I promise.'

What else should he have thought?

They had not spoken of it afterward, he reflected as he left Jakob sitting outside the café and walked through Getreideplatz. And the episode had never been repeated. He was left with a memory which now hung between the three of them, albeit unbeknown to one. Perhaps it had in part prompted the trio's drift into the ambit of their fellow students, the turbulent frothing of whose passions flowed over all three and masked the rifts widening between them. It was easier not to be alone. But they felt this as a renewed interest in their peers rather than as a disenchantment with each other, so that, arriving at the bridge two days later to confirm for themselves what the whole town already knew and finding a group of their friends bathing there, all three experienced and concealed a faint sense of relief. Today at least they would be excused the performance of the intricate dance which they performed only for one another's benefit. When they reached the river-bank, Ruth pulled her skirt up above her knees and waded into the water. Sol and Jakob followed. Her abrupt departure two days before had not been mentioned by any of them.

The water rushed in a glittering sheet interrupted by sandbars and little reefs of pebbles where a few sparse tufts of long grass had taken root. A channel near the far bank flowed slower and was deep enough to swim in. As they approached, Sol picked out the heads of Lotte, Rachel, then Chaim Fingerhut and his sister Lia. Four or five others were lying on the bank, seemingly asleep.

The water flowed around their legs then whorled away downstream towards the stumps of the bridge's piers. A solitary arch had survived the dynamiting and stood midstream to commemorate the triumph of its continued existence. The rest lay in the water, the debris forming an irregular weir.

'The troika approaches! All hands on deck!' shouted Axel Federmann, and the heads of the swimmers turned. Ruth waved. Lotte waved back and sank. The three walked a little way further upstream, trying and failing to keep to the shallows. They were soaked almost to the waist when they clambered ashore, Sol offering his hand to Ruth, who had decided, midstream, to adopt the gait of a decrepit old woman in obscure allusion to one of Ehrlich's productions.

'Oy, how heavy is my back! And how my firewood aches.'

'She's trying to amuse us,' said Jakob to Sol from behind her.

Sol considered releasing her hand to let her fall, with an amazed expression, backward into the water.

'Thank you,' she said, when he did not. She looked back for Jakob, who made the bank in a single stride.

The swimmers were drying themselves when they reached the little group. They had brought blankets and bottles of water. Lia was cutting slices from a loaf of white bread, watched by her brother and Axel.

'A truck arrived from Iaşi this morning,' offered Lia Fingerhut in explanation of the bread. 'It had newspapers, too. *Berlin* newspapers.'

'How did it get through?' asked Sol. 'Newspapers? Did you. . . .'

'All gone by the time I got there.' She passed him a slice. 'Eat.'

The road was open again. Over the past days, those who had fled at the Russians' approach had begun to reappear. They drifted in from the outlying villages to the south, or towns where they had billetted themselves on relatives. Houses throughout the town had been discreetly reoccupied, tools borrowed, repairs begun. Ghostly figures could be spied in the recesses of shops which had been closed throughout the year of the occupation. They wore aprons or long cotton coats and moved slowly around the shelves with pencils tucked behind their ears which they would remove to scrawl figures on their inventories. The returnees delivered themselves to the town they had abandoned, bringing with them canned foods, candles and rumours that Von Rundstedt's army was no more than two day's march behind them and would most likely be in Moscow by December.

'I haven't got a swimming costume,' Ruth appealed to the company.

'Borrow mine,' offered Lotte.

The two of them moved back into the bushes to change.

Sol sat down on the grass next to Chaim and Lia, who asked him if he was going to swim too. He shook his head. Jakob had removed his shoes and socks, clambered back down the bank and was soon wading down towards the bridge, seemingly oblivious to the soaking of his clothes. Ruth scampered past and jumped in, narrowly missing Rachel. Lia followed her and the three girls allowed themselves to drift downstream, only their heads bobbing above the water. Sol lay back and closed his eyes. The morning sun was strong; it would burn the bridge of his nose. He listened to the sound of the shallow water racing around the rocks and shoals, the noise receding of the girls.

'You heard about Erich?' It was Axel's voice.

'Is it true?' He kept his eyes closed, thankful that Jakob was not here.

'I couldn't believe it.'

'He panicked.' That was Chaim. 'I spoke to him a week ago. All he could talk about was his uncle in Berlin.'

'The one who died?'

'The other one. He'd written. Erich showed me the letter. It was very odd. Written from hospital.'

'What did it say?' Sol demanded. He roused himself and sat up.

Chaim made a dismissive gesture. 'It was mad. Just raving.'

'Hey! Look over there!' Axel interrupted, pointing to the far bank.

Half a dozen men wearing suits had gathered by the bridge. Two carried clipboards on which they were writing busily. Another pointed to each of the piers in turn, turning back and forth to address the group. They wore their hats pushed back and used their hands to shield their eyes from the glare.

'Has our mayor has seen fit to return?' wondered Chaim aloud. 'That's Popovici, there in the middle, isn't it?'

Axel nodded slowly, but Sol's attention was drawn by a different encounter. Framed within the the bridge's one surviving arch and silhouetted against the sunlight beyond, two figures were arguing. Sol could not hear what they said but their gestures were expressive: stabbing forefingers and jutting chins. The man – Jakob – stood with his back to the wall, shaking his head while the woman harangued him. The woman was Ruth. Dressed only in Lotte's costume and etched in black against the sunlight, she appeared naked. Suddenly Jakob raised his hand and Sol thought for a moment that he would strike Ruth. But his hand chopped the air, once, twice. Then he turned away from her and strode out into the light.

'If Popovici's back the Germans won't be far behind,' said Axel.

Sol nodded. Ruth was standing in the middle of the arch, staring after Jakob. She seemed to be calling him, but if this were so he gave no sign of having heard. Sol frowned and turned back to Axel. Axel had no more to say.

'What are you all talking about?' Lotte had appeared behind them.

Sol saw Chaim shake his head almost imperceptibly.

'Nothing,' he said.

It was late afternoon before they folded the blankets, picked up their belongings and waded in single file back across the river. An overgrown meadow led up to the road, which led in turn to the station from where they would ride the trolley-car back into town. They walked in damp skirts and trousers and the buoyant mood they had sustained among themselves through the afternoon grew more sombre. When they reached the deserted railway station they threw themselves down on the benches outside, all except Sol who paced about, looking up the hill to Springbrun Platz where the trolley-car would appear before making its way down the last part of the hill.

As he dawdled in front of the others he thought back to the scene he had witnessed under the bridge. Ruth and Jakob sat together, but in silence. They gave no clue as to the cause of their quarrel. All had seemed well that morning: what had happened since? It was his own exclusion, of course, which unsettled him. All three of them had secrets: he and Ruth, himself and Jakob. Now Jakob and Ruth.

Half an hour passed before they realised that the trolley-car was not going to turn up. Reluctantly, they hauled themselves upright and began the climb up the hill into town. They were silent now.

Lia and Chaim Fingerhut bade their farewells at Uhrmacherstrasse. A little further on, some of the others turned off at the old riding school by the Heilige Kreuz church. Lotte, Rachel, Axel, Ruth, Jakob and Sol continued up the steepening slope towards Ringplatz. A few people peered down at them from the balconies of the houses lining the route but the only person they passed in the street was a tiny old woman whom none of them recognised. She looked at them as if they were mad then hurried off down a sidestreet.

'What is going on?' asked Axel. No one replied.

They found the driverless trolley-bus parked in Ringplatz. Gustl Ritter's father was nowhere to be seen. Jakob shrugged and looked about the square, which at this hour and in the last few days had begun to host the same homeward-bound crowds as a year ago. Today it was almost deserted. Only the tables outside the Schwarze Adler were well-patronised, almost half of them taken by a large group of young men.

The six of them walked over. When they had almost reached the outermost tables, Sol grasped the nearest elbow, which belonged to Jakob. The little group came to a confused halt.

The seated men watched them impassively. Their uniforms

were so varied and filthy that they were barely recognisable as such. Only the insignia sewn onto either the arm or the breast pocket of their faded green shirts identified them.

'What is it? What's wrong?' asked Lotte.

'We should go somewhere else,' said Axel.

'The Kaiser?' suggested Rachel.

'Home,' said Axel.

Sol turned and caught Jakob staring at him. There was a strange expression on his face, of resignation mingled with something else. Resentment perhaps. There was no time to ponder it. They shuffled back and crossed the square.

Lotte was still pestering Axel as they rounded the corner. 'What's wrong? Why won't you tell me?'

'They were Iron Guard, Lotte.' Rachel's voice was flat.

The others all lived to the east of Herrengasse. They parted company and Sol took off alone down a passageway which led between yards guarded by high brick walls and overlooked by the backs of tall houses. It was almost dusk but none of them showed lights. He reached Schillerpark and the chestnuts bent their huge leafy heads as though murmuring to him and then listening for his response. There was no one about. He decided to cut through the timber market, which had reopened some days before in anticipation of the German arrival. A back door was usually left unlocked and was guarded only by a nightwatchman, an old man named Hirsch, whom Sol had known since childhood. Hirsch waved as Sol poked his head through the door.

'Solomon, your father was here earlier. Have you seen him?'

Sol shook his head. As a child he had visited the market once a week at least but now he almost never came here. He could not imagine why his father should wish to either. No consignment having been delivered since the departure of the Soviets, there was nothing to broker.

'What did he want?'

The old man shrugged. 'What do you want?'

This end of the yard was occupied by rows of open-sided sheds in which rough-sawn planks were stacked in tiers to season. The air moved slowly through the wood, drawing out the sap, whose faint, bitter smell hung about the yard. Initials stencilled in red paint identified the timber's owners: BvC, BHvC, SLvR. He recalled his father returning once from work with an off-cut salvaged from the mountain of scraps piled up in the south-west corner. He had shown Sol a faded double-eagle beneath which device the letters K-K Ö-U R were just legible. Sol had spelt them out and his father had expanded the initials into the sonorous imperial words: Kaiserliche-Königliche Österreichische-Ungarische Reich.

Other initials, scrawled in yellow wax crayon, were less sonorous. They denoted the brokers who at one time had constituted a floating population of honorary uncles to the infant Sol. HT was Hermann Tischmann who carried sugar-candy in his pockets and used to slip pieces to the boy on his visits to the yard. MW was any one of three Martin Walzes, son, father and grandfather, all trading under the same name and settling each other's accounts. The distinctive A•D•I W had once signified Abraham Wasserstein and his sons David and Isaac, now the sons alone, who were roundly disliked. Sol remembered their father as a huge, devout, terrifying man who had pinched his cheeks and asked if he could recite his 'verses' yet, which being seven years old he could not. He recalled, with a twinge of guilt, his strong sense of relief at the news of Abraham Wasserstein's death. But by then he had not seen the man in years, having stopped coming to the timber market in his mid teens, when, in fact, he had stopped going anywhere his father was likely to be found.

Hirsch had retreated to the cabin by the door. What *did* he, Solomon Memel, want with this place now, on this particular evening? It was almost dark, the broad street beyond the far wall was silent. He should be home. The next shed along was stacked with thinner planks, which having lain here through the winter were now split and warped. The broker's initials were faded and carelessly formed, almost illegible. Sol saw hastiness and ill-temper, and deciphered the letters all too easily. LM signified Leopold Memel.

He had been almost fifteen. Thinking back, he supposed he had begun to spend less time with his father even before their mutual bafflement had turned to antipathy. Perhaps that alone had provoked the events which had followed. His father had dismissed the more outlandish escapades of his son's youth with a tolerant wave of his hand. He might even have taken pride in them. Sol pictured the man standing here in the timber market, slapping his friends on the back, all of them talking over one another and pouring schnapps into their coffee. How would they react to the admission that Leo Memel's son spent his days hunched over a table scribbling verses? It had been three weeks before his birthday. An early present from Papa. He wondered if they had known somehow and teased the broker they had worked alongside for two decades or more. They had been living in Wassilkogasse then, in a cramped apartment in a broad street lined with chestnut trees. His father had built his bonfire in the garden behind the apartment building. Sol remembered walking home from school and somehow knowing what had happened even before he entering the apartment. The smell of smoke was still hanging in the air. So that's how you waste your time.

Something must have triggered the act, he thought now. But what? He turned away and walked towards the machine shops at the eastern end of the yard. They had been plundered by the Russians, who had left behind an assortment of now-useless workshop furniture: empty racks, trestles, work-benches, store-chests. Sol pulled out something that looked like a low crudely-made table and sat on it. Through the railings of the main gate he watched two men hurry past on the far side of Siebenbürgerstrasse, heading into town. Within himself, he could not settle. The presence of the uniformed men at the Schwarze Adler had shaken him, their blank fatigue and the incurious way their eyes had tracked the progress across the square of their little band. Lotte's strained voice echoed in his memory. But the Iron Guard was nothing new, after all. There had been a faction in the town for years, led by a mathematics teacher. Once a month they would conduct noisy meetings in the Deutsche Haus then drink themselves insensible in a café on Mühlegasse called Die Fahne. Would the young men sitting in Ringplatz be content with cheap plum brandy? Or were they thirsty for more than that?

Perhaps Jakob had understood. His friend's strange expression on parting might have meant nothing more than that. And yet the scene he had witnessed beneath the bridge came back to him: Jakob's flailing arms and a seemingly naked Ruth being clothed once again as she walked out into the light after him. Appealing to him? Berating him? They had been arguing and yet they had reached an agreement to conceal it from him. Arguing over himself? Over something best kept from him?

Home, he told himself. Go home.

The beech-scented night air settled around him. In a few more moments he would have risen and made his way back past Hirsch's shed, out into the Schillerpark, along Rutschstrasse to the turning which led to Masarykgasse. His mother would have lit the oil-lamps an hour ago and would be inventing excuses why she should delay supper for just another few minutes, until her son should return. In just a few moments.

But then the silence was broken.

It began as the faintest of hums, at the very limit of his hearing. He raised his head and strained to identify the sound. At first it seemed perfectly even. Then as the noise gained in volume it began to break up and soon enough he recognised the throbbing as the sound of an engine. Then several engines, and then many more than several.

He rose and walked forward, reaching the gate as the first vehicle rumbled past. A convoy of trucks stretched the length of the road, each one illuminated in the lights of the one behind. Their engines thundered and growled, gears crunched and their wheels, each one almost shoulder-high, raised clouds of dust from the road. Canvas tarpaulins covered the roofs and sides but the backs were open and, as each passed, Sol saw the weary faces of the soldiers peering out, helmets off and rifles propped between their legs. They looked like captives while the trucks seemed endless and unstoppable, masterless beasts. Their yellow eyes dazzled him as each cab loomed suddenly out of a concentrated darkness. He stood passively, transfixed, successively washed in light then plunged into darkness. He felt a vast airy weight rise off his shoulders and float away into the night. The waiting was over and whatever would happen next had begun.

*　　*　　*

How was he here?

A gust of wind scudded over the concrete paving in front of the Grand Palais and slapped against the banner stretched across the building's façade. A workman standing on a low tower of scaffolding was struggling to tie down the last corner. Sol watched from across the road as the man reached for the guy-line. The wind was too quick, snatching the light rope away. His arm remained raised in frozen salute as the line whipped about out of reach. Floodlights bathed the workman in their harsh white glare and reflected off the banner's shiny plastic surface. Sol turned up the collar of his coat.

The deepest black imaginable radiated only cold. This was that, Sol thought, looking up at the magnified image. An ember had fallen down a well, its glow adrift, wreathing it in fading heat. The picture's focus was a disappearance, framed by shadowy images which suggested entrails or sides of meat hung from hooks. It was unclear, and properly so. Besides, thought Sol, meat had no particular shape. *Fleisch*. German understood such matters well. French concerned itself with cuts. A further image hid behind the evidence of his eyes, which now saw vaguely-realised columns framing nothing, a flapping shriek of ego daubed in darkening reds on a plasticised tarpaulin. Blood blackened, bodies gaped and one's eyes could lie. The cavity of a carcass? The wind nudged a reluctant ripple across the image and the fabric crackled dully. He imagined he had seen this painting before, but it was impossible.

He had walked down rue La Fayette as far as the Opera House. From there, he had taken to the sidestreets. Place de la Concorde was a waste of wind and traffic, the river a dark channel of silence. He overlooked it from the embankment while cars whined past to his right. An empty *bateau mouche* had slid by. He stood opposite the gallery. Faucher had mentioned the painter's name. The exhibition was to open tomorrow.

He was meant to recall a memory. That was what the painter sought from him; the painting existed for that to happen. Its recessions and dissolves were a kind of mimicry, evoking a generic texture, as if all remembered pasts shared a single sensation. As if memory had a particular shape in mind when it scraped and scrabbled among one's bones. Look at all this glistening flesh! What skeleton should it clothe? The bodies Sol remembered had belonged to his fellow-passengers aboard a Métro train.

He had boarded at Gare de l'Est. A hot late-summer afternoon.

At every stop the carriage gulped humid air from the platforms, then held its breath until the next: République, Oberkampf, Richard-Lenoir. At Bréguet-Sabin the last seats had been taken and those joining the train thereafter had been forced to stand. The two businessmen must have joined the train before then. They had been sitting a little way down the carriage. Every time the train lurched the standing passengers had swayed and momentarily parted so he had caught glimpses of them: dressed in grey suits, one asleep or unconscious, the other red-faced, his tie undone, fanning himself with a sheaf of papers. He had assumed that they were together. A young woman had been among those standing nearest to him, wearing knee-boots, a short skirt and a suede coat trimmed with yellowing fleece, too warm for the time of year. She pouted sulkily, although he would later ask himself how exactly he had arrived at that assumption. She was one of the new young, neither children nor properly adults. They had sprung into existence over the previous year; or perhaps he had failed to notice them before that, the young unkempt men and beautiful women. Sol had amused himself by watching the other passengers' reactions to her, which were complicated and perhaps hypocritical. It was apparent that, beneath her near-transparent blouse, she was naked.

A young workman with untidy black hair got on at Bastille, took one disbelieving look and blushed. He stood rooted to the spot beside her, alternately examining the ceiling of the carriage, the scuffs on his boots and the two men in suits who occupied seats in the next section of the carriage. The head of the sleeping man now rested on the shoulder of his red-faced neighbour, where it rocked according to the motions of the train. The neighbour nudged him but this had no effect. Sol realised that the sleeping man must be drunk and he watched curiously to see how the situation would develop.

As the train neared the end of the tunnel, the drunk made a chuckling sound in his sleep, surprisingly loud, as though mucus was bubbling in his throat. A smartly-dressed woman sitting across from him grimaced. But then Sol had been distracted. The train was approaching a point for which he waited with childish anticipation every time he travelled this line. He would not have let himself be distracted by prudish women or the drunks who offended them, even those wearing business suits.

Shortly after Quai de la Rapée the train emerged from the darkness of the tunnel and seemed to launch itself into space. The carriage's dingy light was suddenly washed away in a flood of sunlight and Sol found himself in mid-air, high above the river, the train curving left then right like a roller-coaster. He twisted in his seat to peer down at the water ten or twenty metres below while the wheels clattered over the ironwork of the bridge.

When he turned back he saw that the red-faced man had stopped fanning himself. Now his face was pale. But of course he had seen a hundred different details. The next stop was Austerlitz. People were shuffling towards the doors, as they always did, elbowing politely for position. They had local trains to catch to Dourdan and Saint Martin d'Etampes, mainline ones to Clermont-Ferrand or even Toulouse. It had been a Friday.

The workman had tired of staring at his boots and, still anxious not to be seen staring at the girl's breasts (was it Sol's imagination which had her thrust them out towards the workman?), had chosen the drunk as the new focus of his attention. But the drunk included the red-faced man next to him. Observation of one necessarily involved the other. As the train shot over the river, Sol saw the young workman swivel around and bend his head as if transfixed by something on the floor. The young woman did not react, but Sol looked for whatever had prompted this odd manoeuvre.

Something was wrong. The red-faced man was no longer red-faced, but pale. He seemed to be in the grip of a convulsion. He bent forward as though to rise to his feet, shrugging off the head of the drunk. But as Sol watched, he slumped back into his seat and the drunk's head fell back against his shoulder. He sat rigidly, enduring this unwanted contact while the remaining colour drained from his face. Now his face was ashen. The woman opposite him had noticed but seemed unwilling to offer assistance. An elderly couple exchanged glances and looked down at their laps. Some of those waiting to get off must have noticed the man's discomfort but now the train was pulling into the station. In a few moments they would be able to pull on the handles and the doors would spring open, releasing them from obligation. The girl was facing away from Sol; he could not see if she was aware of the man's distress or not. Suddenly he clutched his stomach and this time his face screwed up in pain. His drunk neighbour lolled in sympathy. Sol watched discreetly as the sightlines of those nearest wove a fabulous net. They peered out of windows, read advertisements, searched for things in their pockets. Escape from us, they urged the sick man. The drunk's head bounced against the other man's shoulder; the polite fiction that the drunk would wake, would prove to be an associate of the sick man, and thus responsible for him, was tacitly sustained. He would have to deteriorate further before anyone would help him. Sol felt a surge of curiosity. The woman seated opposite kept glancing up at the passengers crowding around the door. She was waiting for one of them to act. But the train was slowing, blurred faces resolving into passengers waiting on the platform. The elderly couple seemed engaged in private prayer. Perhaps they were waiting for the girl to intervene (Sol wished he could have seen her face), or the workman, or even himself. But no one moved. Sol's assumption was that the businessman was having a heart attack.

Then the brakes squealed, the train halted and, as the passengers poured out, the sick man tried to stand.

He heaved himself up by the rail nearest the door then half-swung, half-fell out onto the platform. Suddenly unsupported, the drunk toppled to the floor. Sol rose and hurried out onto the platform.

But the sick man had fallen among the commuters crowding around the doors and, spurred so emphatically into action, they closed about him, calling for doctors and station-attendants and the police. Then, just as suddenly, they sprang back. The man had retched. He knelt on all fours with a filament of spittle dangling from his mouth. Someone offered a tissue. An official trotted up and began to coax the man to his feet, telling the onlookers to stand back, that the train was about to depart. The businessman was muttering apologies and explanations, now anxious only to be away.

Of course he was, Sol would reflect later. Then, however, he saw only that the drunk still lay on the floor of the carriage. The official, who might have been expected to pull him off the train, had disappeared with the sick man. The passengers entering were left to step over the prone figure. A man in blue overalls reached down to shake him awake, but he was holding up the flow and those behind forced him inside. The doors slammed shut.

Standing a little way up the platform, Sol watched the train begin to move off. Then he understood, as he should have done when the 'drunk' had fallen to the floor, or perhaps when he had seemed to chuckle to himself.

But the sick and the drunk were among those whose public signals were to be ignored. They had committed the offence of obligation. The 'sick' man had understood this and had relied upon it. The 'drunk' had been beyond understanding. The train had imparted its own motion to the body whose head had rested on the sick man's shoulder. Of course, Sol realised then, the 'sick' man had known much earlier, perhaps all along. He had decided to choke down his nausea and continue his journey regardless. After all, he must have calculated, the 'drunk' whose presence he had endured, his body pressed against his own, had not looked like a corpse.

Sol never knew what sign alerted the passengers remaining in the carriage. The signals of the dead, he thought later, were as liable to be ignored as the signals of the drunk. Almost as soon as the train began to move, the well-dressed woman looked down at where the man lay, invisible to Sol. Her expression changed quickly from distaste, to bewilderment, and then to recognition. She rose from her seat, her mouth opening and closing. The elderly man shielded his wife's eyes. Others stared. The windows rolled past like frames in a film, each one more frenetic than the last. Sol saw the young workman lunge; he was reaching for someone. The girl, he decided – it could only have been the girl. But she had moved down the carriage. How had he and the workman both failed to notice that? The train was gathering speed. Here she came, leaning casually against the opposite door. But she was paying no attention to the corpse at her feet. She was watching Sol.

He knew now. He knew what the painting on the banner sought among his own particular abattoir of memories. The wind died down. The man standing on the scaffolding grasped the last guy-line and pulled taut the corner of the banner. Sol turned and resumed walking along the embankment. Soon pont

Mirabeau came into view, his apartment block visible on the far side. No lights showed from its windows.

For a week or so after the incident he had picked up discarded newspapers from park benches and bus seats, and had scanned the columns where men bit dogs and long-separated orphans found themselves trapped together in elevators. A man in Clichy had been charged with keeping pigs in his fifth-floor apartment; the son of a postman had discovered 'some roomfuls' of undelivered letters in the house of his late father, and the dwarf-troupe of an East German circus on a tour of its European twin-towns had defected in mid-performance at Braunschweig. But no drunken businessman had died in his sleep on the Métro the previous Friday and no corpse had ridden halfway across Paris, unnoticed or ignored by his fellow passengers. What had happened to those passengers after the carriage had pulled out of Gare d'Austerlitz, Sol wondered. They seemed to have disappeared, carried off down a single-track line to where nothing happened. Where did those tracks lead? The brakes had hissed as they were released and the couplings between the carriages had clattered down the length of the train. He had looked up as the carriage approached.

Her hair had fallen over her face. The girl was now somewhat set apart from the other passengers, who must have shrunk back from the dead man. The corpse had divided the living, as the dead often do, he thought later. There were those who had ignored a man they believed to be dying, and those who had mistaken a dying man for a drunk, and those who had stepped over his corpse. One had tried to help but had yielded to the will of the others. In a moment or two another of them would call for order and calm. A doctor would be plausible, travelling down to place d'Italie for an appointment with his mistress. The others would rally to his call and absolve themselves in hushed concern while the doctor knelt and searched in vain for a pulse.

That would be in a moment or two. For now they played victims and their acting was poor to Sol's eyes. How happily they would have fled their carriage, spilling out of the doors, affecting the stumbling gait of panicked animals or imbeciles.

But who was there to bellow the orders, or bang a truncheon against the side of the carriage? Of the participants in this drama, only he stood outside on the platform. The old couple, pious in their absorption, the bourgeois woman, the young workman rearing out of a fantasy in which he clasped the girl protectively to his chest, or fondled her breasts. Here she came now.

He walked across pont Mirabeau to his apartment block. The outer door resisted, then swung open suddenly when he leaned against it. The antiquated elevator was waiting. The building's other occupants were careful always to close both sets of doors and press the red Bakelite button which sent it back down to the ground floor. Its brass grille clattered shut. Somewhere high above him a cable twitched and the car shivered in response. He rose through the silent building.

If he were honest, he would admit that he had lied. If only to himself.

Once inside, he moved from room to room, switching on every light in the apartment. From the kitchen he took a glass and the bottle of American whiskey, then moved through to the small dining-room, where he settled at a table pushed up against the only window. By day it overlooked the river, the Radio France building and the jumbled roofs of Muette. Now the glass reflected and framed the image of a low-ceilinged room. Next to the door, a row of overcrowded bookcases was partly obscured by a couch and the two straight-backed wooden chairs which faced it across a small coffee-table. The foreground was dominated by the face of a man in his late forties or early fifties with black or brown receding hair. His face. He closed his eyes and the screen went dark. He opened them.

'Good evening.'

Her gesture to the middle-aged man standing alone on the platform had been neither aggressive nor salacious. Himself. Even confined with the other passengers, she was apart from them, as she had been all along. It occured to Sol that if he were to travel this line daily, at this time, for a single week, then he would probably re-encounter everyone in the carriage. But not her. And not the corpse. That was where her allegiance lay, finally. Those two were on a different train. As the carriage had drawn level with him she had shifted her stance and spread her legs a little wider. They had watched each other blankly. Then, in a single casual gesture, she had reached down and pulled up her skirt.

'My name is Solomon Memel,' he said to his reflection. 'For reasons that are obvious, given that I am a Jew and the year was 1943, I left the town in which I had grown up and fled to an area of Greece called Agrapha. It means the Unwritten Places. There I witnessed events experienced by many at that time. In consequence, after the war, I became famous as the poet of *Die Keilerjagd*, of which you may have heard. You may be among the three million or so who own a copy. You may even have read it.'

In the unwatchable black behind the glare of his reflection, the banner masking the façade of the Grand Palais rippled in the wind. The floodlights illuminating the image printed upon it would have been switched off by now, he supposed. Its cracks would be darker, its creases deeper, the ragged tissues smoothed at first, then stretched and split by one of memory's miraculous wounds. Underneath her skirt, the girl on the train had worn nothing. He had stared at her oddly childish body, naked from her waist to the tops of her boots and forked at the gaping split of her sex.

But he had lied to himself, he realised, in recalling that particular moment as though that were the memory prompted by the Englishman's painting. What had he seen when he had looked up at the banner stretched across the Grand Palais's façade? A sexualised gash of some sort, some clottish aping of *L'Origine du Monde*. And what had he remembered? A bizarre moment in an otherwise ordinary Friday afternoon at the Gare d'Austerlitz. That memory was a lie. 'Her sex' had not 'gaped'. He had not seen its 'split'. An untidy nest of thick black hair covered her crotch. He had stared. A second later she would let her skirt fall again. The silly, shrieking passengers noticed nothing. Liars. All of us, he thought. The memory elicited by the English painter's daub lay as far behind the girl's outrageous salute as forgetting would permit. What he had remembered in the dark recession at the painting's centre was a substitute, an effacement. The girl's sex was what he could bear to recall and thus not what he could not.

'Whether you have read my poem or not,' he continued, 'you will know that I wrote of a Greek partisan as both herself and Atalanta. And I speak German as my mother tongue.'

He paused to consider what he should say next and drained his first glass of whiskey.

'The exit wounds inflicted by certain firearms can resemble a woman's sex when aroused: one of war's more tasteless visual puns. But true, as I can testify from experience. Confusion between the two can result in episodes of impotence and delusional behaviour. To which I can also testify.' He refilled his glass.

Ruth had looked as he imagined she would. The years had added definition to her features. He had expected her to be surprised at his own appearance after almost three decades. Presumably photographs of him appeared in America from time to time. Poetry journals requested them. He finished the second glass and poured a third. How odd the people who arrived, emerging out of the features of others. And always uninvited. Sandor's face told him nothing, so many people had passed through it. He wondered if it had been the youthful Ruth that he had recognised in Lisa Angludet, or, just perhaps, the altogether harsher angles of the one whom Ruth hoped to draw out of those soft, over-full cheeks and lips. Her eyes had been right; the rest all wrong. The eyes never change, he thought. Not even in death.

He sought his own eyes in the reflection in the window. His own sought those of a girl on a train. Had he seen her face before that moment? He had no image of it at all. He had thought her 'beautiful' and 'sulky'. But she had stood sideways on to him, her head angled away. A mass of dark hair, the hinge of her jaw and a single high cheekbone; nothing more came to mind. The carriage slid across the field of his vision. She flicked the hair away from her face to reveal a high forehead and prominent brow and cheekbones, a strong face that was barely softened by a full mouth. The dead looking through the living.

But all of this had come to him afterwards. Remembrance, however insistent and unwelcome, could not have come before recognition. Only when she had dropped her skirt had he lifted his gaze from her crotch and looked up. There was no doubt. Framed in the carriage window, her black eyes had followed him as the train pulled her away. She wore Thyella's face.

The young workman had been pressed against the window. Struggling with the catch to let in some air, his cheeks sucked in with the effort. There it went.

'Solomon!' he hissed from too far up the platform to be heard, too deep within the life he had buried. It was Jakob.

'Sol! Did you find my letter?' He grinned. 'Don't forget the truth, eh?'

Then both of them were gone.

*　　*　　*

It was still early. The curfew would not lift for another half an hour at least. Sol glanced at his wrist, forgetting that he no longer owned a watch. He waited behind the row of cottages which formed the southern boundary of Schillerpark.

Ahead of him, the familiar shallow slope of the park led his eye past the poplar trees to the crest of the gentle ridge above which showed the tops of the chestnuts where Jakob, Ruth and himself had been used to sit. But that was in a previous life. In this one the parks were forbidden; he had not set foot in any of them in eighteen months. It had seemed a trivial restriction among all the others, but this Monday morning it was the snare into which he had had no choice but to tread. Regulations interdicted the streets between six in the evening and eight in the morning. They interdicted the parks at any time. They forbade absence from the roll-call, which took place at the assigned workplace at eight sharp.

To be here, or there, or not, at this time or that time: all were offences under the regulations, which had multiplied until it had become impossible to remember them all. The railway station was interdicted, unless one were taken: then it was forbidden to leave. There had been a rumour during the first wave of deportations that a man named Fischl had talked the guards at the station into taking his parents off the train. But Fischl, if he existed, was an anomalous creature; the snares set by the town's current masters were ingenious devices and did not release their captives so easily. Their dogs were tireless and could not be distracted or thrown off the scent. There were new inevitabilities. The thought sank into Sol as a lassitude which rooted him there, suddenly uncaring as to what might happen. To do nothing, to wait passively, merely to exist. What else had his parents done? That, too, was an offence under the regulations.

But a single oversight on the part of the authorities, he told himself, and all might yet be well. A one-line omission in a list of addresses. He fingered the residence papers in his pocket and kept his eyes fixed on the far corner of the warehouse which stood behind the timber market. The ground there was more sheltered; a light frost lay on the grass. Jakob would be unable to pause for more than a second or two. Sol smelt cooking from one of the cottages and heard children playing. Normal things. He was breathing too quickly. Think of Fischl. Even the most painstaking huntsman could glance away at the instant the quarry crossed the break; the animal could slip into the thick woods and disappear amid shadows. But, this hope, he knew, was a fantasy and no more real than the relief he had felt at the beginning. He thought back to the first days of the occupation. Then, at least, the future that awaited them had been plainly laid out, had they chosen to read it. Only afterwards had they been deceived.

'Animals!' his mother had exclaimed. 'Beasts!'

She dropped her voice and murmured something else. The three of them were in the parlour. She freed one hand from the strap of her handbag and wagged a finger. 'But I told you the Germans would put a stop to it. I told you, didn't I?'

Sol's father nodded. 'Of course, Fritzi.' He looked up at his son, who said nothing. 'The worst of it's over now.' His wife pursed her lips.

It had been three days since Sol had returned home with news that the trucks had entered the town. His father had left the house later that night to find out more. The soldiers were Romanians. The Germans were a day behind them. Sol and his mother had digested this news in separate silences. Then his father had mentioned moving out, perhaps to his cousin's house near Sadagora, just to err on the side of caution. For a week or so, no more. His mother had cried. They had got as far as fetching the suitcases from the top of the wardrobe. But then the first noise from the streets had reached their ears.

'No better than animals!' his mother burst out again. Her dark blue skirt was speckled with the face powder which she applied in quick dabs every few minutes. It made no difference: the grey pre-dawn light cast its own grainy pallor over their faces. She had made a distracted attempt to clean the apartment the previous evening. None of them had ventured outside for three days. Apparently posters with the new regulations had been posted along Siebenbürgerstrasse and in Ringplatz.

'Perhaps the Banulescus could go? It's not as if it's far,' Sol's mother suggested. 'Just the end of the road.'

'I'll ask them next time I see them,' promised his father. 'Or it might be easier if I went. I need some air in my lungs.'

'No! . . .'

'Fritzi, for God's sake calm yourself. Sol, go upstairs and ask the Banulescus.'

Sol opened his mouth to protest. A near-imperceptible shake of his father's head silenced him. He rose and began drawing back the bolts and unhooking the chains which his father had hammered into the door after the first rabble had passed the end of the street. They had sung patriotic songs, beating time on saucepans and dustbin lids: a joyless carnival. The shouting and glass-breaking had come later.

Outside, on the staircase, Sol waited for a few seconds in case his mother should think to peer through the letterbox. Her outbursts had subsided somewhat from those of the night before last. She had spent the following day and night sitting rigidly awake. Now she forgets who her neighbours are, thought her son, for she had knocked on the Banulescus' door the night before last. They had heard their upstairs neighbours' footsteps, moving about in the apartment above their own but no one had answered.

His father had nailed the letterbox shut later that night, after Petre Walter had left. His father's drinking partner had knocked softly on their own door in the early hours, then, finding no response, had whispered his name, softly and repeatedly, until the door was opened. Petre's face was bruised. His first words had been to say that Rabbi Rosenfeld had been killed; after that Sol's father had led him down the hallway where they had conversed in whispers. That had been the worst night.

Yet their apartment had not been marked out. No stones had been thrown through their windows; they had not been dragged from their home and beaten in the street. They had not been troubled once. They had only listened. They had heard.

'It's Iron Guard thugs and drunken soldiers,' Sol's father had said when Petre Walter had left. 'And the police just stand by and do nothing.' His mother had cried quietly and his father had put his arm around her. Then he had fetched his hammer and nailed up the letterbox.

Masarykgasse was empty. The sun had yet to rise. Sol walked through empty streets to the main road. To the south, a kilometre or so distant, two military trucks had been parked across the thoroughfare. Tiny figures carrying guns stood in front of them. The regulations were impossible to miss. Up and down the length of the road, large notice-boards had been attached by wire to the lampposts at each junction. Sol's eye skipped over the close-set gothic type: '. . . all resident Jews above the age of five years . . . consist in a six-pointed star with a ten cm. diameter . . . shops or offices of Jews will display visible signs . . . applications for exemptions are unnecessary . . . to be in the streets, squares, or other public places after six p.m. nor to enter the public markets before midday . . . to use the tram system or other means of transportation . . . public or private telephones . . .'

Calm settled upon him as the import of the words became clear. The cool morning air smelt of fine dust. The town was quiet. He turned and walked slowly back home. In their own street, there was no evidence now that anything had happened at all.

'She was right,' he told his father. He glanced towards the back bedroom, into which, he presumed, his mother had retreated. He was unable then to hold back the sense of relief which surged through him and he quickly ran through the list of trivial restrictions by which the newly-arrived administration sought to reimpose order on the town. His father's face cleared for a moment, then his habitual suspicion descended.

'Why would they want our telephones?' he grumbled. 'Who on earth has a telephone?'

But by whom, Sol wondered later, had the deception been perpetrated? For in the weeks and months that had followed, it seemed to him, the authorities had been increasingly explicit in their prohibitions and demands: that 'all resident Jews will move their residence without delay into the quarter of the city designated for them' and that 'all expenses incurred as a result of the above measures will be the responsibility of each Jew'. Even the actions, which began in August and took place, exclusively and predictably, on Saturday nights, were conducted in the harsh white glare of powerful arc lights. No, the deceivers were not Commandant Ohlendorf's black-uniformed officers, who sped about the town in armoured transport cars, nor even the battalions of security police recruited from among the Romanians and Ukrainians. And certainly not the grinning officer who, as the three of them tramped down the staircase with their allotted suitcases, had simply put out his hand for the keys to the apartment. Sol had walked ahead and pretended not to notice as his father surrendered them. He had recognised the man as a colleague from the timber market.

The crowded streets had dazed them. Sol staggered under the weight of the suitcase. He remembered the hurried parting from his friends five weeks earlier, behind Ringplatz, on the day their tormentors had arrived. Since the occupation, and confined by the curfew, he had seen none of them. He could not imagine their lives or guess their thoughts now. They had disappeared. It was easier to learn these new truths alone.

The ghetto had been established in September. The residence assigned to them was a single small room in one of the alleys off Judengasse. Sol had left his mother and father sitting on their suitcases, apparently lacking the will to unpack them, and had walked down into the street. He had made his way first to the hospital, where the office of the Jewish Council had been installed. A crowd had gathered outside the main entrance. Inside, trestle tables had been set up and endless lists of names laid out announcing the work details demanded by the new labour decrees. Sol pushed and shoved with everyone else until he found his name, then pushed and shoved his way out again. As he regained the street the sound of hammering reached his ears above the din of the crowd. He began to force his way forward through the mass of people moving downhill in the other direction. Soldiers were constructing a high wooden barrier at the end of Judengasse. An old man clutching a trunk as large as himself collided with Sol, who struggled to keep his balance. Someone behind him pushed him upright, then grasped at his jacket. He shook himself free without looking around and struggled on. The street was growing ever more crowded. Two small children were being pushed forward by a girl too young to be their mother. All three were crying. Those around them tried to move clear. Sol stepped aside and was about to squeeze past. A hand caught him again and this time would not be shaken off. He turned to confront his aggressor, his own hand raised to free himself. There was a moment of bafflement, another of disbelief. It was Jakob.

But it seemed too disconnected from the circumstances, Jakob's familiar face in the turbulence around them, and what he told Sol in the voice Sol knew so well. These words did not belong in this mouth. Jakob began without preamble, the ghetto walls going up behind them, the crush and panic of the crowds, and the last stragglers being shoved past the cordon by the guards. It should have been said in some other context, where he might have understood it better, but, as the days and weeks passed, he realised that Jakob's words were themselves the only circumstance for their utterance. Only the events yet to take place within that circumstance had been missing.

He had been misdirected by the flat tones of Jakob's voice. For a second or two the simple sentences had made no sense. On the third night of the occupation, Jakob's father had been arrested at his home and taken to the headquarters of the town's new masters in the Palace of Culture. There he had been shot in the back of the neck.

Sol had looked down. He had put his hand on Jakob's arm. The other wore a bemused expression.

'What you or I say, or even think, no longer matters, Sol. Look at these people,' he said with contempt. 'The truth is all around them and what are they doing? Keeping up their spirits, telling each other "Hope for the best!" and "Soldier on!" Idiots! They know they're living a lie and they still can't bring themselves to abandon it.' His eyes were fixed on something in the far distance. 'None of us can.'

But Jakob was wrong, he thought, deranged in some way. Soldier on. Hope for the best. There was no alternative.

The work parties assembled in Mehlplatz. Sol joined a hundred or more men, who, once issued with tools, were marched out of the town by security police wearing a hodge-podge of different uniforms who bellowed at them to move faster whenever the pace slackened. The men carried picks and shovels and, as they continued, it began to dawn on Sol what their assignment must be.

They were led from Uhrmacherstrasse down the steep incline, past the Polish church and through Springbrunplatz, to the foot of the hill. Here they were directed left, towards the railway station. A little way beyond it, a German officer passed them on the road, drawing a ragged volley of salutes from the guards, all save one. A young man near the head of the column looked up too late to give more than a startled wave. The officer glared at the offender, stopped his car and barked at the man, making him salute five or six times in a row. Finally satisfied, the officer had climbed back into his car. The other guards had begun to rib the hapless man and one of the work party, a heavily-built man with a moustache, had asked him what he thought he was doing, hopping about like a frog every time a German snapped his fingers. Sol had had the impression that the young guard and he had known each other in some different context. The guard had coloured with embarrassment, but said nothing.

They had been drawn up in ranks along the river-bank, where a roll-call was taken. Sol called out his name. The moustached man had given the name 'Gert Scholem'. The commander had nodded to one of his sergeants.

There were a hundred different thoughts among the hundred or so men gathered there, Sol thought later. A hundred kinds of apprehension and a hundred half-envisioned futures. But all of them ended with the trudge back up the hill at the end of the day, the pulling off of sodden boots, nourishment, rest. Jakob's unabandoned lies. None of them ended as Gert Scholem's future did. What had been his thought when he had opened his eyes that morning?

Four men had run forward and pulled Gert out of the line. A fifth had clubbed him across the backs of his knees. They had begun to beat him with the butts of their rifles. Sol had watched the guard who had failed to salute. He was tugging on a cigarette, looking away. After that Sol had turned his attention to the ground, noticing how the the turf was already trampled to mud, then to his rust-spotted shovel, to his shoes, already splitting, then across the river to the rows of graves which stretched along the river-bank and extended into the meadow behind. Sol picked out the spot on the far bank where he and his friends had sat and talked in the July heat. That was where Jakob, Ruth and himself had crossed, and there, a little upstream, was where he had pulled her up out of the water. The arch in which she and Jakob had argued still stood. Who had been talking to him? Chaim Fingerhut? No one had seen him since that day. Nor his sister Lia. Everyone else had survived, Jakob had said, without mentioning Ruth. Sol had had to ask after her by name. Sol imagined them all, sitting on blankets across the river and talking among themselves. Around him, the labour detail waited in a thick silence barely broken by the thud of the rifle stocks. Gert Scholem no longer moved. Sol's imaginary companions faded into the grey of the clouds which stretched to the horizon. The commander barked: 'Enough!' Then they were put to work.

Sol shovelled, and as he shovelled, that day and the next and all those that followed, he thought in one way or another about what Jakob had said. There was an insight at the end of his friend's stark equation which resisted him, or which he could not accept. Something inhibited him. His shovel scraped dully under the water. He brought up bricks and fragments of dressed stone and tossed them onto piles which other members of the detail carried to the near bank. A brief autumn came to its end in the third week of October when rainstorms lashed the town for five days and nights. The waterlevel rose to the point where it was no longer possible to work in the river and even the guards preferred to smoke cigarettes under the scant cover of the trees rather than drive them into the swirling flood. The respite had proved brief; the level had soon fallen again and the temperature with it. Sol and the others of the detail felt their feet grow numb in the freezing water.

Sometimes men would disappear: fail to turn up, fall off the roll-call, as if they had never existed. The man who worked with Sol had operated a metal-lathe in a factory. The owner had already been down twice to speak to the guards. A hip-flask had been passed around. The lathe-operator would not be here for much longer, he had confided to Sol in a whisper. For now, however, he raised and lowered a heavy iron bar, driving it into the bed of the river to lever or break up those fragments of brick, mortar and stone too large to lift. Sol worked behind him. They were near the far bank and, as Sol glanced up, he realised that this was the precise spot where Ruth had stood with her skirts gathered. She had offered him her hand and had not looked up, so confident had she been that he was there to pull her up, out of the water, and not let her fall. He was standing on the bank, waiting for her to do just that. Where was she now? He stood in cold water which came up to his knees. There was no one there to pull her up. He was shovelling. He thought, 'We were the liars.' And an instant later, 'But Gert Scholem's murder was true.'

In the spring of the following year, a rumour ran through the ghetto that the town's mayor, Popovici, had prevailed against the wishes of the military governor of the whole of Bukovina and the ghetto was to be dissolved. Sol watched the drawn faces of his neighbours and workmates brighten. He listened to the excited chatter which ran up and down the stairwell as he climbed to his cramped quarters. The arrests slowed, then stopped.

Sol, his mother and father were among the last to receive their papers. They watched the constant trickle of men, women and children puff and pant up the street to the dismantled barricade. Once there, the returnees planted their suitcases on the ground and joined the slow line for the security police to inspect their papers. Those unable to wait any longer pooled their resources and bribed their way out. Finally, their own documents arrived.

'Signed by the mayor himself,' said his father, transfixed by the crudely-printed papers.

They packed their suitcases and walked up Judengasse, presented their permits and continued up to Ringplatz, where the tables outside the Schwarze Adler were filled with citizens enjoying the unexpected March sunshine. The traffic on Siebenbürgerstrasse was light and orderly. The trolley-car passed them with its conductor leaning out from the footplate, just as Gustl Ritter's father once had done. A great clatter from the timber market signalled a load falling from the hoist, as often happened. These were normal and everyday matters. When they reached the apartment in Masarykgasse they found its door intact and its contents untouched.

All lies, thought Sol, while his mother exclaimed over the undamaged china and his father patted clouds of dust from his armchair. Just as the papers in his pocket were lies: drafted by liars and signed by a liar and carried by one who lied in believing them. And in offering the false example of his defiance, Gert

Scholem too had been a liar, if that was indeed the falsehood he had peddled. A further possibility occurred to him as something too fantastical to be entertained: might Gert Scholem have expected to be saved?

He would not join the liars, he told himself. In June, the skies above the town were again lit by the white glare of the arc lights. Those unfortunate enough to have left the ghetto before receiving their papers and residence permits were escorted from their homes and driven down to the station, from where the long freight trains departed for work camps in Transnistria. Sol had returned to their home once to find his father poring over his papers, checking and rechecking the tiny print. His mother had been slumped behind him.

'We never handed in our inventory,' said his father. His voice shook. 'Look here, "All Jews are to declare their assets including real estate, stocks, jewellery, rugs, kitchen utensils, furniture, money, livestock and any other possessions." It should have been, somewhere here, yes: ". . . made in duplicate and presented to the officers of the Jewish Council at the Jewish Hospital."'

'We never noticed it, Solomon,' said his mother. 'Oh God, what are we going to do?'

'It's what I told Petre,' his father said. 'Check your papers. Check your permit. Check it and double-check it.'

Petre Walter had been arrested in an action three weeks before. Nothing had been heard of him since.

'Ignore it,' Sol answered his mother. 'There is nothing to be done.' Then seeing that this had brought her to the verge of tears he added, 'If anyone had noticed, they would have come for us before now. No one is arrested for not declaring their assets. How would they know we have any assets, unless we declare them first?'

No one is arrested for anything, he thought. Or anyone is arrested for anything: having no papers, having the wrong papers, having the right papers, breaking curfew, not breaking curfew. The resolution of these confusions came only at night, in vans filled with security police and under the magnesium glare which bleached the streets and blinded the men, women and sleepy-headed children who shuffled out clutching their suitcases and sacks. The arc lights clarified everything, sweeping over the city and descending where they pleased. What happened under those lights, what was rumoured to happen at the station, what he had first seen happen by the banks of the river almost a year before: these things were true. His father's belief was misplaced that the rules existed to be obeyed, that obedience might keep them safe, that their safety was ensurable, for these things were lies. He understood Jakob's words better and better. They were simple and the situation was simple. Then, in the September of the second year since the Germans' arrival, both became more complicated.

Jakob was late. It must be almost eight now. Sol glanced about him every few seconds. The avenue of poplars before him led uphill to the park proper. To his left, the ground fell away down the slope of the hill. He felt his panic rise again; he could not stay here much longer. He had known what to believe and what not to believe. Now he did not.

Jakob had appeared unexpectedly four days before, falling into step beside him as Sol walked slowly across the square at the bottom of Franzensgasse.

'We need to talk,' he said by way of greeting. Startled, Sol had opened his mouth to speak and been cut off. 'Not here. Turn left over there.'

It was a warm evening and the streets were crowded with men and women hurrying home. A small crowd bunched around a checkpoint at the junction. As they approached, Sol reached in his pocket for his papers and waved them over the heads of two old women. One of the security police motioned him through with his truncheon. He looked around for Jakob but his friend seemed to have passed through ahead of him. He was waiting a few metres further up.

'Come on,' Jakob said. 'There's less than an hour before curfew.'

'What's happening? Where are we going?' asked Sol. They crossed Herrengasse and entered Armenischegasse, where the street narrowed and the passers-by were fewer and all Jews. 'My papers aren't authorised here,' he said.

Jakob snorted. 'Authorised for what? Come on. It's not far now.'

They turned into an alley and continued between the backs of two terraces of tall, narrow houses. Jakob strode ahead as though the route were familiar to him. The alley grew narrower, then ended in front of a high wall. Before they reached it Jakob pushed open a gate and entered the backyard to one of the dwellings. A short flight of metal steps brought them to a door, which opened at his approach. Sol hurried after, the door closed behind him and he found himself in darkness.

A match scraped and flared. An oil-lamp's glow touched the low ceiling then spread over the rough brick walls of the basement. A doorway at the far end disclosed a second room, but it was lightless. A face Sol knew from somewhere replaced the glass hood and looked up.

'I have to go,' Jakob said behind him.

Sol turned. 'Wait, what did you want to tell me? Jakob?' But Jakob was looking at the man who stood over the oil-lamp. The basement was cold, despite the mild weather.

'Have you . . . ?'

The man nodded. 'All done.'

'Pessach will explain,' said Jakob. 'We will see each other again soon enough.' With that he slipped out of the door and was gone. Bewildered, Sol turned back to the man.

'You don't remember me?' He was shorter than Sol, in his late forties perhaps. 'I'm not sure we ever actually met.' He smiled. 'Pessach Ehrlich. The theatre. I used to run the theatre.' He held out his hand.

'The theatre,' Sol echoed, uncomprehending. 'What theatre?'

Ehrlich made no reply. But then Sol heard footsteps tread carefully down a flight of wooden stairs in the darkened room behind the man. A vague movement coalesced into a human figure and Sol's bafflement gave way to understanding. Ruth stood in the doorway.

She was thinner than he remembered. Her hair was cut differently. A thick slash of red lipstick covered her mouth. His first impulse was to go to her but something in her bearing held him back.

'Ruth . . .' He managed after a long pause. He searched her face. 'Where have you been?'

Ruth shook her head and addressed Ehrlich. 'Jakob has gone?'

Ehrlich nodded. Sol looked at them impatiently. 'What are you doing here, Ruth? What is going on?'

Ruth held Ehrlich in her gaze for a second or two longer and Sol wondered what lay between the two of them. There was a time he might have felt jealousy. Now everything was too clear and all too late. Too late for Ruth and him, and for Jakob, the clearest-sighted of them all. Jakob's truth would not be denied, but it was cold and hard. There was a time he could have wrapped himself in warm lies, shut everything out except Ruth and himself.

'Your residence papers were signed by Popovici,' said Ruth.

'Yes,' Sol admitted. 'How did you know?'

'An action is planned for next Saturday,' she said. 'The quotas have been raised.'

The words fell on him like cold water. She paused. He waited patiently, for there was no hurry. He knew now why he was here.

'Your names are on the list,' she said. 'Your mother, your father and you.'

Now it was Monday morning. Jakob was not going to come for him. He had been arrested, or imprisoned, or shot. He was being frog-marched across the courtyard of the Palace of Culture. He was in its cellars with his hands tied behind his back and a question tickling his ear. They were going to beat the truth out of him. Jakob was lost. Sol's uncertainty ballooned and he tumbled within it. He could not stay here a second longer. He breathed crisp cold air and waited under a cloudless blue sky. He listened to the faint din of the timber market behind the old warehouse. The noise from the thoroughfare on its far side was fainter; a truck passing, handcarts rattling perhaps. He tried to think what he could do. Cling to what is real, he told himself. Only what is real. Jakob's truth was harder even than he had suspected. He would not think what Jakob's absence might mean so he wavered, in some intermediate place between the preserve of the non-existent Fischl and the world of the no-longer-existent Gert Scholem. Give up, he thought. Nothing more could be done. There was nowhere left to be. Was that not 'real'? Was that not 'true'?

'You're not allowed in the park.'

He jumped at the sound. Two small boys were peering at him over the back of the fence.

'It's not the park,' Sol managed in reply. 'The park is up there. Now go away.'

'*You* go away,' said the other boy. Then he raised his voice. 'Go on. *You* go away!'

Sol fixed them with a stare. 'You are being very rude. When I tell your parents about this they will be very angry with you both.' He started to walk towards the avenue of poplar trees.

'That's it! Go away!' shouted the first boy to his retreating back. Then encouraged by this success they both yelled as loud as they could, 'Go away! Go away! Go away!'

Sol heard an adult voice shout from inside one of the cottages. He forced himself to walk a few more paces. Then he broke into a run.

'But there's nothing wrong with our papers!' his father had insisted. His mother had stared into a private middle distance and said nothing. She had seemed perfectly self-possessed, as if this was of interest but had nothing to do with her.

'Ruth has found somewhere we can go. It's just for two nights. Saturday and Sunday,' he pleaded. 'It's safe, a factory, empty over the weekends. It's not even owned by a Jew! How can you sit here and wait for them?'

'How do you know this list even exists?' asked his father. Then there was a flash of his old argumentative self. 'And who is this "Ruth" you set such store by?' he sneered.

'Ruth's a wonderful girl,' murmured his mother.

'Listen to me,' Sol started again.

Ruth had told him what he must do, then made him repeat back to her the address of the factory. She had put her hand to his cheek and he had noticed she was wearing scent of some kind. He had forgotten perfume.

'Be there as close to curfew as you dare,' she said. 'It's safer. The factory is empty over the weekend.' There were no choices now. There was nothing to decide. And yet his father prevaricated all that night and most of the next until Sol shouted at him. But even under this provocation, the older man merely waved his hand, warding off his son's words. Through it all, his mother said nothing.

Saturday came.

Sol renewed his campaign, going over the same points, saying the same words until they wore ruts in the sentences they formed and sank to meaninglessness within them. His parents had stopped listening. As the curfew approached, his frustration mounted until he began to berate his father for his obstinacy and stupidity. The older man shook his head wearily. His mother gave no sign of having heard at all.

'You deserve no better!' he cried out finally, then fell silent at his own words.

'Enough Sol. We're tired of all this.' It was his mother who spoke. 'Now off you go.'

She smiled at him but her face was slack and the childish expression seemed to come from one who could no longer see the person who stood before her. This could not be her son; an impostor had taken his place. The person he had once been was long gone. His father looked up at him from his chair. There was a new note in his voice.

'Just go, son.'

Sol turned from them in a baffled rage, pulled open the door and ran down the stairs.

The children's voices faded. *Go away! Go away!* He forced himself to stop running before he reached the thoroughfare. It was crowded at that hour. He drifted along with the men and women until the turning to Masarykgasse. Something was going on outside his apartment building. A cart was stationed outside its entrance. He moved nearer.

Here were the same stairs he had thundered down two nights ago. The outer door was wedged open and men were shouting to one another inside. His father's chair stood on the pavement. Beside it was the dresser in which his mother's best china had once been arranged. They had never eaten off it that he could remember. Now the dresser stood on its side, empty, waiting to be loaded. Packing crates were being carried out of the building. The china would be in one of them. Other articles of their furniture were distributed between this cart and two others further down the street, each with its placid horse waiting calmly in the traces.

The same operation was being repeated up and down the street: men struggling out of narrow doorways carrying tables, beds, chairs, clocks, building little islands of furniture. Other men were dismantling these to load the carts. All the men wore their armbands. Easier than digging rubble out of river-beds, thought Sol. Some of his own possessions lay among the articles tumbled carelessly into the packing cases: an ugly glass paper-weight, some coloured pencils, a children's 'Book of Legends'. He reached down, picked out the paperweight and put it in his pocket. One of the workers coming out of the doorway stared at him in terror. Sol smiled. It was far too late to put anything back.

A little further down the street a black-uniformed officer was talking to a smartly-dressed young woman outside a single-storey house that Sol had barely noticed before. So Jews lived there too, he thought to himself, wondering if he had known them. A large cart stood outside, fully loaded. Two men were preparing to board up the door. He felt the paperweight in his pocket bump against his leg. He walked with his head down. His limbs felt loose somehow. The important thing now was not to think.

'Don't think,' he told himself under his breath, and almost giggled. 'Don't think.' He was going to laugh; he could feel it. 'Don't think and don't laugh,' he muttered. And don't stop and don't run and don't go and don't stay and don't come back and – what else?

'You! What did you say? Come here!'

Don't hope. That was what Jakob had meant. His mother and father had understood. He had not, until now. He turned to face the German officer. His useless papers were in the same pocket as his useless paperweight. He had the sensation that he had let go the last handhold of a torturous ascent. He was falling backwards into space and it felt easeful. For a moment he luxuriated in his abandonment.

'Sol! There you are at last!' the girl exclaimed, turning around.

'That's him?' asked the officer dubiously. He was a short red-faced man. His chest strained at the buttons of his tunic. The girl was Ruth.

Ruth nodded and reached to spin Sol about the way he had come. 'Mumbling to himself's the least of his bad habits,' she explained, smiling. 'Can't you even remember an address?' she chided Sol. 'Come on! We're late enough as it is.'

The sound of hammering began behind them as she walked him back down the street.

'What are you doing here, with a German officer?' he asked when they were clear. 'What are we late for?'

'Nothing,' said Ruth.

Her face was powdered and her lips rouged, as before. She wore mascara that appeared not quite black and which did not suit her. Sol looked up at roofs and windows as they wove a path through the men emptying the houses. The overseers had lit their cigarettes. The action was all but over.

When they were halfway up the street Ruth hissed to him under her breath to pay attention. He glanced at her. There was something on her jacket, something trickling down one lapel. Spittle, he realised, and was strangely embarrassed, wondering how to tell her.

'Your papers are no good.' She spoke without looking at him when they reached the main street. 'If they're inspected, you'll be arrested. Your parents were taken on Saturday.'

He could still hear the hammering, but it was faint now. He said, 'Jakob never came.' It was a long thin smear of silver.

'Turn off here.'

'Where are we going?'

'Never mind.'

They walked slowly down an unmetalled road whose name Sol could not recall or had never known. They passed single-storey cottages with vegetable gardens in front of them. The sun rose higher but took none of the chill from the air. Ruth's lapel was clean. She must have noticed and wiped it, he concluded, and was relieved.

'Where can I stay?' he wondered aloud. Perhaps the factory where he had spent the last two nights. There would be room there. But people worked there during the week. Somewhere else.

Ruth stopped. 'Stay? Sol, if you stay you will be shot, do you not understand that after all that has happened?' She paused, then spoke more calmly, almost to herself. 'But how could you know?'

He shook his head. 'Someone . . .' It was time to mention the spittle on her jacket, although it was gone. Tell her anyway. 'Someone spat on your jacket.' Her face moved oddly. She was about to cry, he realised. 'It's gone now,' he added.

'Not you, Sol. Not you too. Please!' She stopped and turned to him, placing her hands on his shoulders.

'My father wouldn't come,' he said. 'We argued. He burned my poetry. A long time ago. It was nonsense anyway.'

'Listen to me Sol, after the last house there's a track leading down to the left. Follow it as far as it goes. There's a cowshed. Look inside. There should be two packages, I don't know. Clothes, some food. Take them both. Don't stay there.'

The wheels of a passing cart had left ridges and grooves in the soft mud. To the west, the mountains showed sharply against the clear sky, their lower slopes shaded with pines, the peaks of the highest capped with snow. The tracks would meet at infinity, thought Sol.

'Come with me,' he said.

She shook her head.

'Who is the other package for?

'It was for Jakob,' answered Ruth. 'Now go.'

*   *   *

Sol found himself, again, in the climbing dream. Slopes of rough grassland rose before him and his task was to reach their crests, which he did, only to be faced with the next, identical slope. The inclines grew steeper as they repeated themselves; this part was very slow. Then the first trees broke through the turf and he moved uphill through chestnuts and oaks, then thick-barked pines. He reached the heights where only beeches and firs would live and at last not even they. The ground hardened underfoot, becoming stone. The air was thin and cold up here, and turbulent behind the windbreak of the ridge. Snow to come.

All of this was familiar.

Then the first pain would be felt, which entered through the feet, rose and gathered itself in his ankles. His bones bowed and straightened. His footfalls jarred through his frame. The body and its memories. Mine, he thought, nearing wakefulness.

But the body also numbed from below, feet first again, for the same pain seemed to scour of sensation the flesh through which it passed. Feet, ankles, knees, hips, spine. Only the skull guarded its sentience, gauging the sudden blast of air which swept up the slope yet to be descended and the great stepping-stones of its crags and outcrops. But the body it topped was nerveless; a thing that moved according to one thought: the next climb.

The repetition had been the worst of it, he concluded vaguely. Up and down, and always the cold.

He had found the two packages where Ruth had told him they would be. Then his flight had begun.

And there was his journey to the dark tunnel which had proved its terminus, from birthplace to the extinction he had first glimpsed in the barrel of a rifle, thought Sol then, one crusted eyelash ungluing itself and the eye opening on the lowest shelf of the bookcase. His own editions were shelved there, arrayed in order of publication. Their spines rose and fell; an angular diagram of peaks and troughs, climbs and descents. His route in cross-section.

The morning roar of traffic rose from the boulevard below and vibrated feebly at the window. He had fallen asleep on the couch. He had woken to the sight of his own books. *Edo, edere, edidi, editum.* To breathe one's last. To undergo edition.

His first book had come out from Fleischer. The volume began the series: *Memel • Die Keilerjagd,* printed on a dark blue spine with the intertwined hands of Fleischer Verlag's device below it. Let that represent his first obstacle, thought Sol, the range of the Carpathians, after the first weeks of terror on the plain. He had slept in snatches during the days, moving only by night.

Sol's tongue dragged itself free of stale saliva and he swallowed. The whiskey bottle stood empty on the floor with the room bent around the swollen cylinder of its neck. A shoe lay beside it.

Surrer Verlag's edition had succeeded Fleischer's, after the purchase of Fleischer's publishing house. Surrer had then put out the fat white paperback which German high school teachers even now were drumming into the heads of their pupils. In Germany, one 'did' Memel from the age of fourteen. 'It is the same all over the country,' a young doctoral student had once told him excitedly. 'A special day, when every head bends to the same text at the same time.' Like the Roman Catholic Mass, thought Sol.

It was sixteen in France, but not compulsory. *Solomon Memel • La Chasse* had been produced a few months after the German paperback, in a similar format. Together these first three extended a little plateau along the shelf, the place where he had become Solomon Memel the Poet.

This trio would stand for the long southward plunge to the Danube, he thought. If ever a God had watched over him, his hand had descended there. Even if the same hand had also raised the mountains which rose before him afterwards. The mountains which had seemed never to end. The black cover of the next volume rose sheer against the French and German editions, *Solomon Memel • Den Vildsvin Jagt* picked out in red, 'for the blood, and the darkness of the body around it,' as his Danish publisher had explained, in perfect German. *A Caccia di Cinghiale* marked the spine of a pocket edition which had been hastily bound in hard covers when his sudden celebrity had leaped the Alps. An illustrated version from France followed, then the first of the Spanish editions. The outlines of their spines rose and fell along the shelf.

No, the mountains never ended, thought Sol. On they went, rising and falling, on their way to meaningless exhaustion. Editions from Poland, Hungary and Czechoslovakia with no translators credited, a samizdat production from Russia, then the official one towering over it. A first, error-ridden Romanian translation produced by the only surviving member of the Fingerhut family, an aunt of Chaim's and Lia's, and dedicated to their memory, then the bound transcript of its near-faultless successor by a professor at the University of Cluj, which Sol had refused to authorise, and next to that, bunched together, the first Swedish, Norwegian and Icelandic editions. His eye ran along a ridge of right-angles and perfect perpendiculars, peaks and precipitous ravines. He flexed a foot and cramp ran up his calf. He tried to raise his head.

He had spent the first winter in two freezing hideaways. Men with dogs had tramped through the woods around the first, hunting him perhaps. He would never know. He had fled higher, to the second, a long-abandoned shepherd's hut. The cold had reached into him, winding steely fingers around his bones. Here was its faint echo: a piercing rod of pain running through his brow to the back of the skull. His stomach heaved suddenly with no result. Sol breathed in, breathed out, then swung his legs and rolled upright.

He was a quarter of the way along the shelf, less than a quarter through the long march he wanted it to represent. *Solomon Memel • The Boar Hunt* was wrapped in a garish multicoloured dust-jacket. It had quickly been replaced, at Sol's insistence, with a more sober grey design. Together they formed a thick, half-shaded pillar. His eye ran over translations into Estonian, Catalan and Dutch. There had been an argument with the Dutch; he forgot the details. Hebrew, after numerous unexplained delays. Hardbacks and paperbacks, the lattermost printed in alphabets so foreign to him he could not distinguish the words of the title and it was impossible to draw the unmarked frontier where his second collection began, *Von der Luft bis zur Erde.* Not with certainty. The terrain had not changed; only its stumbling pilgrim, who shook from cold he could no longer feel and watched his bones suck the skin tight over his frame as the flesh within it wasted. These volumes stood for the weeks that followed as he had inched his way south. There were less of them: 'An inevitable falling-off ' (*Der Spiegel*). He did not know how long he had walked. He recalled some of the days as lifetimes, while of others he could not recollect a single second. It was not until Reichmann had questioned him that he had traced a tentative southward line and realised that whole weeks had erased themselves from his memory, falling away behind him as though his passing had snapped the last cable of a swaying bridge and sent it tumbling into the abyss it once had spanned. His passage across had left no trace. There had come a point when he had risen each dawn as though from a deathbed, as unsurprised by his continuance as he would have been by cessation. He moved and existed to move. That he existed had been enough.

And I am, thought Sol. His head pounded steadily. He would have to stand soon. He smelled sour. *Steinbrech* mustered fewer volumes yet. By the time of his last volume, published three years and three months ago, his publishers numbered five: Surrer, still proclaiming his genius in quarter-page advertisements with every publication, the impeccably impoverished Editions Maroslav-Lèger here in Paris, a university press in the United States, the unchanged and unchanging Danes, and a hand-bound volume produced single-handedly, it seemed, by the faithful professor from Cluj. His work, he was told, had grown obscure.

The last book on the shelf was different. Taller than the others, and bound in thin green cardboard, it resembled a school exercise book and leaned at an angle against the Romanian edition of *Es gibt so eben*. If he were ever to gather another volume of work, and if it were ever to be published, then this flimsy production would be shunted along the shelf again. It would always be the last of his books. But did it signal the end of one flight or the beginning of another? He had watched Ruth disappear up the hill. He had entered the shed.

The packages were there as promised. They had contained rye bread, onions, coarse sausage meat and a letter from Jakob, written in pencil on pages torn from an invoice book. He read with difficulty, *Solomon, Your 'Rilke' won't help you now, or your 'Goethe', or your poems* . . .

After that, Jakob's scrawl appeared to collapse. It was hard to distinguish underlinings from crossings-out and over the following three pages he could make out only odd words and phrases. Four times 'The Truth' was spelt out in carefully formed letters but the words surrounding it were each time illegible. The last page was covered in scribbling which bore no resemblance to writing at all. The letter had been signed with a character which might have been a 'J', or an approving tick.

So his flight had begun. That first journey's end and his first exhaustion were then still almost a year away. Jakob would be waiting there. In the last days, deep in the Pindus, he had had the impression that the mountains were moving, but very slightly, bending in towards him as if taking strange bows. He remembered a dulled sense of alarm which had accompanied this perception. His movement no longer contained any thought of 'towards', nor had it ever, he supposed. There was an unforseeable place where the interminable distance would give out. *Click.* There. And there was another where he would be unable to continue.

The last book described one of these. He still did not know which.

He remembered becoming aware that the landscape had grown dry, with slopes of rattling scree and grey mosses. He would scrape them out and chew them with handfuls of snow, unable to taste their bitterness. His nose bled and the blood dried, clogging his nostrils. His throat burned from the coldness of the air. He bound his shoes with strips of cloth torn from his shirt.

Feet, thought Sol, pulling off a sock and looking down. A brusque American doctor in Venice had taken one look and told him that he would limp for the rest of his life. Later, here in Paris, he had been lectured by a stern-faced woman surgeon who had waved his X-rays at him and indicated badly-healed fractures, the floating fragments of cartilage, flicking her painted fingernails against the brittle plastic of the transparencies. 'Your feet are your own, Monsieur. Now their aches are yours too.' But there were no aches. The nerves were damaged; he barely felt his feet.

He had reached the brink of a cliff and looked down into a void. A vast crater opened before him, as though a giant hand had scooped a basin from solid rock. Far below, he had seen what he had thought was a track running across the basin's floor. But there seemed no way to reach it. The walls were almost sheer. He must, he thought later, have been close to the end. His limbs were numb with exhaustion or cold; he did not know which. He could no longer remember being able to imagine the life he had left behind. He would sleep now, he had thought, and had turned to find somewhere to lie down. Jakob was standing behind him.

'Get up,' Jakob said. (So had he, Sol, already been lying down? His recollection was otherwise clear but that had been omitted.)

'We have to get down there,' Jakob pointed and said a word that Sol did not understand. 'There's a path and after that we'll climb.'

'Yes.'

There was a path, as promised. There had to have been a path. Then they began the climb, although Sol soon lost sight of Jakob, whose voice drifted up, growing less and less comprehensible. He knew, of course, that Jakob had been taken away, along with all the others, in trains, while he, Solomon Memel, had fled, and so there was no 'Jakob', or 'others'. No 'Mother', or 'Father'. Nevertheless he could move in strange pursuit of this spectre, whose continued being could not be disproved, or not yet, not before reaching the floor which lay far below. A 'Jakob' could live in the depth of the descent, Sol's own slow progress. He slipped once, his shins scraping down the stone. That his hands and feet felt nothing helped him. He was surprised at the ease of it, second by second; only joining the moments together was hard. The last part would see the sheer sides grow ever more shallow until slopes of scree gave out onto level ground. The floor was littered with stones. There was an opening in the face ahead of him and to his left, a sliver of darkness shaped like the blade of a knife. A cave would give good shelter, he thought. There was a past above him that had been expunged; how else was he here, if not by falling down a well of space in which his guide had so briefly existed? There was no 'Jakob' now. Opposite the cave, far off to his right, an answering fissure split the sheer rock from top to bottom. He thought he had seen a track of some kind from the edge far above. There was no trace of it now.

He sat down, knowing as he did so that he lacked the strength to stand again. Fatigue rolled over him and he reached for the package that someone he had known had left in a shed. Long gone. But he was no longer cold. He would sleep now and never wake up.

So it should have ended.

The noise of the traffic outside grew in volume; a grey September sky. Sol pulled off his remaining shoe and sock and reached forward for the first and last volumes on the shelf, Leon Fleischer's volume bound in dark blue cloth, the other in green cardboard which sagged under its own weight: *Die Keilerjagd von Solomon Memel: Eine Kommentierte Ausgabe.*

Underneath this legend was printed the annotating editor's name: *J. Feuerstein.*

* * *

An unfamiliar voice crackled in the receiver.

'Good news, bad news and news neither bad nor good. Which first, Herr Memel?'

After the war, he had travelled from a city untouched by the conflict and arrived in another. The war's sentence was written between them, a repetitious stutter of roofless buildings and cratered roads whose full stop jolted Sol awake as the train juddered over the points outside the Gare de l'Est and slid within its protective shade. The sudden cool, the broad expanse of the platform and the echoing voices mingling beneath the wrought iron and grimy glass of the station's roof many metres above disoriented him for a moment. But in the next instant he felt his new surroundings cloak him and draw him forward into the crowd, which seemed to melt from him. He knew no one. He carried a suitcase of reinforced cardboard and, in the inside pocket of his jacket, twenty-seven pages torn from a notebook, each one covered in crabbed handwriting. His significance, if any, lay there. He was in abeyance. He had come to Paris, he understood later, to wait.

He had taken lodgings in rue des Ecoles. The rooms of the Hotel d'Orléans had been rented by the hour during the war. Now, in its aftermath, they were home to a floating population of sixty or more residents, who shared three bathrooms and one telephone between them. Its previous incarnation lingered in the pale pink, threadbare carpets which covered the floors, walls and even the ceilings, and the deep rust-striped sinks, one per room, their taps rimed with limescale.

The singular telephone was installed in the hallway. Whenever it rang, the ancient concierge would let it sound for a minute or more before emerging from her little room with its smoked-glass windows and shuffling down the hallway. She would interrogate the callers as to the urgency and relevance of their business. If the resident to whom the caller hoped to speak were out, she would mutter 'Busy' and replace the receiver without taking a message. If in, it was 'Wait', while she rested the receiver on a small shelf beside the handset which had been fitted for that purpose, then crept around her glass-walled office to the bottom of the stairwell. There she matched name to occupant, occupant to room, and calculated the necessary degree of volume. Sol's room was found on the fifth floor and so she screamed at the top of her voice.

'Monsieur *Mee*-mel!'

Sol looked up from of the summer issue of *Perspectives*. A small stack of foolscap sheets lay on the right side of the desk, the product of the last six days' labour. Tomorrow he would take down the typewriter from the top of the wardrobe and begin to type out the German text he had translated from the English. The occupant of the room to the right of his own would complain, as he always did, and there would be a terse exchange in the corridor. But that would be tomorrow. He rose, hurried down the flights of steps and took the receiver from the shelf.

'Bad news? What bad news? Who is this?'

'Leon Fleischer, your publisher. I am calling from Vienna.'

'Pardon me, Herr Fleischer. Your voice sounded different.'

'Of course it does, I'm dying. The bad news is that I'm selling the publishing house. You are to have a new publisher, Herr Memel.'

'Dying?'

'Perhaps Surrer Verlag. We are in negotiation.'

'What?'

Sol had sent out the typescript of *Die Keilerjagd* in the winter of 1950, running off purple copies smelling of acetone on the mimeograph machine in the Paris office of *Perspectives*. Surrer Verlag might have been one of the recipients; he could not remember. He had forgotten them all, except Fleischer.

After his arrival in Paris, he had found work translating journals, catalogues, academic textbooks and technical manuals. He pored over the texts he was sent, ate, drank, slept. He waited. Perhaps a different life would begin; he did not know and made no effort to initiate one. Or perhaps his previous life would recommence. At their parting in Venice, Ruth had promised to write to him poste restante in Paris when she had settled anywhere long enough to receive a reply. At first he had made the journey to the Hotel des Postes in rue du Louvre conscientiously once a month. The office seemed always to contain the same half-dozen young men with carefully-combed hair and threadbare suits, the same thin-faced women in headscarves, the same old men with nicotine-stained beards, all in the grip of some private desperation. He would wait in line for his turn at the hatch and his precious few seconds of the official's time. His anticipation would mount, then the official would glance at his *carte d'identité*, disappear for a minute or so, and return shaking his head, already looking over Sol's shoulder for the next petitioner, shuffling forward with hands cupped about his offering of hope.

But hope of what? Sol asked himself. As the months went by the ritual scattering of his expectations seemed to lose its power. Sol would curtly thank the empty-handed official and turn on his heel, irritated that an hour of his time had been wasted in the airless room on the upper floor of the Hotel des Postes. A reversal effected itself slowly in the man who stood in line (less frequently now, perhaps once every two or three months), for a letter which never came. His anticipation as he waited became something more akin to trepidation and, he realised slowly, when the official returned with nothing, Sol no longer felt disappointment, but relief. No letter had arrived for him, from Ruth or anyone else. He felt no lack. He had shrunk to the confines of his elected life. There was no room in him for need. He had not entered the building on rue du Louvre in more than a year.

Leon Fleischer's letter had arrived directly, however, at the Hotel d'Orléans. By that point, Sol had learned to regard such envelopes without anticipation. Those few publishers who had replied had confined themselves to expressions of regret. This time, however, he had read, 'Thank you for your recent submission which is receiving the attention of the editorial committee of Fleischer Verlag.'

'Surrer! Don't tell me you haven't heard of Surrer Verlag.'

'Yes, I have. But what is wrong, Herr Fleischer?'

'Poverty. Why else does one sell one's publishing house?'

'I mean your health.'

'Just age.'

He had received a second communication from Fleischer Verlag in the late spring of 1951. 'Your recent submission has been considered by the editorial committee of Fleischer Verlag in whose judgement it merits publication. Please sign and return the contracts enclosed.' Underneath, a handwritten note from Leon Fleischer had invited him to visit, if ever he were to find himself in Vienna.

Sol had stared at the note then walked slowly upstairs, closed *The Service and Maintenance Manual for the Mauer Large-Particle Filtration Pump (Models P35, PS35 and P55)* and reached into the wardrobe for his coat. He wanted to tell someone, he realised. Or he wanted someone to tell. He had read the note again and then gone to Gare de l'Est to inquire after trains to Vienna.

'Poetry I have. Paper I lack.' Leon Fleischer had waved a near-transparent sheet which drooped like a handkerchief. He pointed a sharp nose in Sol's direction. His small dark eyes swept over his guest. Pinched cheeks and a bald angular head suggested some kind of diagnostic instrument, thought Sol.

Fleischer edged his way around chairs piled with books bound in Fleischer Verlag's dark blue covers, extending a hand towards Sol, who shook it.

'You would be?'

The telephone rang before he could answer.

Fleischer listened for a moment then said, 'Your problem. But my loss. No, I do not wish to speak with Herr Friessner.'

A longer pause followed, during which he motioned for Sol to sit down.

Leon Fleischer said, 'Delivery is not a commutative process.'

The receiver clattered in its cradle.

'Solomon Memel,' said Sol, but then the telephone had rung again.

Fleischer hovered over a crowded desk, the backs of his knees knocking against a wooden swivel-chair into which he seemed always almost on the point of settling. His pen scratched quickly at the blotter while he spoke into the mouthpiece. A number of typed manuscript pages engaged his attention between these interruptions, or perhaps they were themselves the interruptions, for they elicited from him similarly discontinuous volleys of words. He would look up after each outburst as if to include Sol in the private commentary which either text or telephone had provoked. Sol nodded or shook his head as seemed appropriate, understanding only that the editorial committee of Fleischer Verlag, and all others of its officers, appeared to consist in Leon Fleischer alone.

'Nonsense and no,' the publisher said finally, at once dropping the receiver of the telephone and turning over the last page of the manuscript.

'Done. Herr Solomon Memel, forgive me. I did not expect you and I am very glad you have come. On the strength of the work you have sent me, I believe you to be the most significant poet of your generation. Now let us talk.'

Sol had left Vienna two days later. The smart blue volume had appeared from Fleischer Verlag eight months after that, in December. To date, a little more than a year since Sol's first meeting with Leon Fleischer, *Die Keilerjagd* had sold forty-one copies.

Now he asked, 'But what do you mean, Herr Fleischer, when you say "Just age"?'

'Is it the adverb confusing you, Herr Memel, or the noun? Why do poets never wish to hear the *good* news?'

'What is the good news, Herr Fleischer?'

'Reichmann has called.'

'Walter Reichmann?'

'He wants to interview you.'

The following week a broad-shouldered man in a black linen suit stood in the hall of the Hotel d'Orléans. He turned lightly on his feet at the sound of Sol's footsteps. An owlish face was framed by a close-trimmed beard and short grey hair. He smiled, disclosing tobacco-stained teeth.

'Greetings, Herr Memel,' said Walter Reichmann. 'I am honoured to meet the author of *Die Keilerjagd*.'

The two men shook hands.

'There used to be a restaurant not far from here,' Reichmann continued. 'In rue Domat, if I remember correctly. Wonderful spinach. Do you know it?'

The restaurant had changed hands. It was too early in the season for spinach. The two men ate a thick chicken stew and watched each other over their spoons. After his initial burst of bonhomie, Reichmann had made only the smallest of small-talk, commenting first on the framed photographs displayed on the walls, then on the string of pennants which hung above the bar. When Sol enquired after his dining companion's journey, Reichmann replied, with a self-deprecating smile, that it was he who ought to be asking the questions. But he resolutely failed to ask any. Sol watched the interviewer's hands carefully tear the remaining bread into fragments, then drop these into his stew. From time to time the dull clangour of pots being washed sounded from the kitchen. Reichmann had large hands for his size. They were as unexpressive as their owner. The two men were the restaurant's only customers.

'Shall we walk?' suggested Reichmann when the meal was over.

They stepped out into a street of shuttered shops and began an aimless progress in which Reichmann seemed guided by a search for occasions to recall the history of the quarter. Here Verlaine had died, and here an American novelist had lived between the wars, and here Descartes was thought to have

written the *Discourse on Method* ('But this is not true').
Reichmann presented each observation with a little shrug and
Sol nodded or agreed. The irony that he, who had occupied this
quarter for three years, was being shown its sights by his visitor
seemed unremarkable. I have not lived here, he thought. His
Paris flowed around him like air. In which future would some-
one look up at the Hotel d'Orléans and point out the room of
Solomon Memel?

The afternoon wore on. They ambled deeper into the backstreets, their route taking them further away from the river.
Sol's puzzlement at Reichmann's aimlessness became mild
irritation, and finally a perturbed boredom. Something lay
under what Reichmann was telling him and something else
underlay Sol's unease. They were related. Eventually, the two
men arrived outside a door with a tiny grille set into a high
windowless wall. Pink onion-domes rose behind it.

'They serve wonderful mint tea here,' said Reichmann. 'Are
you thirsty?'

But Sol was no longer willing to continue the other's enigmatic charade.

'No,' he said, and pointed across the road. 'Let's go in there.'

An imposing edifice was set back from the thoroughfare by an
open courtyard and a broad flight of stone steps. Fluted columns
rose into the air and supported an enormous pediment bearing
an elaborate frieze depicting animals.

'The Jardin des Plantes?' queried Reichmann. 'But of course. It
will be perfect.'

They entered and climbed the staircase to the first floor. A
varnished wooden sign above a high doorway announced: *Les
Espèces Disparues*. Within, two rows of glass cases ran the
length of the gallery. Sol smelt chalk dust and old air. Inside
the cases stuffed animals were displayed. Their yellowed claws
had been wired to branches to hold them in dramatic poses.
Beneath the faded fur and thinning plumage showed the dull
sheen of embalmed skin. Their glass eyes glittered implausibly,
as if such creatures had never existed at all in nature but had
been constructed here. Soon, Sol thought vaguely, even their
extinctions would be extinct.

The gallery was high and narrow and the least sound echoed in
the glassed roofspace. But it was silent, Sol realised. Reichmann

had stopped talking. *Dodo*, he read. *Quagga.* The dried skin of a
sea cow lay stretched out in a cabinet with a wooden rule to
indicate its length, which was four metres and twenty-two
centimetres.

Enough waiting, Sol thought. He had not understood Walter
Reichmann's small-talk, nor his pedantic commentary during
their tour of the Latin Quarter. Both were clear in the eloquence
of his silence.

'When did you eat the wonderful spinach?' Sol asked.

They were standing a little apart, in front of a cabinet from
which an over-sized bison-like creature regarded them.

*L'Aurochs était un grand boeuf d'Europe, proche du zébu
d'Asie . . .*

'I served here during the war,' replied Reichmann.

Moa. Hydrodramalis gigas.

There was a long silence, which Reichmann eventually broke.
'I have to ask my questions.'

'Of course,' said Sol.

Sol said, 'I do not know, in literal terms, how I arrived at the place
where *Die Keilerjagd* was written, but it had to be written. In the
context of my situation – I may say *our* situation – my journey
was inevitable. One speaks of loss as something one carries, or
bears, but that is not the case. I know that my father died of
typhus in a work camp and that my mother was shot as 'unfit for
work'. To me they have disappeared, leaving no evidence that
they existed. I returned one morning to the place where I had left
them and they were gone. One may approach such realities, but
only by circuitous routes. Such absences, I mean . . .

'When I was discovered by the *andartes*, the Greek partisans, I
was unconscious. I had given up. I did not know what country I
was in, nor how far I had travelled to reach it. I came to the task
with nothing, nothing at all . . .

'There *must* once have been a boar, in some shape or form.
And a hunt. Kalydon was a coastal kingdom, where the Greek
heroes gathered. The boar could only have led them north, into
the mountains. Towards myself. So I saw their fate, instead of
those I did not see. Through them I was the witness of the fate I
had fled, do you follow?

'The situation was confused. I understood little at the time. In the mountains I could not speak the language and in the camp there were only rumours. The Germans were readying themselves for the withdrawal; everyone knew that. Some *andarte* groups were trying to prevent this and others were willing to let them go. Of course there were elements of bluff on both sides. Traps were set. The events in which I was involved formed part of this, I believe . . .

'Eberhardt, Oberfeldkommandant Oberstleutnant Heinrich Eberhardt, to give him his full title, was responsible for the worst. There were military objectives, to ensure the withdrawal, for example, but towards the end even this pretext disappeared. There were no objectives, no purpose, only savagery and waste, a visitation of rage. The boar's mark, as I saw it . . .

'No. I can say no more of Thyella than I have said. She took that as her *nom de guerre*. Her real name was Anastasia Kosta, although I learned it only after the war. It was her arrow that found him, so to speak, just as Atalanta's first found the boar . . .

'But how does one write of a disappearance? What of those events which leave no trace and those beings who leave no footprints? There are terrains which admit nothing and record nothing. Such places do exist. If the poem grows "mysterious", as you say, when it enters the cave then there must exist a mystery to solve. But it is not so. The invisibility of what takes place there is necessary. Some acts will be performed only under cover of such a darkness. I tried to bear witness to what I could not see. To what could not be seen . . .

'No, not quite. Her face was the one I awoke to, but it was only after the attack that I saw it as an image. There were flashes, you see, openings in the smoke. The Thyella of *Die Keilerjagd* is remembered from one such. But I saw the bodies of the partisans in the same way. They had been hung from the branches of a tree. Just a glimpse. Like a grotesque menorah. That image would become the death of the sons of Thestius, high on Aracynthus. The last image was the entrance to the gorge. There was a fissure in the cliff behind the village, with soldiers around it. At its far end was the Cauldron and the cave. I had already passed through the gorge, of course, but unconscious. I would not see it again for a year and a half, and then the circumstances were very different. Then it was we who were hunting. And Eberhardt was the hunted . . .

'Yes, with my own eyes. You asked how?'

'Yes.'

'It was barbaric, of course, but it used to be common practice in the villages outside the town where I grew up. I doubt it was different in the mountains of Greece. The peasants used to say that the meat would be tainted unless it was done while the animal was alive. But to children, especially Jewish children, the allure was irresistible: blood, death, knives. And the sexual aspect perhaps. The genitals themselves. Its being a pig added another illicit thrill. I never actually stood there and watched but she must have seen it done many times, as a child.'

Finally, 'Correct. Just as I described. Then she shot him.'

Reichmann wrote quickly, in a compact hand.

A train stirred beneath the cover of the siding-shed, a train identical to the one that had carried him to Paris. It had rested here for at least the six years since his arrival. Now cobwebs quivered in the angles of its windows. Couplings clanked and fine dust rose from its empty seats. The carriages shuddered as the locomotive's insistence tautened through their length. The long shed wrapped them in darkness but there was a glare of daylight ahead, where the doors had been opened and the track stretched into the distance.

The locomotive's blunt nose emerged little by little into the light, pulling the protesting carriages. Some were windowless, mail-cars perhaps. After that came flatcars carrying the years' accumulated detritus: broken cement sacks, fuel drums cut in half, tar-coated lengths of wood. No one had expected this train ever to move again, but here it was.

He saw that there were already far more cars than could have been housed in the shed. The locomotive was hundreds of metres down the track. It sounded its horn – *mee*-mel! *mee*-mel! – and at that its composition changed again. Closed cars began to emerge, built of rough planks and bearing an encrustation of dried mud for livery. There were more and more of them. The head of the train was almost out of sight now and yet he seemed to be aware of every part of it. The locomotive was approaching the city he had left in favour of Paris years before, the city where Ruth would be waiting. Parts of the train were in tunnels, others slicing through cuttings or passing over viaducts. The rearmost section was still rolling out of the shed. As the closed cars trundled forward into the light they were met by men and women who struggled to keep pace for a while then fell back, exhausted. He was inside, peering out between the planks of the walls. He recognised faces – Chaim Fingerhut was there and Gustl Ritter – but most of them were unknown to him. They were trying to grasp little pieces of paper which he was pushing between the planks. *Mee*-mel! *mee*-mel! *mee*-mel!

The other cars were empty. He had his suitcase, which he was sitting on, and the twenty-seven notebook pages, which he was tearing into fragments small enough to push through the cracks between the planks, knowing that each one would be grasped by a fluttering hand outside, uncrumpled, smoothed and saved. The train was endless. He was its only passenger. He would be back in Venice soon.

Mee-mel! Monsieur *Mee*-mel!

'Have you received Reichmann's article? Ach! The post is a licence to sell stamps and betray. Not at all. Quite the opposite. Yesterday the orders were, wait, let me see. One moment, Herr Memel . . .'

Leon Fleischer's voice had changed again. Now it rasped in Sol's ear as he stood in the hallway. He saw the concierge moving behind the frosted glass, a limbless insect. A truck rumbled slowly past, paused, engine throbbing, then continued on its way. It was two months since he had bade farewell to Walter Reichmann.

Upstairs in his room, the book on the desk was opened at a page with black and white line drawings of a man, a woman and two children sitting down to supper. The legend above read: La Famille: Une Institution Type?' A sheet of paper beside it displayed the handwritten words 'Die Familie: Eine typische Anstalt (?)' Sol's translation of *La Sociologie, une Introduction aux Principes Fondamentals* was all but done. It would, however, never be completed. Fleischer's voice returned and rasped again.

'What? I beg your pardon, Herr Fleisch. . . . Could you, yes. I mean I did not hear you correctly. I see. Yes, I see. No, I'm simply surprised. Very surprised.'

He put down the telephone and stood quietly in the hallway, considering the creature who had come into being in Reichmann's article. A second Solomon Memel had been framed within its columns of text, as he saw when the magazine arrived some days later with his name prominent upon the cover. The protagonist of Reichmann's narrative had created himself in the harsh terrain of the mountains, turned on his enemy and defeated him.

Over the months that followed, he repeated what he had first told Walter Reichmann to a procession of the critic's more junior colleagues and rivals. The face of Solomon Memel looked out from magazine covers and for a few days after each of these appearances he would be recognised in shops and cafés. He was asked to appear on television and refused. Leon Fleischer telephoned with news of the volume's continuing success and the details of his skirmishes with the executives of Surrer Verlag. The negotiations, Fleischer told him with glee, had been transformed by the success of *Die Keilerjagd*.

'They are such clumsy huntsmen, Solomon. Crashing about in the undergrowth. They will never catch your boar.' The publisher's voice grew gravelly through the summer. A breathy whistle appeared in the autumn.

That October a Swiss newspaper published an overexposed photograph of three women standing on a hillside with rifles slung over their shoulders and bandoliers of bullets. The caption read: 'Anastasia Kosta (left), the "Thyella" of Solomon Memel's *Die Keilerjagd*, photographed in the western foothills of the Pindus three years before her death.' The accompanying article claimed that the picture had been taken in the summer of 1941.

Sol had peered at the newsprint reproduction. The woman was the right height. The face was strong, almost too strong to be conventionally beautiful. It might have been her, but the details which would have told him certainly were lost in the glare of sunlight which had flooded the photographer's lens. In lieu of any other image, it was reproduced over and over again. She was sometimes 'the *andartisse* or woman partisan', sometimes 'the Greek resistance heroine', but more often than either she was the 'Thyella' of his poem.

In the New Year he began to search for new lodgings, a process long envisaged and long delayed. The books which had piled up in every corner of the room in the Hotel d'Orléans were packed into boxes. His clothes, he thought, would still fit into the cardboard suitcase which sat next to the typewriter on top of the wardrobe. Lying on the bed with his hands behind his head he looked up at both and realised that almost a year had passed and he had not written a word. Since the day he had encountered Reichmann, in fact. He climbed staircases to tiny mansard attics. His footsteps echoed on expanses of parquet. He looked up through light wells with the proportions of liftshafts at tiny squares of sky. A concrete pillar near Montparnasse had windows instead of walls. The view was invoked. The view of me, he thought, his nose all but touching the glass, which misted then cleared, revealing hundreds of other windows, or thousands, and hundreds of thousands.

In February Leon Fleischer's voice regained the timbre Sol remembered from their first meeting.

'I have "undergone a minor operation", as moribund politicians like to say. In consequence I am dying at the standard rather than accelerated rate,' he explained to Sol. 'Speaking of death and politics, you were quoted in the Bundesrat last week. Misquoted, I should say. Did you see the report?'

'Dying? Dying of what?'

'You are beginning to repeat yourself, Solomon. Normally a trait of older poets. Now, the latest from Surrer. This is quite priceless . . .'

The sale of Fleischer Verlag to Surrer Verlag seemed to have become an all-consuming passion for Leon Fleischer. His telephone calls became résumés of its progress, or lack thereof, for the feints and thrusts of the negotiation seemed to advance nothing, so far as Sol could tell, save the affair's ever-deepening complication. Fleischer's enthusiasm for the negotiation was unquenchable, but not infectious. He would laugh to himself in Vienna while Sol in Paris puzzled over the contractual point that could occasion such delight. He resumed his hunt for an apartment and finally found one, in the sixteenth, which seemed to have nothing to recommend it besides the fact that Sol did not dislike it as strongly as the others he had viewed. It was not available until May. In mid-April, he took the receiver from the shelf in the hallway of the Hotel d'Orléans and found himself speaking to a woman.

'Am I speaking to Herr Memel?'

'Yes, may I ask who is this?'

'Ingeborg Fleischer, Herr Memel. I am Leon Fleischer's wife.'

'Wife? But I didn't know . . . Forgive me, Frau Fleischer, I didn't know that . . . Excuse me.'

'I have never involved myself in my husband's business affairs, Herr Memel.'

Out of the corner of his eye Sol saw someone enter the door to the hallway and hesitate in the gloom.

'Until now,' Fleischer's wife continued, 'when I must. I am telephoning all of Fleischer Verlag's authors to tell them that the house has been sold to Surrer Verlag. Surrer Verlag has assumed responsibility for all contracts drawn up by my husband and will send a more formal notification. I wanted to telephone the authors first. I believe Leon would have wanted that.'

Sol felt a cold wave ripple through him. 'Please pardon me, Frau Fleischer, but do you mean Leon . . .'

'My husband died the night before last, Herr Memel, of complications arising from cancer of the larynx.'

'But he had an operation,' Sol protested. 'He told me he was recovered.'

'The operation was not successful.'

The figure hovering in the hallway was still there. A resident waiting to use the telephone, Sol thought. He turned his back on the man.

'I am very sorry, Frau Fleischer. Without your late husband, I would never . . .'

'I understand, Herr Memel. Many of the writers published by my husband have said as much, but I know that Leon would have been particularly pleased that you acknowledged his support.'

'I am very sorry,' Sol said again. There was an awkward silence.

'Herr Memel,' the woman spoke at last, 'I am embarrassed to say that I never shared my husband's interests.' Ingeborg Fleischer paused. 'I rarely read the books he published. In fact almost never. Books do not interest me very much.'

Sol could see her now. Ingeborg Fleischer was plain, with a kind face, light brown hair which she had curled once a week. Her husband had baffled and fascinated her and now he had baffled her for the last time by disappearing. Sol could hear the shock in her voice.

'But I read your book, Herr Memel.'

Then Ingeborg Fleischer hung up.

Sol replaced the receiver and turned towards the door. The man who had been waiting to use the telephone advanced. Sol stood aside to let him pass. He would go out. Walk. Think. The man was carrying a large briefcase, which he swung out, almost striking Sol. It was Walter Reichmann.

Sol's first thought was that the occasion of the critic's reappearance must be Leon Fleischer's death. His hesitation was that of the bearer of bad news. But his demeanour did not seem consolatory. Anxious, perhaps, as he greeted Sol. No, Sol decided, this had nothing to do with his publisher.

'What brings you to Paris, Herr Reichmann?' he asked.

The critic mumbled something in reply, opened his briefcase and began to rummage, one-handed, within it. He shook his head in frustration as he fumbled after whatever it was he sought, and whatever it was that compelled his presence here. The man was more perturbed than Sol had first thought.

'Herr Reichmann, I have just learned of the death of my publisher, Leon Fleischer. Now, forgive my directness, but why are you here?'

'I am sorry to hear that, Herr Memel.' Reichmann's round head rose from his briefcase. 'I am sorry. I knew Leon Fleischer. A man of integrity, integrity, yes . . .'

'Herr Reichmann, what is the matter?'

'The matter?'

The critic pulled his arm out of his briefcase and handed Sol a book bound in green cardboard.

'This, Herr Memel, is the matter. Or integrity perhaps.'

The thought seemed to be occurring to him for the first time. Sol waited for the critic to assemble his thoughts.

'Integrity is earned over time, Herr Memel. Years. I too like to think I have integrity. A critic's integrity, of course. That my judgements are trusted and believed. That those whose work I endorse are also to be trusted. My integrity depends on them, do you see?'

The critic delivered this little speech to the floor, looking up to face Sol only at its conclusion.

'What is this about, Herr Reichmann?'

'I must ask you something, Herr Memel. Something it pains me to ask; that should never be asked of an artist.'

'Then ask.'

But the critic frowned, pursed his lips, tapped his briefcase against the side of his leg, twisting this way and that in the hallway of the Hotel d'Orléans, in the grip of some internal argument. Or he is mad, thought Sol. But then Reichmann appeared to reach a decision.

'There are no dolphins in the gulf of Corinth, Herr Memel.'

'What?'

Reichmann pointed to the book which rested, forgotten, in Sol's hands.

'In there, Herr Memel,' he said. 'My questions are in there.'

*　　*　　*

The wind had dropped as he descended. The sides of the crater rose around him. At the bottom the air was still.

He looked across a vast floor broken only by stones. He remembered the light had dimmed and its colours seeped away leaving dry stone, the far cliffs, pebbles shifting under his feet. Jakob had disappeared, had never existed here. The last seconds had seen the light's drainage accelerate, a flood of it west and away. A starless black gathered in the sky. He had lain down. No, he had tried to reach the cave and its shelter, but he had lacked the will. Only then had he lain down. The darkness was the closing of his eyes.

There was no up or down in the slow tumble which followed, but there were openings in it, brief glimpses and disturbances, motions and sensations which he registered only as they passed beyond the reach of his senses. He remembered something like animal hair, coarse and fibrous, and a hot sun that made his head throb and dried his tongue. Soft waves of air had broken over him in a rhythm that nudged him gently one way then the other. A grinning man held four fingers in front of his face, said a word, then vanished. The ground was a reservoir of pain. He would reach down to touch it, then the pain would warn him off, but it grew harder and harder to remain weightless. When he opened his eyes he saw railway tracks suspended above him. The next time they were seams of coal. Finally they were smoke-blackened beams. He was lying on straw in a low-ceiling hut looking up into a tunnel of darkness. The tunnel swung aside, becoming the barrel of a rifle.

Click.

The safety-catch. The rifle was lowered. Sol looked up at a woman. She was a little older than himself with long dark hair pulled back from her face, dressed in army fatigues. The eyes which looked down at him were black and betrayed nothing as she fixed him in her gaze. Sol looked up at her. But a moment later she moved beyond his field of vision. The door slammed shut behind him before he could turn his head.

Someone had wrapped his feet in ragged lengths of cloth. There was no sign of his boots. His left foot began to throb as he carefully unwound the improvised bandage. Then the right. Both were swollen and discoloured; the toenails on the right foot felt loose. He lifted his leg with both hands and rested the foot on the ground as gently as he was able. In the next instant something seemed to grasp his foot and crush it. He managed to raise the foot and waited for the pain to subside. He lay in the darkness in a daze while questions circled like kites, high above and unreachable: How far? Since when? For how long?

He had understood that he was dying, alone and very far from home, but he had been wrong. His future still existed. Wrong, all wrong.

The hut was windowless but the roof, supported by the heavy black rafters, seemed to be constructed of turf. Sunlight prickled above him and suddenly he was thirsty and light-headed. His feet were still unbandaged. From last night, he told himself. They had been bandaged an unknown number of nights before that. He had been brought here, wherever 'here' was. He had been found, and that must have been the evening he climbed down into the crater. He would have died that night if he had not been found. Another question. He slept again.

He awoke to the smell of stale woodsmoke. Four men stood over him. Three were dressed in fatigues, as the woman had been; the two younger ones wore full beards. The third was heavily-built and red-faced. He regarded Sol placidly. All three carried short machine-guns.

The fourth man hung back. He was older, but how much older

Sol could not guess. He held an ancient rifle which reached almost to his shoulder. His steel-grey hair was cut close to the scalp and a sharp nose gave him a hawkish look, reinforced by eyes which seemed not to blink. He was shorter than the two younger men, who might have been his grandsons. When he moved forward Sol saw even in the hut's dim light that his eyes were a piercing blue. Sol tried to pull himself upright, then spread his arms helplessly. The old man watched his efforts and Sol was reminded of the woman the night before. Her gaze too had surrendered nothing of her thoughts. He uttered something in a language Sol did not understand, first to Sol, then in an undertone to the older of the others, who nodded and knelt beside Sol, wheezing theatrically. The man's eyes narrowed and his mouth worked silently. He formed his lips around three words.

'I am America.'

Sol stared at the round face which hovered before his own. It wore an expectant expression. To his surprise, Sol realised that he recognised the words. I am. America. He was being addressed in English. Before he could order his thoughts to respond to the outlandish sentence, the man spoke again.

'You are America?'

They began to attempt to communicate, watched by the two young guards and the old man. By 'I am America', Sol grasped, the man meant that he had been in America, or that he spoke 'American', and 'You are America?' asked if Sol did too. Then the man thumped himself on the chest and introduced himself. He was 'Uncle America'. Uncle America grinned at this minor victory over their mutual incomprehension.

The other three did not grin; nor did the young men trouble to conceal their impatience as they waited for these preliminaries to conclude. The old man stood back in the shadows, resting the butt of the long rifle on the ground. For all the inconsequentiality of the words which passed between Sol and Uncle America, the tension in the hut increased as their halting exchange looped them in half-understandings and led them into impasses from which they would slowly retreat to attempt their meanings from some other direction. When Sol nodded to signal that he had understood, Uncle America would grin broadly, quite oblivious to the mood of his companions, and when Sol spoke he would listen with his mouth open and his brow furrowed from the effort of concentration. Sol began to suspect that the man was a simpleton.

From the rear of the room, the old man spoke, quietly but suddenly. Uncle America listened then turned back to Sol. 'You are in . . .' And there he broke off. After a pause he said, 'place', then cupped his hands and spoke a word which Sol knew, or remembered, but did not understand.

'You are in place.' Uncle America cupped his hands again. 'You come to place by road.' He was red in the face now and he no longer smiled. 'But there is not a road to . . .' He cupped his hands and said the word again.

It was the word Jakob had used. *Khax-Arn-Nee*. The non-existent Jakob, who had guided him down an impossible descent to the place in which he was to have perished. He had been saved, however. He understood the words being spoken but not their import. Yes, he thought, I was in place. He began to tell what he remembered. There had been a path around the rim which dropped down, then a climb, how he had fallen once or twice. Uncle America relayed his words in short bursts. But as Sol relived the descent for his silent audience gaps began to open in the story, as though his stride had widened or he had made impossible leaps down the sheer face. He did not know how he had arrived safely at the floor of the crater. He could not remember. He stumbled and faltered. Finally he stopped. The room was quiet.

Its silence was broken by one of the younger men. He muttered something then gestured impatiently at Sol. His thumb flicked the catch on his gun.

But the old man spoke, quickly and quietly as before. Sol saw reluctance in the face of the young man, who stepped aside to let the old man approach. He squatted in front of Sol, holding the antiquated rifle as before, and peered into Sol's face. Once again Sol was reminded of the woman the first time he had awakened. Then, the old man extended his free arm, palm open, as though to slap Sol in the face. It stopped short, however, and rested against Sol's cheek, almost a caress. The old man spoke.

'Say the truth,' Uncle America translated. 'About the place.' The same word again. Axani? Khaxane? The old man's eyes held him, searching his face.

'I am telling the truth,' he said. 'As much as I know it.'

The old man watched him for a few seconds more, then removed his hand and rose to his feet. He said something else, which was not translated, and by the anger which flashed across the young men's faces Sol knew that he had been believed. It was anger, certainly, and behind it was apprehension. But they could not fear him, only what he represented in that question, which he had not been able to answer. He had reached the floor of a basin of stone scraped out of the surrounding mountains. What was there to fear in that?

Over the days that followed the face he saw most frequently belonged to Uncle America, full-cheeked and snub-nosed, his mouth slightly agape as though mildly surprised at anything and everything around him. He would amble in with a gait that rolled from side to side, settle a bowl of cold thin soup on the ground then lower himself with a sigh onto the packed earth and rest his gun on his lap. Then he held a finger up, 'One,' a second finger, 'Two,' a third, 'Three.' After this ritual he would pass the bowl to Sol and while the other ate he would begin to talk.

'Hellas!' Uncle America thumped his chest to indicate himself. 'Greek!'

Sol's first question had elicited an immediate and straightforward answer. His subsequent queries, when he managed to speak over Uncle America's rambling monologue and frame them in such a way that the man might understand, were rarely so fortunate. He had not, Sol finally understood, been to America. He had intended to go, to follow his cousin, or second cousin, who had been brought up in the nearest town and could write. Uncle America had had the cousin's letters read, reread, explained and re-explained many times over to him by the cousin's elderly parents, who were now dead. So the tenuous link with his second cousin, or third cousin, had been severed and the problem of getting to America remained. The war had complicated the issue. Uncle America's English seemed not to extend to any clear explanation of how he came to speak it.

The Germans were a distant presence as Uncle America eked out his store of words and reached after the long vista of his project. But the old man's other enemies were close, he explained. An arm was waved and brought down with a chop. A valley away? The other side of a river? They had joined the Germans because Geraxos was with the *andartes*. That was the old man's *nom de guerre*.

On the days that Uncle America did not appear, young bearded men armed with short machine-guns would bring the bowl of cold soup. They regarded him neutrally, nodded, retreated. He was left alone again in the near-darkness, which was all the darker after these dazzling interludes. As his eyes readjusted, the earthen underside of the roof reappeared, then the blackened beams which supported it. There was no scent of smoke now, though, only a dry animal smell. No one had lit a fire here for many years. A verse drifted in his thoughts, something about the 'black in the smoke being heavy with fat' or 'thick with fat'; it was not quite right. He spent the hours chasing it, and other fragments, until the door opened again. The words and their author eluded him. He wondered if the woman would return.

'One!'

Uncle America unbarred the door and propped it open to admit air and light. He recited the next two numbers. A hunk of dense bread would be produced from the man's pocket and while Sol slurped and chewed the man would begin to talk. Sol listened for dull echoes of the Ancient Greek he had learned long ago at school, but those days seemed even more remote than the language he had carried from them and he deciphered only fragments, which broke through Uncle America's opaque accent then sank again and were lost. There were reticences in his ramblings, or subjects which ran up against the limits of their improvised language sooner than others. He could not tell whether Uncle America truly misunderstood him or only chose to. But when he had finally asked after the woman, he had only needed to trace a rough form with his hands and Uncle America had nodded and replied: 'Geraxos gave her name. She is child of child of . . . other woman.' Uncle America clasped his hands and tried to pull them apart. There was some family bond which he could not unravel.

'Thyella,' the man said. Then his expression grew troubled as though there were something incomprehensible, even to himself, in what he had said. Or in Thyella herself. Then he had begun to explain that if Sol tried to run away the other *andartes* would shoot him. He, Uncle America, would shoot him too.

'But how could I run?' Sol burst out as the other's meaning crystallised. He pointed to his feet. Uncle America appeared baffled. Then, understanding, he began to laugh, for Sol could barely stand unaided. Uncle America supported him when he escorted him outside to relieve himself and even then Sol winced with pain. These, however, were his only respites from the hut's interior gloom. Outside, he could breathe out its fetid air and draw fresh into his lungs. It was mountain air, thin and cold. The land rose on either side of the hut, while the ground before it fell away, widening as it descended to stands of trees below. It was an offshoot of the valley which could be made out behind the trees and thick undergrowth at the bottom. Its mouth thus shielded, it would be hard to tell from the valley below that this place existed. The hut stood almost at its head. There was no sign of any other habitation, or of human presence at all. Once, Sol saw woodsmoke rising in still air somewhere off to the south-west. He assumed it signalled a village, or the camp of the *andartes*. One arm was slung over Uncle America's shoulders; with his other he pointed to the thin plume of smoke. Uncle America grinned amiably and rubbed his stomach. The next day he brought a piece of cooked meat and watched while Sol devoured it then licked the grease from his fingers. But he did not confirm that the smoke indeed came from the *andartes'* camp, or that Geraxos's enemies were in the next valley or across a river. Similarly, it had taken a whole afternoon to explain the relationship between himself, his cousin and his cousin's parents who had lived in the nearest town. But in that time Uncle America had never once mentioned the name of the town.

Sol's frostbitten feet began to regain their normal colour. Two of the nails on his right foot were only loosely attached. He could almost stand on his left foot, although the pain quickly became unbearable. The hut grew more oppressive by the day. Was he being protected, or imprisoned, or only held until the time came to dispose of him? Then, for three days running, Uncle America did not appear and the younger men checked on him in pairs, one remaining in the doorway looking out while the other placed his food on the ground. He remembered one from the night when Geraxos had questioned him but no flicker of recognition passed across the man's face. On the fourth day, two more had come, this time with Uncle America.

'We walk tomorrow,' he said. 'Feet good.' He waved a hand at the back of the hut, meaning north, Sol supposed. The mountains again. There could be only one answer. He nodded quickly. The other two talked quietly among themselves. Their faces were impassive but their movements were quick. One rolled a matchstick between his teeth, took it out, reversed it, tapped it against his leg, replaced it and repeated these actions over and over again.

'What is happening?' he asked Uncle America.

The other shook his head. 'Tomorrow.'

But tomorrow arrived that same afternoon. Sol was standing when he heard machine-gun fire rattle from further down the valley. He lost his balance and let himself fall to the floor. He had rebandaged his feet as soon as the men had left and tried to think what he could do. They would shoot him if he could not walk; that was what the visit had meant. But he could not walk. And tomorrow was already here.

He pushed open the door of the hut and began to crawl around to the side. If he could reach the ridge at the top. . . .

He did not know what he could do if he reached the top. The machine-gun fire was intermittent, short bursts alternating with longer ones from a more powerful-sounding weapon. It seemed to be growing simultaneously both nearer and more distant. He picked out single shots. Nearer. The fighting was spreading. And crawling was as agonising as walking. He was not going to reach the ridge.

He stopped and looked down on the roof of the hut, which was barely distinguishable from the ground out of which it rose. Twenty impossible metres to the top. Perhaps fifty to the bottom. Another burst of gunfire. But where from? Where am I, he wondered. He began to drag himself down to the trees and undergrowth at the mouth of the cutting. Hide there, he thought. Every jolt of his body registered now in his feet. The bones within were being broken into splinters and driven into him. He pulled himself down the slope. There were two kinds of gunfire: near and far. The heavier weapon seemed to have ceased, but the near gunfire was now very near. Another twenty metres to the trees. The heavy undergrowth would hide him. He would be safe. Then an *andarte* stepped out of the cover directly ahead of him.

The man raised his gun and took aim at Sol. But he must have looked up from the gunsight, Sol deduced later. He had faced his intended victim and Sol had seen that the partisan's eyes were blue; the same blue as the old man's. Then puzzlement spread over the *andarte*'s face. He lost his footing and fell, clutching his shoulder. The crack of the rifle came a second later. But not his. The partisan lay on the ground. From somewhere behind him, deep within the undergrowth, a man screamed and continued screaming. Someone barked an order, the voice high and excited. Stand up, he told himself as two soldiers ran towards him, the first swinging the stock of his rifle to catch him in the ribs. He must have stood up. They would have shot him on the ground.

He saw the woman as he fell, for no more than an instant. Thyella was kneeling on the ground in front of the trees, surrounded by soldiers. Her jacket had been pulled open to expose her breasts. Her hands had been tied, or perhaps they were clasped behind her? One of the soldiers had put his rifle to the back of her head.

Flashes, parts of things, all emerging and falling back into blackness. He wanted to hold them still and they would not stop or be hurried into coherence; they gathered at their own pace. In front of his face was hard earth with a single smooth stone embedded in it. He was lying on his front. His head throbbed. So it had been a village, he thought, regaining and surrendering consciousness.

It was still there when his eyes reopened. An area of packed earth was ringed on three sides with cottages built of rough stones. Behind the dwellings rose their raw fabric, a face of grey rock. Some of the soldiers had taken cover in front of the cottages. They looked up nervously at the heights, but there was no firing now. At the other end of the village, a second group had taken up position around a deep recession in the cliff face. A heavy machine-gun had been set up there. Its operator aimed the barrel into the fissure. The cottages were loosely grouped. Their focus was an open-sided structure which appeared to have been built around a tree. A planked roof encircled the thick trunk and was supported at the corners by drystone pillars. Within it was a group of men who wore no uniforms, only green armbands. There were tables and chairs. From his lowly position, Sol could see that they had one of the *andartes* in there. Two of them held him upright before their commander, who sat behind a table. There was something on the table, wrapped in grey sacking. The commander unwrapped it and held it up to the partisan but Sol could not make out the object. At the sight of it, the captive's head began to shake, in refusal, like an animal rejecting harness. The men holding him struggled to control him. Their commander shouted and the partisan was frog-marched across Sol's field of vision, then behind. The captive began to bellow as he was dragged away, the voice growing fainter. There was a brief period of silence, but the final cry reached Sol's ears as clearly as if the act performed on the man had taken place only a few paces away: a high shriek.

He did not know how he was here. He had been pulled to his feet by the same soldier who had knocked him down. The ground drove spikes through the soles of his feet; the world reeled around him. A soldier was being carried out of the trees by four of his fellows. He was screaming, the same scream Sol had heard earlier. Blood soaked the soldier from crotch to knee. His companions struggled to hold him. A voice had shouted in German, 'Put down your weapon!' Where was Thyella, he wondered? Where was Uncle America? The day's flat white light dimmed and surged and dimmed again.

There were two rifle shots, but very distant. The men stationed near the cliff face looked at each other. The men wearing armbands fell silent. Then, from one of the houses emerged two men in German uniform. One shouted an order in Greek to the regular troops. The men in armbands were ignored. Sol watched them approach until they stood over him and he could see only their boots.

'A Vlach, she says,' said one of the officers. 'Crippled. They found him in the mountains.'

'So?'

There was a pause.

'No. Colonel Eberhardt's orders were explicit. We need them all.'

'Haven't Kariskakis's thugs had their fill yet?'

The two men passed out of his earshot. He was 'crippled'. Perhaps he would not have to stand again. The officers re-entered his field of vision as they walked towards the men waiting in the shelter built around the tree. Wehrmacht uniforms: a captain and his sergeant. The sergeant was replacing his pistol in its holster. *So?*

A group of soldiers ran past carrying jerrycans. There was no sign of either villagers or *andartes*. There were men behind him. Someone shouted an order in Greek. The first explosion went off. Sol smelt the smoke before he saw it. A thick black pillar climbed heavily into the air then leaned and fell into the one rising next to it. He heard an engine start. But how? There was no road here. The smoke thickened. He saw the men around the break in the cliff pull back in twos. *Black with fat.* Not black. Why must he think of this? Klopstock? Trakl? Neither. The houses were empty. The smell was mineral, older than flesh. His eyes streamed. The smoke was not 'black', but 'dark'. And the brighter the flames, the thicker the following darkness, which engulfed the houses in a choking cloud, the village, the retreating soldiers and finally even the cliffs which rose above them all.

* * *

Where the rue Cuvier met the rue Jussieu, Reichmann had touched his elbow. Sol remembered it as the first physical contact between them. One after another, three cars nosed their way out of the narrower street and across the stream of traffic to turn left. Horns sounded.

Reichmann asked, 'It might be more correct then to see *Die Keilerjagd* as a witnessing of an annihilation. I am thinking of its first metaphor, this rendering down, this burning which reveals and obscures, very quickly, and then consumes its material. An annihilation of its own poetic material, perhaps. You look doubtful, Herr Memel. I was considering that first adjective, in a work which contains many such compound-words and no adverbs at all. They are held under great strain, their components often in outright opposition. Isn't the whole poem to be read in this kind of light, by this flame which flickers then disappears in the darkness of its own smoke? In an *inevitable* darkness: no fire without smoke, so to speak?'

213

A thin strip of patchy grass ran almost the length of quai Saint Bernard. Men in blue overalls were at work with trowels. Plastic containers filled with brightly coloured bedding plants lay beside them. The river flowed smoothly past, opaque with mud. The two men looked down from the pavement above.

Reichmann exclaimed, 'You wrote your way out! The darkness is not a metaphor, but literally true. Your whole journey was made under the conditions imposed by the cave, where every step was a guess and every direction was taken by chance or in ignorance. Its darkness was your true ignorance. Because what happened to you was real. No, excuse me Herr Memel, because the poem assumes the full burden of your experience, your real experience. It is a map of those conditions, those violent uncertainties. Without it you could not have found your way out. It was an undiscovered trail, a mountain pass where none was thought possible. But it had to be walked to be found and marked. And the region was called?'

Sol told him again.

'Exactly!'

Upriver, the latticed arches of pont d'Austerlitz framed diamond-shaped fragments of a leaden sky. A Métro train rumbled across in a long flicker of electric light.

'Exactly so, and yet you wrote it. Even if you had never committed a single line to paper, you wrote it, Herr Memel.'

They turned their heads at the sound of bells. Notre Dame was striking the hour.

'One might even say that the poem's first image is not the toppling column of smoke, not Kalydon's ruin or the burning of a remote village, but a face. Atalanta's face. Thyella's face. Because *Die Keilerjagd* was lived before it was written, and her face was the first image you saw, was it not? Herr Memel?'

*　　*　　*

Thyella, the opening in the rock and its jagged edges, a tree hung with men. The smoke rolled and broke around him, cloaking then disclosing these images by turns.

It seemed the attacking force had manoeuvred their vehicles up a dry river-bed to within marching distance of the village. The Greek soldiers shouted to one another. They were laughing now and smoking cigarettes. They did not mix with Kariskakis's men, who walked ahead. The German officers were nowhere to be seen.

Five grey army trucks and two smaller vehicles were parked in a semi-circle where a meander of the river had swept out a broad pan of gravel. The soldiers on guard nodded to their returning companions and resumed their scrutiny of the heights which rose on either side, jagged ridges of bare stone. Sol was pushed over a tailgate and pulled forward by the two soldiers guarding the prisoners already gathered in the truck. They were old women and infants. He lay on his stomach and looked up into young and ancient faces, which looked back at him without expression at all.

They waited. The other trucks were turned around. Pebbles crunched beneath their wheels. Then there was a commotion and the two guards began to shout. Something landed heavily on the backs of his legs. He strained to look over his shoulder and Thyella's face stared into his. Her lip was split and one eye almost closed by a black bruise. Someone had rebuttoned her jacket. Her hands were tied behind her back. She was breathing heavily. Then German voices sounded outside.

'No, no, idiot. Get her out!'

There was an exchange in Greek with the guards in which all he caught was the repetition of a name: Eberhardt. The floor of the truck thudded as two more soldiers jumped in. The woman was pulled upright and hauled out. An argument was going on somewhere outside. A dozen or so soldiers climbed in, pushed the prisoners closer together and settled themselves towards the tailgate. The truck's engine started. It was manoeuvred forward and back. The convoy moved off.

The river-bed rolled them from side to side as the truck lurched down the channel and over the boulders left there by the vanished river. The soldiers were silent, looking up at the surrounding mountains. The dry bed was exchanged for a track and the convoy crawled along. Twice they were forced out while the vehicles were nursed up inclines too steep to be taken loaded. When the light failed a halt was called. Sol and the other prisoners spent a sleepless night.

They resumed at first light. The track seemed to deteriorate and at every halt their escorts would finger their weapons and forget the cigarettes which hung limply from their mouths, scanning the upper slopes. The eventual road was little better. The old women clung to the children, rigid with an apprehension that, Sol slowly understood, derived from the vehicle rather than the fate towards which it carried them. Not one uttered a sound. By contrast, the soldiers grew more talkative as the mountains became hills and then a long level road. They drove through clouds of dust thrown up by the preceding vehicles. Sol lay face down on the floor of the truck, hands and feet both numb.

The next thing he knew he was coughing and the trucks had stopped. The soldiers were shouting again, confidently now. He was pulled backwards, by his feet, and deposited on the ground. The old women rose stiffly from their positions, helped by the children. The soldiers waved their rifles.

They were in a compound surrounded on three sides by wooden barracks and fenced with high barbed wire. A bare flagpole stood in the middle of this area and beyond it were the two smaller armoured vehicles, parked in front of a low building protected by sandbags. A radio mast projected from its roof and wires looped from one corner to a nearby telegraph pole. Two unmarked vans were drawn up alongside it. The motor of the nearest idled and a man in civilian clothes sat with his legs hanging out of the open door.

The fourth side of the compound gave out onto a lake, its far shore barely distinguishable in the failing light. A reed-bed had been cut down to afford a clear line of fire, or perhaps only to expose the view. A stubble of green stumps pricked the surface of the water. Across the lake a line of low hills approached, almost meeting the shoreline before veering away. The roofs and low bell towers of a town were visible between their lower slopes and the water.

He sat on the dusty ground. The villagers, young and old, stood in a group behind the truck which had carried them all here. Three human-shaped bundles were unloaded from another of the trucks, much as he had been. One of the old women was retying her headscarf. Her fingers seemed to fumble with the knot. Then Sol realised that they were all looking across the compound.

A procession was making its way past the front of the communications hut towards the vans. Two soldiers led the way, flanking a blindfolded man. A soldier behind him nudged him in the back with his rifle when he wandered to left or right. One arm had been secured behind him; the other he carried in a sling, for his shoulder was dark with blood which had soaked the side of his jacket. It was the partisan who had tried to shoot him, Sol saw. Two more soldiers followed and then, blindfolded likewise, with both her hands tied behind her back, came Thyella.

These soldiers were not Greeks, Sol saw, but Germans. Two of them marched alongside her with their rifles shouldered, holding her by the arms, for she would jerk and shrug every few paces in an involuntary fashion. They pulled her along between them by main force. Two officers brought up the rear.

The van driver had jumped down from the cab and now held open the back doors. As the wounded man was pushed into the interior he gave a sharp cry of pain. Thyella spun about, an answering cry breaking from her. She pulled herself free and kicked out at her invisible captors. The startled soldiers jumped back but then, realising her helplessness, one neatly tripped her and she fell heavily to the ground. She rose, only to be tripped again. The other of the soldiers laughed. At that the captain barked an order and the two bent to pick her up. The doors of the van were slammed shut. The vehicle reversed. She must have understood then that the injured man was being taken away. She began to curse the men she could not see. The soldiers dragged her down the side of the building and out of sight. The two officers watched, then walked back to the communications hut and disappeared inside.

The Greek soldiers swigged water from their canteens and talked loudly among themselves. His fellow prisoners stood motionless and expressionless, even the youngest children, as if none of this existed. As if nothing had happened at all. There was no sign now of the German soldiers or their captive. Then a Greek officer shouted to his men and they sauntered over, six or seven of them, swinging their rifles. Under their direction, the old women and children moved obediently towards the nearest of the huts. Struggling to stand up, Sol felt a hard prod in the small of his back and fell forward onto the ground. As he turned over, he was prodded again, this time in the stomach. A soldier stood over him, rifle pointed at his chest. On the far side of the compound, the door of the communications hut opened. One of the two German officers emerged from the hut and signalled to the Greek officer. He, in turn, pointed to Sol.

Behind the wooden huts stood the nucleus of the original camp: long low structures built of plastered stone and roofed with clay tiles. The white-washed walls of the nearest building were studded with small barred windows. Cells, Sol discovered.

He sat in a corner, rubbing his ankles. The cords binding his swollen hands and feet had been cut. The feeling was returning. It was almost dark outside but a dim square of light showed through the barred opening in the wall high above his head. The heavy door was punctured by a peep-hole, closed from outside. Beyond it was the central corridor which divided the building. As he had been escorted in, a guard sitting outside a cell midway down its length had jumped up, waved them back and pointed to a door two cells before the one he kept vigil over. Sol waited as the door was unlocked. At the far end of the passage was an open door and a larger room beyond it. An old woman wearing a headscarf was mopping the floor, watched by a soldier who sat on a desk pushed back against the wall. A faint smell of urine reached his nostrils. Above the woman's head, two ropes hung down. He dredged three words from his memory and again he could not remember their source. *Tension too decays.*

He heard trucks start and stop, later some shouting, but distant. Something scraped loudly over a stone floor and, a little while after, footsteps sounded outside, the old woman and her escort. They passed his cell and the sound faded. A door slammed and the noise boomed down the corridor. Thyella would be in the cell where the guard had sat, less than ten metres away. But why, Sol wondered, had he been singled out?

He settled back against the wall and fell into an uneasy sleep. He dreamed he was running and it was agony, but it was impossible to stop. There was a long dusty road which led to a range of mountains. He ran through gorges so narrow that he could brace his legs between their sides. There was the village, already ablaze. And there the fissure in the cliff behind. There the tree where a man was being hung, or suspended, but he could not see how. There was blood. Something terrible was being done to him. Was he alive or dead? The waxen faces of those already hanging stared down at him and he ran again. Here was the stand of trees. He had to get through the undergrowth. It seemed to take an age. She was in there, somewhere, crouched over a man whose blood welled between her fingers. The blue-eyed partisan beckoned him forward, a young man. He was in the wrong place. The partisan raised his rifle quickly. There was not much time. The soldiers rushed forward with their injured comrade, wielding him as though the wound in his groin were a kind of weapon. The shells thudded down and the trucks roared like tethered animals, maddened by the noise. Where was Thyella? Everyone was waiting. The last shell whistled through the sky, growing ever more shrill, screaming louder even than the injured man, stretching itself through an impossible duration. There was one figure still standing, further up the slope, above the hut. Get down, he urged himself, cowering, shrinking from the sound. He buried his head in his arms, trying to burrow his way into the cell floor.

The screaming was a siren. The thudding of the shells were explosions; they were going off outside. He heard men shouting some distance away. A flash lit the cell in wan light for an instant. The following thud a second later. He awoke to the realisation that a battle was underway. A machine-gun stuttered dull syllables in his ears. Distant rifle fire. Nearer, an engine caught. Much nearer, he thought. The engine ran louder, then quieter, then louder again. A truck. But no headlights. Something, or someone, scrabbled over the roof of the cell block. He strained his ears but the engine noise drowned out the sound. There was a shout outside, which was repeated, and then an answer came. Her voice. A quick volley of words. Then gears crashed and the engine revved. Suddenly Sol knew what was about to happen. He threw himself across the floor and rolled. The engine drowned out the sounds of the battle as it approached at full throttle. In the next instant his world collapsed around him.

For some seconds there was nothing to see except clouds of dust. He coughed, his eyes streaming. The noise of the truck's impact resounded in his ears. The vehicle lay partly buried in rubble and pinned beneath the collapsing roof. A section of wall larger than himself lay beside him. Smashed roof-tiles covered the floor. They were trying to drive the truck out again but the engine whined where seconds ago it had roared. He felt for his legs, gripping them with both hands, then tried to move forward. His limbs seemed to take for ever to stir.

Outside, the pitch-dark was revealed as a rolling cloud of dust by a flash from the far side of the camp. The driver had cut the engine of the truck. There was movement off to his right. A different engine-noise broke into his hearing and something moved around from the other side, men running, a group of five or six. The vehicle-noise grew louder and then a van identical to the one into which the injured partisan had been thrown drove towards them, its back doors flapping as it bounced over the uneven ground. The gunfire was intermittent now, almost perfunctory. The van skidded to a halt. The figures ran towards it, five men carrying guns. One woman. Sol pulled himself forward, ignoring the pain which stabbed his feet, grunting with effort. The group were climbing into the back. He looked up, knowing he would not reach the vehicle in time.

'Wait!'

One of the men pointed his gun towards the source of the sound. Thyella's head turned slowly. Her eyes found him and her arm knocked down the man's gun. The gears engaged. He drew breath to shout again but the sound never left his mouth. Thyella had raised her finger to her lips, for silence, and the gesture seemed to him so unexpected and unlikely that he obeyed.

He came to his senses as the wheels of the van found purchase in the dry soil. Her face sank back into the darkness and the vehicle carried her away. She and her liberators were gone. He shouted after her. He was still shouting when he heard the sound of men running. A rifle-bolt was drawn back. He turned and raised his hands. The captain motioned his men to stand back.

'A Vlach shepherd who speaks German,' he remarked.

The officer looked up at the truck half-buried in the wreckage of the wall, then down again at Sol. 'You will be questioned in the morning. When Colonel Eberhardt arrives.'

Not tension, but terror. *Terror too decays.* Who though? Because when the second hour had elapsed, the fear that had first gripped him, when they came for him a little after daybreak, would no longer sustain itself. Beneath terror was a well of hopeless boredom. He was afloat in it, for now. The sweat had poured off him at the sound of their footsteps, quick and purposeful over the stone floor. The scrape of the key and the heavy report of the door slamming back against the wall. They had run at him, descending upon him.

He had been frogmarched backwards down the corridor. Fragments of fallen roof-tiles cracked beneath the guards' boots. The smell of urine grew stronger. Damp plaster and stale cigarette smoke. They had pulled the chair forward and tied him to it by the wrists and ankles.

He faced a wall which had been painted pale yellow, then grey, then a dull red and finally whitewashed. The successive skins had bubbled and peeled away in patches. He shifted to dislodge a splinter which pricked his back. It was a heavy chair, made of posts and rough planks, built so that it could not be toppled over, no matter how violent its occupant's exertions. In front of him was the desk he had seen earlier, an ordinary wooden table. Two metal-framed chairs had been placed behind it. A single drop of sweat was creeping down the back of his left leg. He breathed slowly and deeply.

The panic which had seized him at the first sight of this place had not left him, not even when all but one of the men had left the room. They had marched back up the corridor, leaving him with a single guard, who sat behind him, out of sight. He heard the man's chair creak from time to time. The panic only sank and came apart in him. There were stains on the floor, stains which an old woman and her mop could not lift. The terror was there, but it was eventless, a meaningless disturbance. His thoughts were of no consequence. He, Solomon Memel, led to nothing.

An object had been placed on the table. An instrument? He did not know. It was wrapped in cloth. Grey sacking, which he recognised, and which the partisan had recognised too. They had taken him away and killed him. But Sol had not seen what the cloth contained.

The guard shifted and his chair creaked. Time in the room was measured in the relative brightening of the light entering the barred window. Voices sounded outside once or twice, but

Greek voices, and incomprehensible to him. Vehicles came and went at a distance. It would be hot in the sunlight and the lake tempting with its sheet of unbroken cool water. He sank into apathetic languor, an abandonment of the self to whom the next minutes or hours would bring Colonel Eberhardt and what Colonel Eberhardt meant. The guard behind him stood up. Sol felt his skin prickle. The guard stretched and sat down again. Sol's stomach clenched and unclenched. He looked down once more at the object on the table, wrapped in grey cloth, denied him for now.

The prelude would be the sound of the door at the far end of the corridor, then approaching footsteps, sharp and confident. There was work to be done. Whatever casual conversation had been carried on from Eberhardt's arrival would be brought to its conclusion, an anecdote hurried to its end and polite laughter, normal noises. They would remark on the damage done to the building in a matter-of-fact way. Their voices would encourage him in a self-deception that normality might still embrace him too, that he was within its pale. But then, at some point in the corridor, those sounds would end.

The report of the outer door rolled the length of the corridor and reached his ears as an armful of wood dropped on a stone floor. Footsteps, then silence, the guard behind him jumping to attention, the click of his heels, his salute. Underneath the whitewash the wall had been painted red. Grey under the red. Yellow under the grey. The stone had sweated out its salt under the sun which beat outside. The door slammed shut.

Three men had entered: the captain, a Greek and the man who must be Eberhardt. The captain removed first his cap, then his tunic. The Greek wore no uniform, only the green armband. Eberhardt he barely saw. The last two were somewhere behind him. The room was silent. The captain leaned forward, placing his hands on the table to either side of the implement in its cloth wrapping. He looked over Sol's head to those behind him, then down again.

He said, 'Name and rank.'

Sol's response, it appeared then, proved unsatisfactory. His subsequent responses too proved equally unsatisfying, even provocative, repeated as they were three or four times, with increasing degrees of urgency. The questions and his inadequate answers locked them both in cycles of repetition; it was impossible to proceed before he had fulfilled the captain's need for this or that fragment of information. Something was being constructed out of these materials, an elaborate narrative that he could not comprehend. But it involved their escape from these repetitions. The captain wanted something better than the truth, something compelling and plausible. More significant.

'You are either a deserter or a traitor, or both,' began the captain again.

His responses to these points too proved inadequate, or incoherent, and were disbelieved. The surpassing tale which the captain laboured to assemble could not be built from the shoddy materials Sol supplied.

'Geraxos let you live for a particular reason.'

Yes. But why? Why had that happened?

There was a sink in the corner behind him. He had not seen it but he heard water splashing. The captain was washing his hands.

'You thought she would take you with her? She would have slit your throat in a second. Shall we ask her comrade? We have him, you know. Or perhaps I should show you. It wouldn't have been only your throat . . .' He had held up a crudely-made knife with a short hooked blade.

At a certain point, the Greek took over, although it was the captain who continued to ask the questions, or make the statements to which Sol was required to assent.

'Once again. How many? For how long? These are simple questions. We do not wish to hear about the state of your feet. Simply, how many and for how long?'

Then he nodded again to the Greek.

'Once more.'

There would be a pause while they changed position and the man settled himself. The words grew jumbled, seeming to repeat themselves, but with slight variations and changes. He grew confused as to the point when he should attempt to speak and when to listen. His answers grew confused too; inconsistent with each other, which was indicated to him. The captain grew frustrated. His edifice toppled as fast as it rose. Its foundations were rotten. Sol tumbled out material. He said,

'None' and 'No' and 'I don't know' and 'Neither'. But it was no good.

The captain nodded and nodded again.

He said, 'I am not German. I am Romanian.'

He said, 'I am not a soldier, or a criminal.'

The captain nodded for the final time.

He said, 'I am a Jew.'

'Look at him.'

Sol turned his head very slowly to the left, away from the voice, which was Eberhardt's. The Greek was standing against the wall, soaked in sweat from his exertions. The man looked askance at the officer, then relapsed into impassivity. Sol realised that he himself was drenched in cold water. To revive him? His hands and feet had been untied.

'Look at his features, the nose, the brow, the way the eyes are set back in the head. Don't worry, he cannot understand a word we say. Even if he could he would take no offence. Think of him as a domesticated animal.'

Eberhardt reversed one of the chairs across the desk from him and straddled it. The captain had hung his jacket there, Sol remembered. He had removed it when the Greek had set to work.

'And Thoas led the Aetolian warriors, men of Pleuron, Pylene, Olenus and Chalkis by the shore and rocky Kalydon,' recited Eberhardt. He tipped his head to the man standing. 'Look at Homer's warriors now. What have they become? Oh, there is no need to answer these questions. Captain Müller has dealt with all that.'

Sol had moved his mouth as if to respond. It was very important to respond, even if there was no definite answer to give. He relaxed his face, but one of the cuts around his mouth had begun to bleed freely. Eberhardt leaned his elbows on the table and studied the package which still rested there. His fingers toyed with the frayed edge of the sacking. He looked into Sol's face.

'You can survive,' he said. 'You, Solomon Memel, the Wandering Jew from, where was it?'

Sol formed his lips carefully around the syllables. Clarity too was important. Eberhardt nodded.

'As a Jew you would by rights be sent to join your brethren in Salonika, although precious few remain there now. Which means a rather arduous journey north. Even more arduous than your journey south, I would venture. Captain Müller was right to assert that your situation could worsen considerably. But it could also improve, Herr Memel.'

He must have passed out again. The blur of pain panicked him as consciousness returned. Answer, he told himself, answer quickly. But there were no questions. Eberhardt was speaking softly, as if to himself.

'Geraxos is significant. A few hundred men, but the right men and in the right place. The old man knows how to fight this war. You encountered his grandson. Xanthos. The old man will not give him a thought. A good commander knows how to spill blood.' Eberhardt nodded slowly to himself. 'This war will be won in the mountains; the old man knows that. I have seen his handiwork.' His face was inches from Sol's own. 'And hers. Yes, you remember her, of course. Thyella. The Greeks fear her more than him, Herr Memel. Can you imagine? I will tell you why. I will show you. But all in good time.' His hands moved around the cloth package, his fingertips tapping soundlessly on the wood.

'Why would they take the trouble to save you, Herr Memel? You want this to be over. I understand that. It will be very soon, but you must pay attention.'

Sol nodded slowly.

'Good. You are found near death in the mountains of Greece, in a place the local people call Khaxani. It means the Cauldron. By shepherds, our blue-eyed informer has told us, after some prompting. But there are no "shepherds" in the Cauldron. There is no water. Nothing grows. There is nothing but a crater and the cliffs which surround it on all sides. The partisans found you and they took the trouble to carry you out. How, or why, I do not know. There is a gorge. I am told that a man who knows the route well might make the journey in a day and a night. And they carried you out.'

'I . . .'

'Yes, you were dead to the world, unconscious. We have established that. And the gorge is not so mysterious after all. Inhospitable, certainly. Defensible too, at any number of points.

But how did you come to be there, Herr Memel? Geraxos's men use the gorge. The village where they held you stands at its mouth. Their presence is unsurprising. Fortuitous perhaps, for you. But how was it that you were there to be found?'

Eberhardt's voice had changed. There was no speculation in his question.

'There are strategic aspects to this question. Tactical possibilities which, in certain circumstances, would transform Geraxos's little platoon into a force of great significance. Unlikely circumstances, but still . . .'

The silence thickened and gathered in the room. Then Eberhardt turned to the Greek and said something in his own language. The man nodded, clearly surprised, then picked up his jacket and walked out of the room. The two of them listened to his footsteps recede down the corridor. The far door opened and closed.

'He will not be necessary, you might be relieved to learn. Just the two of us for this part, Herr Memel. A way down may also be a way up. A way in may also signify a way out; and if there exists a way out of the Cauldron . . .'

'I don't know.'

He felt the cuts in his mouth reopen and begin to seep. Blood trickled over his tongue: a metallic taste.

'You do not wish to betray your comrades. It is understandable. Even though they would have killed you rather than let you fall into my hands. They are fighting for their country. Even a Jew, who has no country . . . But of course you have not seen their handiwork. Times have changed since Homer, Herr Memel.' Eberhardt smiled sadly. 'You will answer my question now and you will live. You have my word, which will mean nothing to you, but you have it. I have good reason to keep you alive, Herr Memel. I only wish I could tell you it. Your decision would be so much easier.'

There was an error in what the officer said. Thyella had had the chance to kill him last night and she had not. She had knocked away the barrel of the gun. What did that mean?

The Colonel exhaled regretfully when Sol remained silent. His hands moved to the package which lay on the table between them. He began to unfold the sacking.

'Perhaps you saw Kariskakis's men at work in the village. An ugly sight. They are old enemies, he and Geraxos. Kariskakis led an attack on him through the gorge almost a year ago. There was a failure of intelligence. A number of Kariskakis's men were captured, his sons among them. Kariskakis found their bodies hanging from trees outside his village. It was the manner of their hanging, however, for which he seeks revenge. And what had been done to them before their deaths, by Thyella.'

Eberhardt unwrapped the instrument.

Sol looked down. He knew now how the men in the village had been killed, and why the partisan had recoiled.

'Kariskakis removed one of these from each of his sons and vowed to return them in like manner. You see, once driven through, the body's own weight . . . But you understand. Death can be very slow. How did you come to be in the Cauldron, Herr Memel?'

One of Sol's eyes had closed. The flesh of his face and neck throbbed and seemed either to stiffen or swell with each pulse of blood. The room was humid from the water which had pooled at his feet and steamed from his soaking clothes. He saw Thyella's arm pushing down the barrel of the gun, her finger being raised to her lips, for silence. Eberhardt's fingers traced the length of the shank. His thumb pressed lightly against one pointed end.

'There are those among my colleagues who cannot think beyond bridges and railways, roads, lines of communication and supply. They see the barbarism, but they do not understand it. It has always been here, in the mountains. Even before Homer. That is where it comes from; it will be defeated only there.'

Eberhardt was a tall man whose long face seemed to elongate his body further. A high forehead disappeared finally in wisps of black hair slicked down and back over the high dome of his skull. This unexceptional countenance came alive now, as he spoke of a war against all that could not be civilised or tamed. But it was a monologue and Eberhardt was its true audience too, Sol realised. It was growing harder and harder to remain upright. Soon he would have to answer the question put to him, or refuse to do so. He thought back to the few minutes he had spent in the Cauldron before he had sunk to the ground in exhaustion.

'Now, Herr Memel, for the last time. There will be no time to recant once the animals outside are loosed upon you. They wanted Geraxos's grandson, but I have my own plans for him. They wanted Thyella and could not hold her. Only you are left. How did you reach the floor of the Cauldron?'

The officer's eyes fixed on his face. Sol swallowed with difficulty.

'There is a cave,' he began.

He dropped his gaze to the table, where Eberhardt's hands gripped and released the instrument, never once looking up after those first words, for he had seen in the officer's face that his words had been anticipated and believed.

*   *   *

The lights dimmed and for a moment the auditorium was in absolute darkness. The projector whirred; a rectangle of luminous black flecked with fleeting splinters of light appeared before them. It vanished and was replaced by washes of colour cut horizontally across the screen. At the top, a distant mountainous interior stood out against the dark blue of a dawn or evening sky, the farthest peaks snow-capped and pinked with light. The bottom half was water, which rippled and shivered a few metres beyond the prow of the boat, growing smoother with distance. The boat rail was a blurred white bar wavering over a shoreline lost in haze and diluted colours, sandy browns and liquid greys. The boat was changing course, the whole scene slowly sliding to the right and bringing the lights of a small town into view. Beyond it was a wide stretch of water and a headland, but very distant, if it existed at all. A small grinning boy leaped up, waved and fell from sight. There was no sound.

'Antirio,' said Ruth. 'The ferry docks there. Messolonghi is further around the headland.'

'That rise further inland must be Aracynthus,' Sol replied. 'The lower slope.'

'It's called Mount Zygos now,' said Ruth.

They were sitting in plush upholstered seats in the basement of the building. The screen glared and darkened and glared again, washing their faces in light. Sol settled in the soft embrace of the chair.

His taxi had crawled the last kilometre, trapped behind a truck carrying steel sections of an enormous yellow crane. A new business district was rising to the north-west of the city. He had arrived anxious and late at the address on the edge of the seventeenth arrondissement. Ruth had been waiting in reception with Vittorio.

'You made it. I'm happy. We had trouble finding a projector to run this stock. It's an old format.'

Ruth looked tired and distracted. They had been shooting for three weeks. There had been a row on set the day before. Ruth had called a break and telephoned Sol. Now Vittorio reached across to shake hands.

'Let's go. They're ready downstairs,' Ruth said to the two men.

Some brief scenes followed the approach to the coast: a wooden jetty with a large hut beside it; a narrow curving street and children running past the camera; a girl turning back to stare, bewilderment on her face; a crossroad with no traffic in sight but a bench under a tree and three old men sitting on it, all smoking, one either waving or warding off the camera. The film was overexposed and the colours weak.

'Who shot this?' asked Vittorio.

'Local crew,' said Ruth.

'You should have got people from Athens. Angelopoulos. Or Makis Barouch.'

Ruth pursed her lips. 'No budget. Anyway, the later stuff is better.'

Vittorio snorted. Ruth was sitting between the two men and at this she turned from her cameraman to Sol and made a face. Sol smiled back, thinking that he saw the girl he had known surface momentarily in Ruth's features. She turned away.

The next sequence had been shot from the window of a vehicle. The jerky footage showed stunted bushes of indeterminate colour punctuating a parched reddish-brown landscape. The land rose and the road twisted so that the camera swept to left and right in wide pans. Little stalls with wooden tables and roofs of corrugated iron flashed past, all deserted.

The scene changed. The vehicle had been a bus or a coach; its light-blue form crept slowly out of shot. The screen filled with a massive shape which rose in spurs and ever-steepening slopes, reaching higher and higher until its dark vegetation thinned and disappeared. The sky above was intense blue and when Sol turned to Ruth he saw her face tinged with the same colour.

'I know where we are,' he told her. She turned to him but said nothing, most of her face in shadow.

The camera moved slowly back down the mountainside. Sol said, 'That's Aracynthus again, or Zygos. From the south. This was shot from the bridge. The work camp was on the far side and a little way up the valley to the right. Below the ruins.'

Ruth still made no response.

'What ruins?' asked Vittorio after an awkward silence.

'Kalydon,' said Sol. 'There's a stone platform, perhaps forty metres by twenty. It would have been a temple. And the remains of a road; it's just a ridge now. It led up to the city. Parts of the outer wall are still there. They were waist-high twenty-five years ago; the rest was just foundations. We dug up some smashed pottery, a few charred bones. There were coins too, but Roman. Much later.'

'The list in the poem,' said Vittorio.

Ruth's face was turned to him. He gave her a quizzical look and she seemed to pull herself from some private train of thought, then turned back to the screen.

'Yes,' said Sol, turning back himself.

The base of the mountain passed slowly across the screen from left to right until it disappeared and was replaced by the glare of sunlight off the waters of the gulf. The broad mouth of a river indented the distant shoreline and the camera followed its meanders upstream to arrive finally, as Sol predicted, at the bridge on which the cameraman was standing. Then he trained his lens up the valley.

'It's gone,' said Sol.

'What?' Ruth's voice.

'The camp.'

Above the bridge the river unravelled itself into five or six streams which criss-crossed a broad shallow channel. Bushes had taken root where little islands and ridges rose between the streams. Their bright greens seemed too vivid, even artificial, against the dull rusts and browns of the valley and the grey of the stones which lined the river-bed. The image went out of focus, then sharpened again on something further up the valley. A long low rise wavered about the screen.

'Wrong lens,' muttered Vittorio.

'That was the city,' said Sol. 'That flat area in front of it and to the left, that was the platform where the temple would have stood. The huts we lived in were below it. They must have demolished them. The river is just out of shot. On the right.'

He leaned over as though this might bring the river into view. The film ran on for a few more seconds and in the last frames it was as if the camera's attention had been drawn by some anomaly in the barren landscape, for it veered suddenly to the left. But then the screen went dark.

'That's the first reel,' announced Ruth as the lights went up. She stretched her arms and turned to Sol. 'This must be strange for you. To see these places again. Is it as you remember?'

Before Sol could answer she rose and signalled to the projectionist, then looked to Vittorio.

'Well?'

The cameraman thought for a moment. 'The shot of the sky when he pans up the mountain. We could use that. Otherwise nothing.'

'Paul kept looking up the day before yesterday, do you remember? Looking for something in the ceiling. Lisa wants him to say what he's thinking and instead of turning away he turns his head up. I wasn't sure it worked, but perhaps he could be looking up like that and . . .'

'That blue is what he's looking for,' Vittorio interrupted. 'And we balance it with the black. He's falling away from the light, do you see?'

Sol, excluded from this conversation, looked around at the rows of empty seats. Concealed loudspeakers hissed very faintly. Ruth reached down and, to his surprise, he felt her hand squeeze his arm. She smiled at him.

'I'm sorry, Sol. Don't feel you have to sit through all this. You must find these memories disturbing. I wasn't thinking.'

'No, not at all,' he protested. He had forgotten how dark Ruth's eyes appeared, set in her pale face. Where had her freckles gone? She seemed armoured somehow, standing over him in her dark jacket and slacks, waiting for the projectionist to thread the next reel. The disappearance of the camp troubled him, as if not the place but the time he had spent within it had been excised. His

231

poem had been written there, and then, if it had been written anywhere. But it might never have come into existence, for all the mark it had left on the place of its gestation. Even the purposeless trenches they had dug appeared to have been filled in.

Ruth sat down. The next reel was ready.

'What happened on the set?' he asked.

She had twisted about and was signalling for the lights to be cut. 'I'll tell you later,' she said. 'Or see for yourself. We have to go through the rushes after this. You might find it interesting.'

Vittorio laughed. 'The same thing a dozen times over. Fascinating.'

'Or two dozen if necessary,' Ruth replied. 'As many as it takes.'

The room darkened and the second reel began.

This footage seemed more expertly shot. Its scenes changed more frequently than those on the first reel, the images coming crisply into focus and filling the screen with solid blocks of colour: dark green drifts of oak scrub against the harsh white of limestone outcrops rising behind them, or the brushed bronze hummocks of the little islands which studded the green lagoon to the west. Reference points linked the scenes more or less successfully: a crescent-shaped olive grove, a cracked spur of rock with a wind-twisted tree leaning out into space, a blackened slope punctuated by charred stumps.

'Those burnt areas were brushwood,' said Sol. 'There was a kind of thorn tree. They had us try to cut it down, but nothing could get through it. They had to burn it off and then it grew back thicker. Around the next ridge we'll see the lagoon again.'

The screen filled with green. Thick stems swayed like tree trunks in a high wind, but their surfaces were too smooth to be trees.

'This is good,' said Vittorio. 'Now go up.'

The camera rose obediently until the screen was cut in half, a piercing blue sky resting on the green of a reed-bed. The camera glided over the tops of the stems, which shivered when a gust of wind rolled off the lake, bent and sprang back. Then it turned inland, away from the lagoon.

'That I can use,' said Vittorio. 'And this. Is this where the flood happens?'

232

'The Kleisura,' confirmed Sol. 'It cuts through the mountain for two kilometres or so. No one knows how it was formed.'

The new image was blinding white, broken only by a thin wedge of blue. The scene darkened, lightened, then slowly darkened again as the camera struggled with the glare. The sides of the canyon grew more definite, rising sheer to left and right. Sol blinked and looked away. Ruth's face was hard and angular, her complexion bleached, her eyes and lipsticked mouth glossy in the reflected light. The camera moved into the canyon and sought out the broken texture of the stone, sweeping over surfaces which appeared jagged and cracked from a distance but whose sharp details smoothed with the camera's approach. This sequence went on for some minutes and the three of them sat in silence, allowing themselves to be lulled by the repetitious images until a flash of red passed across the screen, breaking the spell. The camera followed. An antiquated truck trundled away down a road which had been kept out of shot. A man leaned out of the passenger-side window, looking back suspiciously. The camera waited until the truck was a dot of shimmering colour in the heat haze and then, just before it disappeared, the walls seemed to rise even higher, their scale blotting out the insignificant speck.

'The sequence after this is the old army camp, at the eastern end of the lake,' Ruth said. 'Agrinion. Where you were interrogated.'

Sol nodded, his attention on the new vista projected before him.

'This is the other end of the Kleisura, on the northern side of Aracynthus. Look how much greener it is. And that's the plain. You can see the lake in the distance on the left.'

'It was by a lake, wasn't it?' prompted Ruth. 'The camp.'

The lake appeared. Trees which might have been willows dangled branches over the surface. Beyond them, thick reed-beds extended out into the waters and, as the camera panned around, a few dilapidated wooden buildings came into view. The camera swung quickly about. Two men in uniform were gesticulating angrily. One walked forward and the ground swung into view as the camera was lowered.

'There was a lot of that,' said Ruth.

Sol turned to her.

'In the original footage,' she explained. 'We cut a lot of it out.'

'This isn't everything?'

'It's everything worth seeing.'

When the sequence resumed the colours were duller. The sky was an opaque white and the lake sat as flat as paint behind the dark spears of the reeds and the solid boles of the trees. The foreground was dominated by a long low building painted white and roofed with red clay tiles. Some of the wooden structures seen earlier were visible behind it. Small barred windows ran in a line across the screen. The camera was static and nothing moved in the scene it recorded. Sol was silent.

'This is where you were taken,' said Ruth. It might have been meant as a question. 'Where you first saw Eberhardt.'

Sol nodded, transfixed by the image on the screen, although it had not changed.

'If I could have walked,' he said. He felt Ruth's hand seek out his shoulder and squeeze it. 'How different everything would have been.'

'Escaped with Thyella?'

'It was all she could do to get away herself.'

He pulled his attention from the screen and spoke more brightly. 'She could hardly have carried me on her back.'

'And if she had you would never have written *Die Keilerjagd*,' Vittorio smiled.

Sol made an effort to smile back.

The sequences which followed were of places and landscapes he did not recognise: sparsely-planted cornfields, olive groves, a windmill rigged with white sails, two crows chasing each other around a bell tower. Vittorio grunted his dissatisfaction or made comments to Ruth about the suitability of these images. When the reel ended he yawned and apologised.

'I have to get back to the hotel for five o'clock.'

He offered no further explanation.

'What about the rushes?' Ruth asked.

'We can't reshoot for another week at least. Even then it depends on the light. I can go through them before that.'

'How? If there's no time to reshoot, when will you find the time?' Ruth's tone sharpened. 'We have a screening room, a projector and the footage right here and now.' Vittorio sighed, already settling back in his seat. Ruth turned to Sol. 'Would you mind? If we ran the rushes now and then watched the final reel together afterwards?'

'Why should I mind? I've wanted to see what you were doing all along.'

He soon placed the apartment in which they were filming. It was on an upper floor of a building which rose grandly on the right bank of the river, about fifteen minutes' walk from his home. He recognised the ornate windows which extended almost from floor to ceiling. As the scene began, Paul Sandor was standing to the side of one of these windows, leaning against the wall and looking out at something. He was dressed in jeans and a tight sweater. After a few seconds he stepped up to the window. Whatever had caught his eye was moving nearer. He pressed his cheek against the glass as the angle grew acute, then drew back suddenly, clearly puzzled, although he was little more than a silhouette. Then something behind him disturbed his train of thought. He turned around to face the camera.

Lisa Angludet stood in a doorway at the back of the room, which was empty except for a group of disarranged chairs. She was barely visible in the gloom but as she walked forward Sol saw that her dress was in fact a man's overcoat which she held tight around her as though she were cold. Her legs and feet were bare. Her lips moved. She was angry.

Sandor shook his head and the two began to circle each other, the camera moving around both in the opposite direction. Their faces appeared and disappeared, his ironic and aloof, hers contemptuous. The light from the window hardened the angles of their faces. Suddenly Lisa looked straight into the camera, made a silly face and started laughing.

'Forgot her line,' said Ruth to Sol.

'What is her line?'

'She says, "I've had it with old men." Paul asks her, "How many times?" Then she tries to hit him.'

The sequence began again. Sandor's interest in the unknown scene outside was more playful this time and the change of mood at Lisa's appearance more abrupt. They circled, mouthing silently at one another. Her arm rose. He caught her by the wrist and the camera pulled back to bring both actors into full-length shot, revealing that beneath the ill-fitting coat Lisa was naked.

They struggled inelegantly, Sandor forcing his partner back towards the window then pushing her against the wall. There was a weariness to his movement, a sense of great weight and effort. Lisa twitched and pulled truculent faces, resisting fitfully. The final shot was taken at head height along the wall: Lisa's head being backed into frame, filling the screen and blocking out the light from the window beyond, then Sandor's blotting her out in turn. He might have been bending to kiss her neck or leaning his forehead against the plaster in exhaustion. The sequence ended.

'It's too complicated. Too busy,' said Vittorio, resting his elbows on the seat in front and cupping his chin in his hands.

'It's when he pushes her against the wall. It goes slack there. Nothing's happening,' replied Ruth. 'She's meant to graze her shoulder, remember? Actually leave a mark there.'

'Wearing a coat?' queried Vittorio.

The sequence began again. To Sol's eyes it was identical to the preceding one, except the apartment itself seemed larger and gloomier.

'That was the last,' said Vittorio when it was over. 'You couldn't print the others even if you wanted to. If we could hang a light outside . . .'

'Can't,' said Ruth. 'I want to see them anyway.'

Sol sat through three more repetitions of the scene. Sandor and Lisa reeled through their allotted seconds, reached their end, then found them beginning again. Time passed around the two actors only in the failing of the light, so that when the fourth take commenced they were little more than masses of shadow. But this time the rhythm was broken.

'What's happening?' asked Sol, squinting at the screen.

'Depends on your point of view,' replied Ruth. 'Either a courageous young woman is making a stand against the forces of the military-industrial complex, represented in this case by her co-star. Or a silly little girl is having a tantrum. Your choice.'

Vittorio groaned. 'She was exhausted. We were all exhausted.'

'She wanted to go and smoke marijuana with her friends, so she broke up the set,' retorted Ruth.

Sandor had hold of one of Lisa's wrists but she was bringing her free arm down around his head and shoulders. He let go and she began to flail at him. Her back was to the camera and over her shoulder Sandor's face could be seen, his mouth open, shouting to someone. In the next instant the foreground filled with out-of-focus shapes, heads and bodies, as other members of the crew ran forward to separate the actors. The camera turned away, revealing coils of cable, flight-cases, tripods and light-stands, all crammed into the one corner of the room which had remained out of shot. Ruth was striding forward from this area. She wore a brown jacket and white trousers. Her hand was raised.

The lights came up. Vittorio rose and stretched.

'Next time we have to start earlier. Or shoot in the morning and use the other side of the window. And we need an Arriflex. The Eclair's too heavy. Now I have to go. Peter's meeting me at the hotel, then we're off to the Grand Palais.'

'The exhibition?' Sol asked.

Vittorio nodded. 'Have you seen it? The new work's supposed to be his best in years.' He smiled. 'I need darkness and gloom. And incoherence.'

'Enjoy,' said Ruth.

Vittorio bent to kiss her on the cheek, then reached across to shake hands with Sol.

'Until the next time.'

'Tomorrow,' Ruth called after him. 'Seven-thirty sharp.' The door swung and bounced off its damper, then closed smoothly behind the departing man.

'The last reel is shorter,' Ruth said to Sol as the screening room darkened. 'They ran into some trouble.'

The white cell-block, in full sunlight this time but already sliding out of shot: a wooden barracks, a tangle of wire, a dirt road running along the foot of a long embankment. The train of images processed in sequence, right to left, then the camera panned up the embankment to the beginning of a long slope. The ridge far above looped between two summits. The next shot was taken from their midpoint. The camera looked out over jagged peaks cut by deeply shadowed ravines. They receded into the far distance, arrayed without pattern or end. The camera swept slowly over this harsh chaos.

'This is what Paul meant,' said Ruth a minute or so later. 'He wasn't doubting you. When I showed him these shots he just couldn't believe anyone could walk through terrain like this.'

The footage quickly settled into a pattern. Shots taken from the bottoms of narrow valleys and gorges showed steep or sheer inclines of bare grey rock rising into the sky. There was no sense of direction or progress, simply a montonous succession of images. Each of these sequences was broken by shots of the villages which punctuated the journey, and these too followed a format which soon grew familiar: the *kaphenion* with the men hunched over tiny cups or glasses, a slow pan around the village, children playing, then a succession of close-ups of the villagers, some talking expressively, waving cigarettes about, others staring mutely into the lens. The villagers were almost all men. The few women glimpsed smiled quickly and turned away. A long shot of the road or track out of the village would end the sequence and then the mountains would rise up again.

'The next is the part I wanted you to see,' said Ruth as the camera panned down to a broad stream. Three children were wading through water which reached to their knees, their arms locked, two boys, and between them a girl. She pretended to stagger and stumble while the boys supported her. Then the camera rose again and found the village with its familiar stone houses and the *kaphenion*, which had been built around the trunk of an ancient tree.

'Bring back any memories?'

Ruth's voice was light, oddly flirtatious.

Sol did not reply. A group of old men were sitting at the tables arranged beneath the tree, a dozen or more of them. They watched the camera without expression.

'Sol? What's the matter?' Ruth asked gently.

'What are you trying to do?'

The question sounded harsher than he had intended.

'If you have a question, why not just ask me?' he continued. 'I've answered plenty of questions in my time. Go on, ask what you like.'

'Whatever are you thinking, Sol?' Ruth replied, her surprise unmistakable. 'What do you take me for? How could you . . .' Then her tone grew more measured. 'The children playing in the river. Don't you see? It's us. You, me and Jakob, when we were children. They were playing the same game. Don't you remember?'

Now a plump face filled the screen, a man in his late forties with an amiable expression on his face. He blinked in the sunlight. He was holding up a hand with one finger extended and saying something to the camera. Sol averted his face and did not speak.

'What do you think I meant?'

He remembered that Ruth's temper rose slowly. It always had done. He had to say something. The man held up a second finger and mouthed something else. He appeared delighted. Ruth's next words were calm, however.

'Solomon, believe me, I have no questions. I don't know how I've upset you but I'm not asking you for anything. I don't blame you for anything and I never blamed you. I'm sorry I mentioned Jakob. Anything you say to me, say it only because you want to.'

'Ruth, I don't know what . . .'

'It doesn't matter, Sol. It honestly doesn't matter. Come on, let's get out of here. This ends in a minute.'

'Let it run.'

'If you like. The villagers turned nasty. This one they're interviewing now was a little simple. The others didn't like it. Here it comes.'

The camera swung around in time to catch five or six young men walking up. The nearest raised his arm. An old man stood a few metres behind them. He was pointing at something. An indistinct shape passed across the lens and then it seemed the camera was pushed down. The ground swung into shot, bringing with it two elongated human shadows. From the arm of one dangled an object which could only have been the camera. Then the screen went dark.

*   *   *

In May of 1953 Sol moved from the Hotel d'Orléans to a cramped apartment in a side street off avenue Victor Hugo. A single taxi journey sufficed to transport his possessions: clothes, books and his typewriter, which was the property of the *Perspectives* office and would have to be returned. The cheaply-bound book Reichmann had handed to him now sat on the tiny table in the apartment's living area, next to Fleischer Verlag's edition and a newly-arrived Italian translation. The critic's anxious face rose in his memory, a looming balloon. *All my questions are in there*. Sol had watched Reichmann reluctantly shuffle out of the hotel hallway. The critic had expected something – an explanation perhaps, or an assuagement. He had received neither.

Sol had retreated upstairs, pausing on the first landing when he recognised the name printed on the green cover. Outside the door to his own room, he had turned the first page in anticipation of stepping inside and settling into his chair to read the remainder. His room was crowded with cardboard boxes which he had collected but had yet to pack. He was to move to the new apartment in two days' time. He read, *Die Keilerjagd von Solomon Memel: Eine Kommentierte Ausgabe*. Below it, *Adler Verlag, Tel Aviv*. He had stood in the hallway, key in hand, reading by the corridor's yellowish light.

The distinction of the edition prepared by 'J. Feuerstein' was apparent at a glance. In the original Fleischer edition, the opening catalogue of the heroes swept down the page in solid blocks of text. The hunt began and then the poem modulated, the conflict spreading through time and space, slowly admitting the more modern war where its main action took place. This section was written in long irregular stanzas. The conclusion, in the darkness of the cave, was a continuous column of text running over a dozen pages: 'A singular shaft sunk to the limit of the speakable whose only handholds are words,' as Reichmann had written, adding, 'Readers must brace themselves and climb.'

The pages of Jakob's edition were divided differently. Sol's words advanced down the page, but rarely reached further than halfway. Sometimes a mere two or three lines perched at the top, and one page contained not a single word, or not of Sol's. Instead, there were footnotes.

His new editor had called a few days later, introducing himself as Andreas Moderssohn. They exchanged pleasantries and Moderssohn expressed his admiration for the poet of *Die Keilerjagd*. His voice sounded young, on the telephone, and Sol decided that his deliberate manner was intended to mask nervousness. They talked of the various foreign editions in preparation and the recent decision that *Die Keilerjagd* should be taught in German schools. The conversation turned to the work of certain contemporary poets – Moderssohn had liked Bobrowski's last collection, Sol not – then to a proposed jacket design for the forthcoming paperback edition, which Sol had not yet received for approval and which Moderssohn described in painstaking detail. Finally they arrived at the weather. It was then that Sol understood his editor's ponderous delivery as procrastination.

'You want to ask me something,' Sol interjected.

There was a short silence.

'We received an edition of *Die Keilerjagd* printed in Tel Aviv,' said Moderssohn. 'A German-language edition.'

'Yes?'

'We simply wondered, Herr Memel, if you had approved this edition. It seems irregular, in certain ways.'

'Irregular?'

'It is a technicality, of course. Obviously an edition like this is intended for an academic market. Surrer Verlag would not dream of impeding the work of scholars dedicated to your work. But in the matter of permissions . . . I mean Surrer Verlag acquired the rights to *Die Keilerjagd* with the purchase of Fleischer Verlag and while we wish to make the poem available as you would wish, we do not want to encourage pirated editions. The mysterious Professor Feuerstein seems to have devoted a great deal of effort to your work. Even so . . .' He left the sentence hanging, then his tone changed. 'Herr Memel, we are asking whether you wish us to begin proceedings against Adler Verlag.'

'Proceedings?'

'Prosecution, Herr Memel. For infringement of copyright.'

He had misunderstood Moderssohn's slow delivery. It signalled nothing more mysterious than the speed of his new editor's wits.

'I grew up with Jakob Feuerstein,' said Sol. 'We were schoolmates and then friends. The best kind of friends. We were separated during the war. I am sure I do not need to explain to you the circumstances at that time.'

'Of course not,' Moderssohn replied. Another pause followed. 'You said friends?'

'We were as close as friends could be. Until I saw his name on this new edition I thought he was dead. Now I find he survived.'

'Forgive me, Herr Memel, but may I ask if you have read Professor Feuerstein's edition?'

'Of course. I have it here in front of me. Why do you call him "Professor Feuerstein"? He trained to be a doctor, a medical doctor, but whether he completed his training . . .'

'The accompanying article calls him "Professor Feuerstein", Herr Memel.'

'Article? Jakob has written an article?'

'He is not quite the author,' replied Andreas Moderssohn in the deliberate tone which had characterised his speech throughout this conversation and which, Sol reflected later, had not faltered once. 'I think it might be simplest if I send it to you.'

Jakob's footnotes began as textual references: thickets of abbreviated names, followed by chapter, section and line numbers. After several pages of these, comments began to intrude, brief interruptions in the near-indecipherable blocks which squatted below the lines of the poem. Short and sparse at first, they expanded gradually into sentences, then short paragraphs, while the textual references from which they were derived were relegated to parentheses. A commentary began to emerge and, as it did so, a smile spread across Sol's face. He could almost hear the arch self-certainty in Jakob's voice; the sound of it was as present to him as if its owner were sitting across from him at a table outside the café in Ringplatz, or with Ruth sandwiched between them on the grass of Schillerpark. But now the irritation he would once have felt at the first note of that voice – its presumption of rectitude, Jakob's blithe indifference to its effect – was displaced by pleasure.

True, Jakob disapproved of his dolphins. He censured his choice of weapons. Composite bows were no more available to the fathers of the warriors at Troy than his 'snub-nosed' machine-guns were to their distant ancestors. His apples were unseasonal and the flora of Mount Zygos simply wrong. A flood sweeping through the Kleisura? Impossible: the local watersheds forbade it. And so on. Had this been the cause of Reichmann's anxiety?

As the commentary continued it seemed that its author's thoughts had been increasingly dominated by details of geography, the placement and orientation of buildings, or the altitudes and aspects proper to different plants. Questions of where things could plausibly exist battled laboriously with where he,

Solomon Memel, had situated them. Of the reed-choked lake where Atalanta had bathed Meleager and whence Thyella had made her miraculous escape, 'self-fading into a darkness she had breathed, fleeing her "I" and mine' (one of the poem's rare ventures into the first-person), Jakob noted the vegetation conspicuous by its absence. Where were the terebinths and oleanders, the club-rushes and knapweeds? The crater of the Cauldron was a geological and cartographical aberration.

But you guided me there yourself, Sol murmured. He imagined Jakob sitting as he did now, turning the pages of his poem. Beginning, then ending, and beginning again. In Tel Aviv! How did he come to be there?

Sol looked up from the closely-printed page. Reichmann floated out of the darkness.

There had been a moment in the Jardin des Plantes when Walter Reichmann's voice had cracked. Sol fancied the man had been close to tears. Now I must ask my questions. He had known him in that instant. Of course he would answer the critic's questions. It was very important to provide answers, he recalled, and promptly too. He would do so. Had done so. Reichmann's war was burdensome enough a memory without the mysteries of its victims.

Sol glanced down at the page before him. Jakob appeared to be buttressing an incident near the end of the poem with documentary sources. A convoluted joke was being played; humour, reflected Sol, had never been Jakob's strongest suit. The footnote advanced solidly down the page, citing this, referring to that. There was something odd about the references, which Sol might have missed had not the last echoed the name of a region and tolled a distant bell in his memory. That was it. The texts Jakob referred to in support of the passage were lost. He closed the book. But Reichmann's strange reappearance at the Hotel d'Orléans remained incomprehensible.

The article that Moderssohn had promised was in fact a clipping from a column which had appeared two weeks before in *Maariv*. A translation had been stapled to it, together with a message from his new editor asking him to telephone once he had read 'the attached'.

'With editors like Professor Feuerstein of the University of Tel

Aviv who needs enemies? After the spelling has been corrected, the grammar untangled, and the right number of commas sprinkled over the text, what is an editor to do with himself? The answer, according to Professor Feuerstein, is notes!'

'Readers will remember the stir caused last year by Solomon Memel's sensational poem *Die Keilerjäger*, and the even greater stir caused by its author's wartime reminiscences. But while we marvelled at the exploits lying behind that masterwork, Professor Feuerstein wondered at them. It seems those "exploits" might have been remembered just a little differently from the way they really happened. Who knows the truth of the matter? Professor Feuerstein, it seems.'

Jakob was quoted: 'The truth is always both self-evident and obscure. But assertions are correct or incorrect. Proven or provable or not. I have applied simple criteria to a well-known text, a poetic text because poetry is an occasion of truth, the place where it becomes tellable. Or so it claims.'

'So now we know!' the anonymous columnist had commented. His, or her, jaunty tone sat strangely with the gnomic comments of 'Professor Feuerstein'. A few minor factual inaccuracies were quoted, or misquoted in one instance. The piece ended, 'Who knows, perhaps there never was a hunt?'

One rhetorical question too many, thought Sol. Jakob sounded pretentious and deliberately obscure, the columnist frivolous and unconvincing – even unconvinced. The examples did not make the points that the argument, such as it was, tried to draw from them. They were directed differently, although Sol could not make out the direction. The whole article rang false. Why had Moderssohn bothered him with this?

He picked up the article and Jakob's edition, put on his coat and left for the café on rue Spontini, which he had begun to frequent after his move from rue d'Ecole. It was mid-morning and the café was quiet. He sat down and read the article again. He would have to reply to it, he supposed, and began to compose a letter in his head. It occurred to him that no mention was made of any relationship between Jakob and himself. The columnist surely would have included such an irrelevant tidbit. Why had Jakob concealed it? The paraphrase from Rilke's elegy could only have been intended for himself. What was Jakob trying to tell him? Even after a decade, and at a distance of a thousand miles, Jakob could still exasperate him. He flipped open his distant friend's edition and began to read the notes once again. They were subtly different now, clouded by the columnist's silliness. But here were the familiar culprits: the dolphins who never ventured into the gulf of Corinth, the mountains which must have rotated on their bases, the sun which rose in the west and set in the east, the impenetrable darkness of the cave.

Then he stopped. Suddenly he understood why the columnist's twitterings had seemed so unconvincing and Jakob's utterances so pompous and empty in their context. The columnist had misread his source. As had Sol. Jakob's factual corrections were innocuous. His painstaking reconstructions were exercises in futility. None of the points he raised mattered. The elements of his poem were either as he, Sol, had described them or slightly different. The poem might have been written to accommodate both possibilities, and the events it described happened as securely as they ever had. Jakob's drift was different.

Sol read more carefully, understanding now the subtlety of Jakob's commentary, how it accrued its authority under cover of a leaden-footed hike through sources and references and facts, how it seemed to march towards its pointless end while bending its course towards a far less obvious destination. As he read on, he saw his work begin to change shape before his eyes, growing independently and gaining a resilience he had not conceived. Here the heroes gathered, and here the hunt began, and here the boar's rage broke through the thin turf, with its back bristling and its tusks stained with old blood, its snout sniffing for new. Its violence was inevitable, as was its death. Atalanta and Thyella sprang forward and matched each other stride for stride, racing into their respective darknesses. The cave was waiting for them all.

But this was not Sol's poem. Or not the poem he had intended to write. Atalanta's arrow sped towards its mark, still undeflected by the change in its landscape. The tale stood, and stood alone. And now could only stand alone. The consequent realisation came slowly.

Jakob's arrow sought not the tale, but its teller. Its accusation was directed at himself. These events took place in an impossible country, said Professor Feuerstein of the University of Tel

Aviv over the course of a hundred or more footnotes, a country whose weather was impossible, whose plants could not grow, whose geography was unmarked on any map. The 'reality' behind the lines of *Die Keilerjagd* was distant, as though transcribed from far away, or long after the events. But not by one who had played a part. Not by one who had witnessed them. Jakob's hunt was for a different Solomon Memel: one who had never been there.

Sol's eyes skated over the surface of his poem, searching among its images for the ground from which they had sprung. But his words resisted him now. Jakob had written a different country over his own. It was as if – his distant annotator implied – he had never set foot there at all.

Moderssohn did not telephone until the following week. His voice sounded as slow to Sol's ears as before.

'We have received a number of enquiries. And a strange message from Walter Reichmann,' said Moderssohn.

'He turned up here two days before you last called,' said Sol. 'With this new edition. He behaved rather oddly.'

'I'm sure he did. Professor Feuerstein, or someone at this Adler Verlag, has sent copies of it to most of the newspapers. There is an unhelpful article in today's *SZ*.'

'What does it say?'

'It questions Reichmann's judgement. He must have anticipated something of the sort. We have been talking here about taking legal action, as I mentioned.'

'Of course,' said Sol.

'But we think, in the current climate, it would be inadvisable, Herr Memel.'

'Inadvisable?'

'The damage has been done. It might seem that we were trying to suppress the edition for dubious motives, and there might be difficulties mounting a local prosecution in any case. As far as we know, Feuerstein's edition has not been put on sale. I'm sure you would agree that it might do more harm than good, at this stage. Of course we are making it clear that Feuerstein's allegations are groundless. There is no question but that Surrer Verlag stands behind its authors.'

'I see.'

246

'We must, however, make a difficult decision on the matter of the edition in preparation for the schools,' Moderssohn continued. 'As I said, the question of our authors' integrity does not arise at Surrer. This would be a postponement, not a cancellation. Of course there will be a schools edition. At present, however, the feeling is that it might prove counter-productive to bring out such an edition now.'

'What are you trying to tell me, Herr Moderssohn?'

'I'm afraid several of the journalists have sought comments from the board responsible for the syllabus and as a result *Die Keilerjagd* has been withdrawn.'

After a brief silence Sol said, 'There is no truth in any of this.'

'Of course,' said Moderssohn. 'I am very sorry, Herr Memel. If Jakob Feuerstein was your friend, why is he doing this?'

Reichmann's odd manner grew more comprehensible when the post brought the first batch of newspaper clippings, forwarded without comment from the offices of Surrer.

When even a critic with the acumen of a Walter Reichmann slips up, what hope for the rest of us? Last year's protégé, Solomon Memel, has come back to haunt the great Herr Reichmann. Pushed and puffed to fame and acclaim, it now seems there may be rather less to Solomon Memel than first met the eye. A new edition of Die Keilerjagd *has made it clear, in not so many words – but plenty of footnotes – that Solomon Memel's memory contains some awkward gaps.*

One or two of the journalists speculated on the motives of 'the independent scholar affiliated to the University of Tel Aviv' or 'the indefatigable annotator of *Die Keilerjagd*', but the story was stronger with Jakob Feuerstein as a distant, somewhat mysterious figure. Through May and June most of the fun was had at Reichmann's expense, who did not reply. *Der Spiegel* did not deign to mention the affair.

Sol, too, maintained his silence, mindful that no one yet had actually voiced the implication of Jakob's work in terms explicit enough to answer. At Andreas Moderssohn's urging he spent a week composing – and destroying – letters to Jakob. The message he finally sent, addressed to 'Professor Jakob Feuerstein of the University of Tel Aviv', read:

'Dear Jakob, We have survived. Now we must talk. I will meet wherever you wish. Please write to me. Yours in hope, Solomon.'

He received no reply.

In the slack newsdays at the height of summer, several of the broadsheets ran long densely argued articles on the supposed authenticity of *Die Keilerjagd*, or on the integrity of its author. A fellow poet 'defended' Memel's right 'to invent his life alongside his art'. An Austrian academic made the (carefully generalised) point that deliberate falsehood in poetry could be seen as a reaction against the unexamined normative falsehoods of everyday life, and thus as a higher form of truth. The only clipping that gave Sol any cheer was a letter addressed to the editor of *Der Standard* in Vienna:

'Sir, My late husband, Leon Fleischer, would never have published the work of a charlatan. Solomon Memel is a great poet.'

The editor had commented below Ingeborg Fleischer's letter: 'This newspaper upholds the right of all great poets to be charlatans, and vice versa.'

Sol spent his days working, in a desultory fashion, on translations of French poets – Char, Larbaud – and his evenings in the café on rue Spontini. When sleepless, he poured himself measures of American whiskey and wrote through the night, one measure per page. The work which resulted was formal, almost musical, with noisy bursts of strange imagery. He would wake late, sometimes slumped at the desk, and read through the night's yield. Invariably, come the morning, it was worthless.

By the autumn, the newspaper clippings no longer arrived in thick packets from Surrer. October saw only a mention in an academic article chiefly concerned with a literary controversy which had taken place in Australia in the 1920s. November brought nothing at all. Then, in the last post of the year, a letter arrived from Tel Aviv. His own letter fell from the envelope. It was unopened. A covering note had been typed on headed paper from a Professor Zvi Yavetz of the Department of Philology. It read:

'Please find enclosed your letter addressed to "Professor Jakob Feuerstein of the University of Tel Aviv". This institution wishes to state that Professor Feuerstein neither gained his professorship from the University of Tel Aviv, nor has he ever been employed by or affiliated to this university in any way. We dissociate ourselves from the comments he has made and note that his publication(s) have not been published under the auspices of this university.'

Underneath, in handwriting composed of large, untidily formed characters, Professor Yavetz had added, 'I and the Hebrew Writers Circle of Tel Aviv salute you, Solomon Memel. We have spent many hours discussing your work and wish you well in this time of trial.'

A Parisian Christmas passed, Sol's fifth, he realised as he listened to the bells ring out. He decided to open the whiskey bottle earlier than usual, in a secular celebration. Later he scrawled 'Happy Christmas' over Professor Yavetz's letter and addressed an envelope to Andreas Moderssohn at Surrer Verlag. His editor had not telephoned since . . . He could not remember. November? October?

'Happy New Year, Herr Memel!'

'What?'

'Happy New Year! This is Andreas Moderssohn. Did I wake you?'

'Yes. I mean, no. Happy New Year, Herr Moderssohn.'

It was January the ninth or tenth. Morning, he supposed.

'Herr Memel, *Spiegel* has broken its silence. There is a long article. A wonderful article. Can you find a copy there in Paris or shall I send one?'

The vendor at the International Presse kiosk at Gare du Nord looked at him curiously after he had cut open a bale and handed Sol the magazine. Sol glanced down and saw his own face staring up at him, 'The Memel Affair' stamped across his features. He walked across the road to the brasserie beneath the Hotel Terminus. Several of the interviews after *Die Keilerjagd*'s success had been conducted among the mirrors of its back dining-room. He recognised the *maître d'hôtel*, but was not recognised in return. He ordered coffee at the bar.

To his surprise, the article was not by Walter Reichmann, although the critic appeared as an actor within it. It was credited to 'Slavko Mihailovic', who began by recounting the familiar story of how *Die Keilerjagd* had come to be written, then published, how its success had been assured by a 'ground-break-ing' article by 'Germany's most respected literary critic and journalist'.

Then the fall. Jakob's edition had appeared from an unknown Tel Aviv publishing house 'in circumstances almost as mysterious as those of the text upon which it commented'. Mihailovic analysed how the edition made its allegations under cover of a disinterested process of bland annotation and how the cumulative effect of Jakob's corrections and quibbles resulted in a fatal undermining of the author of *Die Keilerjagd*. But then he broke off this analysis.

'All this is beside the point. Jakob Feuerstein's charge is made implicitly; it is nowhere stated in his text. Nor has it been stated elsewhere, save by innuendo, rumour and slur. It is this: that the success of Solomon Memel's poem, *Die Keilerjagd*, derives not from its formal strengths but from its authenticity. It must be document as much as poem. Memel himself has spoken of the events lying behind his lines, the hunt for Eberhardt and his own part in it. Thyella herself has gained an iconic status. No one disputes that these events occurred, not even Professor Jakob Feuerstein. The charge is against their witness, Solomon Memel: that, contrary to Memel's own account, given to Walter Reichmann and published in this magazine, he was not there and so played no part in the events that inspired *Die Keilerjagd*. His poem rests thus on a falsehood, or has already sunk within it.

'But Feuerstein's allegations are baseless, as even the most cursory examination would have shown. It has not been performed, until now.'

Sol drained his cup and ordered another. As he read on, he reflected that 'cursory' hardly did justice to the extent of Slavko Mihailovic's 'examination'. The journalist had travelled to Greece with what he called 'a simple question needing a complicated answer' and had set about disentangling the true from the false, the false from the merely mistaken and the merely mistaken from the wilfully misunderstood. Perhaps predictably, this project had led him into a morass of conflicting detail over which neither Jakob's account nor his own could claim greater authority.

But as Mihailovic had slowly worked his way around the

locations of the poem, he had come upon two witnesses more compelling than the mute mountains and misplaced vegetation of the Greek countryside. The first was an emigrant to America who had returned to Greece in 1937 and claimed to have fought with Zervas during the war, until an injury had lamed him. He had worked briefly as an interpreter at the British Military Mission in Messolonghi and had been present at the interrogation of a young man in 1945 by a British intelligence officer. 'But it was not an interrogation. They drank tea and talked about the war. He did not need an interpreter. He spoke good English. Better than mine,' Mihailovic quoted his witness as saying.

The tea never came, thought Sol, recalling the man, and the British Captain who had questioned him.

The unneeded interpreter had remembered the young man's name but had no memory of his face and could not identify Sol from a photograph. In fact, he might not have remembered the incident at all if they had not spoken about Thyella. 'Of course everyone knew about Thyella; there were a lot of rumours about her around that time,' the man had said. 'No one knew then what had happened to her. They talked about Colonel Eberhardt too. All we knew about him was that he was gone, along with the rest of them. And the young man was about to leave too. His papers had come through, from the Americans.'

Mihailovic's second witness had been encountered fortuitously. The journalist had headed north, into the mountains, in defiance of the military restrictions on travel in the area. Here his questions had provoked an increasing reticence among the villagers. Occasionally this reticence had become alarm. When he had persisted, he had been threatened and even chased out of one village. He had retraced his steps to Karpenisi, where he had been arrested after an argument with his guide and held overnight. Here, the reactions of the villagers had grown more comprehensible. The irritated chief of police had told him that he had 'had enough of mad Germans' before releasing him on the payment of a fine. He had been reminded that the area was closed to foreigners without permits and had been put on a bus back to Messolonghi.

Mihailovic spun out the rest of his detective story over more than a page, but its dénouement was already clear. After a number of false leads, he had finally run his quarry to ground in Naupaktos. The 'mad German' had, of course, been Jakob, although he had been travelling on an Israeli passport. He had been hospitalised in the port town after 'a nervous collapse', according to a doctor there who had treated him. The doctor was quoted:

'He was brought in by a woman who claimed to be his wife. There had been an incident at their lodgings. He was unable to give any coherent account of his movements and the woman was obstructive. He had suffered a complete collapse. His symptoms were characterised by paranoid delusions which he could not distinguish from reality. We sedated him. He was here for four days, after which an ambulance arrived from Athens and he was discharged.'

'And this,' Mihailovic commented, 'is the witness we have preferred over Solomon Memel.'

The article concluded with an attack on those 'domestic cultural commissars' who had proved so eager to vilify one of Europe's finest poets, and Mihailovic finished with the hope that they would now prove equally eager to recant.

'But why?' said Sol, aloud, and in German, drawing a glance from the bartender. 'You never asked why he did it, Herr Mihailovic.'

He closed the magazine, placed some coins in the saucer, and walked out.

'Now is the time to speak out,' Moderssohn exulted.

It was three weeks since the *Spiegel* piece had appeared. In the intervening period, most of the major newspapers and magazines had run shame-faced pieces on 'The Memel Affair'. Today it was the turn of the *FAZ*, who had hidden their blushes behind a bloated survey of literary hoaxes stretching over three full pages. It had ended with the pious caveat: 'Now the stakes are higher. These literary games are no longer games. It is our history we are playing with. Let us never drop it again.'

'Are they playing catch or roulette?' asked Sol when Moderssohn read the concluding lines over the telephone.

'They want to run an interview too,' said Moderssohn. 'But then, all the papers do. I have been speaking to my colleagues.

We should choose eight or nine, not even the most important. Some smaller magazines.'

Moderssohn sounded youthful again, but his delivery was as ponderous as ever. The conversation was taking a long time to arrive at the point where Sol had chosen to wait for it. The previous day he had returned to the Hotel d'Orléans to collect his post from the ancient concierge.

'Telephone rings a lot,' she had grumbled, pointing a bent forefinger at his chest. 'Always you!'

Moderssohn was now listing the possible journals, in order of preference. Eventually, Sol was able to interrupt the inexorable flow.

'I do not think this arrangement will be practical, Herr Moderssohn.'

'Not practical? No, of course it would be tiresome to repeat the same thing so many times. A press conference might be better. We could hold it here at the publishing house and invite some of the other journalists.'

'Herr Moderssohn, you've misunderstood me. A press conference will not be any more practical.'

'Herr Memel, the statement will be far more effective if you deliver it in person. But, if you do not wish to, we could simply distribute it in the normal way.'

'Statement?'

'Your statement, Herr Memel.'

'I have no statement, Herr Moderssohn.'

'But there must be a statement. You have been vindicated.'

'I have given my last interview,' said Sol. 'I have answered my last question. I have made all the statements I am ever going to make.'

That summer, *Die Keilerjagd* was added to the syllabus for secondary schools in Germany. Austria followed in the autumn and France the following spring. A trickle of postponed translations became a spate. He received a substantial cheque from Surrer and bought an apartment in a modern block overlooking pont Mirabeau. His second book, a collection of shorter poems, appeared and gained respectful notices. He arranged his editions along the lowest bookshelf in the living-room, placing Jakob's last. There had been no word of him since Mihailovic's article.

But Mihailovic himself did appear, in person, a small sharp-faced man who introduced himself as 'Slava', rising to shake hands over the restaurant table where the two men had arranged to meet.

'I don't know why he is so determined to speak with you,' Moderssohn had told him. 'It's not an interview, Herr Memel. Perhaps it's the other way around: he wants you to interview him.'

Slava spoke broken German, but excellent French. Sol politely congratulated the journalist on his article. Slava shook his head.

'Reichmann wrote it,' he said. 'You didn't guess?'

'No.'

'I was sent to Greece to find out what I could. I find things out, sometimes. I put people together. Fix things. I work for *Spiegel* now and again, and others, in the background. Reichmann wanted my name on the article. Or not his.'

Slava leaned forward over the table, eager to convince. His hands fluttered as he spoke. He wants me to like him, thought Sol. But that is not why he is here.

'I didn't get as far as I had hoped, in the mountains,' Slava said. 'My guides refused to take me beyond Karpenisi. Do you know it?'

'Only by name.'

'It doesn't matter. I was arrested there, just as Feuerstein had been. The rest was simple.'

'The interpreter, then the doctor in Naupaktos.'

'The doctor didn't want to talk. I was frank with him, told him why I was there and what I was doing. At first, all he would say was that his patient, Feuerstein, had been delusional, had made a partial recovery, and then had been discharged. But when I mentioned your name he reacted strangely. He said that he had tried to contact you at the time, and had written later but got no reply.'

'Written to me? But how?'

'He gave me the address,' said Slava, reaching into his brief-case and bringing out a battered notebook. He riffled through its pages. 'It was Masarykgasse 10.'

'My family's address, before the war.'

'I see,' said Slava. 'The doctor asked if "Memel" was a

pseudonym. On the hospital form, Feuerstein had named you as his next of kin. Or whoever had filled in the form for him. The doctor refused to show it to me. But he said that under "Nature of Relationship", Feuerstein had put "Brother". You have no brothers?'

'No,' Sol confirmed. 'What about the woman? The woman who was or wasn't his wife.'

'Reichmann insisted I include her, but I think the doctor invented her. There was no record of an ambulance to Athens, just his word for it, and of course the hospital didn't want him there. I don't know how he left, or where he went.'

'Tel Aviv, evidently,' said Sol. 'He still had his notes to write. His edition to publish.'

The two men were silent.

'I was puzzled, you see,' Slava continued when the pause became awkward. 'Because it was obvious that Feuerstein knew you in some capacity. It fitted with what the doctor said about his delusions. But you never defended yourself. If there was a history between you and Jakob Feuerstein, why did you never reveal it? It would have explained why he wrote this nonsense about your work. I never understood that.'

'This is not an interview.'

'Monsieur Memel, please believe me. I am here to pass on what I learned. Only that.'

'The fact that Jakob Feuerstein knew my address from a decade ago, that he wrote my name on a hospital form, that he called himself my brother, these things prove nothing. They carry no more weight than the delusions you allude to.'

'If I have offended you by raising these matters, please accept my apologies. I do not mean to make a mystery of any of this. Obviously, Jakob Feuerstein's delusions would take you as their focus.'

'Obviously? How, exactly, do I fit into my non-existent brother's non-existent fantasy, Monsieur Mihailovic?' The words marched out too quickly for him to smooth them. Slavko Mihailovic looked down.

'According to the doctor, Feuerstein thought he was hunting for you. He spoke of having lost you in the mountains, during the war. He had come to Greece to find you.'

As the two men parted, Mihailovic apologised for any offence he might have caused. Sol assured him that he had not. Mihailovic pressed a card into his hand. The address was in Trieste.

'I do not live there, but my mail is forwarded regularly,' the man explained. 'I am often in Paris. I am often in many places. If you need my services, Herr Memel, I can be contacted there. I arrange things. Bring people together who wish it. I work where I can. You understand, I'm sure.'

Sol listened politely. He had realised what he must do and now his thoughts were only of that course of action. It was a simple matter. The two men shook hands. It was barely four in the afternoon but the sky was already darkening. He found a taxi on avenue de Breteuil and cursed softly to himself when the traffic ground to a halt behind Gare d'Orsay. The car crawled forward. Place de la Concorde was a chaos of ill-temper, where the taxi stopped and started, inched forward then braked. Sol pressed his fingers to his lips and leaned forward in his seat. Car horns bellowed their ritual protests as the herds converging from north and south merged and jostled. Once across, the reluctant driver took the backstreets at Sol's urging, but they were no better. The traffic solidified around the Banque de France and they sat there for five minutes, Sol's impatience and the driver's irritation at his passenger growing apace. But it had been almost three years since last he had made this journey. His impatience was absurd, and rue du Louvre was only two streets away.

Sol paid the driver and made his way up rue du Bouloi, then crossed the road and pushed through the rush-hour crowd to climb the steps of the Hotel des Postes. The collection office was a large windowless room on the first floor with a hatch set into one wall. Nothing had changed since his last visit. Sol took his place at the back of the line. When his turn came, he handed over his identity card to a capped official who scrutinised it. Yes, Sol thought to himself, the poet. The official looked up, nodded curtly then disappeared into the depths of the building. Through the hatch Sol saw long rows of shelves, built floor to ceiling, upon which rested sheaves of letters, small parcels, loose papers and cards which might have been either mail awaiting collection or part of the Hotel des Postes' system of classification. The men and women behind him were silent, as he had been. The official was gone a long time.

Not Rilke. Not Klopstock. Not Trakl.

Above the ruins rose hills covered with thick woods. They were not permitted up there. Below, the floor of the valley broadened. This was where they worked. The river running through it meandered, carving multiple channels in a wide gravelly bed. The Naupaktos–Messolonghi road crossed it at its shallowest point by a low bridge supported by stone arches. Tufts of stringy grass stitched the reddish-brown soil on either bank, the land rising gradually towards the valley's sides, where olive groves clustered in the shade cast by Varassova to the east and a spur of Mount Zygos to the west. The river widened further as it neared the coast, then emptied into the gulf through a confusion of channels and banks. From the edge of its mouth curled a tongue of land which enclosed a reed-fringed lagoon to the west. Down there were marshlands, salt-pans and the short-lived silty beaches washed down by the river, which was called the Evinos, or Evenus, or the Phidharis, or once, long ago, the Lykormas.

But the bridge marked the lower of their two boundaries. The band of territory permitted them extended from the crossing-point to the ruins further up, and stretched across the width of the valley. Within it was the Kurtaga Work Camp.

Heads and shoulders rose out of the ground then fell again. Seventy-five men worked here, a fact they were reminded of daily at the roll-call. Other men watched them, fifteen or sixteen of these. They leaned on their rifles and looked idly about, now and again removing their caps to mop their brows. Sometimes one of the guards shouted at the men digging nearest him, and sometimes this ritual outburst would pass all the way down the line. The men digging appeared to pay no attention. The shouting concerned only their guards; it was internal to them, because they were few in number and their rifles were old. Most were from Naupaktos, which was a day's walk east, around the back of Varassova. The men of the Kurtaga Camp were from Messolonghi and Aitolikon, black marketeers, curfew-breakers, petty thieves, relatives of men suspected as partisan sympathisers, and Sol.

The men lived in four wooden huts which stood behind the

spur of the Zygos and which were overlooked by a small farm-house where their guards were billeted. A barbed-wire fence encircled the huts and defined the inner perimeter of the Kurtaga Work Camp. The guards shared the duty of walking its perimeter in pairs during the hours of darkness. The prisoners inhabited the huts between Monday, when they arrived, and Friday, when they were marched back along the coastal road, past the outskirts of Messolonghi, to a much larger camp where the barbed-wire fencing was more formidable, the huts longer and more crowded and the stench of ordure stronger. There, groups of women and children would wait outside the main gate for their arrival, often after nightfall, and would rush forward and press small parcels of food into the hands of husbands, fathers, or brothers, sometimes exchange a few words with them, then be pushed back by the guards while the prisoners were marched inside.

The Messolonghi camp had been built about an abandoned monastery. A swastika flying from an improvised flagpole tied on top of the bell tower looked as though it had been raised by children for a prank. Sol had been taken there three days after his interrogation. He had stood to attention while a German officer read several handwritten forms then looked up at him curiously.

'You will not be joining your comrade,' he said, 'Fortunately for you. But you will work.'

Sol had nodded. His 'comrade' must be Xanthos.

He had been escorted out by two Greeks, detainees like himself, who had shown him his bunk then had gone through his clothes in a systematic, impersonal fashion. Finding noth-ing, they had left him there. The barracks' other inhabitants had returned at sunset, stamping their boots and beating the dust from their clothes. They had passed Sol without a glance and thrown themselves on their bunks. Sol fell asleep to the rise and fall of breathing all around him. Then, at some point during the night, he had been awoken by a hand on his shoulder. Someone had knelt behind him and addressed him in quick, but heavily accented English.

'You speak this language?'

'Yes.'

'Tomorrow you will be assigned a work detail. You cannot be protected here.'

'Protected? From who?'

'Geraxos has enemies here. Do not mention him, or Thyella, or Xanthos. Say nothing about where you have been.'

'Xanthos?'

There was a short silence and Sol, fearing that the man would slip away, turned and found himself looking at a slight, bespectacled man with a sharp face.

'He is with the politicals in the Upper Compound. Forget him. He cannot be helped now. Find me if you believe yourself in danger. Say that you know something about a man called "Miguel". Just that. I will hear of it very quickly.'

The next morning, as 'Miguel' had predicted, he had been called out by a Greek officer and assigned to a work detail. The other men had stared at the bruises and cuts on his face. Sol had ignored their curious stares.

The first months had been spent carrying buckets of stones. Large piles had been deposited by the side of an unmetalled road which climbed from the head of the lagoon up a long slope to a dip in the ridge three or four kilometres away. Teams of prisoners carried the stones from these piles to the road, where other teams raked them level. One day a team of German engineers had arrived with surveying instruments. There had been a fierce argument with the overseer and the work had come to an abrupt end. After that his work detail had been set to clearing brushwood, which was harder than carrying stones. The gnarled bushes had sent their roots deep into the soil in search of water and the spiny oak scrub cut their hands as they bent and twisted the woody stems until they split and broke. They grew back as quickly as they could be removed. Their guards seemed to acknowledge the pointlessness of the work by standing about in groups, sharing cigarettes, rather than driving their charges to greater effort. They laboured through a mild winter. Then they were moved along the coast to the valley of Kurtaga where a network of lines had been marked out with posts and white twine. There they were told to dig trenches.

Not Eisinger, he thought. And not Kittner. The column of oily smoke had cleared and the vista beyond it was clear and bright, as though the memory were his own.

Warm winds blew in off the gulf some kilometres to the south, sometimes bringing rain. The trenches filled with water.

At night, when the winds abated, cold air rolled down the valley and the men shivered and caught chills. April brought a period of drier weather followed by meridian storms, the clouds gathering inland over the mountains each morning and either receding by midday or breaking overhead to send down torrential showers. The men drove their shovels through the thin turf into clay, snapping off old roots and grubbing up stones. Sol's Greek workmates affected not to notice the weather, which could not be changed or guarded against.

He understood little or nothing of the men who worked around him and they, in turn, viewed him with wary incomprehension. The disparate words and phrases which simple repetition lodged in his memory would not cohere. Their arguments and chatter were so much noise. He drove his shovel into the earth, stepped back and leaned his weight on the blade, levered, lifted and tipped out the load. This was his rhythm and that of every member of the work detail. But the lines unfurling themselves before his mind's eye were his, their music his. Not Klabund's. Not Hauff's. Not anyone's but his own. They had belonged to this place once, long ago, and might do again. But the men toiling to either side of him were not the ones to enact them. Their names had no place among the words he muttered, only to himself, from daybreak to sunset.

The men dug trenches which were one metre and sixty centimetres deep and half as wide. One of the guards carried a stick marked with these measurements which he would drop into the excavation, then lay widthways across the top. By summer, Sol noticed, he would drop his measure into the deepest part of the trench and drive it into the bottom, giving the man leaning on his shovel below a conspiratorial wink, which was not returned. The trenches were intended as a line of defence against attack from the coast. But there was nothing to defend here, the men grumbled to each other, sitting outside the fly-infested huts with their bare wooden bunks. Nothing to defend but a farmhouse and some old ruins. That, at least, was what Sol assumed was said. He tried to follow their words. These were not just any old ruins, one man broke in. And then another began to tell the story, but in a purer, more elevated Greek, because it was an old story which had taken place here in the vale of Kalydon. Someone tried to interrupt, but the man continued despite this, and then Sol listened, realising that the fragments he understood belonged to a story he had once known, which he had perhaps read. The old tale peeled back its freshly inked page leaving alien characters on the opposite leaf of his waiting memory.

Summer advanced and the sun rolled overhead, pressing down on the sweating men who shovelled earth. The trench stretched arms towards Varassova and Zygos without ever reaching the havens of their shade. The wooded heights shimmered and narrowed to a hairline crack of imagined cool in a baking haze. The waters of the gulf shielded themselves in glare. Long lines of transport planes began to appear, travelling in single file across the cloudless blue of the sky to the west. They hummed and buzzed through the mornings and then, as the weeks went by, their lines grew longer and sometimes stretched into the afternoon, when the air itself seemed to turn to heat. Convoys of military trucks rumbled over the bridge below, never stopping or slowing. The woods, the shade, the ruins of Kalydon, the water, the heights which rose around them: these were the places denied to Sol. Beyond their horizons was the darkness into which Thyella had disappeared.

The guards drank more heavily. Their laughter reached the ears of the men in the huts, more often their angry shouts as they argued or even brawled. One night three of them appeared in the doorway of the hut where Sol slept, shouted incomprehensibly, then staggered out again. They were older men, those who could be spared for a defensive line which, all knew, would never be defended. There were hushed discussions among the other prisoners in which Sol was not included. The Germans were pulling out. The Allies had landed in Epirus, or Thessaloniki, or were sure to land soon.

Then, late in August, they were marched back to the camp outside Messolonghi to find that the grey uniforms of their German captors had been replaced by the civilian clothes and green armbands of Greek ones. A ring of sandbagged gun emplacements had been thrown up around the perimeter. Sol's workmates eyed the new guards cautiously. They were marched into the crowded camp at rifle-point.

Sol looked further up the hillside to the Upper Compound, where the politicals were held. Nothing moved behind the

double fence of barbed wire. The guard towers were now manned by Greeks.

'Be ready.'

A foot hooked around his ankles as he was nudged in the small
of his back. He fell forward. He scrambled to his feet but his
assailant had already disappeared into the mass of men behind
him. He searched the faces nearest him, wondering why Miguel
should wish to deliver his message in so enigmatic a manner. Sol
had recognised the voice.

He did not set eyes on the man in the following weeks,
although he looked for him. Rumours ran through the camp
like fevers. A skeleton force of German troops was still garri-
soned in the monastery building. The main camp was guarded
by Security Battalion men. The barracks grew crowded as more
contingents of men were marched up the dusty road to the
camp. For several nights running the inmates heard gunfire in
the far distance. There was no water for a day and most of a
night. A man was shot on the wire.

The heat increased. Men wandered aimlessly looking either up
at the heights of the Zygos or down to the tantalising waters of
the lagoon below. Columns of grey trucks moved along the road
which followed the shoreline. The guards now patrolled inside
the wire in groups. A man started shouting from the roof of one of
the barracks and a large crowd gathered and cheered. The guards
manning the watch-towers of the Upper Compound loosed
volleys of machine-gun fire into the air. Then, one morning, Sol
was woken by angry shouts. Men were running to the northern
fence. A crowd had already gathered and were shouting through
the wire at a line of Security Battalion men who faced them
through the sights of their rifles. A line of men was being
escorted from the Upper Compound by a mixture of Greek and
German troops, the latter armed with machine-guns which they
trained on their prisoners, although many of these walked with
difficulty and had to be supported. Pressed in among the crowd,
Sol craned his neck, scanning the faces for the one he sought. The
mob shouted louder as the men were led past. A man standing
beside Sol saluted. There was a truck waiting further down the
hillside and when the prisoners reached it the mob, which had
now grown to include almost all the men in the camp, fell quiet.
The men were pushed into the back. Sol found him then.

Xanthos's left arm hung limply at his side and he wore the same fatigues as when Sol had last seen him, blindfolded and injured that time, at the camp by the lake. The partisan was pulled up into the truck. The German troops left with their prisoners and, that afternoon, Sol watched the machine-guns being lowered from the Upper Compound's watch-towers. He felt drained of energy and returned to the barracks, where he fell into an uneasy sleep.

That night was the first in which he dreamed himself climbing. The rock was rotten with frost and crumbled under his feet. Fragments tumbled and bounced down the mountainside, setting off small avalanches of stones and boulders. Great crashes thundered up from the bottom of the gorge far below, where tiny figures cowered from the debris smashing down around them. How could he see them, he wondered? No matter how carefully he proceeded he could not help but send down a deadly rain. And he had to proceed. Their courses were bound to one another's.

He was awoken by the sound of rifle fire. Someone's footsteps thudded on the planks of the floor. The door of the barracks opened and banged shut again. It was night. He rose, his legs shaky and his head throbbing.

Be ready.

Outside, groups of men ran past. Others crouched behind the barracks. Sol smelt smoke. A barracks lower down the hillside was on fire. As he watched, the roof buckled and split, sending a tongue of red flame high into the sky. The camp was bathed in the light. More gunfire sounded then, from a position high on the hillside. A heavy machine-gun answered from below. Men were shouting to one another. There was no sign of the Security Battalion troops, or their assailants, only the sounds of their gunfire and answering fire from somewhere beyond the flames.

Sol began to make his way across the camp, darting between the buildings. Crouching men looked up at him. The gunfire came and went.

On the southern side of the camp half a dozen men were pulling at the concrete posts of the fence. They threw themselves to the ground as small-arms fire crackled nearby. There was no sign of the combatants, whose fates were being settled beyond the reach of the red flames and faint moonlight. The uprooted posts hung between those still standing, dangling from the uncut wire. Shadows shaped as men moved around him. Something glinted at the edge of his vision, two red reflections of the firelight. When he found their source, Miguel's bespectacled face had turned away again. He was kneeling by the corner of the last barracks, pointing up the hillside to half a dozen men. Several nodded and the group set off up the hillside. Sol followed.

The fence at the top of the camp had been cut. Miguel pointed again and the men split up. Miguel alone made for the Upper Compound, whose gates stood open. When he reached the first of the brick buildings he turned quickly and beckoned to Sol, who had thought himself unobserved; he ran forward a few paces then stumbled on the uneven ground. When he got to his feet Miguel had drawn back around the corner. Sol advanced cautiously. The fighting seemed to have moved further down the hillside. There was the man, a dark shape close against the wall.

'Where is he?' asked Miguel.

Sol stopped. 'Who?'

Miguel said nothing. He shifted position, fumbling with his jacket.

'Who?' Sol repeated. 'Who do you mean?'

Miguel raised a pistol to Sol's chest. Then, before Sol could speak, Miguel's silhouette disappeared within a greater one, which appeared to wrap itself about the man, then detach itself with a sound like a boot being pulled out of wet clay. The figure stepped back. For a second Miguel did not move, then he rolled around to face the wall and slid slowly to the ground.

Sol began to back away, but Miguel's assailant ignored him, hunched over his victim and reaching into his jacket. Then he moved with surprising speed. Sol staggered backwards. Why could he not run? It was if the strength in his legs had drained into the soil.

A familiar, untroubled face emerged from shadow. The man glanced at Sol, then looked around the deserted compound and nodded, satisfied.

'Take,' said Uncle America, handing him Miguel's weapon. He mimed the action to pull the trigger. 'Pauff!'

Sol began to shiver as they descended the hillside. They stopped at one point and Uncle America whistled softly. They waited in silence. Then three *andartes* appeared. Uncle America took out his knife and had Sol show them the pistol, then the five continued down the hillside. They heard machine-gun fire below and behind them, but distant.

Twenty or thirty *andartes* were gathered by the shore, near the head of the lagoon. A burning smell reached Sol's nostrils. He sat and hugged his knees to his chest. Behind him a second group of partisans were at work setting up a gun emplacement at the entrance to a canyon which seemed to have been cut from solid limestone. The moonlight was stronger, or seemed so, reflecting off the white stone. He asked himself, What must happen here? An engine fired and there was a thin cheer. Uncle America emerged from a crowd of men and walked towards him.

'Where?' asked Sol, pointing first into the canyon, then across the lagoon. He was cold and yet soaked in sweat. Cold meant the mountains; his sweat Kalydon. He had fallen behind.

Uncle America nodded amiably. 'We find Eberhardt,' he said, and turned away to wave to someone. Men moved aside and a small truck inched forward, its windscreen smashed. Sol rose at Uncle America's insistence and the two of them made their way through the crowd of partisans which had closed behind the vehicle.

Sol heard a crash and another, louder cheer. A little way down the road, a truck lay on its side. Partisans were trying to push it off the thoroughfare. The back of the transport had been blown off; charred fragments lay scattered over the ground. The burning smell had come from there. Another group surrounded a smaller piece of wreckage, which might once have been a car. Other, less identifiable debris littered the area, which was cratered where shells had fallen or mines had gone off. A line of bodies lay by the side of the road.

Geraxos was standing over the corpses. He held his long rifle in both hands, letting its muzzle roam over them. At Uncle America's approach, he looked up and his blue eyes swept over Sol, who thought he saw regret in the man's face. But the moonlight was weak and the blue of his eyes too must have been remembered from an earlier time. The boar does not die here, thought Sol. Not here and not yet. Where was Thyella?

Geraxos and Uncle America spoke together in an undertone. Sol looked down at the dead men. They wore grey combat uniforms or the civilian clothes and armbands of the Security Battalion. A number of *andartes* had gathered around a corpse which was set apart from the others. Men would walk up, work their way through their murmuring comrades, then look down. As Sol waited his turn, he caught her name, confirmed between two of the partisans. Thyella? Thyella. The partisan in front of him stepped aside and Sol looked down at the corpse of a tall man in his late forties with thinning hair, dressed in full uniform. He seemed untouched. Only his cap was missing. Sol felt a hand on his shoulder. Uncle America appeared at his side. He too glanced at the dead man, then drew a finger across his own throat and grinned.

'Thyella,' said Uncle America. He pointed at the corpse. 'Eberhardt.'

Sol looked at the dead man's face and shook his head. 'This is not Eberhardt.'

In the pre-dawn light the lake appeared as a field of slate. The truck emerged from the wooded country into which it had plunged after the ghostly canyon and climbed a short steep rise to a road which hugged the shoreline. The camp was visible as a collection of blockhouses, oddly regular against the curve of the shore and the mountains behind. The first sunlight touched the tops of the highest peaks as the truck and its human cargo approached.

Sol sat braced against the tailgate surrounded by wounded men. They had been lifted in and settled together at the canyon's entrance. The jarring of the truck had drawn low grunts of pain as it rumbled slowly over the broken road. They had passed checkpoints manned by partisans. At each stop the driver had shouted ahead, been answered, and then they had been waved through. The passenger seat was occupied by a man whose head was almost completely wrapped in bandages. Uncle America rode on the footplate beside the driver. Sol watched the little buildings grow in definition. There were the rows of barracks, there the open square with its flagpole, although no flag flew now, and there the large hut from which a radio mast had risen. The mast he could not see, nor the cell-block, which was shielded from his view. He clutched the heavy pistol. His shivering seemed to have stopped.

As they pulled up in front of the communications hut, men ran towards the truck and began to carry out the wounded. Uncle America swung down from the footplate and the two of them walked inside.

A man dressed in faded fatigues looked up from a map that was spread over a large table. Behind him, someone was kneeling on the floor, attempting to repair a field radio, which hissed and crackled from time to time. Three others stood around the table, talking urgently. The commander nodded to the two of them, then resumed his discussion. Sol occupied himself from the far side of the room by trying to pick out their position on the map. He followed the coast to the lagoon of Messolonghi. He fancied he could make out the canyon through which they had driven. The lake was obvious and the camp was here at its eastern end. His eye wandered north, into the mountains, but that region was unrepresented. The centre of the map was blank.

An hour passed. Now and again the air over the lake carried the faint sound of gunfire from the town on the far shore. The sun rose and glowed off the distant roofs. Eventually the three partisans grunted their assent to whatever had been resolved, saluted their commander, and left. The man looked over at them and Uncle America began to speak. Soon the officer was shaking his head in exasperation, as though a request were being made which he could only refuse. He barked a few words in reply and Uncle America fell silent, neither angry nor disappointed. Instead he leaned over the map on the desk, then slapped his palm down on the centre.

As they emerged from the hut, two trucks were drawing up from which more wounded men were lifted out. Others arrived during the course of the morning, either on foot or in the battered trucks which drew up to disgorge their passengers then set off again. Sol walked around the communications hut to the cell block. A patch of new brickwork formed a red scar in the centre of the wall. The roof had been patched with corrugated iron. He continued around to the lakeward side and lay down in the shade.

The next thing he knew, he was being shaken awake. The sun

was in his face. Uncle America and the three *andartes* stood over him.

'Where is she?' he asked, confused for a moment.

'We go,' said Uncle America.

Geraxos was standing behind him, his eyes fixed on the mountains.

They would pass through villages where blackened foundations marked the positions of the dwellings. Sometimes chairs and tables were set up, as though people were living in the ruins. From a distance, a church built on a high ridge seemed purposeless in its isolation. Drawing nearing, they found the cottages of its parishioners strewn around it. Not one stone stood on another. They traversed a hillside strewn with smashed furniture and pottery which seemed to have fallen from the sky. There was no sign of the houses which must once have held these contents. Their inhabitants had vanished. Further on, the six men looked down into a steep-sided gully where a stream raced. Uncle America took the heavy pistol from Sol; a shot resounded. Why should these things have printed themselves in his memory while so many others left no trace? His fever abated but he had been weak and light-headed.

The air thinned as they moved higher into the mountains. There was a junction in their journey; it was somewhere ahead, but before the entrance to the gorge. At that point their route must intersect that of Thyella and Xanthos. The boar was run to ground in the marshland about a lake where reeds grew. Peleus loosed the first spear and missed, then Atalanta her arrow, wounding the beast. Ancaeus would be the first of his victims. It fell to Meleager to kill him. But the lake was far behind them now. Instead there was the river-bed, which more than a year ago had been dry enough for the trucks carrying Geraxos's enemies to use as a road. Now a shallow sheet of clear water ran over its stones. Sol knelt to dip his hand in the water, which felt warm and cold at once. The hunters must gather here.

They camped in the ruins of the village, beneath the charred tree which had once supported the roof of the *kaphenion*. Sol shivered and dreamed that men were stepping carefully about him and his prone companions, placing their feet in the narrowest spaces: the crook of an elbow or knee, between barely separated legs. A heel descended and fitted itself in the cup of his chin and breastbone, lifted and disappeared. They were the same footsteps, repeated over and over again.

When morning came he had stopped shivering, but the sickness was still there, a tight cord strung through his frame. The intervals between bouts were briefer and briefer. Uncle America sat on a low wall. He nodded to Sol. Geraxos and the three younger men stood behind him. Sol got to his feet. The rock face rose above him, more irregular than he remembered it. His limbs felt loose, weightless.

Sol remembered the entrance to the gorge. The ground sloped up to a lip and then appeared to fall away. The old man and the three andartes strode forward, then dropped out of sight. Sol and Uncle America followed until they stood at the point where the gorge began.

Sol looked down. Every step hence would incur debts he could not repay on his return. The old man was halfway down the descent, which was a steep slope of crumbling earth punctuated by narrow ledges and outcrops of rock. He leaped from point to point, his rifle held balanced in one hand. The younger men followed in his footsteps.

Uncle America gestured to the vista before them. Crags jutted from the sides of the gorge, which were fissured where frost had cracked the dark grey stone. Sol thought of what lay ahead, the space into which he was falling. He could not stop now. The four men who had preceded them were shrinking figures in a waste of boulders and scree through which a black stream curled. What did this place mean, except that a twisting cord of water had cut its way through the rock over the millennia? Sol heard something catch in Uncle America's throat, a sound he did not recognise. The older man pointed down into the bare, sunless place. Then they began the descent.

*   *   *

Flights of stairs fenced with elaborate wrought-iron balustrades and bannisters rose through the building. Their steps sagged where the human traffic had worn down the stone. Sol took them two at a time, pausing midway to catch his breath. At the top of the final flight, a young woman sitting on a plastic chair looked up from a paperback novel.

'Madame Lackner telephoned,' he began to explain.

Before he could finish the woman got to her feet and put out her hand.

'You're Solomon Memel, of course. I'm Elenie, Madame Lackner's assistant.' She picked up a clipboard from the floor and made a tick against a list of names, then smiled. 'Door duty today. Come with me. They're between takes.'

She led the way down the landing, edging past a depot of metallic cases draped with cables and stacks of bright orange plastic crates with the legend *Cine-BGT* and a telephone number stencilled on the side. She knocked softly on the door at the far end and there was a murmured exchange. Elenie turned back to Sol with a smile.

'Please, Monsieur Memel.'

She stood aside to let him pass, drawing in her breath as though the passage were too narrow for them both. Sol slid around the door and found himself in a room he recognised. This was where Paul Sandor and his co-star had circled each other and grappled, five times over: the light-filled space which had appeared in the dark of the screening room. Now it contained a dozen or more people, the nearest of whom was Lisa Angludet, sat in front of him wearing shoes, blue jeans and nothing else. A woman was dusting her shoulders with powder.

The actress looked up at Sol as though her state of undress were perfectly unexceptional. They exchanged greetings. Sol looked around the room, which was larger than had been apparent in the rushes. Two doors led to further rooms, on either side of this one. It was warm, but the dull light entering by two high windows at the far end seemed to chill the air. Vittorio was standing in front of the left-hand opening with another, younger man, whom Sol recalled from the restaurant. They held up instruments to the light then examined them intently. The younger man scribbled in a notebook. Rolf? Ethan? In front of the other window Ruth crouched beside a chair in which sat Paul Sandor.

The actor was bent forward, elbows propped on his knees, fingers interlaced behind his head. Ruth spoke to him, then rose and patted him on the back. Sandor straightened and stretched his arms. Ruth looked quickly over at Vittorio, who shrugged, then at Lisa. The girl was watching Sol. The make-up artist dabbed ointment on her face and retouched her lipstick. Sol smiled uneasily. Ruth mouthed a silent greeting as she approached, then addressed the girl in the chair.

'Five minutes, Lisa. We have time for three more takes, maximum.' Ruth's voice was brittle.

'Three?' The girl stuck out her lower lip.

'Yes, I know. Life is terribly hard. Is she ready?'

The make-up artist looked the girl over and nodded. Behind Ruth's back, a man walked in carrying a soundboom. Vittorio followed him with a large camera, which he waltzed around the floor for a few seconds. No one laughed. Sandor glanced over his shoulder, then looked away again. Men walked in from the adjoining room carrying chairs which they positioned carefully according to marks chalked on the floor. Ruth watched these preparations and waited, her lips pursed. Eventually, everyone found their place.

'Please everybody,' she said. 'No mistakes.'

The scene began as Sol remembered. Sandor stood by the window, first craning his neck then pressing his face to the glass as whatever it was that had captured his attention approached down the street. He was dressed in the same sweater as before but the trousers were darker and cut more formally. This time, when the object of his interest disappeared from view, Sandor's face dropped and then puzzlement surfaced in his features, slowly becoming surprise. The actor's character had understood something, thought Sol, who was sitting on Lisa Angludet's stool among the gear piled in the corner. Vittorio stood back from the actor, the sound-man with his boom beside him, Ruth behind both. All three turned slowly away from Sandor.

Lisa stood with her arms crossed over her breasts and a creased white scarf wrapped about her neck. Now Sandor's surprise meant something different. He smiled theatrically at her appearance. Lisa was looking around the room. No overcoat this time, noted Sol. Was she more naked in jeans, or less so?

'Where is everything?' she demanded.

'Come in, come in. You must be cold.' Sandor skipped forward, the eager suitor. 'We had too many things. Far too many, don't you think?'

Lisa wore mules. Her footsteps resounded around the room as she walked over the floorboards. Vittorio pulled back slowly.

'No. I don't think.' A look of disapproval spread over her face. 'What's wrong with you? Why don't you get rid of me too?'

Sandor pretended to look shocked.

'What do you want?' Lisa went on. She was trying to work herself up but she was tired. Their affair was tired?

'You know what I want,' Sandor growled.

He moved around Lisa, who stepped back. Suddenly he pulled a face and made as if to grab her breasts, flexing his fingers, a silent-movie villain. Lisa crossed her arms more tightly. Sandor changed tack.

'What do we care?' he exhorted her grandly. 'We still have chairs. Wonderful chairs!'

He threw out his arm to indicate them, hamming up his character's performance. He was drawing the girl in, Sol saw. Making her react to him. The two actors circled each other.

'I don't care.' Her voice was sullen. 'I've had enough.'

'My thought entirely.' Sandor was spritely, still. But there was an edge to his voice now.

'I've had enough of you. I've had enough old men!' She was going to burst into tears.

'Oh really? And how many old men have you had?'

'Enough!' she shouted, and lunged at him. Vittorio, the boom operator and Ruth moved back at the same moment. Lisa hit Sandor on the side of the head before he caught her by the wrist and pulled her towards him. They struggled clumsily, stumbling towards the window. Lisa made listless attempts to free herself but they were no more than gestures. Then she gave in. Sandor pushed her slowly, heavily against the wall. Lisa stared over his shoulder then grimaced in sudden pain. Ruth guided Vittorio closer until the camera obscured the actress's face, then manoeuvred the cameraman around to the side. Sandor bent his head to the wall, rested it there for a moment, then pulled both him and Lisa towards the centre of the room, out of shot. Ruth stepped back.

There was silence.

'Getting better,' Ruth announced, and clapped her hands.

A dark smudge now stained the wall between the windows at shoulder height, like a bloodstain that had been rubbed in, then allowed to dry. As Lisa walked back to reclaim her stool he saw that the same substance, a kind of oily chalk, was smeared over her back. He stared at her, puzzled. She caught his eye.

'Your shoulder.' He touched his own. The make-up artist was preparing her alcohol wipes and cotton wool.

'They paint this stuff on the wall, then paint white over the top,' she said, as Sol rose to his feet. She scratched at her back and held up her fingers. Behind her, Vittorio was playing his camera over the stain, back and forth. A man carrying a paint-pot waited for him to finish.

Sandor looked across the room and raised his hand in greeting. Sol walked over as Ruth reappeared. Vittorio made a final pass over the wall then lifted the camera from his shoulder.

'You came,' said Ruth.

'Of course,' Sol replied. 'I said I was curious.'

'Yes,' said Ruth. 'That's what you said.'

'We've saved the best till last,' said Sandor. 'Or the last till worst.' He looked tired, and older than he had appeared a few minutes earlier. He was wearing face-powder, Sol saw. A young woman hovered behind the actor carrying a bag of pots and brushes. 'That's what I need,' he said, nodding to the man now dabbing paint over the stain on the wall. 'A good coat of white-wash.'

'It was much better,' said Ruth. 'We'll get it next time.'

She looked anxiously out of the window, then beckoned Sol to follow her into the adjoining room, where a table and chairs had been set up. A woman hunting through a long rail of clothes looked over her shoulder, smiled at Ruth, then resumed her search. The two of them sat down. Ruth sighed and rubbed her eyes.

'Difficult day,' prompted Sol.

Ruth glanced back into the next room as though this thought had only just occurred to her.

'You don't see anything in what we're doing, do you?' she said. 'Of your work, I mean.'

The question caught him by surprise. 'Am I meant to?'

'I don't know. It depends.'

'On what?'

'On what happened. On where we are, the two of us.' She thought for a second. 'These are your memories, not mine.'

'I wanted to talk to you. That first night.'

'Yes, I know.' She looked up. 'I wasn't delayed. I said I was. At the airport . . .'

She would have said more but then someone in the next room called her name. She smiled apologetically at Sol.

'We can talk tonight,' Sol said. 'After you're finished here.'

Ruth nodded. 'There's coffee,' she said as she pushed a chair aside.

Sol sat at the table. Members of the crew walked in and out. Then the room beyond went silent, the door was closed and Sol listened for the scene to begin again. This time, however, the two actors had hardly begun their dialogue before there was a muffled thud and Ruth's voice sounded.

'Shit! Can someone please tell me why this is happening?' Her voice rose. 'Anyone?'

The door opened and Vittorio's assistant marched in shaking his head. Ruth spoke more calmly.

'OK. We go again. Last chance everyone. We need one take, just one.'

'I need to pee.' Lisa Angludet's voice.

'Too late. Positions everyone.'

'*Merde*. I said *I need to pee*.'

'Positions.'

'The light's hopeless,' said Vittorio's assistant to someone behind Sol. 'We're not getting anything.' He picked up something from the floor and walked out.

'Calm down,' Sol heard Sandor tell someone. 'We just move through this together. One, two, three.' The girl.

There was silence and then the scene began again. Sol listened to the actors' ballet, the wooden reports of Lisa's footsteps as she approached across the room, Sandor's retreat, a feint, then the struggle. They stumbled, stopped and stumbled again. A short silence meant she was pressed against the wall, which would graze her shoulder. The mark she left was a quotation from the poem's concluding section, when Meilanion grazed himself in the cave. It stood for evidence.

Then, in quick succession, Sol and everyone else in the room heard Ruth say, 'That's it, get her face now,' followed by Sandor's voice, 'For Chrissakes, Ruth, what are you doing?' and an instant later Lisa Angludet who shouted, 'Get off me! Get off!' Her voice broke into sobs.

Sol jumped up and opened the door as the girl freed herself and ran across the room, one hand to her face, the other pressed to her crotch. Sandor turned from the wall, his face red. Ruth stepped back, nodding to herself.

'Jesus Christ, Ruth.' Sandor was shaking his head.

Ruth ignored him. 'Did you get it, Vittorio?'

The cameraman looked down at his camera as though noticing it for the first time. 'I think so.'

'Did you get it or not?'

Vittorio nodded.

Ruth smiled. 'We're done. Break camp. Saddle horses. Thank you everyone.' She clapped her hands, seemingly oblivious of the silence in the room, or perhaps determined to break it. The crew turned away and began to pack up.

'You're a fucking piece of work, Ruth,' growled Sandor as someone handed him a jacket.

'We need to write you some new lines, Paul,' she said, walking past him to Sol. 'I'll get things organised for tomorrow, go over some things with Elenie. Then we can go. Will you wait for me?'

'Of course,' said Sol stiffly. He went back into the adjoining room and sat down again. People came and went. Sol heard three dull clangs as the chairs were stacked. A trailing plug scraped over the floor and banged against a plastic bucket. Someone dropped a teaspoon in a cup. The crew swapped 'goodbyes' in a mish-mash of languages to a flushed urinal's distant crash of applause. He sat in the company of the empty costumes hanging from the rack behind him. The afternoon reached its final shade of grey.

Several minutes of silence had passed before Sol rose and walked into the main room in search of Ruth. It was empty. He crossed and opened the door opposite. Beyond it was a corridor with doors off to the left. A fragment of plaster crunched beneath his heel. There was a skylight at the far end, whose weak illumination fell on what appeared to be rubbish sacks.

'Ruth?'

275

No reply came from the corridor. He tried the first door, which was locked. The second swung open on a bathroom. A pull-cord lit a bare bulb hanging over a bath of yellowed enamel. The mirror's spotted silvering gave him his face in a spray of shrapnel. Perhaps Ruth was waiting for him outside, on the landing.

'Ruth?' he called again.

'She's gone.'

One of the rubbish sacks rose. Lisa Angludet walked towards him. 'There's no one here,' she said.

She wore a military jacket and a towel wrapped around her waist. Her jeans swung from one hand. 'They won't dry.' She pushed past him. Sol followed as she walked, barefoot, back into the main room.

'Gone where?' he asked.

'Just gone,' she said, glancing around from the place of her earlier humiliation. 'So she plays these games with you too?'

The main room was almost dark. Yellow palls of street-light entered by the windows and fanned across the ceiling. Sol leaned in the doorway.

Her jacket was an approximation of Wehrmacht uniform. The cut was wrong and there was something that looked like a medal ribbon, red and white, on one of the breastpockets. The girl stared at him, a strip of her skin visible between the lapels of the unbuttoned jacket.

'There's a rack of clothes through there,' he said, indicating the opposite door, behind the girl. 'There'll be something you can wear.'

'What do you want to see me in?' The girl smiled. 'Help me choose.'

'Play those games with Ruth,' he told her, walking into the centre of the room. The mark by the window was still there. Evidence.

'She told me what you said. Wrong tits, wrong ass. So what? I'm not so stupid.' Lisa wrapped the jacket more tightly about her and walked quickly into the far room. 'You don't know what she's doing to your work.'

He paused, for a second or two, or longer perhaps. Her jacket was draped over the back of the chair he had sat in, waiting for Ruth. The towel lay on the floor beside it.

'I've seen you before,' he said.

She put her finger to his lips.

'Shush.'

She dropped to her knees in front of him.

'I saw you in a Métro carriage. You pulled up your skirt.'

Her fingers were fumbling with the zip on his trousers. She was clumsy.

'Imagine I'm her. You can do what you want. Like on a train.'

'I remember your face,' he said. But he did not remember.

'Imagine me.'

What did she mean? He felt numb. He did not want her. He reached down and touched her hair. 'Who should I imagine? Who are you?'

The girl made no reply.

In the next instant the room was bright with electric light. Ruth stood in the doorway. She looked down at the girl. Lisa sat back on the floor, making no attempt to cover herself.

'She's whoever you want, Sol. Me, if you like.'

Ruth flicked off the light, plunging them both into darkness.

'Enjoy her.'

*   *   *

Letters and small packets received poste restante at the Hotel des Postes were held awaiting collection for one year. A 'year' in the poste restante office, however, was a variable quantity, running at least from 14 July, when the last current-year arrivals were received, to the first week following that date in the following twelve-month period. Only then were the previous year's arrivals audited and thus the minimum 'year' allotted to each letter and small packet was effectively defined as at least 368 days and sometimes as many as 376, depending upon which day of the week 14 July fell on in that particular year.

A uniformed official explained these matters to Sol through the hatch in the wall. Sol glimpsed long rows of racks which stretched away behind the man. Ruth's letter would have lain there, somewhere. He directed his gaze back to the official, whose explanation had not finished.

It followed that a letter or small packet arriving on 15 July 1952, for instance, would wait in the poste restante office of the Hotel des Postes until 14 July 1954, and, that date being effectively any day in the week following, the office's maximal 'year' could sometimes stretch to more than twenty-four months. Thus, continued the official, the Ministère des Postes et Télécommunications, which undertook to receive, store and disburse those letters and small packets entrusted to it poste restante during a period of one year from receipt, actually exceeded its legal obligation in all cases, sometimes by as much as a second additional year, free of charge.

A note of apology had entered the man's voice.

There were different rules for parcels, which could not be sent (or accepted) poste restante, mostly for reasons of space, although sometimes they were held for a certain period if the offending dimension (any one exceeding forty centimetres, or any two exceeding twenty-four) was either negligible or a result of deformation in transit. The official had returned empty-handed from the gloomy rows of shelves. Might it have been a parcel that Sol was expecting?

Sol sensed the restive queue behind him. Letters came here to wait. Their recipients waited for the news which had waited for them. People had died and been born and moved house and separated and married: all these things were waiting to happen here. He had expected Ruth. But if Ruth's faraway life had ever come here in search of him, it was now gone. He told the official that he had not been expecting a parcel.

'Then I am sorry, Monsieur, but there is nothing.'

'What happens to letters after a year?'

'They are returned to the sender, or sent to Neuilly. There is a form.'

Sol took the form and tucked it inside his coat. The rush-hour traffic was in full spate when he walked back down the steps of the Hotel des Postes. A light drizzle fell, the buoyant droplets whirling in the cones of streetlight. The crowd flowed around him, then eddied behind him. He walked to Châtelet and took the Métro home.

And perhaps there had been no letter from Ruth, he reflected in the quiet of his apartment. It was almost ten years since they had parted in Venice. Perhaps they both preferred to remember the people they had been rather than encounter those they had become.

The form was printed on stiff brown paper, divided into boxes, gummed along one edge and scored so that it could be folded in three. A pre-printed address ensured delivery to the office at Neuilly, which would 'remit any letters or small packets'. He printed his name. He wrote '6, avenue Emile Zola, Paris 15e' and ran his tongue along the sour gum. Five weeks later a slim bundle secured by a perished rubber band was delivered to the apartment above pont Mirabeau.

'That is correct, Madame. Eight-two-eight. Nine-two. Seven-eight. Yes, I understand. Thank you. Yes, I will be here.'

Sol replaced the handset and sat back. The overseas lines were busy and he would have to wait. The operator would call as soon as a connection could be made. He drummed his fingers on the desk and thought of the bottle sitting behind the dusty glasses in the cabinet in the kitchen. The telephone would ring and the operator would tell him that the connection had been made to the number written on the back of the envelope in which Ruth's letter had arrived. Then he would tell Ruth.

The first letter in the bundle from Neuilly had contained a review of *Die Keilerjagd* clipped from a German newspaper and a note hoping that 'as the author' he might find it of interest; it was signed 'An Admirer'. The second and third letters were both from a female relative of Chaim and Lia Fingerhut, who wrote to inform him that 'someone found your book in Bucharest. We are very proud, and I have translated some of it into Romanian (difficult!)'

The fourth letter bore an American stamp. It was from Ruth.

An hour passed. Sol fetched the bottle from the kitchen and set it on the desk in front of him. It was almost nine o'clock. The city's lights tinged the sky with dull yellow. He stared at his reflected self, unmoving, suspended outside the window. His image picked up the whiskey bottle and poured itself a measure of liquor. His mouth opened and swallowed. A floating telephone did not ring.

Ruth's letter had crossed the Atlantic three times, for, returned to sender after its incalculable sojourn in the Hotel des Postes, it had been marked 'Not known at this address' and sent back. A telephone number scribbled on the back of the envelope had connected him to an unknown woman who had paused for so long after his initial question that he had thought the connection broken.

'No one by that name lives here,' she replied eventually.

'I am calling from Paris. Can you tell me where she does live?'

There was another long pause.

'I don't know where she lives. I don't want to know where she lives, either.'

'I knew her before the war,' said Sol. 'I apologise for troubling you.'

The woman sighed theatrically, then said, 'I heard she was working out of Hartwood's office. Number's in the book.'

Then she had hung up.

Sol drank steadily. At some point he carefully disentangled the telephone cable from the snarl of wires behind the desk and placed the instrument on the floor. At full stretch, the cable almost reached the couch, where he had taken up his new position. It would be better if the telephone was on the low table in front of the couch, he thought. Easier to reach when it rang.

But the telephone remained on the floor and did not ring. Sol lay on the couch and drank until the words he would say to Ruth dissolved. It was too late. The titles in the bookcase swam in his vision, composing and recomposing themselves. The characters spun and whirled, leaping up and down the spines like acrobats, vaulting the peaks and bounding out of the troughs. They would not stop now he had set them in motion. Their clangor rang in his skull. *Get up! Get up!* A short silence, then, *Get up! Get up!*

He rolled off the couch and felt the bottle topple. The last of the whiskey spread a tongue of liquid over the floor. The telephone was ringing. He lunged for the receiver.

'Ruth,' he mumbled.

'Your call has been placed, Monsieur. Shall I put you through now?'

'Ruth.'

'Sol? Are you there? Is that you?'

'Ruth, I can . . . I can't hear you. I can't hear . . .'

It seemed as though the telephone was still ringing, but it was impossible. He was speaking into the mouthpiece. Ruth's voice.

'. . . you've heard? How did you find. . . . It was last . . . alone? How can you talk to me about this?'

Talk to me. You have to find. Say something. *I shot him.*
'He was dying anyway.'
Had she hung up?
'Ruth.'
The room sagged and the woman's voice came in waves, breaking over his head. He held the telephone in his lap. The receiver felt hot and slippery with sweat from his fingers. He could not speak, or listen to the woman who spoke to him from thousands of miles away. Wake up, he told himself. Wake up. What was she telling him?

But when he did wake up, the telephone lay on its side on the floor. He was in a room smelling of liquor, in soiled clothes, one foot bare and his shoe resting next to the empty bottle. He lay on the couch across from the long row of his editions. What had he said? He remembered pronouncing her name, but then? He reached for Ruth's letter. He had written her number on the back of the envelope. *How can you talk to me about this?* What had he told her? He could not remember what he had said.

He took out her letter:

Dear Solomon,

All post-office workers hate Jews. They claim you do not collect these letters then send them back to me, whose life is hard enough. I am still married, but not for much longer. I am going to get a divorce from John (the ex-Major) and take all his money. I told you I would. It's the American way. I have a swimming pool, a huge motor car, and a smile as wide and perfect as Ann Sheridan's, who is my co-star in my latest film, *Just Across the Street*. I say co-star, actually she's onscreen for about ninety-four minutes and I'm the twenty-eighth one on the left in a cinema queue, but who cares? It's a sugary mess. I make poor John get me these parts and then he makes me do them. We really are quite unhappy with each other.

Otherwise life is easy here and I am becoming American, which I like. Do you understand? I hope so. I cannot think about the war any more but I need to talk to you to stop thinking about it. As I said, life here is easy and I would like to live like that now. How are you living? Please find the place for the Tellable as soon as possible, if you get this. This is the third letter I have

written, my dear Solomon. The others came back. I don't think
I'll write again.
I send you my love,
Ruth

PS. Even if you get the chance, please don't see *Just Across the
Street*. I actually have a small speaking part, which makes it
even more dreadful than it is anyway.

*   *   *

Dear Ruth,
I am sending this letter to your 'aunt' in Venice, to Ehrlich,
and to Auguste Weisz at the Schwarze Adler. I hope one of these
places is where you are. And the same letter to Jakob.
I am in a Displaced Persons camp a little way north of
Messolonghi. No one seems to know whether or not the war has
ended; I have decided to believe that it has. I hope that you are
safe. The stories I hear are very bad.
I have been very ill but have now recovered well enough to
do what I have done through most of this war: digging. I do
not know how long I will be here. The choices are repatriation
(to Soviet 'Chernovtsy'), or Palestine. Please write to me and tell
me that you and Jakob are alive. There are two addresses:
Solomon Memel, Int. 0551, Agrinion Camp (DP-Transit), c/o
British Military Mission (Greece), Messolonghi, Greece, and,
as above, c/o International Red Cross, Mainland Greece
Mission, Messolonghi, Greece. The post arrives here from
Athens once or twice a month.
I think of you every day.
Solomon

When he was strong enough to stand, Sol had wrapped himself
in blankets against the January cold and taken his first unsteady
steps from his palette-bed to the window. As the frost melted
under his breath he had looked out on a reed-fringed lake and a
distant town. He pressed his face to the cold pane. A different
flag hung from the flagpole and the communications hut was
a pile of blackened timbers, but the camp was otherwise unchanged. The plastered walls of the cell-block in which he had
been held were streaked with soot.

Now they housed the administrative offices of Agrinion Camp (DP-Transit) and the personnel who hurried in and out of its doors wore Red Cross armbands or Greek Army uniforms. The soldiers provided food, or at least transported it, arriving weekly in a battered German military truck and offloading sacks of rye flour, which came from Canada. Greek gendarmes from Agrinion came now and then and were shouted at by a stocky woman with short blonde hair, the camp's director, who was Swiss. There were fewer than five hundred men in the Agrinion Camp when Sol became aware again of his surroundings, perhaps a hundred more by the time he could walk unaided. When he was strong enough, or bored enough, to present himself for work, the number must have reached a thousand. But thereafter, the numbers fell.

He had had rheumatic fever and pneumonia in both lungs, the nurse in the hospital wing told him. She spoke a slow, stilted Greek he could understand. She was from Trieste. He said nothing then. He was lucky to be here, she added. They had not thought he would recover. The nurse smiled and walked away.

The numbers fell because the camp's inmates left, in groups of a dozen or more in the same supply truck which wove its way over the cratered road skirting the southern shore of the lake. Once its sacks and crates were unloaded, it returned by the same route with a different cargo. Some of the men it carried away hung out of the back, waving caps and shouting to their friends; others climbed aboard in silence and departed without a backward glance. But none returned, and those arriving at the camp, in battered ambulances, under escort, on foot, by mule, injured, diseased, speechless, numbered fewer and fewer. Sol did not know how he came to be there, nor where he might go when he left.

Fields stretched away behind the camp. He worked with the other able-bodied men, and they were paid, though in thick piles of drachmas, which were worthless. Sol lifted tussocks of grass, knocked dark red soil out of their rootballs and muttered to his shovel.

The departures gathered pace through late spring. There was a rumour that under a lottery scheme free passage could be had to America, and from there one could send for one's family. Some men spent whole days sitting in the cold outside the administration building. As Sol understood it, one presented oneself there and waited for a long time, perhaps as long as a day. Then, for a much longer period (certainly weeks, perhaps months), nothing happened. But papers of some sort arrived, in time, and then one walked into one's hut, clutching or waving them, packed one's belongings, or simply stuffed them into one's pockets, and climbed into the back of the truck, never to be seen again.

'Who is your sponsor?' asked the Red Cross officer from behind a desk stacked with neat sheaves of papers. He made notes in pencil. There was a box of pencils beside him, another of notebooks. Wooden crates filled with papers crowded the floor to either side of the desk.

'Visas are almost impossible, even to return to your own country, let alone travel permits. And there are no trains running north of Arte at the moment. Let me look at your file.'

Sol's file contained only two sheets of paper.

'You've already been interviewed, but there's no clearance marked here.' The man looked up, puzzled. ' "Failed to respond" it says here.'

'I was ill.' He tried to distinguish the faces that had floated before him during those weeks. 'What is a clearance?'

The official was nodding. 'Ill. Yes, I see. Clearance from the Greek authorities. It can take months. Better to try the British.' He looked again at the papers and frowned. 'They're going to talk to you anyway.'

'I've written letters,' said Sol. The man looked at him blankly. 'I want to send these letters.' He passed them over the desk and the man shuffled through them, then rubbed his eyes.

'Forget these,' he said, offering back all but one. 'Anywhere east of Vienna's impossible. They'll sit in Athens for the next ten years.' But when Sol did not move to take them, the official sighed and put the letters in a sack behind him. He considered Sol again.

'This room was used for interrogations,' said Sol. 'There was a mark on the wall behind me, different colours where coats of paint had peeled away. I can't remember the colours. Green was one. On the floor there were other marks.' He stopped. The official was looking at him strangely. 'I was interrogated in this room.'

He twisted about to point out the patch on the wall.

But the wall was white. There were no marks, or stains.

'It was repainted,' the official said after a pause. 'We know what happened here.'

There was a short silence.

'We will do what we can.'

'Can you give me a notebook?' Sol pointed to the box on the desk.

The official hesitated, then handed one across the desk.

Two months later Sol was summoned back to the administration building, where a different official led him down the same corridor but this time stopped short of the room at the end. The former cell was shelved along one wall and the shelves filled with filing boxes. There were two chairs, but no desk. The official shut the door.

'You are to take the truck tomorrow,' he said in faintly-accented English. 'Take your possessions with you, whether you are told to or not. Colonel Ward wants to talk with you in Messolonghi.'

'Clearance,' said Sol.

'No, that's done here.' The official paused, as if unsure how to proceed. 'It's very irregular. The circumstances in which you were brought here are not recorded in your file. There's nothing unusual in that, but you should assume that Colonel Ward knows something of those circumstances. Do you understand?'

'Who is Colonel Ward?'

'Never mind. Just answer his questions as fully as you are able.'

'And who are you?' asked Sol.

The official looked surprised. 'Dahlberg. Liaison.' When no reaction was forthcoming from Sol he added, 'From Sweden.'

There was much confusion with the check-list before the British Captain, a plump bespectacled man with a red face and bristly light-brown moustache, had a tick next to all the names.

'Memel?' he pointed to Sol, who nodded. The Captain tried to explain something in very bad Greek. Sol nodded again and climbed into the truck with the other men. They sat around him, clutching their bundles and grinning while the truck lurched and swayed out of the camp to begin the drive around the lake. After less than an hour they turned south into flat marshland. The road ran over a low causeway. Out of the open back Sol watched Agrinion shrinking and the mountains behind, which seemed invariable. It was late afternoon before they reached the lagoon. The truck rounded the shoreline to enter Messolonghi from the north and a short time later they pulled up outside a large brick building. The men climbed out of the truck and stretched their legs. Most of them were continuing on to Naupaktos, where their homeward journeys would properly begin. Sol jumped down and looked back. The heights of Zygos rose behind him.

'Follow please,' said the British Captain in his almost-Greek. They walked into the building.

A large room with benches on either side was deserted save for two Greek women dressed in black, one young, one old, and three silent young children who sat between them. They looked up as the two men passed through. Sol and the Captain climbed a staircase. Rooms to either side of a corridor had been outfitted as offices. Sol caught glimpses of uniformed men hunched together over map-tables and desks. One appeared to be taking a telephone to pieces.

'Ward about? Colonel Ward, anyone?' the plump Captain called out as he bustled through. Men shook their heads, or looked at him curiously.

'Pandazis then? Anyone seen him?'

'Upstairs,' a voice said.

The Captain beckoned to Sol, an exasperated expression on his face, and they climbed to the top floor.

'Pandazis! Where the . . . Ah, look, explain to this chap that Colonel Ward wants to ask him a few questions. Let's sit in here, shall we?'

Pandazis was a small neat man. He arranged three chairs around a desk at one end of the spacious room. Above the fireplace, a large-scale map of the Gulf of Corinth caught Sol's eye.

'Tell him not to look at that, Pandy. Classified.'

This was translated into Greek, then the interpreter said something else, which Sol assumed had to do with Colonel Ward's absence.

'I speak English,' said Sol.

'Well!' exclaimed the Captain. 'That's going to make life easier, if Colonel Ward ever gets here. He's got a few questions for you.' He enunciated his words precisely. 'Pandazis here does the interpreting around these parts. I'm Captain Montgomery. No relation, worse luck. Now let's see if we can get some tea while I track down Colonel Ward.'

Two hours passed. From time to time, Captain Montgomery put his head around the door to deliver the news that the lines were still down, or that the vehicle which they had heard outside, which should have contained the missing Colonel, in fact did not and that Colonel Ward was, all in all, not to be found. Eventually Montgomery returned with the intelligence that the elusive Colonel seemed to be in Patras and thus would not be back that night.

'We're just going to have to make the best of it,' announced the Captain to Sol and the silent Greek. 'Memel, isn't it? You probably know what this is all about. I'm deuced if I do. If Pandazis here takes the notes we can get through it one way or another. Let's start with the Kurtaga camp, that's where you were, wasn't it?'

Sol nodded.

'Good, that's a start. Write that down, Pandy. Now, after that . . .'

'You want to know about Eberhardt,' Sol interrupted. 'Or your Colonel Ward does.'

This seemed to irritate the Captain.

'Look Memel, I don't pretend to know any more than the average British Army officer posted out to clean up somebody else's mess. If you're so sure that Colonel Ward wants to know about this Eberhardt fellow then blast away by all means.'

Pandazis spoke then. 'Colonel Eberhardt was an Abwehr officer here in Messolonghi. He ran a number of agents and ordered some of the reprisal actions north of Karpenisi.'

'I see. Well, that sounds like Colonel Ward's department. What can you tell us, Memel?'

Sol told the two men what he knew of Colonel Eberhardt.

'Is that right, Pandy?' asked Montgomery when Sol had finished.

The Greek shrugged in a non-committal manner.

'I must say, Memel, it does seem odd that this Eberhardt was here so late in the day. Getting caught out like that. Worse than careless. You say the partisans caught his unit, up by the lagoon was it?'

'There had been a fight there. He got away with a few of his men,' Sol tried to lead the Captain back to the subject at hand.

'Let's be clear about what you're telling me, Memel. You weren't there at the time, but you know that he escaped, and who killed him, but you don't know how he died. It doesn't matter to me which of those statements is true, and I doubt it matters to Colonel Ward either, but even a Captain in the British Army knows that they can't all be true. Simple logic.'

'He was killed by a woman partisan who fought under the name Thyella . . .'

'This girl you say tried to help you escape?'

'Yes.'

'And you know this how?'

'He had been mutilated, in a particular way.'

'Let's stick to specifics,' said Captain Montgomery, leaning forward.

'Eberhardt had been castrated.'

Montgomery's expression did not change. 'One wouldn't want to meet her on a dark night. And what became of this Thyella after that?'

'She's dead. She went after Eberhardt, just as I told you.'

As he spoke, Sol caught a movement out of the corner of his eye. The Greek had given a tiny shake of the head to the Captain.

'You saw her body too?' Montgomery pressed him.

Sol did not answer.

'Come on Memel. Simple question. Yes or no?'

Sol turned to the Greek.

'You're not an interpreter.'

'Steady on there, Memel. Speaking out of turn won't get you . . .'

But the Greek had raised his hand. Montgomery sighed and sat back in his chair. The Captain and the interpreter exchanged glances.

'You already know about Eberhardt and Geraxos and Thyella, don't you?' Sol continued.

'Anastasia Kosta, to give her her real name,' the Captain said. 'Yes. And we've heard your name too, Mr Memel, although you seem to grow more mysterious by the minute.' He smiled, then spoke in a businesslike manner. 'Colonel Heinrich Eberhardt was an executive officer of the Militärverwaltungsstab-Messolonghi reporting to the Oberfeldkommandantur here. Responsible for internal security, in other words. How he was able to issue orders to a Greek Security Battalion, as you suggest, is something of a mystery. Wouldn't have made him very popular with the SS men. Bit of a loose cannon. What I'd like to ask you, what we would both like to ask you,' he nodded his head to the Greek, 'is why Eberhardt had a Jew with known affiliations to a local *andarte* commander assigned to a low-security labour battalion instead of shot?'

Sol looked from one man to the other. Their expressions were mild. Curious.

'Eberhardt interrogated you personally.' Montgomery continued. 'We know that. He also put his name to papers describing you as a "Temporarily Displaced Romanian National". Has a better ring than "Jewish Communist Partisan", wouldn't you say?'

The Captain regarded him evenly. The buffoonish manner of a minute ago had disappeared.

'He wanted something from you, Herr Memel. What was it?'

Sol kept his silence, which grew to fill the room and press on all of them. At last, the Greek broke it. He rested his elbows on his knees then spoke slowly and softly.

'There was a table in front of you, and on the table there was something wrapped in cloth, wasn't there?' He looked up for Sol's confirmation before continuing. 'An instrument of some kind. Before he showed you what it was, he told you what it was for. That was the order, wasn't it?'

Sol nodded again.

The Greek reached down and fumbled with the laces of his right boot. Montgomery pushed his chair back, stood up, and walked to the window. The Greek peeled off his sock to expose his foot.

'Look,' he said. 'That is what it was for.'

Sol glanced down, then looked away.

'Some things cannot be withstood,' said the Greek. There are places where we cease to be ourselves. It makes little difference now what you did, or said. And it will have no repercussions. Or not for you.'

The Greek pulled on his sock and pushed his foot back into his boot.

'Eberhardt died by the lagoon,' said Captain Montgomery from the window. 'We have that much. The Kosta girl too, most likely.'

'You know that's not true,' said Sol.

'Really? Please tell me why.'

Sol shook his head. Men's voices drifted up from the street outside. A horse's hooves clopped as it pulled a cart up the slight incline. These sounds only magnified the silence in the room. The two men let it continue.

'Well, we can't force you to talk to us,' said Captain Montgomery at last. 'No butchers' hooks here. No doubt it'll all be cleared up sooner or later. Or not.'

Sol looked up.

'As I said, I'm only a British Army Captain posted out to clean up a mess. In the end, none of this will amount to much. But wars rumble on for a while, Memel. They don't just stop.'

The Captain nodded to himself, then walked over to the desk and opened one of the drawers.

'Now, a final mystery. A United States Army Major in the – what is it?' He looked down and read aloud, 'The "Internal Film Information Services Unit". Major John Julius Aubrey Franklin II, no less! Now why would he be so eager to meet you?'

Montgomery handed a sheaf of papers across the desk.

'Travel warrants. Entry permit. Even some US Army meal vouchers in there somewhere. The full works.'

The Captain was easing himself back into character. Sol looked through the documents one by one. The bold peaks of the Major's signature repeated themselves across the pages, dwarfing the scrawls of the co-signatories, which were mostly illegible. He looked up, baffled.

'Don't look to me for answers,' said Captain Montgomery. 'Questions more my line. I'd try and ship out to Taranto, if I were you. Get a troop train up the coast.'

The route he eventually took, while indeed passing through

Taranto and continuing up the eastern coast of Italy, would prove considerably more complex than the simple sentences of advice offered by the Captain in the upstairs room in Messolonghi had suggested. It would be autumn before an over-worked locomotive heaved its mixed train of battered carriages and freight-cars across the plain of Lombardy, pulling into sidings to allow the passage of the westbound trains and stopping for the work-gangs who appeared to line almost the whole route. The line was single-track for long stretches. The mountains visible to the north and the sheet of water to the south encroached and receded, squeezing and releasing the neck of land over which the train passed until a long bend in the track directed it south and shortly afterwards they were passing over open water. The tired and sprawling men raised an ironic cheer. The train slowed to little more than walking pace to cross the causeway. Long minutes later, yellow stucco walls rose around them, then fell away just as abruptly. The carriages and cars shuddered over the points outside the station.

Sol showed his papers to a succession of baffled Italian gendarmes until, after a long wait, two white-hatted American Military Policemen were summoned.

'Major Franklin, huh?' said one, looking through the dog-eared bundle. He pointed to Sol's name. 'This you?'

Sol nodded.

'Should have a photo and a stamp.' He spoke briefly with his colleague as to whether civilian transport passes required stamped photographs or merely photographs without stamps. They decided the former.

'Get a photo,' said the colleague. 'Get it stamped.'

They led Sol out of the station into a bicycle-crowded square and then through streets which narrowed and widened unpredictably. They pressed themselves against walls to allow passage to the oncoming traffic, then crossed smaller squares where the only sounds were the reports of his escorts' boots and the softer slap of his own. An instant later the crowds would surround them again: men pushing handcarts, young women carrying children, or bundles of wood, groups of American servicemen. They turned corners. They crossed canals. Tattered laundry hung from lines strung between the buildings' upper storeys.

'Where are we going?' he asked.

'Major Franklin, right? The film guy?'

'Yes,' said Sol.

'That's where we're going.'

They exchanged glances and Sol had the impression that some laborious joke was being played on him. Or perhaps on Major Franklin, the 'film guy'.

The policemen stopped at last outside a pair of wooden doors set into a large archway. There was a bell-pull, but one of the men hammered on the wood with his fist. They waited. After a minute or more, a woman's voice called out something in Italian.

'Americano,' replied the hammerer. 'Got someone for Major Franklin.'

A small door set into one of the larger two opened and a very small, very old woman peered out, looked the three of them over, then nodded.

'There you go,' said one of the policemen, ushering him inside. 'Don't forget that photo either.'

Sol assured him that he would see to it, then ducked through the doorway.

A short archway led to a courtyard enclosed on three sides by walls and shuttered windows. On the fourth, balconies rose in tiers, supported by elaborately carved pillars. The old woman bolted and barred the door behind him then said something in Italian.

'Franklin,' he said, and tried to show her the name on his papers. 'Major John Franklin.'

The woman began to speak rapidly, incomprehensibly to Sol. Perhaps this was part of the policemen's joke. A water trough stood in the middle of the courtyard. He would sit on that and think. The old woman followed, still talking, or complaining, or threatening. It was hard to tell, with her jabbering in his ear. Suddenly his patience ran out. He stood upright and shouted.

'Ruth!'

The old woman closed her mouth and began to back away. He drew breath to shout again, louder this time. As loud as he could.

'Ruth!' he bellowed at the top of his voice.

The noise echoed around the courtyard. The old woman stared at him as if he were mad.

'Here, Sol.'

She was leaning over the second-floor balcony. He would remember a navy-blue towelling bathrobe, a light-coloured towel, and the bright red of her fingernails. She wore her hair short.

'You've had your hair cut,' he said. 'It suits you.'

Ruth turned away for an instant and then was joined on the balcony by a middle-aged man with dark slicked-back hair.

'Sol, this is John. Major Franklin, I should say.' She nudged him with her elbow.

Major Franklin waved his hand in welcome. 'You're Ruth's cousin?' asked the man. 'We're glad to see you at last. Let me tell you.'

'You're sleeping with him.'

'I am not!'

'You're in love with him.'

'Don't be ridiculous. He's in love with me.' She poked her head around the door. 'I'm going to marry him and live in Hollywood. With a swimming pool.'

Sol laughed.

'I'm serious!'

Sol and the Major had sat awkwardly together on the balcony while Ruth dressed. The Major had made conversation, telling Sol about his unit's assignment, which was to produce short films about the lives of ordinary people coping with life in liberated Italy. The Major spoke modestly and wittily. Sol nodded and grew ever more conscious of the dirt ingrained in his skin. He must smell, he thought. The urbane, softly-spoken American seemed a creature from another world.

'The game is finding people with the same attitude Americans hope they would have if they found themselves in, say, a ration-queue in Venice, if you see what I mean. Then we have to persuade them to be filmed. They're a little hard to find.' He smiled at Sol. 'But that's where Ruth comes in,' he said, as Ruth reappeared. 'Don't know what we'd do without her.'

Ruth had smiled back, meeting his gaze. She wore clothes Sol had not seen before.

'We'll put Sol in my aunt's apartment, shall we?'

Had the Major nodded, or had his head dropped a little at that,

Sol asked himself, recalling the moment. He lay with his own head resting on the lip of the bath-tub. Grey soapy water swirled around him as he lifted one knee and scrubbed lazily, listening to Ruth rearrange furniture in the next room. After a disorientating walk, the two of them had climbed a narrow twisting staircase. Ruth had unlocked a door at the top and ushered Sol through. He had blinked in the sudden brightness. Windows opened over rooftop vistas to either side. Light flooded the rooms, a soft golden light which warmed everything it touched.

'There's only us,' Ruth had said, behind him. 'She was a pretend aunt, remember?'

Sol fumbled for the plug. When he emerged from the bathroom, Ruth was opening the windows. He stood before her, newly-washed, dressed in a clean soft cotton shirt and dark grey slacks.

'John's clothes?'

'Whose else? You can't wear the rags you came in.'

'I'll wash them.'

'I've thrown them out. They had lice. I took your bits and pieces out of the pockets.' Ruth moved briskly around the room then stopped and looked him over. 'Sol, what happened to your feet?'

The bundle she had earlier pushed around the bathroom door included a pair of soft leather shoes, which had proved too small. Sol looked down at his bare feet. Clean, they appeared more misshapen than he remembered.

'Walking,' he said. They looked at each other across the room. 'How did you come to be here, Ruth?'

She shook her head and began to make up a bed on the couch.

'Stay here as long as you need to. John can fix it.' She unfolded blankets.

'Ruth. . . .'

She stopped, her back turned to him.

'None of them came back, Sol. Your parents, mine, the Fingerhuts, Gustl, his father. They took Ehrlich only a month before the end.'

'And Jakob?'

'He was arrested the night before you left.'

*

294

His sleep was a slow fall into welcome darkness, down and down. He did not know how far. At some point in the night Ruth came to him. He awoke with the palm of her warm hand in the small of his back. She touched her lips to the back of his neck. He turned his head.

She knelt by the side of the couch, a dark shape against the outer dark of the window. He reached back and she took his hand in her own. Then, in a single quick movement, she slipped beneath the blanket and fitted herself against him, her breasts pressed against his back, her legs bent to his. She freed her fingers and stroked his stomach, then his ribs, slowly, as though she were counting them.

'Do you remember?' she whispered. 'That night in Flurgasse, walking back from the theatre?'

'Your play,' he murmured, still drowsy and willing to let happen whatever might take place.

'I wanted you. You remember how it was? You're so thin now. I'm going to feed you up.' She stroked his stomach again.

'You're going to America.'

'Hush.'

Ruth reached for him then, and for some time there was silence. She kissed his shoulder, then rested her lips against the base of his neck.

'I'm sorry,' he said eventually.

'I'm happy,' she whispered. 'I'm happy that you're alive.'

She was crying.

*   *   *

Sol heard Paul Sandor's voice issue from the loudspeaker in the side of the tape recorder:

'What marks our passing? A cracked window-pane, a mark on a wall, the ring in the bath-tub, and a smear of lipstick? Everything we have spilled, or spoiled, or let fall. The dust settling in our footprints. The marks we leave behind us fade, or are blown away. Is this how we survive?'

The spools turned slowly at one end of the room. At the other, an awkward procession was underway. Vittorio crept across the floor, his camera held waist-high and the viewfinder angled up. He hunched to peer into it, glancing up every few seconds. The lens glided over the surface of the wall, almost touching. Behind him, one of the young men Sol remembered from the week before mimicked his movements. He seemed to have no function until Vittorio muttered something when the camera moved closer yet. Then the young man reached over and twisted something on the lens. The last person in the procession was Ruth, who directed the movements of both.

'Go in closer, Vito. Enough, now up in a curve. That's it. Pull back a little.'

They inched their way along the wall.

This time no one had been waiting at the top of the stairs to check Sol's name off a list. The orange plastic crates had gone and the actors had disappeared. Ruth had turned from the window as he walked in.

'I can't offer you anything to sit on, I'm afraid.' She had spread her hands in apology. The three chairs had been removed, along with everything else, even the chalk crosses which had marked their positions. Ruth walked across to embrace him, as if nothing had happened. 'We shouldn't even be here,' she said.

There had been a terse telephone call three evenings ago.

'I overreacted, Solomon.'

'Nothing happened, Ruth. And nothing was going to happen.'

'It wouldn't matter if it had. It's none of my business.'

'It didn't.'

'I know.'

They had listened to one another's breathing over the telephone line which connected them across Paris. Ruth had talked about the English painter, whose lover had killed himself in a hotel bathroom. There had been pictures. A remote electrical wind blew in their ears.

'We're out of time.' Ruth's voice crackled through the disturbance.

'I have time,' said Sol. The interference reached a peak and abruptly disappeared.

'Not us. The crew. The set. Paul starts shooting in Mexico in ten days. He tells me he hasn't even read the script. We're out of money. The production office can't write cheques.' She chuckled to herself. 'Sets are supposed to be struck, Sol, but they never are. They fall apart of their own accord.'

'I'm sorry.'

'It's always like this.'

He said, 'I still have time.'

There was a long pause.

'I've tried to be honest, Sol.'

He said nothing, waiting for her to speak again.

'We'll be shooting until late tomorrow night. I'm on an early flight back to the States on Saturday. You know where to find me.'

She had ended the call abruptly.

Now she, Vittorio and the assistant moved down the wall, keeping to the side of the window where Sandor had stood. Vittorio clicked the viewfinder back as he angled the camera down, taking the lens to within a hand's-breadth of the floor.

'Very slowly now Vito, at a diagonal to the floorboards. Then curve around. Make the gaps between the boards look solid. Solid as railway sleepers. Cut straight across them.'

'There's not enough light,' said Vittorio. 'No contrast.'

'Doesn't matter. Keep going.'

Sandor's voice continued: 'What of the gaps in our account? The edges of our "Ands" and "Thens" or "Otherwises"? Who'll read our signs, or see us in what we leave? There are no truthful silences. Look back now, look at our trails and their scattered possibilities. We took so few of them.'

'The light's going,' said Vittorio.

Only the machine responded: 'Step into darkness. Nothing betrays us there. Walk into silence. Leave nothing. Be among the lost.'

'Light's going,' Vittorio repeated.

'Let it go,' said Ruth.

The lens moved back and forth over the floor, recording nothing. There was no stain on the wall and no crack in the window-pane. The light fell and fell.

Sandor's voice ceased. The turning spools drew blank tape through the machine. Sol thought of the moment in the screening room when Ruth had prompted him for his memories. Three flickering children playing in a grainy river and their resonant ghosts: himself, the woman beside him and Jakob. A train whistle sounded its thin note from further up the valley. He pulled himself out of the chilly water and the sun shone out of a cloudless sky, stinging his wet skin. Had he been hot or cold?

But they were not children. They had never been three children playing in a river. Ruth was right, he thought, as the shadows lengthened, forming two figures on the rough ground where he had once lain. It was honesty, of a sort.

The last of the tape unwound.

'That's it,' said Ruth. 'We're done.'

The two men straightened slowly.

There was a muted leave-taking. Vittorio and his assistant packed their equipment, slung the padded cases over their shoulders and edged their way out of the door. Ruth and Sol listened to their footsteps as the two men walked away down the corridor.

'Here is the time,' he said.

'What?' Ruth looked distracted.

'There's no crack in the glass, Ruth.' He pointed. 'There's no mark on the wall either. I didn't understand before.'

'Because they've gone. The lovers and the tracks they left. They've disappeared, like your Greeks.'

'That's not what you say. You say they never existed. That none of it happened.'

'Do I? Did they? Thirty years ago, or three thousand?' Ruth was silent for a moment. 'But you're right, Sol. I've deceived you.'

'Take my name off your film. Let me disappear too.'

Ruth smiled to herself. 'Not the film. The footage I showed you from Greece. I took it, with Jakob. You guessed, didn't you?'

Sol stared at the woman who stood by the window.

'Why have you done this, Ruth? Why did Jakob. . . . What does he want from me?'

'Nothing.'

'Then why . . .'

Ruth shook her head.

'Jakob doesn't want anything from anyone. Not anymore. He shot himself in a cellar in Tel Aviv in 1955,' she said. She held herself erect and expressionless. But then her face crumpled.

He took a step forward, as if to hold her. She raised her hand.

'No.'

'I wrote to him,' Sol said. 'The letters came back.'

'It would have made no difference. He had to see things as they were. He only wanted the truth. Don't you remember how he was? He thought you would be the one to tell it, Sol. Oh God, you don't understand a word of what I'm saying, do you?'

Sol shook his head. He tried to summon the Jakob of thirty years ago; Jakob and his unlivable truth. When Ruth spoke again her voice was calm.

'When you telephoned, I thought you had heard. Nothing you said made sense. Jakob wrote to me, insane letters. That's how they traced me. They were all about you, Sol.'

'But you believed him.'

'He didn't even believe himself. I think he hoped to find you there. But you were gone and there were only the places you had been. The camp. The village. The mountains.' She looked across at him. 'Of course you were there, Sol. I've known that all along. It was never you I doubted.'

He waited while Ruth locked the outer door of the apartment. They walked down the stairs and into the street. He offered her his arm but she refused. Cars sped past. On the other side of the road, the river was a silent cut in the city's noise and motion.

Ruth began to speak about the time in Greece. Her memories broke off and resumed abruptly. From time to time she would address a comment to him but before Sol could reply she would be led down some other train of thought or would chase after some other recollected fragment. Sol walked beside her, awkward in his indecision. They crossed pont Mirabeau.

He pushed open the door to the apartment block and pressed the button in the elevator. They rode up in silence. When they entered the apartment, he saw her brow furrow as though she had formed a thought and were debating whether or not to express it. She did the same again when he returned from the kitchen with the whiskey bottle and two glasses. She nodded for him to pour.

'But when the night-hunter loses the trail,' Ruth said deliberately, as if in conclusion to an argument that they had conducted between them many times, 'what then?'

Sol stared at her in bewilderment.

'There had to be a boar. And hunters to hunt him,' she said. 'But when the light fails and the tracks give out.'

'What are you trying to say?'

Ruth looked up, surprised. But at what? To find him sitting there? He did not know the woman who sat opposite him.

'Of course you were there, Sol. And there was a woman, called Thyella, or Anastasia Kosta, or Atalanta. And you were her night-hunter. It's not so different: a film is only a trace, a scattering of shades and colours. A succession of moments. I understood what you did.'

'And what did I do that you understand?' Sol broke in. 'How do you film the dark, Ruth? How do you catch what is not there?'

'Then the truth is just silence. Or darkness.'

'And what is lost is lost? Those who disappear may as well never have existed. Or do you think the boar remembers his victims? The boar only remembers his victors, Ruth.'

'Like Atalanta? Like your Thyella?'

'Yes.'

'But the closer you got, the less there was of her. Her tracks grew fainter and fainter. And at the very end, she disappeared. There was no "Boar", no "Atalanta", no "Eberhardt", no "Thyella" . . .'

'You're as insane as Jakob. I saw with my own . . .'

'Stop! Stop it, Sol!' Ruth burst out. 'Don't ask me to believe what you saw with your own eyes. Eberhardt was killed outside Messolonghi. He was escorting a group of prisoners to a camp further north. He was an Abwehr intelligence officer, an ineffective one, according to his records.'

He stared at her across the table.

'Jakob,' she said in explanation. 'He knew all of it. There was no record of "Thyella". People remembered her in Messolonghi. They described her much as you do and told the same stories you tell. But when we travelled into the mountains she faded. The villagers knew less and less, or would not talk. Until we reached the gorge and the village there.'

'It was her village. Eberhardt razed it. He gave the order. I saw them do it.'

She nodded, not looking at him. 'It was burnt down during the war. They told us that.'

Ruth picked up her tumbler and raised it to her lips. He saw her mouth distort through the glass as she sipped.

'Thyella's name meant nothing to them. You see, I understood why you needed her, and what you needed her to be. You think we should have fought like her,' Ruth said. 'In our Bukovina, and your Agrapha, and everywhere between. Better to have left our mark like that.' She smiled sadly. 'Such romantic dreams. You wanted us too, to march through Ringplatz with our bows and arrows and spears. We could never be the heroes you needed. Nobody could. Not Thyella. Not me. I'm sorry, Sol.'

'Please stop, Ruth.'

Ruth picked up her tumbler and raised it to her lips. He saw her mouth distort through the glass as she sipped.

'You liked my hair short, Sol. In Venice, do you remember? You should have seen me when it was cut. It was the officer you found me with the day you left. They did it after the Germans had gone. They pulled me out and shaved my head in the street.'

'Enough, Ruth.'

'I'm not ashamed.'

'You had no choice.'

'We choose the people we become. I chose to survive. What did you choose, Sol?'

'Thyella killed him.'

'The truth is now, Solomon. Not then. Here is the time for the Tellable. Your Thyella never existed. Your "boar" was an insignificant desk officer. The boar didn't die at all, Sol. The boar won.'

She fell silent. He watched her waiting for him to answer.

*   *   *

A lake of stone had drained away. This void remained to mark its passing. The floor of the Cauldron was a plain of stones enclosed by rising cliffs. There was no scale. Their first footsteps over the loose rocks and smooth grey pebbles sounded at once too loud and too puny. The six men walked out of the gorge and stopped.

Sol let himself sink slowly to his knees, hearing small stones crunch and grind beneath him as he settled. The air was cold and very dry, and burned his lungs when he drew it in, each breath an effort now. The shivering had stopped and started throughout the previous night. They had risen at first light and continued their progress, Sol's limbs floating out from him then drifting back. He wondered if he might drift upright again. Uncle America said something to the men in front and they turned to look down at him, the old man, the three *andartes*. Uncle America's hand descended and hooked itself under one arm. He was lifted to his feet.

His head fell back. The sky hummed and thickened, luminous one moment, opaque the next, a curving vault of blue. He closed his eyes and felt his skull's weight roll forward. Open them. There was the cave. It seemed too narrow: a black blade hundreds of metres away. He might have mistaken it for a shadow. The grey cliffs rose above it and pressed down but its darkness was dense and resistant. There was no colour here. The old man's eyes did not belong. The wrong eyes, he muttered, as one of the younger men turned away again. A dark plant was blooming in his face. The wrong colour.

No, he thought. The wrong time. That had come later.

They advanced, the two younger men out to the left and the other to the right, the old man between them. He and Uncle America walked behind. Their footfalls clattered over the stones. Red belonged here no more than blue. What did the old man see?

And then. That was the moment.

One of the *andartes* spun around, as though something had caught his eye, some movement. Dark red petals were flowering in his face, shooting roots and sprays through his head and into the air behind him. Sol felt something strike the backs of his knees. He fell, as a hard crack rolled around the surrounding cliffs. The echoes died slowly. There was a moment's silence, then Uncle America began firing. The two remaining younger men opened up too. The old man held his fire, his rifle flat to the ground, motionless. The noise went on and on, returning off the unyielding stone in tumbling volleys that merged and roared in his ears.

How long? Counted in heartbeats, or gauged against the slow fading of the light. A minute?

Little explosions of dust curved towards him, their arc seeming no more fearsome than the splashes of a waterfowl beating its way into the air. Uncle America grunted and shifted position.

His gun chattered again. The two younger men had moved forward. One turned his head, looking back for Uncle America but finding only Sol. He shouted something, a strange grin stretched over his face. Uncle America shouted back. He too had moved forward. But the old man remained where he was, still kneeling, his long rifle held down, watching the cave. The gunfire came in regular bursts now, swapped back and forth between the three men, from the left, from the right. Sol raised his head.

The entrance to the cave was both larger and more distant than he had thought. The cleft in the rock dwarfed its defenders, who were specks of movement against the darkness behind them. Twitching disturbances. Then, suddenly, one of them was still.

The old man raised his hand. A last burst of noise rolled around the walls and broke apart. The guns fell silent. Look at us, thought Sol. What sign do we form? And the crouching silhouette against its blade of light, the ripples in its outline as it shifts. The old man stood up. All wrong, Sol thought. He might have spoken aloud, for Uncle America turned back to him and said something he did not understand. All of it lost. The old man faced the dark break in the rock and called out.

Slowly and unsteadily, something rose from the floor of the cave, a shape which at first made no sense to Sol. Uncle America was already standing. At the appearance of the distant figure the younger men rose too. They watched as the figure stumbled down the slope from the entrance, fell heavily, and then appeared to break in two.

The old man began to walk forward. The others followed.

Two bodies had come to rest at the foot of the slope. One lay motionless where it fell. As the five of them approached, the other stirred, then rose.

Thyella got to her feet and walked back to where the dead man lay. She bent to lift him again, hooking her arms under the dead man and dragging him slowly away from the cave. Nothing moved there now.

They halted a little way short of the woman. The old man spoke. She let fall her burden then turned to him. The old man looked into her face, then down at the dead man. He shook his head and said something. Uncle America reached inside his jacket, then pointed towards the cave. He took Sol's hand and pressed the revolver into it.

Her eyes had passed over him then. Her face betrayed no sign of recognition. She had raised her hand to her mouth and placed a finger to her lips.

Sol glanced down at the weapon. The old man reached out with his free hand and touched his palm to Thyella's face. The two had looked at each other.

Sol walked towards the cave, past the dead man, who was Xanthos. She had closed his eyes. He reached the slope which led up to the entrance. Loose stones rolled under his feet. The air inside was colder, and damper, and their discarded weapons lay on the ground among drifts of spent cartridge cases. He looked back once before walking into the darkness. She was walking away from them across the floor of the Cauldron. She had almost reached the centre. The old man raised his rifle to his shoulder. She came to a halt. Sol turned away before the shot.

*　　*　　*

Sol said, 'I know that her name was Anastasia Kosta. She took the name Thyella and fought with the *andartes* in the region of Greece known as Agrapha from 1941 until her death in 1944. I believe she was the lover of an *andarte* who fought under the name of Xanthos. He was wounded and captured in an action ordered by Colonel Heinrich Eberhardt in the summer of 1943. Thyella was captured in the same action, as was I. She escaped. I and Xanthos did not. Perhaps she was allowed to escape. I do not know.

'Eberhardt was an intelligence officer attached to the German headquarters at Messolonghi. He was killed during the German withdrawal in September 1944, either outside Messolonghi or in the mountains north of Karpenisi. If Thyella betrayed her comrades to Eberhardt in exchange for her lover's life and, by chance, my own, I do not know how. If she killed a German officer so that his corpse might pass as Eberhardt's, I do not know why. If I was her night-hunter, as you said, I proved a poor one. I know that she was executed without trial in a place called the Cauldron in the autumn of 1944 and that, before she died, she asked me for my silence, which I have kept.'

Here is the place. Here is its home.

Sol looked around the empty room. He heard the distant thud of the lift and wondered for a moment if Ruth might have decided to return. But the whine of the electric motor passed his floor and continued up through the building. He rose from his chair, walked to the window and looked down.

Ruth was crossing the bridge. She appeared and disappeared, moving through the pools of streetlight and their intervening darknesses. She had waited long seconds for his answer. Then she had risen to her feet.

'How could I have answered you, Ruth? Our memories never tell us the stories we need. Our heroes never live the lives we require. Such lives leave no trace for those who follow. Their true acts take place in darkness and silence and their untellable stories rest with them, in the cave. What could I have shown you of that?'

PART III

Agrapha

The damp was animal. The air he breathed had been breathed before. Latent in the soured air was its fizzing rush through living blood. Standing in the cave's dead lung, his own lungs pressed the cage of his ribs, relapsed, and pressed again. The other's old breath flowed through him.

He walked forward and the light died. His eyes strained against a darkness he knew to be absolute. He closed them then advanced, feeling his way forward, taking slow steps. A loose rock rolled beneath his foot and rattled over the cave-floor, which was ribbed with little humps and ridges. The passage dropped, then slanted, leading him deeper into the darkness.

His progress slowed, or seemed to. There was no time here. He felt for the crevice or crack that would trap his foot and trip his weight forward, sending him headlong into space, or nothing, his own blindness. *The night-hunter tracks by the light of the moon. . . .* No moon had ever shone here. His palm swept over the stone's cool surfaces, which erupted into pitted honey-combs, then smoothed themselves, or broke into fissured patterns which his mind's eye could not assemble. His arm reached into breaks in the walls and emerged again. He continued.

The cave narrowed. For a few brief steps, with arms outstretched, his fingertips would touch both sides. Then it widened again. He stumbled, once, falling and grazing himself on the abrasive stone. The floor yielded nothing to his padding footsteps; their soft scraping and his breathing were the only sounds. The cave's course began to twist. He slowed his pace again. He was patient. Nothing could happen here, except his own creeping progress away from the light. There was no trail to follow now and nothing more to know.

He thought the cave grew warmer, but it was not so. It was a smell proper to warmth, faint in his nostrils. Musty and dry. Proper to the warmth of an animal's body.

He reached up and touched the roof of the cave, then traced its orbit around him. He gulped air and held his breath, listening, then dropped to his hands and knees. The smell grew stronger.

He reached out his hand. Nothing. The cave's cold stone. But he heard breathing now, toneless and rhythmic. In, and then out. He moved forward and reached again. His hand closed on living flesh. The boar stirred.

The movement was enough to shrug him off. He crept closer, his fingers tingling as they felt their way forward. A hoof. Its cleft, then the dew claw above it, an ungrown bud at the back of the hind leg. The hair on the haunch was matted with filth or blood. The boar lay on his side, his breathing quick and shallow.

He felt for the animal's belly, where the hair was sparsest and the skin beneath fine-grained. His palm stroked the fibrous bristles above. The boar shifted again, raising his head then letting it fall. A tusk scraped on the stone. He reached for the hackles. They lay flat along the line of the back, thick as goose quills. Then he lowered his head until the coarse bristles of the boar's flank scratched against his cheek. He settled and ran his fingers into the softer wool beneath. He felt the boar's fading heat pulse through the hard armature of his fat. The lungs rose and fell, each inhalation jostling his head, each exhalation shallower than the last. In, and then out. He was in time. The boar's heart thudded, slower and slower. He waited for its silence.

Now.

ABBREVIATIONS

SIGLA

ad	ad
aliq.	aliquando
ap.	apud
cit.	citation
cf.	confer
dieg.	diegesis
ff.	following
fort.	fortasse
fr.	fragment
ibid.	ibidem
id.	idem
q.v.	quod vide
Schol.	Scholiast
schol.	scholion
s.v.	sub verbo
vid.	vide

AUTHORS AND WORKS

Ael	Aelianus
Nat Anim	De natura animalium
Var Hist	Varia historia
Aesch	Aeschylus
Ag	Agamemnon
Cho	Choephoroe
Eum	Eumenides
Sept	Septem contra Thebas
Pers	Persae
Prom	Prometheus

Aeschin	Aeschines
Alex Pleuron	Alexander Pleuroniensis
Ant Lib	Antonius Liberalis
Anth Gr	Anthologia Graeca
Anth Pal	Anthologia Palatina
Antig Car	Antigonus Carystius
Apollod	Apollodorus
~	Bibliotheca
Ep	Epitome
Ap Rhod	Apollonius Rhodius
~	Argonautica
Apostolius	Michael Apostolius
Ar	Arrian
Cyn	Cynegeticus
Arat	Aratus
Phaen	Phaenomena
Archil	Archilochus
Aristoph	Aristophanes
Ach	Acharnians
Eccl	Ecclesiazusae
Eq	Equites
Lys	Lysistrata
Nub	Nubes
Plut	Plutus
Thes	Thesmophoriazusae
Vesp	Vespae
Aristot	Aristotle
Ath Con	Athenian Constitution
Gen An	De Generatione Animalium
Hist An	Historia Animalium
Meteor	Meterologica
Nic Eth	Nicomachean Ethics
Poet	Poetics
Rhet	Rhetoric
Athen	Athenaeus
~	Deipnosophistoi
Bacch	Bacchylides
CAF	Comicorum Atticorum Fragmentae, ed. Kock

Callim	Callimachus
Aet	Aetia
Hec	Hecale
Hymn	Hymns
Choerob	Choeroboscus
Clem Alex	Clemens Alexandrinus
Protrept	Protrepticus
CQ	Classical Quarterly
Cy	Cougny
Epig	Epigrammatum Anthologiae Palatinae Appendix Nova
Dem	Demosthenes
Dict Cret	Dictys Cretensis
Dio Chrys	Dio Chrysostomus
Or	Orationes
Diod Sic	Diodorus Siculus
Diog Laert	Diogenes Laertes
Eratos	Eratosthenes
Cat	Catasterismoi
Eur	Euripides
Alc	Alcestis
Andr	Andromache
Bacch	Bacchae
Cyc	Cyclops
Elec	Electra
Hec	Hecuba
Hel	Helena
Herc	Hercules furens
Hipp	Hippolytus
Hyps	Hypsipyle
Ion	Ion
Iph Aul	Iphigenia Aulidensis
Iph Taur	Iphigenia Taurica
Med	Medea
Mel	Meleagros
Or	Orestes
Ph	Phoenissae
Rh	Rhesus

Suppl	Supplices
Tro	Troades
FrVk	Fragmente der Vorsokratiker, ed. Diehls and Kranz
FrGrHist	Fragmente der griechischen Historike, ed. Jakoby
Hdt	Herodotus
Heph	Hepaestion
Ench	Encheiridion
Hes	Hesiod
Ast	Astronomia
Cat	Catalogus Mulierem
Melamp	Melampodia
Sh	The Shield of Heracles
Theog	Theogony
WD	Works and Days
Hesych	Hesychius
Hippoc	Hippocrates
Epid	Epidemiae
Hom	Homer
Hymn	Homeric Hymns
Il	Iliad
Od	Odyssey
Hor	Horace
Ode	Odes
Hyg	Hyginus
Ast	De Astronomia
Fab	Fabulae
Iamb	Iamblichus
Pyth	Vita Pythagorae
Inscr Kos	Inscriptions of Kos, ed. Paton and Hicks
Isoc	Isocrates
Lact Plac	Lactantius Placidus
Lesches	Lesches

Il	Ilias Micra
Luc	Lucianus Samosatae
Dial Deorum	Dialogi Deorum
Lyc	Lycophron
Alex	Alexandra
Mar Par	Marmor Parium
Mus	Musaeus
Hero	Hero and Lyander
Nepos	Nepos
Tim	Timoleon
Nonnus	Nonnus
Dionys	Dionysiaca
Op	Oppian
Cyn	Cynegetica
Hal	Halieutica
Ov	Ovid
Ars Amat	Ars amatoria
Fas	Fasti
Her	Heroides
Met	Metamorphoses
Pal	Palaephatus
De Incred	De incredibile
Parth	Parthenius
Er Path	Erotica Pathemata
Paus	Pausanias
PEG	Poetae Epici Graeci, ed. Bernabé
P Berlin	Berliner Klassikertexte, ed. Schubart
P Grec	Papiri Greci et Latini della Societa Italiana, ed. Vitelli et al.
P Hibeh	The Hibeh Papyri, ed. Grenfell and Hunt
Pind	Pindar

Porphyr	Porphyrius
De abstinentia	De abstinentia
Quaest Hom	Quaestiones Homericae
P Oxy	Papyri Oxyrhyncus,
	ed. Grenfell, Hunt, Bell et al.
P Petrie	Petrie Papyri,
	ed. Mahaffy
Prisc	Priscianus
Inst	Institutio de arte grammatica
Pron	De Pronuntiatione
Proc	Proclus
Chrest	Chrestomathia
Prop	Propertius
P Ryl	Catalogue of the Greek Papyri
	in the John Rylands Library,
	ed. Hunt, Johnson and Martin
pseudo-Aristot	pseudo-Aristotle
Mirab Auscult	De mirabilibus
	auscultationibus
Ptol	Claudius Ptolemaeus
~	Geographica
Quint Smyrn	Quintus Smyrnaeus
Posthom	Posthomerica
Sen	Seneca
Ag	Agamemnon
Her Oet	Herakles Oetaeus
Quaest Nat	Quaestiones Naturales
Serv	Servius
SIG	Sylloge Inscriptionum
	Graecarum,
	ed. Dittenberger
Sim	Simonides
Soph	Sophocles
Aj	Ajax
Antig	Antigone
Elec	Electra
Eriphyle	Eriphyle

Ich	Ichneutae
Mys	Mysoi
Oed Col	Oedipus Colonus
Oed Tyr	Oedipus Tyrannus
Philoc	Philoctetes
Trach	Trachiniae
Statius	Statius
Achill	Achilleis
Theb	Thebais
Stes	Stesichorus
Suoth	Suotherai
Strab	Strabo
~	Geographia
Suet	Suetonius
Tib	Tiberius
TGF	Tragicorum Graecorum Fragmentae, ed. Nauck
Theocr	Theocritus
Theod	Theodosius
Can	Canones
Theog	Theognis
Thuc	Thucydides
Tit Liv	Titus Livius
Tzet	Tzetzes
Chil	Chiliades
Varro	Varro
Re Rust	De Re Rustica
Virg	Virgil
Aen	Aeneid
Georg	Georgics
Xen	Xenophon
Anab	Anabasis
Cyn	Cynegeticus
Cyr	Cyropaedia
Hell	Hellenica

Mem	Memorabilia
Sym	Symposium
Zen	Zenobius

ACKNOWLEDGEMENTS

Thanks are due to Roger Cazalet, Billie and Joe Lintell, Neil Taylor and, most of all, Vineeta.